CECE DOWNING'S

Start Over Summer

CECE DOWNING'S

Start Over Summer

A NOVEL

SOON WILEY

DUTTON

DUTTON
An imprint of Penguin Random House LLC
1745 Broadway, New York, NY 10019
penguinrandomhouse.com

Book design by Katy Riegel

LIBRARY OF CONGRESS CATALOGING-IN-PUBLICATION DATA
has been applied for.

ISBN 9780593185179 (trade paperback)
ISBN 9780593185186 (ebook)

Printed in the United States of America
1st Printing

The authorized representative in the EU for product safety and compliance is Penguin Random House Ireland, Morrison Chambers, 32 Nassau Street, Dublin D02 YH68, Ireland, https://eu-contact.penguin.ie.

For Jennifer

AUTHOR NOTE

While I have done my best to portray New London and the surrounding area as faithfully as possible, I have taken some liberties with the nature and function of Mamacoke Cove. Given its status as an Important Bird Area by the National Audubon Society and its designation as a natural area within Connecticut College's Arboretum, it is highly unlikely that Richie Rayburn's oyster farm expansion would be approved. However, for the sake of the novel's plot and setting, this allowance was necessary. Changes were also made to the dates of the reunion weekend at Deerfield Academy. Any other errors or oversights in the novel are my own.

There is this quality, in things, of the right way seeming wrong at first.

—JOHN UPDIKE, *Rabbit Run*

I am always tying up
and then deciding to depart.

—FRANK O'HARA, *To the Harbormaster*

CECE DOWNING'S

Start Over Summer

June

1

Even with the benefit of hindsight, Cece Downing can't seem to grasp how she's arrived at this particular moment—renting an ivy-smothered pool house month to month in the backyard of a pleasantly deranged botany professor in New London, Connecticut—and yet, here she is, recently fired, newly single, and for the first time in what feels like a lifetime, without a plan.

The property runs parallel to the street, and from her spot on the rickety front deck, Cece has a good view of the road, just beyond the rebellious shrubs and arrowheaded hostas. Bernard, her parents' ornery three-year-old beagle she's agreed to watch while they're on vacation, expels a half whimper from underneath her chair, alerting Cece to his desire for dinner, preferably sooner rather than later. But Cece has other ideas.

Of late, she's been fantasizing about how she can use Bernard to meet a guy who lives six houses down. She's considered letting the dog dig up the man's flower beds so she has an excuse to knock on his door and apologize. More than she cares to admit, she's hoped Bernard might slip the leash on their daily walks and tear after the chipmunk that lives under his deck. And sometimes, when she can't sleep, the slap of the pool water tedious and dull, her mind drifts to more desperate ideas, like dropping the dog off in the man's yard, outfitted with a new collar and tag with her address, and waiting for him to show up, Bernard cocooned in his burly arms.

This last stratagem, in all its foolishness, is almost enough to make Cece feel reckless—almost. Cece's been thinking a lot about risk lately. She's been thinking about all the preparation, all the calculated decisions she's made over the years to avoid it, and how they've proven ineffective against the yawning chasm of uncertainty and improbability that now spreads out before her like an impenetrable mist.

If everything—all the carefully crafted plans, the necessary sacrifices, the well-worn paths Cece's taken—led her to this, what was it all for? What did any of it mean?

Like it was yesterday, Cece can still remember her confusion and anger during an eighth-grade English class when Mr. Gordon, a stuffy man with smudged glasses and thinning hair, introduced their new poetry unit by reading aloud Robert Frost's "The Road Not Taken," his voice scratchy and saccharine. With equal parts horror and disbelief, Cece watched as her classmates clamored to agree with Mr. Gordon: Life *was* best lived when you chose the unfamiliar, the unknown. A life spent following in the footsteps of those who went before you was a wasted one. Cece had disagreed vehemently with Mr. Gordon, not only about his dangerous outlook on life, but with his interpretation of the entire poem, Even so, she'd said nothing, fearful it would negatively impact her current grade of an A.

It's the first Friday of June, and Cece's rushed home from her job across the river in Noank to catch a glimpse of this mystery man who cruises by her pool house in his pickup truck every weekday at 5:30 p.m., like clockwork, on his way back from the shipyard that lies at the bottom of the street. Naturally, she's taken to calling him Mr. Shipyard.

Chilled Pinot Grigio sweats in the early evening heat, and Cece's day job is a distant memory—the stench of the rubber gloves and waders scrubbed clean (she hopes), the clatter of oyster shells a mere rumor, the persistent cramp in her hands nearly gone. Cece hadn't been expecting anything glamorous when she'd applied for a seasonal job at the oyster farm, but somehow, she's still shocked at the toll the menial tasks have taken on her body. The ache in her lower back, the knotted muscle behind her shoulder blades are constant reminders that at thirty-two, Cece can't bounce back like she used to, at least not like when she was a D1 athlete, her body a temple, a muscle-toned missile cutting through water.

She sips her wine judiciously. Nothing good ever comes from drinking on an empty stomach. And yet, here she is. A cool breeze arrives off the Sound, brackish and sweet. Cece loves living near the water, and even though the pool house is shabby, with its musty carpeting, Formica-topped junior kitchen, and cramped bedroom, she's grateful to the landlord for renting it out on such short notice.

Bernard's whines grow louder, and no sooner does Cece head

inside to give him his kibble does she hear the low rumble of Mr. Shipyard's pickup truck. It starts in her chest, and as the horsepower gets closer, tremulous and teasing, Cece swears she can feel the vibrations all the way down to her crotch. She checks her phone: 5:25. He's early. He's never early, at least not on any of the eight weekdays she's been doing this—this stupid, necessary thing. Sensing Cece's excitement, Bernard abandons his food bowl for the screen door, where he mashes his wet nose against the screen. "Back!" she shouts louder than she intends. No matter how authoritative she makes her voice, the commands have no effect, with Bernard only growing more frantic. What the hell, she thinks, clipping the leash onto his collar. A dog can't hurt her chances. If anything, he'll make her look normal, less tragic. Less tragic would be most excellent right about now.

Through the verdant foliage, a sight to see: The turquoise hood of Mr. Shipyard's pickup crests the hilly road just as Cece gets settled in her chair, Bernard underneath her legs, tongue lolling from the heat. It's an old Ford Ranger with more rust than paint. He's smoking a cigarette, his arm dangling out the window like a weathered tree limb, tanned and speckled with paint. He drives slowly, hand on top of the steering wheel—a veteran captain, guiding his ship into port. Cece imagines his eyes behind those sunglasses, yellow and red-rimmed from welding or staring at the white bottoms of boats all day. His long, black hair looks wild and unkempt underneath his baseball cap. Stop staring, Cece thinks, stop staring. But the Pinot Grigio tells her otherwise, and all she can do is smile.

As the truck passes, Bernard lets out three piercing yaps. Nails scrabble across the deck, and the only thing that stops him from launching off the top step is Cece's heel on his leash. "Cut it out," she growls while still trying to maintain her smile. She hopes Lorraine, her landlord, can't see the spectacle from her bay window. The more Cece tugs the leash, the more he yaps.

Mr. Shipyard turns their way and raises a hand and smiles, his teeth obscured by a thick beard. Cece tucks a piece of stray hair behind her ear and waves back, her cheeks warm and itchy.

"Well done," Cece says. "You've made a display of us."

Bernard bashfully lies down and sets to licking the tops of his paws.

"What? Not my type?" She scratches him behind the ears.

The beard, the smoking, certainly the derelict truck—just one of these things would have been enough to turn Cece off in previous years. Dealbreakers. Nonstarters. But where had those rules gotten her?

Even when it came to hookups in college, Cece had played it safe, avoiding anyone who seemed like an artist or an activist, people her mother referred to disparagingly as bohemians, people who didn't have a clue how the real world worked. And if they weren't going to have a viable career, if they weren't going to make money, then Cece had no reason to waste her time and energy dating them. She still remembers the first thing her mother said when her acceptance letter arrived in the mail from Bucknell: "Think of all the opportunities you'll have, all the fine young men you'll meet." Cece understood. *Fine* didn't mean nice or fair-looking. *Fine* meant rich, or even better, wealthy. A part of Cece wishes she could blame her current predicament—single, a dead-end job, mounting student debt—on her mother, but the truth is, Cece was more than a willing participant. When it came to romantic partners, Cece, from the earliest possible age, had always sought stability and predictability. Her first crush, Jack Heinz, had caught her eye in the sixth grade because of a successful bake sale he'd organized for the baseball team, demonstrating his keen sense of fiscal responsibility. In ninth grade, she fell for Paul Peters, a milky-faced boy who was running for class president. In a dank gymnasium in front of a raucous crowd, he'd delivered a rousing—at least to Cece—speech on his plans for Tappan Zee High School: a more efficient lunch line design, a responsible fundraising campaign for their eventual prom, a car pool initiative. He was a boy with a plan, a vision for the future. There was nothing sexier, Cece thought, than preparedness.

But things are different now. With her funds dwindling, her once-promising career up in flames, Cece can't help but acknowledge there's no path left to follow, no plan to make everything right. Failure, in its many forms, is something Cece has never been well acquainted with, and this realization only pushes her further into a place she cannot name.

Even with her entertainment for the evening out of sight, Cece can't help but keep thinking about Mr. Shipyard, biceps like whiskey barrels, hands the size of spiral hams. As if to prove he's telepathic, Bernard lets out a low and airy whine, garnering a half-begrudging pat on the head. Distractions are important these days, and as far as distractions go, Cece could do much worse than Mr. Shipyard.

In the direction of the main house, beyond the rusting chaise lounges and prodigious vegetable garden, footsteps sweep through the tall grass in need of a good mowing. Lorraine emerges from a thicket of hydrangeas, her bouncy salt-and-pepper hair held captive under a sun hat. They've spoken little since Cece replied to the post on Craigslist: Seeking independently minded boarder with a sense of adventure for New London pool house. Utilities included. Men need not inquire. Initially, Cece had been wary of renting a place on the same grounds as the owner, but what choice did she have? Lorraine accepted cash, didn't need references, and didn't ask any questions.

Lorraine's Crocs make a squishing noise the closer she gets; a noticeable musk (wet earth and coffee grounds) emanates from her. "Came by to see how you're settling in," she says, digging around in her overalls for something she's misplaced.

"Fine," Cece says, "just fine."

Lorraine looks to the street, eyes narrowed, crow's feet tucked deep into the corners of her eyes. Nostrils flared, she sniffs the air like one of Bernard's brethren. "I don't like that man."

Cece knows exactly who Lorraine's talking about, but she feigns ignorance.

"I have half a mind to call the DMV and report his truck. No way that vehicle passes an emissions test."

Maybe Cece's losing her faculties. She can't smell a thing. Regardless, she needs to stay on good terms with her new landlord, no matter how nutty. "I was wondering what that smell was."

"Men," Lorraine says, screwing up her face. "They're not happy unless they're destroying something."

There are so many questions Cece yearns to ask—how long has Mr. Shipyard lived on this street, has Lorraine ever seen him with anyone, does he seem like the kind of man who'd entertain a summer fling?—but she resists, nodding in silent agreement instead.

Lorraine leans from one leg to the other, looking like she has something to say but doesn't. Cece is keenly aware of how quickly her living situation might go wrong, and she's intent on staying on Lorraine's good side. Their agreement is strictly verbal. There was no lease to sign, only a handshake and a long and ponderous up-and-down assessment from Lorraine when they first met.

"I better get back," Lorraine says. "Groundhogs aren't gonna trap themselves. I was hoping your dog there would scare them off."

Cece apologizes for Bernard's canine inadequacies and watches Lorraine lope back to the house while she nurses a second glass of wine, mosquitos nibbling at her ankles. She resists the urge to take a stroll by Mr. Shipyard's house, the wine goading her on. Too soon, she thinks. Way too soon.

Back inside, Cece sits at the banquette and eats Chinese food leftovers for dinner. She forces herself to see the good, the silver lining, the glass half-full. Her confines are cozy, bespoke, vintage even! People would kill to have a place by the water for the summer (even if it's a dingy pool house), especially all her friends who are stuck in the city, sweating it out with everyone who can't afford to escape. Except that none of Cece's friends live in the city anymore. They've all grown up, married, moved to not-so-far-flung places like Hastings and Tarrytown, Rye, and Beacon. Long gone are the heat-soaked days of July and August in cramped apartments, battling the oppressive humidity with early-morning walks in Central Park, taking turns in front of the air conditioner, catching the Jitney out to the Hamptons for one, maybe two, measly days. Cece hasn't spoken to her friends of late. They still think she's gainfully employed, engaged to Jonathan, planning a wedding. They'd all sounded so excited, almost relieved, when she'd told them the good news. They're still waiting for their save-the-dates, eager to slip the cards from their thick envelopes and proudly display them to their husbands—their last friend, the final holdout, getting married. It's finally happening!

Through the window, tree limbs crisscross the darkening sky in menacing silhouettes. With only yellowed light from an overhead ceiling fan, the living space feels menacing and strange, unpacked boxes sending shadows up the wood-paneled walls, dusty valences hanging above the windows like morose specters. Cece gathers Bernard up in her arms for his walk. She pauses on the deck, the night warm and deep. She's embarrassed, a grown woman afraid of the dark. For now, she's glad Lorraine's nearby.

Before she knows it, she's passing Mr. Shipyard's house, a ramshackle Cape with weather-beaten cedar shingles and a sagging roof. Scaffolding adorns one side of the home, running all the way up to the chimney draped in a plastic tarp. Out front, the yard is littered with pieces of freshly cut wood—molding, from the looks of it. Despite the carnage, there's something charming about the picture, and Cece wonders how long he's been working on it. She wonders what allows a person to see the beauty and potential in run-down things. Potential isn't something Cece's ever put much stock in.

No lights are on, as she suspected, but Cece still stands there for a moment, letting the breeze cool her aching neck, and she imagines what's behind those walls and under that roof. She imagines the smell of the house, the muskiness, and she wonders if Mr. Shipyard dreams. And then she's wondering whether it's too late to start her life over, or if she ever started at all.

2

Sticky and hot, the base of her skull throbbing, Cece wakes to the whir of cicadas outside her window. Bare walls and a curtainless window—it takes a moment for her to remember where she is. Without a proper box spring, the mattress is strangely close to the floor, causing Cece to feel as if she's been jailed in a bottomless pit. Then she remembers—the walk by Mr. Shipyard's house—and suddenly she feels deserving of this punishment. The cicadas crescendo, the hundred-strong *thick-thick-thick-thick-thick* mocking and cruel. At least they get laid before they die, Cece thinks, rolling onto her back and examining the ceiling.

What was the probability, Cece wonders, that she'd end up here? Alone, mired in debt, fired from the only profession she's ever known. Hadn't she taken every precaution, done everything right, to avoid this very outcome? As early as middle school, Cece found refuge in numbers and mathematical formulas, even while most of her girlfriends gravitated toward the fiery heroines and impenetrable poems in English class, or studio art, with its emphasis on creativity and self-expression. Her preference for logic, deductive reasoning, and probability only grew in high school. Back then, the world seemed a chaotic and terrifying place (Bush versus Gore; 9/11; the war in Iraq), and what better place to find solace and refuge than in cold, hard numbers, equations, and solutions—inarguable facts, the truth?

Cece's phone vibrates from under her pillow. She can already hear her mother's voice: *Don't sleep with that thing so close to your head. It'll give you a brain tumor!*

Still groggy, Cece makes the mistake of swiping open the message before looking at the sender. It's from Jonathan, her ex-fiancé: Just checking in. I know you said we shouldn't talk, but I'm worried about you. Is this really what you want?

Rage detonates in Cece's chest. The wording of the text, the blatant disregard for her feelings, the presumption! It's all so Jonathan. He always knows best, and not just for himself, but for everyone. Cece had told him—in the plainest of terms—they were done, finished. She'd given back the ring! And yet, here he is, only a few weeks later, pretending as if their breakup, the implosion of their four-year relationship, was a mere bump in the road, something to be repaired, filled, and tamped down like an irksome pothole.

Dragging the sweat-dampened pillow out from under her head, Cece places it firmly over her face, making sure to yank down on either side for the sake of the neighbors, and lets forth a guttural scream. Why does he insist on being so willfully dense? Does he really think he knows what's best for her? But even as she laughs at the absurdity of Jonathan's message and squeezes her hands into fists, Cece catches herself, ever so briefly, wondering if he does, in fact, know what's best for her.

Before Cece can consider whether to text back or block the number, a call comes through. It's Santiago, the supervisor from the oyster farm, and he doesn't sound pleased. It's Saturday, but Cece had picked up the weekend shift to earn extra money, which means—she checks her phone—she's already fifteen minutes late. Not a great start.

Cece takes a frantic shower, all the while fighting the urge to assume the fetal position. It's foolish—bathing before a job like this—but she can't bring herself to show up in her current state: bloated, sunburned, somehow hungover. She throws on a pair of sweatpants, a threadbare T-shirt, and takes Bernard for the quickest walk of his blissful canine life, tugging him along even as he stops to mark every tree and bush, eats two pieces of toasted white bread with cold butter, slugs a glass of tap water, and jumps in the car.

The docks are deserted, only moored boats and placid water—the occasional wheeze of a straining bowline. Cece yanks on her rubber waders in the dusty gravel parking lot. Two figures watch her impassively from the shade of the warehouse, its metal doors swung open below a faded sign: Rayburn Oyster Company. As she approaches, Davi, the boy, heads off without a word toward the dock, his gait slow and resentful. Santiago, his father, leans against a steel drum, a scar running ragged through his patchy beard.

"Sorry," Cece says, weighing whether to make some sort of excuse.

Santiago gives her a shrug, as if to say, *It's okay—we don't expect much from greenhorns anyway.* He digs around in the blackened pouch of his sweatshirt before producing a pack of cigarettes.

"It makes no difference," he says. The tone of his voice reflects the unseriousness of Cece's work. "Richie said you wanted extra shifts, so we waited."

Cece's face burns. The irony is not lost on her that all the years of schooling, the job experience, the accolades at her firm are worthless in this particular moment. Santiago points to the stack of black crates woven from plastic mesh. "Same gig as yesterday. Power wash those. Fix any holes with zip ties."

Cece wants to say she's ready for some real responsibility, a challenge. After a week of the same tiresome routine, she wants to get out on the water and show Santiago she's capable of more, but he's already walking to the boat, motioning, cigarette in hand, to his boy, who starts the engine, pale gray fumes curling upward.

The oyster crates are heavier than they appear. When she'd started work at Rayburn, she thought they'd looked flimsy and light, but now she knows they're cumbersome and heavy, stinking of rotting seaweed and sea scum.

So, they're not letting her on the boat until she's proven herself. That's just fine, Cece thinks, unhooking the first cage. The pressure washer is where she left it yesterday. She wheels it outside and starts it up, the sound deafening and terrible in the morning calm. She'll clean the whole stack before Santiago and his boy return. She can't give them an excuse to tell Richie she's no good, worse than inexperienced, lazy.

Basket after basket, Cece's back is tight, and even after a break, her forearms still tingle and quiver from the power washer. It's only nine, but the day is already warming. Cece pulls her T-shirt over her nose to check her BO, but all she smells is the ocean. On her eighth bag, Cece encounters the first sign of damage, a hole the size of her fist in the plastic webbing. Without gloves, the work is slow going and painful, the stiff plastic cutting into her hands, the zip ties sharp and unforgiving. It's not long before blisters bloom and reopen on Cece's soft palms, but she persists, cursing herself for not buying gloves in a foolhardy attempt to exude toughness.

If Kim, her mother, could see her now . . . would Cece's work ethic elicit pride? Doubtful. More like shame, and most certainly a scolding. *What was the point of sending you to that fancy college if you're going to end up with rough hands and a farmer's tan?* Cece can hear her saying. *If your grandfather were alive to see his granddaughter doing manual labor . . . I'd never hear the end of it.*

The eldest of three, Kim was born and raised in Providence. Her father was a sanitation plumber for the city. He retired with full pension benefits at the age of sixty with forty-two years of experience. He died a year later from complications related to pneumonia. Kim was convinced his early death was connected to his work and exposure to toxic chemicals, but her mother refused to sue the city. She was a quiet but stern woman who lived her life guided by three principles: Go to church, donate to charity, and don't blame others for your own misdeeds. Kim couldn't get out fast enough when she turned eighteen, putting herself through school—two years at the local community college and then finishing up at URI.

Determined to avoid her father's fate—body hobbled by decades of work, in the grave before he could enjoy retirement—Kim went straight to law school in New York City, dissatisfied with Rhode Island's provinciality. Her mother thought she was mad, spoiled even, for leaving. What was so special about New York City? How did she intend on paying Fordham's hefty tuition, renting an apartment? Kim took out loans, got roommates, hustled, lived in the library, worked harder than she ever thought herself capable of, because that was her only advantage—her tolerance for asceticism in all its forms. The sacrifices—missed family vacations, skipped holiday parties, ignored flirtations—they were all necessary if Kim wanted to craft a better life for herself. She was wholly alone in her efforts. There was no family name, no legacy, no plan she could consult. Much later, Kim would recount these events back to Cece before she went to college—a college Cece suspected would stretch her parents' finances—as if the selective details of her mother's life might help Cece understand a simple truth: For people like them—people without family legacies, people who had yet to forget the dirt under their grandparents' fingernails—college was about stability and guaranteed success. College was how you made sure you never tended bar or painted houses for a living. College was where you met fine men and drew a blueprint, for you, yes, but also for those who would surely come afterward: your children, and their children, who would know nothing of dirt.

With her ear plugs in, the roar of the pressure washer is reduced to a murmur. Despite arms turning to jelly and her back barking like a rabid dog, Cece falls into a rhythm, dragging a crate forward, unlatching it, hosing it down, then checking for holes and repairing anything that looks like an oyster might slip through. She's not thinking about the sweat stinging her eyes or the sun beating down. Instead, Cece's thinking about how there are parts of herself, parts she'd forgotten about, that prefer this kind of work. Sure, it's difficult and grueling, but there's something deeply rewarding about watching the stack of crates grow. This is *real* work, Cece thinks to herself. Tangible. There's nothing theoretical about the progress she's making, no hypothetical scenarios to determine or consider.

Cece wishes she could pinpoint the moment she decided to become an actuary, but like most things these days, she finds herself unable to remember it clearly, to differentiate between the world's desires and her own. She wishes she could blame her overbearing parents—Kim fixated on Cece graduating with a "useful" degree, her father, Barry, content, as long as she kept his D1 swimming glory days alive and well—but Cece can't. She knows, in the innermost curvatures of her heart, that from her earliest days, she's always moved through the world like a drowning swimmer toward a life raft, toward safety. What was the point of striking out on your own when a perfectly good path, traversed and mapped, lay before you? Was that not prudent, wise even?

Cece had always done the right thing. The safe thing. And where had it gotten her? What impeccable results had it produced? After all the assurances, the silent nods of approval from gray-headed relatives during Thanksgiving and Christmas about her sensible major (statistics), recession-proof career (an actuary), and eventual hard-won promotion to senior manager for Ernst and Young's East Coast risk management division, Cece, incomprehensibly, had found herself out of a job, proven redundant and too costly after a corporate merger. It didn't matter that she'd spent nearly a decade at the company. Nor did it matter that she'd passed all seven actuary exams, in six years no less, a feat accomplished by no other employee at the company. In a cruel twist of fate, it was Cece's accomplishments that seemed to make her an easy target for cost-cutting measures. Her new superiors were less enamored with her credentials and more worried about her salary.

When Cece had met with the new higher-ups, she'd had the distinct feeling, sitting at an almond-shaped table in a conference room overlooking Lexington Avenue, that they cared little for her expertise or professional achievements. And yet, she'd felt confident. Unlike most of her colleagues, who'd fallen into a sort of paralyzed panic after news of the merger, Cece had felt secure in her position. Fired? Let go? An impossibility. What company didn't value loyalty, production, and consummate professionalism? As it turned out, the three baby-faced men across from her at the table did not, and before she could fully process what had transpired, Cece found herself nodding and saying needlessly polite things like "I understand you're in a difficult position," and "I see your point," and lastly, as she was escorted out of the room, "Thanks for taking the time." So confused, so utterly befuddled was she that it never crossed her mind to question or challenge them.

Cece might have been able to shoulder the weight of her unceremonious dismissal from the only company she'd ever worked for; she might have been able to weather the catastrophic setback like a veteran mariner guiding their ship through a tempest, updating her resume, collecting a superb and impressive list of references, and arranging interviews. She might have come out the other side, battered and bruised but stronger and wiser, had it not been for Jonathan's reaction.

Even now, hands cramping around the pressure washer trigger, head woozy from gas fumes, she can hear his voice clearly, unbothered and patronizing. Only when Cece reaches for another crate and clutches air does she realize she's done. Flipping a switch, the motor comes to a halting stop. Cece tugs her earplugs out and massages her jaw. Quiet. Water laps pilings. In the distance, a buoy bell clangs, rhythmic and known.

ON THEIR EVENING walk, Bernard and Cece make a pass by Mr. Shipyard's house. Even after a long, hot shower, Cece's muscles—muscles she never knew existed—still ache. She is tired—no, exhausted—but unlike the nights when she'd come home late from the office, the glowing computer screen imprinted on the inside of her eyelids, the dreaded ding of incoming emails sounding in her head, she feels energized, antsy.

Mr. Shipyard's truck is in the driveway, but all the lights are off in the house. Before she can think twice, Cece's on the front porch, her knuckles brittle against the solid oak door. Lungs in her throat, she waits. Bernard whines, no doubt resentful his walk has been cut short. Nothing. She resists the urge to peek inside, through the cockeyed shades. Bernard tugs at the leash. Cece wonders if Mr. Shipyard has a girlfriend. She didn't spot a wedding ring; Cece remembers that much.

On the second lap around the block, Cece recalls an old bar nearby on Williams Street. It seems like the type of establishment Mr. Shipyard would frequent, and even if he isn't there, it might be nice to meet some locals. There's something else, too. A desire, a need, lingering in the crevices of Cece's mind, to *do* something, something foolhardy and unpredictable—something, anything! That might distract her from the current state of her affairs.

Even for a Saturday, downtown feels desolate. New London, like Fairhaven and New Bedford, has seen better times, a boomtown funded by the long-forgotten whaling industry.

The bars and restaurants won't fill up until the fall, she's been told, when kids descend from the college up on the hill, with its verdant quads and imposing oaks. Cece downshifts as she descends, passing the inexplicable grouping of Citgo, Sunoco, and Shell gas stations, each offering up wildly different prices.

The Whaler is sandwiched between a barbershop and the Chinese restaurant Cece's been ordering from in a run-down mini strip mall. There are plenty of nicer spots to drink in New London, places with craft beer and thin-crust pizza, but Cece's in the mood for cheap bottled beer, poor lighting, and Mr. Shipyard, of course.

It takes a moment for her eyes to adjust once inside, the air stagnant and sweet. Two old-timers are at the bar, suspenders stretched over their lumpy backs, white wispy hair peeking out from under their stained caps. Plumbers, if she has to guess. Above the backlit liquor bottles, the Yankees are playing Baltimore on mute. No Mr. Shipyard.

"What can I get you, love?" the bartender says, her pack-a-day voice thick and raspy.

Cece plops down on a black vinyl stool at the end of the bar and asks for a Coors Light, an order she hopes will endear her to the Whaler's patrons. Either deeming her too young (she hopes) or just out of their league, the men have already gone back to their game, grumbling about how it's no fun to root for the Yankees anymore. "Look at those yuppies. Too busy texting and eating sushi. It's all gotten too damn corporate."

Jonathan was, still is, one of those yuppies. His firm is always giving seats away: courtside at the Garden, luxury suites in the Bronx and at Arthur Ashe. They'd gone to a Yankees game once, seats behind home plate, and Cece had been astounded by the pop of the catcher's mitt. And even though Jonathan had silenced his phone to give Cece his full attention—a not-so-insignificant gesture, given the number of work calls and emails he received on an hourly basis—Cece caught herself gazing out toward left field, where the bleachers, fueled by fandom and beer, bellowed and churned with life. She felt ungrateful then—Jonathan asking if she was cold, offering his jacket, his eyes blue and kind—for wishing she were out there, far away, faceless in the crowd, a collective roar in her throat. Surely this seat, cushioned and plush, this view, unobstructed, oozing with verisimilitude, was better. And yet, Cece couldn't shake the feeling this wasn't where she belonged, even as she sipped wine from a plastic cup and nibbled on vegetable crudités.

"What've they got you teaching up there at the college?" the ruddy-faced bartender asks.

"Oh," Cece says, flattered for some reason, "I'm not a professor."

The bartender eyes Cece's soft hands. Cece feels something close to resentment. She wonders how many college kids and local hipsters come to drink at the Whaler ironically, as if slumming it were a performance, one to be documented, played out in snapshots on phone screens and seven-second reels.

Desperately, Cece wants to say something, anything, to make this woman understand that she's closer to *this* world—the flimsy red cocktail straws, the grizzled patrons with their grime-smeared necks, the hand-scrawled signs (POLITICS-FREE ZONE; UNSUPERVISED CHILDREN WILL BE PUT TO WORK; NO DRINKS ON CREDIT)—than she appears, even if she's spent the better part of her life trying to escape it. Everything in this bar (the dust-covered speakers, the peeling tin ceiling, and wobbly high-tops) reminds Cece of her grandfather, long dead, who'd bounce her on his stomach when she was just a child, his beard thick with the smell of Marlboro Reds, fingernails grooved and split.

"I'm working at Rayburn," Cece says, "over in Noank."

The bartender's face softens. "Right, then. Hope he finally gets his second operation up and running. The rich folk and college wiseasses have been fightin' him on it."

"He has more than one?"

"You don't know?" the bartender says, scrunching up her lips like Cece's just asked a real dumb question. "Richie's been trying to get approval to install some oyster bags just up the river in Mamacoke Cove. You'd think something like that would be a no brainer, but like I said, the undesirables have been raising hell. God forbid we get a few more jobs around here."

"What are their objections?"

"God knows. Last time I heard, they were squawking about the cages ruining the natural beauty of the cove, and something about their recreational space being reduced, as if they can't go kayak somewhere else."

"Can they really do that?"

The woman huffs and wipes down the bar with a suspect-looking dish towel. "Money and time. If you've got enough of it, you can pretty much stop anything from getting done in this country. It's not like they're putting landfills and power plants in the nice parts of town . . . Apologies . . . Didn't mean to lump you in with that lot. We mostly get locals and boat-industry folk coming in here. The college crowd prefer those snooty spots farther downtown and over in Mystic. Ya know, those cafés with tiny coffee cups and bars with mixologists in leather aprons."

Cece wonders what it is about her appearance that gives it away, this unbelonging, other than her soft hands.

A few other customers dribble in, sidling up to empty stools or drifting around the pool table. A young guy in an auto mechanic jumpsuit lights a cigarette and is promptly shouted out into the dusk. Someone asks the bartender for five singles, and soon enough, Tom Waits is growling overhead.

Cece catches her reflection in the desilvered mirror, her dirty-blond hair and drawn face. Her highlights are growing out, have been for the last two weeks, but she hasn't had the motivation to get her hair done. The things women do: dyeing, waxing, lasering—a war of attrition, Pyrrhic victories at every turn. She still has her looks, but lines are starting to crease her forehead and mouth, giving her face a faint sour look. Cece's never considered herself beautiful, at least in the traditional sense. She never ran with the popular girls in high school or college, the ones who'd cut you down with a single look or comment: *I love that you're bringing that haircut back. It's so inspiring how you embrace your curves.*

It really shouldn't have gotten to Cece. Those curves, her broad back and unhideable thighs, were the reason she was at Bucknell with a scholarship to begin with. And even though she was named captain her sophomore year, even though she could hold her breath underwater longer than anyone else on the team, nothing terrified her more than the roving cliques of yoga-pant-clad, flip-flop- and Ugg-wearing blonds who patrolled the halls and quads of her alma mater, their waists impossibly narrow, breasts inexplicably perky. They were another species unto themselves. Cece takes a long swig of her beer, brooding. Curvy. Those bitches. Back then, curvy meant you weighed above 110; curvy meant you didn't look like you subsisted off salads and freshly squeezed fruit juice. Curvy!

"Everything all right here?" A voice pushes into her rage. Mr. Shipyard is elbowed up to the bar, a faded plaid shirt buttoned haphazardly, hair darkening his already deeply tanned chest. He looks at the beer bottle whose neck she's wringing and smiles cautiously, like someone who's trying to befriend a feral cat.

Cece tells herself to release her grip, but she finds herself unable. "Hi" is all she manages.

"You're Lorraine's friend, right? I've seen you on our block," he says, and points to Cece's beer when the bartender comes over.

"No," Cece blurts out, "not a friend. I'm just renting her pool house." She needs to put as much distance as she can between her and the resident crazy. "It's a temporary arrangement."

If he's dissatisfied with the vague answer, Mr. Shipyard doesn't show it, asking if she's waiting for someone.

Just you, Cece wants to say, but instead she takes a long swig of her beer and shakes her head. At the moment, she's got the power, the high ground, or at least that's how she feels, and she'd like to hold on to that feeling, a feeling she'd nearly forgotten, for as long as possible. Be cool; be aloof, pretend this wasn't exactly what she was hoping for when she drove downtown. "You live around here?"

Mr. Shipyard reaches over the bar and snags a handful of paper napkins. His arms are somehow even larger up close. He rubs the top of his beer clean. "I'm a few houses up from you. The Cape. Currently under construction. A real eyesore, I know."

Cece orders another beer and a water. She needs to keep her head clear. They touch glasses. The bar's emptied out, Waits replaced by the Yankees game, which is tied up in the eighth. Mr. Shipyard doesn't glance at the television, which Cece appreciates, even though she's not in any kind of position to care. The old-timers nearby are arguing about whether Aaron Judge is Black. "The kid is White—just look at his skin." "Yeah, but what about the hair?" If he hears them, Mr. Shipyard doesn't let on. With his salt-and-pepper beard and deep tan, it's hard to tell, but something about the subtle flatness of his nose and almost-wavy hair makes Cece wonder about his background.

"So, you're teaching up at the college?" he asks, giving his beard a scratch.

Cece can't help but stare at his hands, calloused and roughed up every which way. "Do I really look that snobby?"

Mr. Shipyard laughs, a single howl, light catching his smile, teeth askew and imperfect in the most charming way. "Not what I meant," he says. "You just . . . Never mind."

"What?"

He shakes his head, like he's scolding himself. "It's nothing bad. You're just nice-looking. I assumed you worked at the college. Not much around here for gainful employment. You're either working at the hospital, building subs, or teaching up on the hill."

Cece wants to linger on the *nice-looking*, but she's doing her best to stay levelheaded. The beers aren't helping. Desire flickers. How long has it been since she's flirted with someone? When was the last time she'd elicited intrigue and curiosity? "Is that what you work on? Submarines?"

"What? I can't be a radiologist at the hospital?"

Now it's Cece's turn to apologize, but Mr. Shipyard is already waving her off. Letting her know it's all in jest. "Neither, actually. I work down at the boatyard at the bottom of our street." He extends a big hand. "I'm Morgan."

Cece takes it, shocked by its warmth, and reminds herself to say her name.

"Nice to meet you, Cece," he says. "That short for something?"

"Claire," she says, "but only family call me that, and even then, I hate it."

The bartender makes her way toward them, but Morgan shakes her off. "I've got a one-drink maximum at this place," he says. "Never a good idea to get too comfortable at the bar within walking distance of your house."

"Right. Totally," Cece says, trying to hide her disappointment, which is odd, considering she doesn't even know what she's doing at this bar, talking to a man she barely knows but could give a 99 percent accurate police sketch of his face if asked. And why not? She's studied it nearly every day at exactly 5:30 p.m. for the last two weeks from her front porch. Morgan. Mr. Shipyard. Mr. Forearms like Artillery Shells. Mr. Laugh That Turns Her Knees into Tapioca Pudding.

Stool pushed back, Morgan stands and leans into Cece, his voice like nearing thunder, like railroad stakes thumped into the hard earth. "Could always do a nightcap at my place or yours," he says.

WHILE MORGAN SLIPS into his house to make two of his "signature cocktails"—he won't tell Cece what they are—she stops off at her place and gets Bernard. No lights on in Lorraine's house, thankfully. One less question Cece will need to answer in the morning.

Their nightcap has gone mobile for the sake of the dog's bladder. Cece doesn't trust herself to make good decisions (whatever those are) around Morgan. Weren't these urges supposed to fade by adulthood? If Cece's being honest with herself—something she's trying to do more of lately—it's the perfect rebound. There doesn't seem to be a better way of forgetting about Jonathan than slipping into Morgan's bed. How easy it would be!

On their walk down uneven sidewalks bathed in living-room light spilled across water-parched lawns, Cece feels giddy, juvenile. Now that the moment's here, some knowable, rippling energy between her and Morgan, she remembers how lacking things were with Jonathan toward the end.

Bernard, usually belligerent, seems happy to walk at their pace. Not looking at each other, seven and sevens in hand, the neighborhood muted and hushed around them—it's easier to take in the silence. Cece is wary of saying too much, ruining this good thing with talk and understanding. Down the tree-lined hill, passing lifted junkers on cinder blocks and half-filled kiddie pools, they make their way to the water, where the wind gusts and the oppressive mugginess lifts up to a near full moon, fanciful and garish. They slow, then pause, Bernard zeroed in on a stop sign. Cece asks Morgan how close they are to the boatyard and what exactly it is he does there. Something like a frown passes over his face to her question.

"A little bit of everything. Jack-of-all-trades-master-of-none type of thing."

"Did you always want to work on boats?"

"Can't say I have," Morgan says, hand scratching his ropy forearms in the half dark. "Huffing epoxy and diesel fumes isn't exactly what I had in mind growing up."

"Sorry, I didn't mean . . ."

Morgan touches her elbow. "Don't sweat it," he says. "I'm not taking offense. My old man worked on boats. I grew up around it."

"I like that you work at the boatyard," she says because it's true.

"You sure you're not confusing my job with something else? Maybe you're thinking I'm one of those yacht owners," he says with a smile.

"I'm not confusing you with anyone," Cece says, moving closer to Morgan, his heady, tobacco musk mixing with the Seagram's, smelling like a forest fire. And because she's just the perfect kind of tipsy and the moon is just bright enough for her to see Morgan's lips, she kisses him, leans in, his chest sturdy and thick, like an oak table. His beard is prickly, and she tries not to giggle as it tickles her nose. She keeps her eyes closed, trying not to sway too much, the dog leash twisting around her legs.

3

Above the towering bramble, only Lorraine's straw hat is visible, a steady stream of expletives tumbling forth between caught breaths. After some thrashing, she emerges, forearms scratched scarlet, loppers in hand, a half-filled mason jar of something swinging around her neck. Cece's having second thoughts about agreeing to help with the yard work, but there's no backing out now.

"Japanese wineberry," Lorraine says, tossing a handful of the magenta vines onto the yard. "It's invasive. Impossible to get rid of the stuff once it gets established. Beating it back is a yearly tradition."

Digging the plants out at the roots makes more sense to Cece, but Lorraine doesn't strike her as the kind of person who takes suggestions well, and she's in no shape for a debate, so she just puts her head down and keeps cutting. She wouldn't say she's hungover; then again, she wouldn't say she isn't. It's more the lack of sleep than the alcohol that's taking its toll. Cece surreptitiously slid out of Morgan's bed around three in the morning. An awkward conversation was the last thing she'd wanted. The night had been blissful, the sex, mind-numbingly good—why ruin it?

"A little hair of the dog?" Lorraine asks, offering Cece the mason jar after unscrewing the lid. The women are sitting on lounge chairs around the pool, taking a spell.

Cece isn't sure what to be more confused by—the offering from around Lorraine's neck or how she knows Cece's business.

"Sheesh," Lorraine says, "you should see your face."

Cece does her best to smile, but all she feels is tightness.

"I was awake when you got in last night. I can't seem to get more than three hours of uninterrupted sleep anymore. Don't ever get old."

Cece has no reason to feel guilty or embarrassed. She's a grown woman. Yet here she is, feeling like a college freshman caught making the walk of shame. "What's in the jar?"

"Hard kombucha. Brew it myself."

"I'll pass."

Lorraine stands and rubs her hands on the seat of her overalls. "Suit yourself."

The women work steadily in silence, the block waking up slowly, screen doors wheezing open, newspapers swept up from driveways, the pleasantly tedious drone of lawn mowers. Cece allows her mind to drift back to last night, Morgan's legs between hers, his thick fingers unhooking her bra with shocking nimbleness. It was strange and exciting all at once, being with someone else after four years with Jonathan, not enough time for things to have grown rote and stale, but somehow, they had. It wasn't that things were particularly bad in bed with Jonathan; it had all just become so routine—a task to be checked off their to-do list. Even on the rare occasion when spontaneity struck them, Cece found herself able to predict his every move: the hurried kisses on her neck, his preference for her right breast, his insistence on taking a shower immediately afterward. If she's being honest, Jonathan's militant commitment to postcoital hygiene didn't bother Cece all that much since it gave her just enough time to lie in bed and finish the job he'd started. Cece cringes, thinking about her desperate attempts for excitement and unpredictability toward the end, when their relationship was on life support: tugging him toward the bathroom at his company's holiday party, a suggestive smirk on her face, donning a plaid skirt and knee-high socks on a Friday night and surprising him. Both instances had failed miserably, Jonathan looking sheepish and uneasy. He'd given her a peck on the forehead, hands resting lightly on her hips, as if to say, *I won't have my future wife and potential mother of my children demeaning herself.*

When they'd first met, Cece had been enamored, seduced even, by his normalcy and uncomplicatedness. Here was a mature, well-adjusted adult. Here was an unrelenting optimist, a man with a fifteen-year plan, a son who loved his parents unconditionally. He was an actuary's dream, an exception to the risk model, an unprecedented piece of data that all but guaranteed compatibility in Cece's love life. So taken with him, or perhaps the idea of him, Cece had overlooked a few not-so-insignificant potential red flags: his disinterest in her career, his inability to allow Cece to pay for a single thing whenever they went out, and an unhealthy obsession with having exactly three kids so that he might replicate his own idyllic childhood. It wasn't that these characteristics were all that terrible, but they were nonetheless worrisome. Yet she was afraid of complaining to her friends or Wynonna, her sister. Jonathan wanted to take care of her and start a family. Was that so bad? Wasn't that what Cece was supposed to want? And if so, why did it make her feel small and insignificant? It spoke to a deficiency on her part, Cece thought. What else would explain what happened between them after she was fired?

On that day, Cece caught the train home after clearing out her desk. Surprisingly, all her personal effects—her framed college diploma, a bronze paperweight in the shape of a swimmer perched on a starting block, a photograph of her and Jonathan atop the Empire State Building with matching I HEART NYC T-shirts back when they liked to pretend to be tourists for the day—fit easily into a single cardboard box. Surely there was more to show for her eight years at the company, but it seemed not. She made certain to use the service elevator, for fear of running into anyone on her team.

At the time, Cece and Jonathan were living in Stamford, sharing a two-bedroom apartment in one of those snazzy new high-rises in the South End catering to the young professionals who weren't quite ready to give up proximity to the city for the suburban dream. Jonathan's private equity firm had offices in Greenwich and Manhattan, but on most days, he worked from home, the second bedroom affording him comforting views of the Sound and, beyond, Long Island. It was only midday, and Cece had lingered in their neighborhood, walking among the monochrome buildings and bustling lunch crowd. People with places to go, things to do. What would she say to Jonathan? How would he take her firing? She imagined him rallying to her cause and savaging the higher-ups: *They're threatened by you, Cece! This would never happen if you were a man! I wouldn't be surprised if they're begging you to come back in a week!*

Standing outside her apartment door, the carpeted floor freshly vacuumed, Cece tried to collect herself. People like her didn't get fired; people like her weren't left in the lurch, without a plan—yet here she was. Cece had always adhered to the belief that if she worked hard, if she committed herself, she would be compensated fairly; she'd be valued. And if people were laid off, if they were pushed out, it was for a good reason; they weren't innocent victims of a laissez-faire market; they were incompetent or inflexible—but now, she couldn't be so sure.

Before Cece could fully compose herself, the door swung open, and Jonathan appeared, earbuds tucked into his ears, a black athleisure top zipped to his stubbled chin. All the words she'd planned were of no use, and she crumpled into his arms, tears welling from a source she never knew existed.

Cold ice water pressed into her shaking hands, a seat cleared on their downy sectional, tissues retrieved from the bedroom, Jonathan patted her knee and asked what was wrong, what had happened? His eyes were somber, his voice low and steady. Cece felt something like comfort then, reassurance that at least she had Jonathan, someone who understood. It was one of the qualities she admired most about him: the ability to stay calm and collected even in the worst situations. There was the flight to Milan when their plane got hit with extreme turbulence. As the oxygen masks tumbled from above, he'd helped untangle Cece's and secured it before putting on his own. Wasn't that the thing they told you in the safety videos never to do? As luggage tumbled from overheads and prayers swept through the cabin, he held Cece's hand, just tight enough to reassure her but not raise alarm. Then there was the time her dad burned the turkey at Thanksgiving, and while her family devolved into recriminations and excuses, Jonathan ran out to the closest Boston Market and returned triumphantly with a rotisserie bird, endearing himself forever to Cece's parents. That was him—always looking for the practical solution while everyone else was panicking.

After Cece had blown her nose and dried her eyes, she told Jonathan she'd been fired. She explained what the executives had said about cost cutting and the nature of mergers. She was at a loss. She didn't understand how this could happen; she didn't know where to go from here.

Jonathan did a strange thing then, relief flooding his features, shoulders relaxing, hand pushing through his brown hair—he smiled. "You had me scared there for a minute, Cece. I thought something truly awful had happened."

"Something awful *has* happened."

"Of course, but you'll find a new gig. There's always demand for actuaries."

Cece fiddled with her engagement ring. She still hadn't gotten used to wearing it, often finding herself surprised by its shiny existence. "That isn't the point. I know I can find a new job."

Jonathan looked as if he wanted to say something, but he kept his mouth closed and buried his hands deep into the pockets of his joggers. He'd offered his solutions. What else did she want?

"They had no cause. I worked there for eight years."

"It's rotten. But you'll be better for it. You don't need them!"

"Why do you have to do that?"

"Do what?"

"Put a positive spin on everything. Why can't you just listen and agree with me, for once?"

"I *am* agreeing with you."

"It doesn't feel like it," Cece said, annoyed with herself for getting annoyed at Jonathan. He was just trying to help.

"I'm sorry," Jonathan said. He pulled her close then, pinning her arms against his chest. "Really. They had no right. You deserve better."

Cece softened and buried her face in the crook of his arm. Makeup be damned. "It isn't just a job to me, you know? This is my career."

"I get that, Cece," Jonathan said, taking her by the elbows and putting some distance between them, "but maybe this is a good thing."

"You're doing it again."

"I can't help it," Jonathan said, his voice rising excitedly. "There's so much we've got to look forward to—planning for the wedding, and we'll be house shopping soon enough. It wouldn't be the worst thing to not be tied down."

"What are you saying?"

"I'm saying you can take some time off if you want. Get some perspective. Reset."

"You don't think I should try to find another job."

Jonathan's face was taking on a vague look of exasperation. "You don't have to worry. Not anymore. I mean, don't get me wrong, I appreciate that you work. I respect it. Do you know how many of my friends' wives have never lifted a finger? It's one of the things I've always admired about you—your work ethic.

But it's not like you need to hustle anymore . . . I mean, you don't need to prove yourself to anyone."

The tears had long dried on Cece's cheeks. Something hard and sharp was forming in her chest. She resisted the urge to scream. "I like being an actuary. I'm good at it."

"Well, sure," Jonathan said, "but you'll have to take time off when we start a family."

They'd discussed the possibility of children, although the conversation had always felt more hypothetical than realistic to Cece, as if it were one of many possibilities for their future. It wasn't that Cece was opposed to kids; she just wanted them to happen on her terms. There was so much more she wanted to accomplish and achieve before she was known only as a mother, a singular identity. She thought Jonathan had understood this—she'd voiced her feelings more than once, and he'd always agreed, nodding vigorously, as if she were making the most obvious of points. But now, with Jonathan pacing before her, she understood that he'd always had certain expectations about the life they were going to lead. Cece saw that once they were married, there'd be little financial need for a job. In a down year, Jonathan made ten times her salary, but she'd never imagined putting her career on hold. She never imagined he'd suggest such a thing. Didn't he know her better than that? It was the feeling that Jonathan had never really taken her career very seriously from the start that gnawed at Cece while she sat in the tenuous silence. Hadn't she had these doubts before? Why had she ignored them? Or worse, why hadn't she recognized them until now?

The disparity between their families had always been a point of concern. Jonathan could trace his heritage back to the Puritans. Their name adorned the new dining hall at Deerfield Academy, as well as the new wing of his hometown library in Newton. As for Cece? Maybe her mother's father chipped the family name into some subterranean brick. Had her father's name been chanted to the rafters of University of Tennessee's natatorium by his teammates after breaking the school record in the two-hundred-meter breaststroke? This was the extent of her ancestral legacy. But these concerns had remained idle worries, background music to their flourishing relationship. Money and comfort had a way of gilding everything in gold, and Cece had found it difficult (she's ashamed to admit) to stop, to question, while summering at Jonathan's parents' house in Weekapaug, touring Christmas markets in Germany, and swimming in the ice-chilled waters of Lake Como, Jonathan on a pebbled beach, Aperol spritz in hand, his sun-splashed face at once expectant and unassuming. How nice it had been! The little luxuries Cece had never known: steaming hand towels in first class; hotel rooms with their own dedicated entryways; the food . . . the food! How easily these things (so many things!) smoothed the edges of Cece's concerns. Of course, it wasn't just about the money—that would have made things clearer in Cece's mind. It was how Jonathan made her feel most of the time—secure, self-assured, good about her life choices—that made things more confusing.

"And what if I don't want that?" Cece heard herself say.

"Want what?"

"A family, a house in the burbs . . ."

"You're saying those things like they're bad."

Cece didn't know how to help Jonathan understand, to make him see. He's just trying to help, she told herself, gnawing the inside of her already pulpy cheek. With every solution Jonathan proposed, every ounce of positive spin, Cece felt like she was drifting further and further away from the adult version of herself she'd always imagined: independent and strong, sole author of her story. But why did it matter? She loathed herself for resisting an outcome most women her age would kill for. She could hear her sister's voice, warning Cece not to sabotage a good thing. Was that really what she was doing? And if this was right, why did it feel so terribly wrong?

"I just told you I was fired," Cece said, her cheeks burning. "Your response can't be that everything'll be okay because you're rich and I can have babies."

Chin to the ceiling, Jonathan pushed out a long whistle. Later on, Cece would wonder if this outcome was unavoidable, whether all their seemingly inconsequential disagreements and quarrelling had brought them, inescapably, to this moment, or if it had all been preventable if she'd held her tongue, excused Jonathan's well-meant solutions, considered the beautiful panoramic view afforded by their luxurious apartment.

"You seem determined to have a fight," Jonathan said in that maddeningly calm and measured voice of his. "Is that what you want? I'm trying to think constructively here."

Without a plan, Cece gathered her things and stood. Even in the bright and airy apartment, she felt suffocated, as if someone had been covertly siphoning oxygen from the room. "I'm going out. Since when did explaining yourself constitute starting a fight?"

"Be reasonable, Cece. You just got here."

Was she being unreasonable? Even in hindsight, Cece can't

be entirely sure. Jonathan's proposal a few weeks ago had suddenly put everything in perspective, and imagined or not, she was staring down the barrel of a marriage tinged with quiet desperation. "I think you just like the idea of me, Jonathan," she said, and opened the door to leave. "You say all that crap about supporting my career, but you don't mean it, not really. You'd rather just throw money at the problem."

If Cece's intention was to make him angry, she was successful. "Just for reference, Cece," Jonathan said bitterly, retreating into their apartment, "things like families, like homes . . . traditions . . . you know, happiness . . . those are things that normal people want. Money's got nothing to do with it."

At first, the walk around their neighborhood was only meant to clear her head; Cece had every intention of returning home and apologizing to Jonathan. She was being unfair. Through the prism of their engagement, everything had suddenly appeared permanent and immovable. She'd panicked, but the feeling would pass. Jonathan would understand. If anything, Jonathan was understanding!

Raindrops spattered the wind as sidewalks turned to dirt paths. Birds, atwitter, rose from the reeds, and Cece realized she'd walked far from the apartment, through Kosciuszko Park, where she stood at the water's edge. Scrambling over the darkened rocks, she moved closer, until the Sound lapped the tips of her shoes. She felt the chilled water soaking her socks. Someone called from the path for her to "watch out," and Cece stepped back, but not before slipping the ring from her finger and burying it in her jacket pocket. She would go back, but only to pack her things and tell Jonathan it was over.

"WHAT DID YOU say was in that stuff?" Cece says. The women are taking another well-earned break after their second battle with the Japanese wineberry. Cece's lying on a lounge chair, her thighs pushing through the bottom where it's missing the plastic bands.

Lorraine, sun hat nudged back on her forehead, offers the jar again. "A little sugar, black tea, yeast, and bacteria culture."

"Never mind. I thought I'd changed my mind."

Lorraine shoves off her Crocs and begins to unclip her overalls. "I'm going for a dip."

Cece does her best to hide her alarm.

"Relax," Lorraine says, jettisoning a sock with a flick of her foot. "I've got shorts on underneath."

"I wasn't worried."

"Sure," Lorraine says, lumbering to the shallow end, where she lowers herself in with a grunt, grime-smeared shirt and all. "Where did you end up finding a job? Or do I need to worry about you making rent this month?"

Cece remembers what the bartender told her last night, about the neighborhood tearing each other apart over Rayburn Oyster's planned expansion. Lorraine's a scientist; surely, she knows all about the ecological benefits of oysters, and it's not like her house overlooks the cove. Still, Cece treads carefully. "Sure did. At an oyster farm nearby."

"As long as it's not with Richie Rayburn, you're good in my book."

"Never heard of him," Cece says quietly.

"Lucky for you. He's a real SOB. Thinks he can just bully his way into our community. But we're organizing." Thankfully, Lorraine doesn't seem interested in expounding on her hatred for Cece's current employer. First Morgan, now Richie. Some luck Cece's got.

"You really aren't coming in?" Lorraine asks as she bobs in the water. "It's touching ninety already."

Cece shakes her head. She hasn't so much as dipped a toe in a pool since blowing out her shoulder (for the third time) her junior year during a tournament in Albany. It's not the injury that stops Cece; it's the memory of her father, calling her a quitter for refusing to get another surgery, the look on her mother's face while he berated her, passive and indifferent. It's also the extra loans she'd had to take out after quitting the swim team and losing her athletic scholarship. It's a lot of things, but Lorraine doesn't need to know all that.

Back inside, Cece decides she can't ignore Wynonna's phone calls anymore. By her count, there are at least four she hasn't returned. Since the breakup, her sister has made a habit of checking in on her, a gesture Cece finds herself simultaneously appreciating and resenting. She's the older sister; shouldn't the roles be reversed?

The sound of shrieking children fills the background when Wynonna picks up.

"Just returning your calls," Cece says, "but you sound busy."

There's some shuffling and muffled castigating. "I'm always busy. I can't believe Devin talked me into a second kid. It's madness . . . How's . . . Where are you again?"

"New London."

"What's in New London?"

Cece resents these simple questions that lay bare the inadequacy of her plan. "Nothing. I just had to get out of Stamford."

"Do you have a job up there or something?"

"Kind of."

"What's that mean?"

"I'm working on an oyster farm."

"Are you okay?"

"Why does everyone keep asking me that?"

"Who's everyone?"

Cece draws the blinds on the cottage windows. "Mostly you and Mom."

"You've been through a trauma."

"Don't you think that's a bit dramatic? I'm the one who left Jonathan. You remember that, right?"

"Of course, Claire, of course, but that doesn't mean it isn't still hard."

Cece hates it when Wynonna uses her full name. It makes her feel like she's in trouble, like she isn't the older sister, like she wasn't the one who carried all their parents' expectations, their aspirations and anxieties. By the time Wynonna arrived, Barry and Kim had mellowed: no AP classes, no hard push to pursue sports, no early curfews. It was as if they were raised by wholly different parents, and on more than one occasion, Cece must remind herself that none of this is Wynonna's fault.

"I'm fine," Cece says. "Can we not talk about this? How's North Carolina?"

More muffled threats, something about eating food off the ground. "Sorry, what? Were we always such a nightmare as kids?

I swear, I can't remember ever putting Mom through the stuff these two get up to."

"That's because it was usually Dad taking care of us. Mom was always at the office."

"No way. Mom was in the city a lot, but we always had sitters."

"Yes, he did, Wynonna. That was when his business was still getting off the ground and he worked from home. You just don't remember because you were too young."

"I think I would have remembered something like that."

This is typical for their conversations, unable to agree on even the simplest of facts. They're blood, and Cece loves Wynonna, would do anything for her, but sometimes she can't fathom how sometimes it feels like they're living on separate planets governed by completely different rules. None of this should surprise Cece. They've never rowed to the same cadence, so it was predictable when Wynonna settled down soon after college, moving to Charlotte, where she had zero job prospects or friends to raise a family. "All Devin's business is down here," she'd said. "It just makes sense."

Cece had tried not to judge, but she couldn't help question whether Wynonna was actually happy. Marriage, popping out babies, furthering the species in the face of most certain climate destruction—did any of it make sense?

"Let's just agree to disagree," Cece says.

"You really aren't gonna tell me how you're doing?"

"Hey, don't tell Mom or Dad about the oyster farm, okay?"

"I thought you were joking."

"Well, I wasn't."

"Have you been responding to her emails?"

"Which ones? I can't keep up with all of them."

"She's gonna flip about the oyster job."

"Not if she doesn't find out."

"Your secret's safe with me."

"Is it, though?"

"It is if you actually tell me how you're doing."

Even though she isn't so sure, Cece reaffirms that she's fine, never been better, in a lighthearted voice she summons from some unknown source.

"So, it's over. He hasn't tried to contact you at all?"

Maybe because Cece hasn't thought about Jonathan since yesterday morning, or maybe because she doesn't have anyone else to talk to about this stuff, she finds herself telling Wynonna about his text message and trademark concern.

Wynonna doesn't see a problem with any of it. Unlike Cece, who initially found it all infuriating and mildly controlling, Wynonna thinks it makes him seem genuine and thoughtful. "He made you happy, Cece," Wynonna says, "maybe not all the time, but most of it, and that's pretty good these days."

"Is this why you called? To take his side?" Cece says bitterly, even as she remembers the good times: Jonathan spending the day on the bunny hill with her at Stowe during a family ski trip; Jonathan going across town to pick up dinner from her favorite Indian spot when she had to work late; Jonathan listening to her father's old swimming stories at Christmastime, all with a smile on his face. It seemed impossible to wholly villainize the man. Of course, there was good in those four years, even if Cece doesn't want to admit it, lest it confuse her.

"We're sisters. I'm always on your side. Whether you think so or not. Breakups are hard, even when they make sense."

Cece says nothing, fearful of the weakness pooling in her stomach like a clandestine lake, vast and unseen. Questions invade her consciousness like nosy specters: Was she asking for too much out of a romantic relationship? Has she ruined the only good thing in her life? Would Jonathan take her back?

Wynonna's now talking about how she can't ever imagine Cece being fired. She knows how much the job meant to Cece. She knows how hard Cece's worked for her career. And she isn't wrong. But Cece doesn't have the energy to share her sister's outrage, her gripes and grievances, so she gives a few assurances and slides off the phone, sending love to Devin and the boys, whose faces she can't quite recall, and promises to call next week.

After depositing her dirty yardwork clothes in the hamper, Cece takes a long, cold shower, doing her best not to think, just concentrating on the water drumming her eyelids. Cece's never been one for meditation or the latest trends in mindfulness, but right about now, she could use some expertise.

Hair dried, armpits freshly scraped, Cece sits cross-legged on the twin bed and stares at her phone: I'm worried about you. Is this really what you want?

Want. Such a fickle word. Had she been too rash? Is she being too cruel? Why does Jonathan's concern elicit such anger? Why is she so hell-bent on making a clean break . . . What exactly is it he's done?

Cece doesn't want to remember the specifics, pushing the ring into Jonathan's palm and telling him it was over, insisting on staying at a Holiday Inn Express while she got the movers sorted.

She hadn't handled the situation with grace or maturity, but Jonathan hadn't given her a choice, refusing to believe she was unhappy, unsatisfied with her reasons for wanting to break up.

The truth is, Jonathan's response to Cece's firing had given her a preview, the veil had been lifted, ever so slightly, and Cece hadn't liked what she glimpsed for her future. It was a good future, a stable and productive future, but it was also a stifling one, a future in which she might find happiness, but only if she forgot herself. And how does one say this to their partner of four years, a man whose only fault is that he is himself? Cece certainly didn't know how, and so she'd fled, U-Haul trailer in tow, up to this cramped cottage in New London, where she presently finds herself somehow still slightly hungover and wondering if she's really thought all this through, and whether seeing Jonathan might not be such a bad idea after all.

Cece's fingers hover over the keyboard, tantalizing and seductive. In seconds, she can communicate every wish and whim and expect an immediate answer. What a terrible gift. I'm okay, everything is fine, she thinks to herself, sliding the phone under her pillow and closing her eyes for a midday nap, the sound of Lorraine's rusty loppers starting up again. Everything is fine.

4

Santiago is waiting for Cece when she arrives at work on Monday. She's expecting more of the same: no real responsibility, mucky plastic crates stacked ten high, ready to be cleaned. Davi is already down by the docks, walking the length of the boat and eyeing the sputtering outboard engine, a black cloud painting the sky ominous. From the doorway, Santiago glares at Cece while she puts on her rubber waders and roots around in a drawer for safety goggles. Ignore him, she thinks. He's just pissy she's still showing up. No doubt he assumed she'd quit once the novelty of the job wore off. The pressure washer isn't where she'd left it. A tremor pings at the back of her neck. It has to be here. Had someone moved it? Did she forget to lock up? Santiago hasn't budged, his beady eyes tracking her every move. Dread seeps in. Cece turns slowly to face him.

"Where is it?"

He crosses his sinewy arms over his chest. "What?"

"The pressure washer."

"You didn't hear? Some ninny forgot to turn the water off

when they were done with it on Saturday. Do you know what happens to that piece of machinery when you don't cut the water source?"

Cece, chin to her chest, shakes her head.

"Lemme tell ya," Santiago says almost gleefully. "That pressure builds up and has nowhere to go. Eventually all the seals and gaskets get blown out."

"Is that what happened?"

"You betcha. We dropped it off to get repaired this morning, but I wouldn't be surprised if it's completely shot."

"I'm sorry," Cece says, because it's the first thing that comes to her mind. "I could've sworn I disconnected the water."

"Sorry?" Santiago chuckles and tugs a cigarette from his shirt pocket. "Sorry's got nothing to do with it."

"Please don't tell Mr. Rayburn. I'll pay for the repair myself."

"You've got that kind of money?"

Cece doesn't have that kind of money; she doesn't have a clue how much such a repair will cost, but she can't have Richie finding out about this after he took a chance on her. "I'm good for it."

Santiago smirks and heads toward the boat, stopping halfway and turning to say, "That'll be difficult on account of Richie being the guy who's tryna fix it."

He's nearly out of earshot when Cece asks him what she should do.

"Nothing," he says. "The last thing we need is you breaking more stuff. Maybe you can organize the tool wall or go get us lunch when it's time."

Watching the boat labor out of the harbor, Santiago's and Davi's bodies suddenly lithe and gleeful on the water, Cece slumps against the rank crates. How could she have screwed up something so simple? All she's done is confirm Santiago's doubts.

Better to get out in front of this, she thinks. Rip the Band-Aid off. She takes out her phone. Richie sounds more disappointed than angry when he answers, which feels much worse, Cece realizes. "Maybe you just aren't cut out for this sort of thing," he says.

Cece picks up a handful of gravel and sends it tinkling across the parking lot. She tells Richie she very much is. This was a simple mistake, an oversight. Even to herself, Cece is unwilling to admit the cause of her absentmindedness: Jonathan, Morgan, all of the above.

"I took a chance on you," Richie is saying. "There's no shame admitting you're out over your skis."

Cece assures him she's perfectly capable and promises to pay for the repair. Richie seems dubious. "That would put you in a mighty big hole before you get your first paycheck."

"I'll pay in installments," Cece says firmly.

"Well, all right."

"I'll make it up to you, Mr. Rayburn."

Papers shuffle in the background, an office chair creaks. "That's, uh . . . that's not necessary," he says, his voice distant and gauzy. "Just do whatever Santiago tells you to do, and don't touch anything with an on-off switch for a while." The line goes dead.

A SHADOW PASSES over Cece. She must have dozed off. Santiago, backlit by the sun, looks down at her, a toothy grin cut into his tanned face. On her feet, Cece looms over him. She wonders if this is why he doesn't like her. Wouldn't be the first man to resent her vertical superiority.

"We had to turn back. Boat engine's acting up. I need you to run it over to the boatyard."

Why the sudden trust? Cece is suspicious.

"Think you can handle that?"

Cece ignores the sarcasm. "No problem. Where's the engine?"

Santiago jangles a set of keys before tossing them to her. "Pickup truck."

It takes all the self-control Cece currently possesses not to betray her panic. The Rayburn work truck is a heavy-duty pickup with dual rear wheels, side mirrors the size of traffic lights, and a hood impossible to see over. It's a behemoth, a colossus on wheels. It also happens to be brand-new, not a scuff or dent on it.

"Don't crash. Richie'll have your head."

So, Santiago is trying to get her fired. That's his angle. "Where am I going?" Cece asks.

"New London."

"Across the bridge? There's gotta be a closer boatyard."

"Oh, there is, but Richie had a falling out with the owner. He's got a feud going with half the locals, and we pay the price."

So she'd be taking the highway, which means she'd be merging, changing lanes, and exceeding speeds of thirty-five miles per hour. Images of a five-car pileup, twisted metal, and smoldering wreckage play out in Cece's imagination. The ruse is up. Why had she thought herself capable of this kind of work? What level of delusion and desperation had led her here? But it's too late now. It really isn't, but Cece needs to feel like it is. She's walked out on Jonathan, uprooted her life, somehow convinced Richie she's a capable employee. If she can't complete a simple task like driving a truck, she might as well give up this entire enterprise, whatever it might be.

"Which boatyard is it?"

Santiago shrugs. "It's near the college and the Coast Guard Academy."

Cece is certain she's misheard. "Which college?"

"The only college over there."

A panicked thrill coils in Cece's stomach. She hasn't seen or spoken to Morgan since she snuck out of his bed. It isn't that she didn't enjoy herself. She did, immensely, it's just that she doesn't want to give him the wrong idea—about what they are, what they could be. There's something else too, a fear, a silly, irrational fear that Cece won't be able to control herself when she sees him, and she's promised herself their night together was something casual and unsentimental. It was too good to just be a one-off, but Cece's determined for it not to become a regular thing, a habit, where feelings might blossom. This summer . . . this moment—living in Lorraine's pool house, working at Rayburn Oyster Company, taking stock—is supposed to be about finding clarity and purpose. She can't afford attachments right now, no matter how good they might feel.

Clutching the keys, Cece stalks off toward the truck.

"Don't forget to use your mirrors!" Santiago calls after her.

THE TRUCK'S EASIER to drive than Cece thought. Everyone gets out of your way when you're the biggest thing on the road.

Towering over the other cars, Cece feels an intoxicating sense of power and superiority. Is this why everyone drives these things? No matter how absurd they might look? A few sharp turns on the smaller roads prove difficult, and Cece cringes as shrubs and tree branches scratch and scrape. At first glance through the dirt-flecked windshield, the boatyard is abandoned. Cece double- and triple-checks her mirrors to make sure she's got the clearance while she rolls through the entrance, the chain-link gate mere inches away. She cranes her aching neck to see over the hood. Sailboats sit aloft, supported by rusting metal cradles, their bottoms faded and stripped, looking naked and strange without water beneath them. In the distance, a blue crane cuts into the sky, yellow boat slings dangling from it like confetti. Cece aims for an empty parking spot in the corner of the yard, forever thankful that she doesn't have to parallel park.

Underfoot, the shifting gravel announces Cece's arrival as she walks in the direction of the main hangar. Inside the dark and cavernous space, her eyes adjusting, she makes out shapes, men on the job, crude banter mingling with sweat and bravado. A few look up from their work, sanders whirring, torches glowing bright, mechanical parts strewn across makeshift plywood tables. No sign of Morgan. Cece asks where she should drop the engine, but her question goes unanswered, hanging in the heavy air. Even in her baggy T-shirt and loose-fitting jeans, Cece can feel their eyes on her. A lanky teenager with a welding helmet pushed up on his pale forehead gives her a begrudging nod toward the white double-wide trailer outside in the parking lot.

Making her way back to where she came from, Cece can't help but admit her disappointment. Maybe he's on his lunch break;

maybe he took the day off, but to do what? To go where? Cece's curiosity gets the better of her, imagining Morgan's life—where he's from, what he did before this, whether he's sleeping with anyone else. Cece isn't proud of that last question. She has no right to wonder about it—but there it is.

The trailer appears empty, but Cece still gives the flimsy door a good knock and pauses, shifting her weight from one leg to the other. A gruff voice from within follows the sound of rustling paper and slamming drawers. Cece runs her tongue along the back of her teeth and prepares for the worst: a grumpy foreman; an old-timer with some questionable views on women in the workplace. Part of Cece enjoys these newfound sparring sessions, proving men wrong with her gumption and stick-to-itiveness. At least down here at the shipyard and with Santiago and Davi, the men are up-front, almost charming about doubting her capabilities, and perhaps for good reason. At her old job, the men had attended enough mandatory HR training sessions to know how to disguise their dismissiveness, unless Cece had a good idea—then they were happy to be collaborative partners, magnanimously offering to let her take the lead and do all the work in the name of equity.

The door swings open, and it takes Cece a moment to realize Morgan stands before her, pencil behind his ear, a V-neck T-shirt stretched across his chest. For one brief moment that doesn't feel brief at all, the two take each other in, and Cece struggles to find an explanation for her presence. Morgan smiles, hands in his back pockets.

"I meant to give you a call, but I never got your number," he says finally.

"Oh, no . . . I'm not here . . ." Cece says, mortified to think how desperate she must seem. She points to the white pickup truck, as if it might explain everything. "I'm here for work."

Is it disappointment flickering across his bearded face?

"Let me guess. Busted engine and you can't take it anywhere else because Richie's got beef with someone?"

"How'd you know?"

Morgan steps down from the trailer, the flimsy stairs bending to his weight. "It's a regular occurrence. Nice guy, but he drives a hard bargain, and that was before this whole Mamacoke Cove shitstorm. Now everyone's got an opinion, especially if you've got a nice little house on the water up there."

"You mean the new oyster farm?"

Morgan gives a stiff nod. "Bit ironic if you think about it, boat-repair fella not wanting another oyster farm. More oysters, more boats. Then again, he's the one with the million-dollar view . . . But yeah, we can take the engine off your hands."

They make their way over to where Cece parked.

"I didn't realize you were the supervisor," she says.

Morgan puts two fingers in his mouth and whistles in the direction of the hangar. "Just whenever the owner isn't here. Plus, it's not like these guys need a ton of help."

They stand by the truck and wait. Morgan runs his hand over the engine, saying something about the make and model, but Cece isn't listening. She's too busy trying not to remember their night together, sheets twisted between her legs, soles of her feet cramping.

"You left pretty early on Sunday morning," he says.

Cece's face warms. "I didn't want to wake you."

"And here I was planning on making you breakfast . . . Thought I'd dreamed the other night until you showed up just now."

Two workers emerge from the hangar, their gait slow and plodding. Cece tries to calculate how much time she has. "I didn't want you to get the wrong idea . . . Things are complicated."

"No explanation needed. I'm a big boy."

"Thanks."

"For what?"

"Making this easy."

"Maybe I'm like you. Trying to keep things simple."

Cece finds herself smiling for no particular reason.

Morgan drops the tailgate with a clang. "Have you been out on the water this summer?"

"Not even for work," Cece says. "They've stuck me on dry land."

"Why don't we go out this weekend? The owner lets me borrow his boat whenever he's not using it."

"What happened to keeping things simple?"

"Being out on the water is as simple as it gets."

Cece can only look at him, unable to find a reasonable reason to say no.

"I'm taking the silence as a yes."

"Sure," Cece says.

"Meet me down here on Saturday. Let's say sunrise," Morgan says, before turning to the approaching men. "Busted engine from Richie. And Mickey, let's try not to fuck this one up more than it already is."

It's strange to hear him giving orders, his language rough, his tone stilted and ill-tempered. The man Cece presumes to be

Mickey scowls at Morgan from under a mop of brown hair. "I didn't do nothing."

"Next you're gonna tell me the drive clamp screws stripped themselves."

"I already told you that was Wesley."

"Okay, Einstein. Don't forget. Righty tighty, lefty loosey."

Morgan already seems to have forgotten about Cece while he helps the men carry the engine. After muscling the tailgate shut, Cece gets in and watches him in the rearview mirror. After dropping off the engine, he stalks through the yard with purpose, arms swinging ever so slightly against his boxy frame, checking the undersides of boats, rubbing his hand along the bottoms. He climbs ladders into raised motorboats, walking the length of the spacious decks and inspecting whatever work's been done. Back on solid ground, he makes a phone call to the owner, Cece presumes, and starts gesturing to the water and then to the enormous crane above. Another worker comes out and offers a smoke. Morgan hangs up and the men stand there surveying the yard, arms crossed over their chests, sun beating down on their shoulders. Cece wonders what they're talking about in that strange language that men use with each other. Before Morgan notices her lingering, Cece starts up the truck and heads back to Noank, hoping Santiago will be impressed she didn't crash.

LORRAINE HOVERS OVER the stove stirring red sauce with a comically long wooden spoon, the fragrance of fire-roasted tomatoes and sautéed garlic filling the air. Cece had been wary of getting too close to Lorraine when she'd first moved into the cottage. An old, eccentric ex-hippie landlord hadn't exactly been Cece's idea of a friend. Plus, she wasn't intending on staying very long. But apparently, all it takes to sway Cece from her convictions is a decent home-cooked meal and an invitation. There's also the prospect that Cece is simply lonely, but she doesn't allow this thought to linger.

While Lorraine shuffles around the island, Cece peruses the sitting room. The coffee table is littered with old newspapers and magazines, mostly *National Geographic* and *Fine Gardening*, a stray *New Yorker*, by the looks of it. It's not exactly the house of a hoarder, but it's close. On the walls, faded posters for Woodstock '69, Earth Day, and the Altamont. A giant flag hangs over the sofa: SAY NO TO NUCLEAR POWER.

"I've been meaning to get those framed," Lorraine says, appearing at her side, spoon held out to Cece, "just haven't gotten around to it. Taste."

"Perfect."

"Not too spicy?"

"Bring on the heat."

"I lived in Calabria for a while after college. Let me tell you. Once you taste food like that, you can't go back. Everything's gotta have spice."

"What were you doing over there?"

"My former botany professor. She was working at the local university. She hired me as a research assistant. But mostly, I just remember drinking some incredible wine and eating the best meats and cheeses I've ever had in my life."

The only times Cece's left the country were with Jonathan.

She'd never considered studying abroad. It hadn't seemed financially feasible. As for traveling after graduation, taking three months off to backpack Europe or Southeast Asia didn't exactly seem like the most responsible thing to do. Gainful employment was her highest priority. What good was her degree if she couldn't make money and pay off her loans? Now Cece wonders if she'd made a mistake. If she'd traveled more, gained worldly insights, would she be stuck in her current predicament? Or might she have found the courage to strike out on her own? Compared to Lorraine's, her life feels quiet and small. The thought depresses Cece. Isn't she too young for such regrets?

"These posters are great," she says, hoping to change the subject. "Very vintage."

"When you're old, everything you own is vintage," Lorraine says, and drops a handful of salt in a pot of water. "That last one . . . the Altamont. Hells Angels were doing security. Beat my best friend into a coma . . . Animals. You don't ride motorcycles, do you?"

Before Cece can answer, her pocket vibrates. "I gotta take this."

Lorraine shoos her out the French doors onto the deck. "Dinner's being served in fifteen minutes, with or without you."

Outside, the pool looks almost inviting, framed by a wrought-iron fence and flower beds sporting vertiginous Russian sage and floppy catmint. Cece loves these long summer evenings, when the night deepens, the sun clinging to the horizon. They make her feel like she still has time, like her life's not rushing by. She thinks about sending the call to voicemail, but that'll only make things worse. Cece wonders how much Wynonna's told Mom.

No doubt they've been strategizing about how to get Cece back on her feet or, more precisely, back with Jonathan.

"Hi, Mom," Cece says, trying to sound aloof.

"How's the job search coming?"

From the steady whooshing on the other end of the line, Cece assumes her mother is driving home from work. Manhattan to the suburbs—a commute she would wish on no one. Her parents still call Tappan home, a hamlet lodged in the southern tip of New York, where Cece and her sister grew up. Even though it meant an hour-plus commute for her father to his job in Newark, higher taxes, and a mild strain on their finances, Cece's mother had insisted on living in the Empire State (a harbinger of Kim's expensive taste and general desire to always have what she couldn't quite afford). Money was plentiful back then, or at least Cece couldn't remember any fights about the lack of it. Business was booming for Barry's print advertising business with clients like Exxon, Nabisco, and Seagram's. The company had recently secured a major deal with *Bon Appétit*, and there was talk of moving headquarters to Manhattan.

"It's practically the same town," Barry said, pouring coffee into his travel mug. "We move a few streets over and save ten grand on taxes. Even the schools are better. So what if it's New Jersey?"

"It's a matter of principle, Barry," Cece remembered her mother saying while she smeared cream cheese on just-toasted sesame bagels.

"Careful now. You're starting to sound like a snob."

Kim shooed Barry toward the door with his briefcase and

newspaper. "It's not snobbery. It's called having standards. I'm not raising our girls in the armpit of America." Just the word *armpit* was enough to get Cece and Wynonna giggling. "Armpit! Armpit! Armpit!" they yelped in unison.

Barry held up his hands in cheerful defeat and blew kisses to the girls before pushing his way out the front door through the maze of shoes and abandoned toys. The moment is one of Cece's first memories, or at least one of her earliest happy memories, when she and Wynonna were still a team, when they laughed at everything because they didn't know any better.

Before answering her mother's question, Cece quickly runs through all the things she can't tell her: the job at the oyster farm, Jonathan's efforts at reconciliation, certainly not Morgan, or the palpable feeling that she's making mistake after mistake. What does that leave to discuss? Not much.

"Job search. What's the news?" her mother repeats, her voice louder this time.

Cece can see her leaning forward, lips nearly touching the center console, seat belt straining against her clavicle. "Hi, Mom. How was your vacation? It's nice to hear from you. I'm well," Cece says in a mocking tone that surprises even her.

For a moment there is only the hush of traffic. "The vacation was nice. Thank you. I'll speak with your father about when we can pick up Bernard."

Cece kneels and runs a finger over a rusted nail sticking out from the warped deck. She presses down hard on it, but to no avail. She'll have to tell Lorraine about it later.

"Well?" Kim says impatiently. "Job update. What's happening?"

The idea of returning to an office—chilled air pumping indiscriminately, murmurous meetings behind thick walls, the smoosh of beige carpet underfoot—brings a sudden wave of nausea. "I'm not rushing into anything."

"What about health insurance? You can't not have health insurance, Cece."

"I've got time to figure it out. There's a grace period before I lose coverage. And there's always COBRA."

"That's hardly a plan, Cece. There've got to be a hundred places looking for actuaries."

"What if I'm not interested in being an actuary anymore?" The question isn't a serious one. In Cece's mind, she hasn't quit the risk management world permanently; this is just a break, but her mother, whom she wants to antagonize, doesn't need to know that.

She doesn't go for the bait. "Don't be ridiculous. Let me talk to a few colleagues. I'm sure they know places looking for your expertise. It's impossible to find good employees these days. I swear, the paralegals at this firm are barely literate."

There's no use in telling her mother she doesn't need to find Cece a job. This is the only way she knows how to help. "How's work going?"

"Oh, you know," Kim says, her voice going flat. "It's the same everywhere. The associates do all the work while the partners get all the credit."

Ever since Kim didn't make partner back when Cece was in high school, this has been the common refrain, although the complaints have grown more bitter and resentful of late, a fact Cece attributes to her mother's expectation that she'd be long retired by now. The plan had always been for Barry and Kim to start their golden years early, splitting their time between New York and a summer cabin up in Maine. The internet had other ideas, however, and by the early 2000s, it was clear print advertising was a losing proposition. Barry shuttered the Manhattan office, cut his staff, and hung on for dear life. There were vain attempts to digitize, misguided efforts to learn graphic design. By the time Cece was applying to college, Barry's once-proud business had been reduced to designing ads in local magazines, and Kim was working more than ever to make up for the reduced income and to keep up appearances. There were certain luxuries—a newly leased car every three years, a perfectly manicured lawn and garden, her membership to the local racket club—she'd grown accustomed to and simply couldn't live without. And while Barry had seemed more than willing to adjust his spending and slip into social obscurity, Kim suffered from that uniquely pernicious conundrum of the American upper middle class—just wealthy enough to appear financially unburdened, but below the surface, paddling frantically, like a duck swimming against the current.

A knock on the glass pane. Lorraine holds up five fingers, tomato sauce and olive oil dotting her already-stained apron. Cece summons a smile and gives her a thumbs-up. "I gotta get going, Mom. I'm in the middle of dinner."

"The cottage has a kitchen?"

"Sort of."

"Have you spoken to Jonathan?"

Cece doesn't know why she's surprised. Of course Wynonna's told their mother about Jonathan's recent overtures.

"Why would I? We're broken up."

"You know we just adored Jonathan."

"You've said so many times."

"I just hope there's a chance for reconciliation."

"He didn't make me happy," Cece says, even though she's not certain it's true. "Don't you want me to be happy?"

"You seemed plenty happy. You wouldn't have stayed with him for four years otherwise. You wouldn't have said yes to his proposal. And not that you're asking, Cece, but let me tell you, happiness is overrated. Happiness is fickle. And you know what isn't fickle? Family, money, and stability. Jonathan had all that in spades."

"That's why you married, Dad, right? For his family name and all that money?"

"Things were different back then. It was the seventies. But if you must know, I thought your father would be an incredibly successful businessman. And he was! He didn't have much when we met, but he had vision. It's not his fault the internet decimated his business."

"How romantic."

"Being an adult is about compromise, Cece. You should know that better than anyone. You're an expert in the field of reality. Managing outcomes, differentiating good and bad risk, gaming out future assets and liabilities. Adulthood, marriage—it's no different, especially for women."

Kim is right, of course, so then why does Cece feel the need to resist? Why is she suddenly repulsed by the prospect of a job she once coveted? Has something actually changed, or is she just being foolish again?

"Just think about returning his text message, Cece. That's all I'm saying. You're smart enough to at least hear him out. Don't let your pride get in the way."

Cece feels herself itching for a fight. She wants to start digging up the past. She wants to ask her mother if all this well-meant advice is merely an accumulation of her own marital disappointments. As children, Cece and Wynonna were never made to believe their mother's long-simmering disappointments were anything serious. Their father would frame Kim's desire to build a screened-in porch, celebrate Christmas in Venice, or buy the girls matching Coach baguette handbags as whims, fleeting desires that weren't to be taken seriously. Kim and the girls would jokingly refer to him as "Mr. No." As in *I'd love to take you girls shopping, but you'll need to ask Mr. No.* Or *Will Mr. No let us go out for sushi tonight?* And *Is Mr. No going to spring for the cabin with air-conditioning this summer?*

Once Kim started working more and business at the print ad agency slowed to a trickle, Barry lost the power of the purse and grew more withdrawn when it came to family expenditures. He was never nasty about it, but Cece sensed he was worried. Initially, her swimming had been about challenging herself, building healthy habits, and teamwork, but as college loomed, Barry spoke often about scholarships. He somehow grew even more intense about her workout routine and swimming drills that left Cece trembling like a leaf and on the verge of blacking out. He was tough on her, questioned her commitment; they fought bitterly, but Cece always got back in the pool, and when she received a scholarship to Bucknell, it all seemed worth it, even if resentment lingered. Swimming was the one arena where Kim steered clear, more than happy to abdicate any and all responsibility—Cece sees that now. Like so many things, there are moments, snippets of time long gone, more recent interactions between her parents that take on a different shade, a different meaning entirely.

It seemed to Cece then, as it seems to her now, standing on Lorraine's deck, peepers chirping in the dusky darkness, that her mother feels cheated somehow by the luck of the draw, the inevitable gamble everyone takes when they marry someone. Barry was favored to win, the safe bet. If only she'd been more ambitious in finding a partner, Kim must think to herself. That's why she is where she is, and now she'll do anything to ensure her daughter, her promising, driven, smart daughter, doesn't make the same mistake.

LORRAINE'S CLEARED THE table of old newspapers and wicker bowls filled with stray coins and double-A batteries. After slapping down a wooden trivet, she maneuvers an orange Dutch oven onto the table. When Cece asks what she can do to help, she's ordered down into the cellar where Lorraine says she can pick any red from the top three rows. "You'll understand what I mean when you see it," Lorraine says after Cece gives her a look.

The cellar is dark and dank, something mossy and pungent in Cece's nostrils. She flails for a light, her hand catching air until finding a slender string dangling from the ceiling. Dark splotches and ringed light—it takes a moment for Cece's eyes to adjust. She makes out an imposing wine rack running from wall to wall, floor to ceiling. Under the cobwebs and dust, sideways bottles gleam dull light. Cece knows nothing about wine, but even she can tell she's looking at a small fortune. She counts carefully down from the top before picking something.

Dinner is delicious, and Cece forgets all manners and decorum, agreeing to seconds and then thirds, heaping freshly grated Parmesan atop her spaghetti and meatballs along with basil from the garden. According to Lorraine, Cece's picked a perfect wine pairing for their meal—a Pinot Noir from Veneto.

"It's from a former lover. The wine," Lorraine says, loosening her belt from under her apron.

Do people even have lovers anymore? Cece wonders. Her curiosity about Lorraine only grows, but she's hesitant to pry. Questions will only beget more questions, and Cece isn't entirely certain she wants to tell her landlord about the chain of unfortunate events that've landed her here.

"We met ages ago. He was a visiting classics professor at the time. I'd just gotten tenure and bought this place for a pittance. Anyway, he was always bringing back wine with him from his travels, or his friends would visit, and they would bring bottles as gifts. We amassed quite the collection."

"Where's he now?"

"Greece, I think, with his wife and kids. I only found out about them later."

"God, that's awful," Cece says before she can catch herself. The wine and spaghetti have lulled her into a false sense of security. Get a grip!

Lorraine holds a speckled hand over her mouth. "Oh, no. You

misunderstand. If anything, I was relieved. I remember being terrified at the time that he was going to do something idiotic like propose. I was even more opposed to marriage back then than I am now. No—it took the pressure off, knowing he already had a family. We could just have fun."

"Opposed?"

Lorraine sloshes more wine into her glass. "This country is obsessed with marriage. Sometimes I wonder how it's reached such a venerable status. Of course, I know how—it's a Goddamn national interest as far as the American government is concerned. Marital tax deductions, social security and healthcare benefits, family leave—the list goes on. But I still can't wrap my head around it. What makes people want to follow that crap? That's what we were all asking ourselves back in the sixties. I guess we were the crazy ones."

Something in Lorraine's words—the anger, the disbelief—tap something deep within Cece, but before she can respond, Lorraine's swatting the air. "That was a hypothetical question. Don't answer it. Sometimes it's just hard not to get riled up, especially when things don't turn out the way you thought."

"I get that," Cece says.

"Nah," Lorraine says, wine-stained teeth showing through her smile, "you're too young to understand nonsense like that."

Cece is somehow simultaneously flattered and offended. "What's the deal with that house that's getting fixed up down the street?" she asks, hoping to change the subject.

The mention of Morgan's home sends Lorraine into another diatribe, mostly about the scaffolding and the ruckus caused by the plastic tarps when the wind blows hard. She's called the town on numerous occasions, but no one seems interested in doing anything. Cece asks if she's thought about talking to the owner.

"I've only seen him a handful of times. He drives that awful truck that makes my windows rattle. He's nothing but trouble."

Cece's cheeks burn, her neck undoubtedly red and splotchy. Red wine does this to her.

"There was an incident back in January. I remember it because it was right after a big snowstorm. The cops showed up outside his house. I asked the neighbors, but no one knew anything for certain. A few people said it was a domestic disturbance."

"A disturbance."

"Yeah, like a fight between family members."

"I see," Cece hears herself say.

"I swear, all those shipwrights are philistines. They'd rather compensate for their tiny manhood in those big trucks than breathe fresh air. They're the type to tell you global warming is a hoax when it snows."

A cold sweat seeps out along Cece's hairline. Her heart thuds in her chest, thinking about her plans with Morgan. Why had she agreed so readily? Was she really that bored? That desperate for attention? Hadn't she had every intention of putting distance between them? Then again, it's summer, and after the shittiest spring in recent memory, isn't Cece entitled to some fun? And if she can't take up a guy's invitation to go out on his boat, what *can* she do? Still, her doubts remain, clinging to her like cobwebs. "You've never actually talked to the guy, right?"

Lorraine drains her glass. "Don't need to. You get to my age, and you can tell a thing or two about a person. They resent us. That bunch."

"Us?"

"People who work at the college. All the townies hate anyone who teaches up there. They blame the college for the town's financial woes. Sure, blame the tiny liberal arts college on the hill, not their own government passing NAFTA, repealing Glass-Steagall, or giving tax cuts to corporations."

"Sounds complicated."

"Trust me. It's not. I've had a few run-ins with their ilk at the monthly commission meetings. That's where I first got wind of Richie Rayburn's plan to expand his oyster business. All I did was ask a few questions and they got bent out of shape. They're not a smart bunch. They'd cut down a forest if it meant they had a job for a week."

"I suppose they need the work."

"Richie claims his proposal will create more jobs, but I've seen that before. It's Pfizer all over again. Why don't you come with me to the next meeting? I could use a set of fresh eyes on the situation. Maybe you'll see something I don't."

See? Cece thinks to herself, This is why you don't agree to have dinner with your crazy, Croc-wearing landlord. "I might have work stuff, but I'd love to check it out."

"No problem if you can't," Lorraine says. "You can help get signatures instead."

"For what?"

"The more signatures we get, the more pressure we can put on the members of the zoning commission. If we can show that Rayburn's project is unpopular, the proposal might be rejected.

But we need more signatures! Once we get enough, I'll write a formal objection, and then we'll attend the public hearing in force. And if all else fails, we'll gum up the works, request an environmental-impact study, a congestion study . . . whatever it takes."

"It sounds very involved."

"Glad to have you on board."

On her way back to the cottage, her head heavy from the wine, grass tickling her ankles, Cece tries to picture the police outside Morgan's home, lights painting the walls red and blue. She tries to remember what his house was like on the inside, but all she can remember is *him,* the touch of his hand, whiskey on his breath. She tries to imagine him and his boatyard buddies griping about the college and people like Lorraine. Before she can get her key in the lock, Cece hears Bernard's paws at the door, frantic and eager. He should've been walked hours ago.

Leash looped around her wrist, Cece closes the wooden gate behind them and stands on the sidewalk. Bernard lets out an impatient whine and tugs them in the usual direction, toward his favorite stop sign. "Let's take a different route tonight," she says. They turn left instead of right. The dog follows tentatively, ears perked, nose in the air, questioning the motivation behind such a change. Better not to walk by Morgan's house tonight, Cece thinks to herself.

5

Before Cece wakes up, there's the briefest of moments—lying in bed, the world gauzy and hushed through closed eyelids—when she misses Jonathan, his arm slung over the small of her back, the bedsheets always freshly laundered and starchy against her cheek.

They'd been set up by friends, and despite Cece's misgivings about blind dates and the usual entanglements that accompanied involving friends with her love life, she was ready for something serious, and Jonathan, she'd heard, was as serious as they came.

"In a good way, obviously," they said. "He's got his life together."

At the time, serious sounded nice to Cece. After nearly half a decade in the New York dating scene, serious seemed like the only sensible option. She'd concluded that there were simply too many beautiful women in the city. It was a numbers game, and no matter how Cece looked at the equation, she was drawing the short straw. There were no consequences for men who couldn't commit, men who didn't believe in marriage, men who wanted to just be friends who occasionally slept together. No matter their outrageous demand, no matter the astounding level of ambivalence, they knew there were a dozen beautiful women just around the corner if they were kicked to the curb. After looking at the situation from a purely statistical point of view, Cece had a hard time holding it against them. Which made it all the more surprising when she met Jonathan at a Japanese restaurant in Alphabet City and found him to be direct, decisive, and yes, serious.

He was sitting at the sushi bar dressed like he'd just come from work: brown loafers, gray slacks, and a navy blue button-down shirt complete with a gray Patagonia vest. It was an unremarkable outfit, a bland, inoffensive style made ubiquitous by finance bros. Cece remembers thinking that if she'd passed Jonathan on the sidewalk every day for a week, she might have never noticed him. But that wasn't the point! Where had carnal attraction gotten her? What had her previous judgments and aesthetic tastes produced? *Nothing* was the short answer. She told the hostess she was meeting someone and breezed into the cramped restaurant and gave her best smile when Jonathan saw her. She hoped she lived up to whatever picture her friends had shown him. And then a marvelous thing happened: Jonathan stood up, shook her hand, and took charge, and suddenly Cece felt foolish and superficial for caring about something as frivolous as a vest.

"It's lovely to meet you," he said. "I was just thinking . . . Sushi is a terrible idea for a first date. I can't believe I suggested it."

Cece was still lingering on the word *lovely.* Who said that word aloud anymore? "This is fine. I heard good things."

Jonathan was already putting a few bills down on the bar.

"I've got nothing against the food. I was thinking more about the chopsticks, and the fact that we can't sit facing each other."

"I hadn't thought about that . . . It'll be hard to find a table anywhere else. It's prime dinnertime."

"Way ahead of you. I managed to get us a table at an Argentinian steak spot just up the street. You aren't a pescetarian or anything like that, are you?"

Cece was impressed by his preparedness and his ability to pivot. But mostly, she felt like he was thinking about her—what *she* might want, how *she* might feel. "Sounds great."

"I know steak's a bit heavy, but it beats being humiliated when they inevitably offer me the kid chopsticks."

"How can I say no?"

"Perfect," Jonathan said with a grin, his teeth impossibly white. "We can always walk it off. The restaurant's right by the park."

They'd yet to have a proper conversation, and here Jonathan was, adding to their date, a first date at that! And yet, it didn't feel presumptuous or arrogant. Cece got the distinct sense that Jonathan wouldn't be offended or hurt if she declined to join him. He struck her as the kind of man who wasn't afraid to say aloud what he wanted, even if it meant failure or rejection.

They never made it to the park. They remained at the restaurant until they closed, which was only possible because Jonathan bribed the hostess to let them stay well beyond their reservation slot. He was fascinated by Cece's job and had to cut himself off after asking too many questions. "It never crossed my mind that you could assess uncertainty, not just in financial or insurance markets, but in life," he said, cutting into his steak with zest, "but of course you can!" As someone with two brothers, he wanted to know what it was like to grow up with a sister. He asked what her parents did and whether she was close to them. He spoke excitedly of the future—a five-year plan that involved making senior VP at his private equity job, crossing Venice, San Sebastián, and Marrakesh off his travel bucket list, and finally beating his best friend at tennis, something he hadn't accomplished since their days at Deerfield—and Cece listened intently. Except for swimming in high school and college, her own goals had rarely extended beyond the professional. As someone who saw the future as risk to be predicted and avoided, she was taken with Jonathan's approach. Here was someone who imposed their will on the complete unknown, willing the desired outcome into existence. Data, models, predictions—Jonathan used them, but he didn't let them stop him from taking action. It wasn't a matter of if his goals would come to fruition, but when.

Cece was genuinely impressed. "Those are some grand plans."

"Indeed. Although not very much fun when done alone," Jonathan said while he looked around the empty restaurant.

"I suppose not," Cece said, wary of the somber tone their conversation had taken. It would be just her luck that she finds a driven, serious, good-looking guy, only to discover he's a depressive.

"I hope this isn't too forward, but I'd like to see you again. I can't tell you how long it's been since I've had a good conversation on a date."

Prior to leaving her apartment, Cece had made numerous promises to herself: Don't be afraid to bail early if the date's a disaster, don't ask him questions and make him feel overly important, and upon pain of death, do not, if asked, agree to a second date. Something in her face must have betrayed her trepidation.

"What's that inane rule men are always following? Something about waiting at least forty-eight hours before calling someone after a date. I never understood that . . . Look, our friends set us up, which means they pity us, which means we've been on the dating scene far too long, which means we're either damaged goods or just way too picky."

Cece laughed. "Some friends."

"I don't want to waste your time or mine. I'm looking for something serious, and I think you are too, so let's find out if something's here. And if not, that's okay. But at least we'll have eaten some good food and gone on some fun dates."

Put this way—so matter-of-fact, so simple—Cece could find no plausible reason to decline the invitation. And after they'd exchanged numbers and Jonathan walked her to the corner of A and East Sixth and put her in a taxi, she thought about what he'd said and how it had put her at ease. Through the smudged windshield, traffic thinned, and green lights stretched for what seemed like miles, and the cab rolled on, jostled and bumped by the rutted streets. The cabbie got a call and began speaking with someone in his native tongue. Cece liked to think it was his wife, calling to check in on him during his shift. She leaned back in the unforgiving seat and closed her eyes. Jonathan, with his forthrightness and maturity, felt like the perfect match for someone like her, someone who craved predictability and security. It didn't hurt, of course, that he had a good job, had attended a reputable college. It was obvious he came from a good family, a family that no doubt occupied a social class well above Cece's. If she had to guess, Jonathan's parents lived the kind of life her mother wished they could afford to live, which meant her mother would approve of him. These weren't the most romantic notions, but where had romance gotten her?! She was ready to settle down, even if that wasn't the phrase Cece would have used, not in a hundred years. At last, she was ready for something simple and good.

Luxuriating in a Saturday off from work, the dark shape of Bernard snoring at the foot of her bed, Cece stretches her legs out until they're hanging off the twin mattress. She wiggles her toes, touching air. A mosquito whines somewhere in the room. Cece flails for a flip-flop on the floor and hucks it in the direction of the incessant drone. What has she done? Why is she here, in this room, alone? She wonders what Jonathan is doing at this precise moment, and then, before her mind can wander, she wipes the thought, like a hand across a foggy windowpane.

The sky is streaked the most glorious daffodil yellow by the time Cece makes it down to the boatyard. Last night over text, Morgan had insisted they leave at some ludicrous hour, and now Cece finds herself grumpy and resentful until he puts a warm mug of coffee in her hand and says good morning, boyish cheer on his face. Lorraine's gossip fades faster than the foghorn somewhere in the distance.

Underfoot, waves slap the dock, wooden planks warped and curved. Shells and algae cling to pilings, ashen and still. Wind bends off the water, and Cece shivers, cursing her insistence on wearing a pair of jean shorts and abandoning all practicality for the feeling of Morgan's eyes on her legs. By the time they board the imposing white powerboat, Cece's teeth are chattering, and she does her best to smile while Morgan unties knots and tosses buoys. He checks the outboard motors before pressing the ignition button, purple diesel fumes gurgling upward. After throttling up, he bends down and digs through his backpack, moving invisible objects with ease. "Here we go," he says, and tosses Cece a pair of sweatpants. "You might wanna throw these on, at least until the sun comes out."

If she weren't still waking up, Cece might have blushed, feigned ignorance, but for now she's just grateful to be warm as she slips on the sweats.

The boat cuts a V down the Thames, sending ripples across the placid water. Under the two steel truss bridges, I-95 rumbles overhead, steady and deafening. The current swirls, turning back on itself and around the concrete piers to their right and left. Morgan guides the boat with equal parts caution and confidence. He knows these waters, where the river runs deep and the shallows rise up without warning. Ahead, the sun hits the first Cross Sound Ferry departing New London, lighting it up like a polished cumulus. Out into the Sound, past the lighthouse, Morgan opens up the throttle, the twin motors roaring to life. With the wind in their ears, it's impossible to talk, and Cece's happy just to sit on the white leather seats in the stern, sun on her face, while Morgan takes them southwest, following the coastline. On the port side, Long Island, slender and green, slips in and out of view.

An hour later, they drop anchor near Duck Island. Cece admires the flocks of great egrets nesting among the dark, junglelike foliage. With their slender necks and bright yellow beaks, there's something prehistoric about the birds.

Morgan emerges from the hold wearing only his bathing suit and black flip-flops. "How about a swim?"

Cece turns away and looks intently at the water. Nothing sounds better to Cece, which surprises her. She can count on her hands the number of times she's gone swimming since Bucknell. She's kept her promise, her petty revenge: never to dip so much as a toe in a pool again, but the ocean is different, dark, and endless, no lanes, no colored floats bobbing in uniformity.

Diving off the back of the boat, Morgan's the first one in, his body surprisingly lithe and elegant as it knifes into the water. For a moment he doesn't come up, the water going placid and smooth. Cece watches for air bubbles, strains to see into the murk, her chest suddenly tight, breath frantic. Then he emerges, shoulders breaking the surface, thick black hair plastered to his skull, and Cece finds she's relieved, which makes her feel foolish and flustered. Before Morgan can recognize the look on her face, Cece crouches and launches from the deck, arms out in front, one hand over the other, chin tucked to her chest, hips high, like she's done a million times. The water is colder than Cece expected, and for a moment, gliding under the surface, eyes scrunched shut, it takes her breath away. Then she's emerging, everything sharp and bright.

They swim, tread water, do laps around the boat, dive under and come up on the other side. Cece stretches herself, breaststrokes long and sweeping, legs thrumming. Morgan spouts water at her, laughing as he crawls away. The water tastes salty and good in Cece's mouth, and for a moment, with the boat bobbing blissfully beside her, the sun cleaving up into the sky, she is present.

Lunch is egg salad sandwiches on whole wheat with a cucumber dill salad and potato chips, washed down with seltzers. They sit in the stern wrapped in beach towels, sunglasses shading their eyes.

"You swim well," Morgan says, backhanding some mayonnaise from his mouth.

Cece nods and squints.

"Like, really well. I was practically doggy-paddling next to you."

"I swam in college," Cece says.

"I'm guessing that's how you got those?" Morgan says.

Cece pulls the towel over her shoulders to hide the purple-hued scars in the shape of boomerangs.

"Sorry. I didn't mean to . . . Sometimes I talk without thinking."

"It's okay," Cece assures Morgan because it is. She doesn't mind how the scars look; she just doesn't like being reminded of that life.

Morgan is standing and hiking up his trunks to reveal a gruesome burn scar on his thigh, the skin—pink and yellow—cratered and pocked. It takes all of Cece's self-control not to gasp. From above, Morgan only grins. "Now we're even."

The logic isn't entirely flawless, but Cece has to admit she feels better. Imperfect and damaged, the both of them. "How'd you get that?"

Morgan licks egg salad from his thumb. "Iraq. Basra, to be more specific. Humvee we were riding in got hit. We did okay, though. Everyone walked away."

Cece still remembers the night the country went to war: missile strikes on television, the night vision footage grainy and green, sporadic explosions turning the screen a sickly yellow. The chyron scrolling in patriotic reds, whites, and blues: Operation Iraqi Freedom. Everyone knew there weren't weapons of mass destruction, and yet, somehow, the country had still gone to war. She'd participated in a high-school-wide protest.

Cece's never met anyone who's served in the military. Should she thank him for his service? For protecting her freedoms? She remembers when everyone in her town tied yellow ribbons around trees to support the troops.

"But enough of that," Morgan says, seeming to sense a shift in the mood. "Now that we've both revealed our deformities, we can enjoy each other's company."

Cece snorts with laughter, sending seltzer up her nose.

"Hope you're still hungry," Morgan says, producing a cornucopia of crackers, cheese, and olives. He lays out a red gingham blanket on the leather seats and starts setting up a crude charcuterie board. Cece retrieves a bottle of chilled white from the hold, and they sit in the sun and eat with their fingers. Morgan sends a few olive pits over the side. "I wasn't sure which cheeses were good, so I just got the ones with the names I couldn't pronounce."

Cece thinks about saying something, about how she was terrible at French in high school, about how her pronunciation was awful, but that isn't true at all. She was top of her class! Why is she compelled to minimize their differences? Morgan doesn't seem bothered in the least.

Morgan cuts a mini wheel of Brie like a pizza with his multitool. "When I've got time, I like to come out here by myself and eat this sort of thing and pretend I'm on the Amalfi Coast, or somewhere in the south of France."

Cece tries to imagine the sea warm as bathtub water, cerulean and glimmering. "Sounds nice."

"This is nice, too," Morgan says. "Long Island Sound. The Mediterranean of the East Coast."

They laugh and eat and fall into silence. The boat rocks to the waves, and Cece leans back, skin tight from the drying salt water.

"I wish I could do this forever," Cece says, before she catches herself. That word loaded and expectant, *forever.* She cringes, hoping Morgan isn't listening. But of course he is listening.

"Which part?"

Cece crams a few crackers into her mouth to buy herself some time. What's wrong with her? A boat trip and free lunch and she's already planning their future?

"I'm just messing around," Morgan says, like he means it.

"This just doesn't seem real."

"Why?"

"Because I'm happy, and until today, I don't think I've ever really thought, I mean really thought, about what makes me happy."

"You're saying it like it's a bad thing."

"If sitting on a boat, eating sandwiches, and swimming all day is what makes me happy, I think I'm in trouble because last time I checked, there's not much money in summering."

"That's the funny thing about money," Morgan says. "The more you make, the more you worry about it. Not that I've ever had very much of it."

The more time Cece spends with Morgan, the more she likes him, his unadorned behavior and rough edges, the way he speaks, directly, without agenda or self-concern. Cece wonders if Morgan shares this newfound sense of hopeful intimacy. She's never been good at this sort of thing, navigating the liminal states, the precursors to dating and more serious endeavors. Then again, she isn't very good at those, either. Just ask Jonathan.

If Cece were younger, if she'd never become an actuary, she might call meeting Morgan serendipitous. If she'd never put her faith in numbers and logic, she might be able to stop herself from calculating all the ways in which they will fail before they ever get started. Oh, how cynical she's grown! But is it really cynicism? Or is she just being a realist?

Morgan dries his sunglasses with a towel. "I don't usually do that sort of thing. If you were wondering," he says, keeping his head half-turned.

"What sort of thing?"

"Us. The other night."

"I wasn't wondering."

"Then I guess I was," he says sheepishly. "Silly, I know. I'm just having trouble calibrating things in my head."

"Well, if you must know, then yes, every summer, I travel up and down the northeast coast visiting dive bars and sleeping with anyone who buys me a drink," Cece says. Humor feels like the best defense. Laugh away the moment and all the real reasons.

Morgan chuckles. "Okay. Got it."

"*Me neither* is the short answer," Cece says after taking pity on him.

"How'd you end up working for that Richie Rayburn? Doesn't seem like your usual line of work."

"What gave it away?"

"Now you're just searching for compliments . . . Your hands mostly."

Two weeks of oyster work and her hands are still in good shape, except for a few new callouses and chipped nails. Cece does her best not to weigh the cost-benefit analysis of being truthful in this moment. Be honest, she thinks. What do you have to lose that you haven't already lost?

"I saw an ad online and was desperate to try something new and get out of Stamford. My fiancé and I broke up a month ago. We . . . he lives there."

Morgan looks out at the water contemplatively. Cece can't tell how this news has landed, his beard making his face inscrutable.

"I also lost my job. He didn't react well," she says before he can respond.

"Sorry to hear," Morgan says. "Getting fired's no fun."

"You've had experience?"

Morgan grins. Those perfectly skewed teeth again. "God . . . more than I can count. Waitering gig at this real hoity-toity spot in Provincetown. A roofing job up in Portsmouth for a total crook. Then there was a welding apprenticeship . . . So yeah . . . I've been fired a few times in my day."

Cece waits for him to say something or ask her questions about the implosion of her engagement, but he doesn't. His seeming disinterest is so palpable, it makes Cece wonder whether she said it aloud at all. Waves slap against the boat's prow, a hypnotizing rhythm. "It was my decision to call it off," she says, unable to resist to urge to clarify her situation.

"It's still hard to end things, even when it's the right thing to do."

That's the problem! Cece thinks. She doesn't know whether it *was* the right choice.

"But whatever reasons you had," Morgan continues. "I'm sure they were the right ones."

Cece wonders if he's just saying all this to make her feel better but decides not to question him. It *is* making her feel better. Isn't that what matters? "Thanks."

"So what was the gig you got fired from?"

It takes Cece a moment to understand Morgan's moved on to the next subject, no longer interested in the juicy details of her failed relationship. Surprised, but mostly relieved, she tells him about her career in what feels like another life.

"An actuary . . . Aren't those the people who help insurance companies predict when you're gonna die?"

"There are different types," Cece says, sounding more defensive than she wants to. "You're talking about a life actuary. They make sure the insurance company models are sustainable. But we do all kinds of work: pensions, property insurance, risk management. It's just the science of risk."

"Science of risk."

"Using statistical tools to determine the probability of something happening."

"Sounds complicated."

"Not really," Cece says. "I mean, you don't even need an advanced degree for it."

"You shouldn't do that."

"What?"

"Make yourself small. Belittle your accomplishments, at least on my account."

"Force of habit," Cece says. "I guess I'm still figuring things out."

"You ever wonder if that's just life? Figuring things out? Like maybe there's no moment where you eventually wake up and everything makes sense."

The idea terrifies Cece, but she cracks a smile anyway. With Morgan here, now, such things seem possible. He's different; he listens, not just to what she says, but how she says it. Cece gets the sense that Morgan would treat her the same whether she'd attended Harvard or the community college up in Norwich. And if she's being honest with herself, which isn't always the case, she doesn't understand how someone can be so unpretentious and secure.

On their way back, Morgan wants to know why Lorraine hates him so much. Cece says that *hate*'s a strong word but that the ongoing house renovation isn't earning him any allies in the neighborhood. There's more to it, Morgan says, that she'd begrudge him even if he had the nicest house on the block. "All those professors act like the college is doing the town a favor," he shouts over the chop of waves and whistling wind, "like the townies should be grateful for the part-time jobs in their dining hall." There is a hard bitterness to his words, and for a moment, Cece wonders if *this* is the real Morgan, underneath the kind and mellow demeanor. She thinks about what Lorraine told her about the police showing up outside his house.

As quickly as it appears, Morgan's hostility melts away, and he shrugs his shoulders, defeated, as if to say, *This is just the way of the world.* Heading up the river, Morgan lets Cece take the wheel and shows her how to read the water. He runs through the terminology: starboard, port, stern, and bow. Approaching the shipyard, he teaches her how to throttle down and reminds her to throw the rubber fenders over the side before bringing them up against the mussel-covered pilings. They walk the length of the boat, and Morgan instructs Cece on how to tie a bowline knot and then a cleat hitch, the rope heavy in her hands. He stands behind her, beard tickling her neck, and recites a trick to help her remember, his voice thrumming against her back: "Up through the rabbit hole, round the big tree; down through the rabbit hole, and off goes he."

"Or she," Cece says.

Morgan chuckles. "Or she."

Cece leans back into him then, his chest sturdy and wide, and for the briefest of moments, she allows herself to imagine what this kind of life might be like—risk be damned.

6

The high season is in full swing in Mystic, Main Street already clogged with eager, boxy-shirted tourists weighed down with triple-scooped ice-cream cones and bags of saltwater taffy. On the sun-drenched sidewalk, crowds gather outside Mystic Pizza, snapping photos of the façade and peering inside, hands to the glass, as if Julia Roberts herself might appear, slinging pizza with her radiant smile and poofy '80s hair.

The traffic is interminable, inching over the river at an agonizing pace. In front of Cece, a contractor drums an impatient beat with a paint-speckled hand against the side of his pickup truck. Kayakers and paddleboarders, necks and noses slick with sunblock, slip underneath the drawbridge, making their way upriver. Mystic, with its charm and whimsy, is nearly unrecognizable from its neighbors—Groton and New London—with their industrial ports and rugged self-reliance, and Cece wonders whether she'd be happier in a place like this, not that she can afford it!

The office for Rayburn Oyster Company sits on the second

floor of a redbrick warehouse on Holmes Street. It's Sunday afternoon, and Richie has summoned Cece to the office. He didn't say what the meeting was about; he didn't need to. The pressure washer had required significant repairs, and while Cece has proven herself capable to drive the company truck, she has no illusions about Santiago's opinion of her. If anything, her responsibilities have shrunk, relegated to hosing down the boat, stacking crates, and tidying up. Despite her dwindling sense of usefulness, there have been little pleasures, of course, unexpected rewards: the way she collapses into bed and sleeps a dreamless sleep; the way her worries evaporate under the beating sun and whistling wind; the way blisters have transformed into thick calluses on her palms. There is nothing abstract or theoretical about this work; it is real, undeniable. Still, she wants more, more time on the water, a better understanding of the oysters themselves, these organisms they're all working so hard to grow. Taking the stairs two at a time, stomach in her throat, Cece prepares for the worst.

Sitting behind a metal desk littered with papers and cascading manila folders, Richie, peering at the gargantuan monitor of his ancient desktop computer, appears indifferent to Cece's presence. He gestures for her to sit down without taking his eyes away from the pixelated screen. There's an audible crunch—a pretzel, a potato chip maybe—while Richie, muttering to himself, navigates the mouse on his crowded desk.

With shoulder-length gray hair and unruly sideburns, Richie doesn't look like a Richie at all. When she'd answered the initial job listing, Cece was expecting someone much younger, someone wearing sneakers and khakis, a gingham button-down tucked into a rope belt. At the time, her only reference for oyster farmers were the occasional stories in *The New York Times* about disillusioned millennials who'd given up their white-collar jobs to take over struggling agricultural businesses in an attempt to return to their agrarian roots. There were never any follow-up stories about these people, only their initial burst of inspiration, when hope sprang eternal, when every challenge and failure was an opportunity to learn. Cece can only assume this is the case because the ventures didn't last long. Is she any different from these people? The fear lingers. Will she scuttle back to her old life whenever this performative venture has lost its luster? In the oyster business for nearly twenty-five years, Richie doesn't share these concerns. He is a man whose only mission is to return the Sound and its tributaries to their former oyster glory, when bivalves once littered the banks and shoals, when the water was so clean it was said the Dutch could see straight to the bottom from their tall ships. He is a man obsessed, who cares for little, unless of course it concerns oysters. Sitting down at his desk, Cece hopes she can use this to her benefit, appealing to his passions rather than rationality, where she stands little chance of remaining employed.

While Cece sits, Richie pulls a pencil from behind his ear and looks over a yellow legal pad. A teardrop-shaped oyster shell dangles around his neck. Whatever is on the paper is displeasing, and he gnaws at the bottom of his already ragged lip. "You did a real number on the pressure washer."

"I'm sorry about that," Cece says hastily. She can't get the words out fast enough. "It was a rookie mistake, and like I said before, just take out whatever you need to pay for it."

"Don't think you'll have much left over."

Cece swallows her panic and shrugs. "No worries," she says, even though she'd been counting on the first paycheck from Rayburn to bolster her dwindling checking account. Breaking up with Jonathan had proven more costly than she'd anticipated. There'd been moving expenses and half the monthly rent for the remainder of the lease. Jonathan didn't need the money; he'd even rejected it when she'd first offered. But she'd insisted. It was the principle of the matter. Then, of course, there'd been dog food for Bernard, an unforeseen car repair, and more than a few profligate purchases from the local wine store.

Richie pushes papers around on his desk.

"I'm good for it," Cece says. If times get tough, or tougher than they already are, she can always draw on her 401(k). A proposition she can't believe she's considering, and for what, pride? After scrupulously saving for nearly a decade, she's miraculously managed to build a modest nest egg. It was never too early to start saving for retirement. She truly believed that. When it came to getting old, money seemed like the great equalizer to Cece, the only tool at her disposal to combat the terrifying unknown future that was growing infirm in the United States of America . . . She must be nuts.

Finally meeting her gaze, Richie looks up and takes her in, his deep-set eyes lingering on her hands and shoulders, like she's a racehorse past her prime. "We could just call it even. There's no shame in cuttin' your losses."

When she'd climbed the rickety stairs to the Rayburn office, Cece had thought being fired was the worst outcome of the current conversation, but she'd been wrong. Being pitied by Richie is far, far worse. He feels bad for her, so bad that he's willing to forgo a few thousand dollars—just to be rid of her. She'd rather he cuss her out, threaten to garnish her wages . . . anything but pity.

"If it's all the same to you, I'd like to stay on," Cece says, annoyed by the quaver in her voice. Countless data presentations, panels moderated, conferences attended—and this, bizarrely, is the most nerve-wracking thing she's done in recent memory. She's never had to advocate for her own usefulness; the actuary exams did that—all seven of them. The very nature of actuary work was indispensable to the insurance industry. But this . . . her . . . She's dispensable. There are a hundred people who could do a better job than her. That much has been proven.

A dubious frown works its way across Richie's face. "Well . . . I—"

"At least let me pay you back in full for the pressure washer, and if you still want to let me go afterwards, I'll go willingly."

"I'm not really the one you need to convince."

"Santiago."

Richie nods.

"I'll handle it," Cece says, even though her determination is already crumbling.

Richie stands up and wipes his hands on his light denim jeans held up by red suspenders. Along with a pilly button-down, he isn't so much wearing his clothes as they're dangling off him, like laundry drying on the line. The crown of his head nearly touches the lamp hanging from the ceiling, and Cece thinks she can smell burning hair. He reminds her of a Puritan preacher, about to rain fire and brimstone from the pulpit, cursing his parishioners for their sins. Cece's persistence seems to fluster him while he rummages through his shirt pocket for something. "It's nothing personal," he says, giving Cece a forced smile full of tobacco-stained teeth.

"I understand."

Richie digs out a toothpick from a shirt pocket and pops it cavalierly into the corner of his mouth. "If you can sort it out with him, I'm good with it."

Cece thanks him and leaves before he can change his mind. Aware Richie might be watching, she holds her head high until she's out of view. Not until she exits the warehouse into the blinding sun, jumps into her suffocatingly hot car, and puts the windows down while she drives out of town, avoiding the drawbridge in favor of the interstate, does she allow the disappointment to wash over her like a thunderous ocean wave.

THE IDEA OF winning over Santiago seems nearly impossible. Cece is caught off guard by her emotional investment in the job. What had initially seemed like a good way to pass the time and disengage from the tumult of her life feels suddenly urgent and necessary. Even if it just means getting to work on the dock with the sorting equipment, Cece wants to feel like she's making progress, learning something, proving everyone wrong. The urge is juvenile and petty, but there's no way around it.

Thankfully, Cece can't linger too long on her conversation with Richie. Dinner with Morgan is tonight, and she finds herself excited and hopeful. At first, she'd balked at the idea, fearful that she might be giving him the wrong idea. Or was it that she was fearful of giving in to an idea, a feeling, that had felt wrong since they'd met? Cece isn't foolish enough to think she can sleep her way through her current problems, which is why she set ground rules: no sex, no sleeping over, under any circumstances. At least she won't have to cook dinner. Pulling into the gravel driveway, she thinks about potential reasons for going out, just in case Lorraine's home and asks where she's headed. If possible, she'd like to avoid the distinction of fraternizing with the enemy.

CECE CAN SMELL the cooking before she knocks on the door. From an open window: the aroma of butter and garlic wafting out into the summer night. Morgan appears, kitchen towel slung over his shoulder, a large Band-Aid on the top of his hand. Nothing serious, he assures her. Just some culinary hubris.

"It smells delicious," Cece says, thankful she doesn't have to lie. In her experience, when men say they can cook, they usually can't. How many mediocre meals had she sat through? A pleasing smile on her face. Can cook, Cece thinks, adding the attribute to the positive category. She's decided to keep a mental checklist in her head, weighing Morgan's qualities. It's a crude but necessary tool to combat her current state of confusion. And yes, Cece is willing to admit she's confused—confused and intrigued all at once. Why else would she be here?

The inside of Morgan's house is nothing like Cece remembers. Then again, the only room she can really recall is the main bedroom. Perhaps she'd had more to drink than she'd initially thought that night. Thankfully, she'd had enough time to shower before dinner, but Cece still sniffs her armpits when Morgan isn't looking, paranoid she smells like sea scum. While he grabs them drinks from the kitchen, she takes the time to look around the living room.

Contrary to its run-down exterior, Morgan's home is warm and inviting inside, with its new hardwood floors and freshly painted walls. A worn but sturdy leather sectional dominates the living room. A grand white ash coffee table rests in the center of a circular jute rug. Shelves on cinder blocks form makeshift bookshelves and line the walls. To Cece's astonishment, they are overflowing with books of every shape and size: thick encyclopedias, clothbound atlases, humble dog-eared paperbacks, and well-preserved hardcovers. Next to the couch, more books stacked in precariously leaning towers along with piles of newspapers, creased and ruffled. Before Cece can examine the shelves more closely, Morgan returns with her beer. For a moment, Cece thinks he'll say something about the books, but he doesn't; instead, he offers her the tour. She considers making a joke about already having done the tour, but she holds her tongue, not wanting to ruin the moment. Between the living room and the kitchen, Morgan's demolished a wall and used the extra space to install an oversized island crafted from repurposed wood, ruts sanded smooth, knots swirling and dark. The rest of the house is still very much a work in progress with rooms that more closely resemble a construction zone than a home: the guest bedroom with Sheetrock for walls, the powder room floor, stripped of its linoleum, a plastic tarp in its place, a slop bucket catching water from the suspect plumbing underneath the sink. Even with the inescapable whiffs of paint and plaster, Cece feels at ease here, where she can't be reminded of her previous life.

Back in the kitchen, Morgan uncorks a bottle of white and gives the saucepan of steaming clams a splash. "Any dietary restrictions the kitchen should be made aware of?"

Cece tugs at the strands of her jean shorts. "All sorts. Unless those clams have lived fulfilling lives, I'm afraid I can't eat them."

Morgan gives a hearty laugh and checks on a large pot of boiling water, turning up the flame. He moves through the kitchen with supreme confidence, pulling a colander and cutting board from the cupboard, slicing lemons and chiffonading handfuls of parsley at a speed that almost alarms Cece, the knife blade small and nimble in his big hands.

"Where'd you learn to cook like that?" Cece asks, after they've taken their bowls of linguini and clams out back.

Morgan's set a crude picnic table made of cast-off lumber and steel drums for them. Citronella candles burn bright in colored glass.

"You get real good at cooking when you live alone," he says, raising his beer.

"I beg to differ."

"To a good home-cooked meal, then," Morgan says.

They toast and fall to eating. Pasta twice in the last week, Cece thinks. Too many carbs—then again, she's burning more calories than she's ever burned with the oyster crew. She can't help but observe Morgan eat, chapped elbows on the table, twirling heaping mounds of slick linguini on his spoon, chewing thoughtfully, his eyes playful, garlic bread crumbs in his beard.

Even though they've already slept together, even though she can remember the way his voice felt against her back—*Up through the rabbit hole, round the big tree; down through the rabbit hole, and off goes he*—she's pushed off-balance by the strange intimacy of the moment, sharing a meal, eating quietly, only the whine of frustrated mosquitos. When Cece accepts the offer for seconds, the reason is twofold: The dinner is utterly delicious, and she'll be less likely to break her own promise not to sleep over with a full stomach.

When they've finished for good, Cece helps clear the table and leaves the dirty dishes in the sink at Morgan's insistence. Admitting defeat to the insects, they move to the living room couch, where Morgan's laid out the home's original blueprints, along with some future design concepts. He explains his vision to Cece, where he wants to install skylights, a half wall, and crown molding. There's even a sharply drawn design for a screened-in porch. He wants to do everything himself, down to the roof work. Cece marvel's silently at Morgan's ingenuity and skill. How does one accrue such knowledge? she wonders.

Looking over his plans, Morgan seems to grow bashful, hastily rolling up the papers and securing them with a worn rubber band, like he's embarrassed by his own optimism.

Cece can't stop thinking about how the more time she spends with Morgan, the more questions she has. Part of her thought everything would make itself plain upon stepping foot in his house again—but nothing could be further from the truth. The sketch Cece's been working on of Morgan—rough-around-the-edges, blue-collar bachelor—is getting hazier by the second.

She looks around the room again. "Have you read all these books?"

"Sure," Morgan says, eyeing the shelves like he's seeing them for the first time. "Half of them are cheap mysteries. The kind you used to be able to buy at the supermarket. Why? Think they're just for show?"

Cece worries she's gone bright red. "No, no. Not at all. I was just wondering."

"You can check," he says, nodding playfully toward the shelves. "They're real, just like in Jay Gatsby's library."

Cece tries to hide her confusion and ignores the literary reference. Why *is* she confused anyway? Has she really become that snobbish? What was she expecting? Cable news stories and NASCAR highlights? The guy went to high school. He probably went to college, too! Get a grip! Cece thinks to herself. "No. I mean . . . it's impressive. I just haven't met anyone in a while that reads much. I don't think I've read a book in five years."

"It's a good way to pass the time as any other."

"Better than binging terrible reality television."

Morgan promises he isn't judging her TV-watching habits, which only makes Cece feel worse. He brings out coasters for their beers that are sweating on the coffee table. He doesn't make a move to get closer, which brings Cece a sense of frustrated relief. Instead, he picks at the label on his bottle and says, "I was thinking more about your old job. About how hard it must have been."

"The hours weren't great, but I loved it, and I was good at it," Cece says.

"I guess I was thinking more about all that data. Those numbers and percentages. I mean, if I knew all the ways something might go wrong or fail, I wouldn't be able to get out of bed in the morning."

"That's where we differ. I find all that data reassuring. Otherwise, I'm flying blind."

"You've got some serious guts. Doing what you're doing. I'd be jumping right back into my comfort zone and my old career, but you're doing this oyster thing. You're actually trying something new. You're here, even though I bet all the data is telling you otherwise."

"I guess I never really thought about it like that," Cece says, growing self-conscious. Is what she's doing courageous? Mostly, it feels reckless. "Makes me feel a little better about camping out in Lorraine's backyard."

"My nemesis."

"How long have you lived in the area?" Cece says, anxious to switch subjects.

Morgan stands up and heads to the kitchen and comes back with a bottle of bourbon and two glasses. "Going on three years. I was up in Providence before that. Drink?"

"I'm not staying over," Cece says, trying to hide her smile. What is she protesting? What is she trying to stop?

"Fine by me."

The heat of the day has burned off, and Morgan opens the living room windows to the cool night air. "I grew up in Wellfleet. My family's in the boat-building business. Really just the repair business these days. We've been up there pretty much since the beginning, or at least when they first started fishing for mackerel. I don't necessarily love the work, but it's what I know, and that counts for something, knowing a trade."

The wind picks up and rattles the screens in their old window frames, bringing with it hints of summer: barbecues and bug spray, the shrill shouts of the neighborhood kids playing manhunt. It's hard to imagine the humidity that had clung to Cece like a waterlogged coat just last week, and Cece finds herself relaxing, the bourbon unknotting her from the inside out, while she listens to Morgan tell her about what it was like growing up on the Cape, catering to the rich in the summer and doing his best not to become a full-blown townie in the winter, when the weather was wet and cold and the idea of fun was a couple of thirty racks in a half-built house. The new-construction homes were plentiful. New York and Boston money always wanting more square footage, more three-car garages, more wraparound driveways.

Cece thinks back to college, when half the campus would return from summer break, bronzed and sand-scrubbed, throwing around names like Wequassett, Great Island, and Chatham, as if they meant something. Cece wonders if she has more in common with Morgan than either of them knows, but she doesn't say anything. Instead, she leans forward and learns that Morgan grew up with two half brothers. His father remarried soon after his mom died. Cancer. She learns that Morgan signed up for the National Guard on his eighteenth birthday, partly because of the GI Bill, and partly because he couldn't stand the idea of sticking around Wellfleet his whole life. He made it close to two years before being discharged. "Drugs," he clarifies, "but not the scary kind."

"That must have been hard," she says instead, "growing up with half brothers."

Morgan swirls his bourbon. "Maybe," he says, "but I don't think I had it worse than anybody else. It's all relative."

Cece doesn't know where she's going with her line of questioning, maybe she's just bored, but she wants to unearth something in Morgan, some vulnerability, some weakness. A secret just for her. "Still, blended families can be difficult to navigate, especially for a young kid."

Morgan chuckles. "Is that what they're calling them these days?"

"I think it's supposed to sound better than whatever we used to say."

"I never really understood the difference between a euphemism and a lie, but yeah, family's tough. Even when they aren't all mixed up."

Morgan's voice is like molasses, syrupy and sweet, mixing with her half dreams as Cece's head grows heavy, her eyelids fluttering. Be careful, Cece thinks, sinking into the crook of Morgan's arm, his worn T-shirt feathery and smooth. But she is tired. Tired of being careful. Tired of thinking rather than doing. "I'm just going to close my eyes for a second," she murmurs. "Keep talking."

When she wakes, the room is painted in shadow. Cece doesn't know where she is, heart thudding in her ears, and she is possessed with the urge to get up, to run. But then she makes out the familiar bookshelves, the coffee table. She spots her toes sticking out from under a thin blanket Morgan must have covered her with, and wiggles them, just to make sure she isn't dreaming. The house is quiet. She rises, her mouth thick from the bourbon. Moving slowly down the hall, she reaches out and touches the walls, a single night-light guiding her way. She tells herself she's sleepwalking, moved by some force other than her own volition.

Morgan stirs when she gets to his bed, shedding her socks and shorts before sliding in. She reaches for him in the darkness, pulling him close. He mumbles something about Bernard. "I took him out earlier," Cece says.

"What happened to not staying over?" he says, lips on her jaw and then her neck.

There's no time to answer, breath catching in her throat, hands on Morgan's chest, warm to the touch. Leg sliding over his bare stomach, Cece moves on top of him, pinning his arms against the lumpy mattress. She likes this best—in the darkness, invisible to each other, blank canvases of possibility. She lowers her face to his, his breath quickening. "I like this," he whispers.

"Me too," Cece says.

They laugh between kisses, front teeth knocking.

THE BED IS empty when Cece wakes, a still darkness beyond the shades. The house is quiet. Cece rolls over and dangles off the bed, searching her shorts for her phone. Empty. Peering through the window, she puts the time around five. Plenty of time to get to work. When was the last time she woke up of her own accord? No alarm blaring. Where's Morgan? she wonders, head foggy, inner thighs tender from last night.

On the kitchen counter, a hand-scribbled note in thick carpenter pencil lead: *Went into town to grab breakfast sandwiches.*

Cece runs her fingers over the lettering, impressed by Morgan's superb handwriting. Alone, she moves through the house, pulling books off the shelves and thumbing through them, opening the kitchen cabinets, surprised by the neatness and organization. She tells herself this isn't snooping; she tells herself she deserves to know a bit more about the man she's just slept with again, against her better judgment. Catching sight of herself in the bathroom mirror, she considers taking a shower but decides against it, opting for a finger smear of toothpaste. Bad breath currently seems like the greater threat.

It happens without Cece thinking. The faucet still running, she picks through the medicine cabinet. She doesn't know what she's looking for until she finds it among the bottles of extra-strength Tylenol and Icy Hot: foundation, a few bottles of nail polish, and mascara. Her heart tumbles, ever so slightly. Why is she surprised? What was she expecting? Cece finds her disappointment annoying and immature, and she fights against the urge to wallow in self-pity. Water off, she listens for his truck—nothing.

You've already gone this far, Cece thinks to herself, kneeling and opening the doors to the bathroom vanity. You can't sink any further. The items in the cabinet can be explained away, left by an ex-girlfriend, one-night stands, but Cece is in search of something else, something more definitive, and then she finds it, stashed behind rolls of toilet paper: boxes of tampons and a toothbrush in a plastic travel case, its bristles worn and frayed. The moment Cece sees the items, she hates herself for even looking.

Outside, a truck door slamming, heavy work boots on wooden steps.

"You awake?" Morgan calls, his voice bright and hopeful. "I've got breakfast."

Cece gently closes the vanity and collects herself in front of the mirror. Smile, Cece thinks to herself. You've got no right to do anything else. Smile!

7

Confronted by the prospect of losing her job, Cece deploys a three-pronged strategy (bribery, reciprocity, and flattery) to keep her summer gig at Rayburn. She isn't about to get fired from two jobs in a month. Last week's conversation with Richie still fresh, she arrives at the docks in Noank just after sunrise, determined to win Santiago and Davi over. What better way to show her commitment than doing their jobs for them? She runs the risk of breaking another piece of equipment or forgetting a step in the process to get the boat ready, but she's got nothing to lose.

The sun is only a suggestion along the horizon when Cece tops off the gas tank with diesel, checks the fuel lines, and hoses down the deck just for good measure. Where there is grime or scum, Cece lets the hose run and scrubs at the areas with a brush. It won't be anywhere near spotless, but she wants it to look cleaned up by the time Santiago and Davi arrive.

The morning's busywork serves another purpose, too—it keeps Cece's mind off Morgan and the contents under his bathroom sink. The tampons, the toothbrush—incontrovertible evidence of another woman, and not just any woman, but a woman who'd spent the night and didn't care if keeping her toiletries at his house made her look clingy. Cece has no right to be disappointed, and yet she is, which only irritates her more. She's the one who was worried about Morgan thinking this was more than a fling. She should be elated!

Cece doesn't know whether they're dropping racks today, but she's gotta keep moving and heads back to the warehouse and starts stacking them, one after another, ten high. Afterward, she heads inside the workshop to organize the tools, a task Santiago had asked her to do already but that she'd half-assed. This time around, she takes her time and works meticulously. She even organizes all the loose screws and nails that are scattered across the plywood worktable. Nothing is left unaccounted for. And by the time she hears Santiago's truck pull in, she steps back to admire her work on the pegboard. It's a wonder of efficiency and organization: zip ties, hot glue guns, measuring tapes, and spatulas for spreading fiberglass filler on the left side, and on the right, in descending order of size, hammers, wrenches, plyers, grippers, and socket wrenches.

The door cracks open and Santiago pushes his head inside. Lips pursed, he gives Cece's efforts a once-over and nods before closing the door. Cece follows him, eager to deploy her other strategies of persuasion. She hurries to her car while Santiago heads to the boat. Davi is already on board and pacing the deck. When she opens her car door, Cece's greeted with an aroma of dough and custardy goodness. She hopes the pastries are still fresh. That morning, she'd dragged herself out of bed at four a.m. and driven to Hartford. She used to work with someone who was from there who'd raved about a Portuguese bakery just off Park Street. The place didn't open until six, but Cece had taken a chance. She'd expected them to treat her like a crazy woman, knocking on the finger-smudged door at five in the morning, offering cash for their freshest batches of *pastel de nata* and *bola de Berlim*, but they couldn't have been more pleased. They'd even given her extra when she mentioned they were for some Portuguese oystermen she worked with. This, too, was a risk, but a calculated one. Santiago and Davi might not be Portuguese at all, in which case, Cece would be accused of all sorts of awfulness, but she'd heard them speaking to one another in a foreign tongue and was fairly certain she'd identified the language correctly; either that, or they were the tannest Russians she'd ever seen.

Paper bag in hand, Cece approaches the boat where Davi is talking to his father and pointing at the deck of the boat, mystified by its cleanliness. Something like pride swells in her chest. The two regard her with skeptical indifference.

"I brought you something."

The gesture flummoxes Santiago, who stands with his hands on his hips. Davi eyes the bag like he has X-ray vision.

"Breakfast," Cece says. "Pastries."

Foot on the gunwale, Santiago leans over and retrieves her bribe. If the immaculate boat, tuned-up equipment, and organized tool wall don't convince him to keep her around, maybe these will. He hands the bag to Davi, who eagerly opens it.

"Pastel de nata!" he shouts, holding up the golden custard in the morning light. "Your favorite."

"We already ate breakfast."

Davi stalks to the back of the boat.

"Where did you get those? There isn't a Portuguese bakery for miles."

"Hartford."

"I guess you think because you brought me some baked goods from the motherland, tidied up, and cleaned the boat I'll let you stick around."

Fury builds in Cece's chest, but she pushes it down, drowns it. "I don't really care what you decide, but I'm here, so you might as well put me to work. And those pastries weren't for you. They were for your son."

They aren't on speaking terms for the rest of the day. Cece stays on land, carrying out the same menial tasks she's done for weeks while Santiago and Davi head out on the boat. When they return with a few racks and set to cleaning oysters in the tumbler, Cece keeps her distance, wary of pushing too hard. Every few hours, Davi looks over in her direction, as if to apologize. Cece wonders if Santiago let him eat the pastries, or if he tossed them overboard out of spite. They cut out early at four o'clock, stripping their rubber waders off and carrying them to their truck.

"I'll see you tomorrow," Cece says to Santiago as he walks by.

"Suit yourself."

The day had been an utter failure. Despite her best efforts, Cece's made little headway. If anything, she's in a deeper hole. She hadn't even been able to deploy her last stratagem: flattery. It wasn't really her fault. Altogether unappealing, rude, and pompous, Santiago was impossible to shower in adulation, real or imagined.

That night, long after Cece's collapsed into bed and fallen into a fitful sleep, she's jolted awake, heart pounding, sweat-soaked sheets clinging to her chest. For one brief terrifying moment, the bedroom is nothing but patchy darkness, and Cece doesn't know where, or who, she is. The unfamiliar confines—the claustrophobic low ceiling, the steady drip of a showerhead, a tinkling wind chime—bring a swift sense of dread, and Cece lies still, straining to identify whatever's shaken her from sleep.

At Bucknell, wake-ups for swim practice were between 4 and 5 a.m. Cece used to revel in the predawn silence of campus while she made the long walk to the athletic center in her sweats and hoodie, drawstring bag hugging her armpits. Back then, her first year on campus, before the shoulder surgeries, before she told her dad, tears in her eyes, enough was enough, she thrived on routine and structure. Even without her father's dogged encouragement, Cece likes to think she would have pursued swimming. Within those lanes, goggles pressed against her eye sockets, hair pulled in a tight bun under her swim cap, the world nothing but a murmur beneath the water, Cece excelled. Swimming suited her—a sport where all the variables are controlled, where the only competition is yourself. It wasn't so much the winning that drove Cece, although she did do a lot of that, too; it was the idea of improving against a fixed unit, of honing her craft to be faster than the time before. While some of Cece's teammates got nervous or fidgety before a big meet, these were the rare moments when Cece experienced a profound sense of calm. She'd already done everything to be prepared; the pool was the same length, the lanes the same width, even the water was the same pH and alkaline levels as it always was. There was nothing to fear—no unknown. Was there anything more beautiful than things going to plan? Back then, Cece didn't think so.

It was after Cece's third torn labrum, when she was still mulling surgery and the prospects of another lengthy rehab isolated from her teammates, that she began to imagine life outside swimming. Even with a practical degree in statistics, the world beyond the college's idyllic campus seemed erratic and arbitrary. There were no guarantors of success, no rules to play by, only the promise of hustle and free-market systems. Cece's lack of social capital and familial relations had only become more glaring during her time at Bucknell. Unlike many of her classmates, there was no friend of a friend at Goldman Sachs, no VP at J.P. Morgan in the form of an uncle, which was fine by Cece. It just meant she had to work harder, prepare.

Like many anxious soon-to-be college graduates before her, Cece sought the help of the college career office. The staff were a genial bunch, middle-aged women armed with turtlenecks tucked into corduroy pants and endless patience for helping squirrelly undergraduates. After countless meetings, in which she grew increasingly anxious over the uncertainty of her future, one of the career officers, in a last-ditch effort, put Cece in touch with her brother who worked as an actuary.

Donald was a life actuary, he explained, dragging out his vowels like a true Wisconsinite over the phone. He worked for Nationwide developing life insurance and annuity policies for people based on risk factor data.

"So, you're predicting the future?" Cece said excitedly. She was holed up in a cubical on the second floor of the library where normal speaking voices were allowed but frowned upon.

Donald gave a titter. "I wouldn't say predict. Maybe forecast is a better way to phrase it."

That was all Cece needed to hear. She thanked Donald profusely and promised to keep him updated on her career trajectory. He told Cece he'd be happy to help her in any way he could, which struck Cece as about the nicest thing a stranger had offered to do for her, and she chalked it up to his Midwestern roots.

Mitigating risk, determining outcomes through preparation and statistics—what could be more appealing? It was swimming all over again, except the world was her pool, and all Cece needed to do was dive in.

"ARE YOU HUNGOVER? You sound hungover." Wynonna's voice is obscene and accusatory, especially for—Cece checks the time with one eye—6:00 a.m. on the weekend.

"I'm not remotely hungover," Cece croaks, "and what's with the early-morning wake-up?"

"This is the only time I have to myself, Cece. The kids will be up in thirty minutes, an hour if I'm lucky, and then it's go, go, go."

Cece keeps her eyes closed, refusing to accept the daylight. She's still aspiring to fall back asleep. "Don't waste it on me, then."

A blender whines in the background. "Don't be crabby. Have you talked to Mom recently? I just got off the phone with her, and she sounded weird."

"Weird how?"

"I don't know. Just off. She wouldn't stop complaining about

Dad. Something about him leaving his dirty socks around the house."

Cece hasn't had her coffee yet and is ill-equipped to assuage Wynonna's trivial concerns. "She's always complaining about him."

"This was different. She was going on and on."

There's a long silence, and Cece imagines her sister sucking her green smoothie through a comically large straw with determination and focus.

"I don't know," Cece says, "sounds like their usual bickering."

"Well, I just thought you should know."

Cece can feel the lethargy lifting, wakefulness intruding. "And I appreciate it."

There's a commotion on the other end of the line. The kids are awake, it seems.

"I'm going back to sleep," Cece says before hanging up.

THE LATE-MORNING SUN pries through the shades. Cece picks the crust from the corners of her eyes. Insomnia. The call from Wynonna feels like lifetimes ago. She'd tossed and turned so much Bernard had lost patience and retired to the floor. In the late-night hours, worries consumed Cece: her impending dismissal from Rayburn, looming financial ruin, and ruminations on her family's advice, urging her to grow up and recognize life for the compromise it is. There was another moment, too, one of weakness, one she'd neglected to tell Wynonna. In bed, she stared at Jonathan's text message: Just checking in. I know you said we shouldn't talk, but I'm worried about you. Is this really what you want? Fingers ghostly, she'd typed and erased, typed and erased. What could she say? She had no right. Why did he insist on still caring, even after she'd jilted him? Why did he insist on being so good? Was Jonathan really worried about her, or was this all ego, disbelief that anyone might be uninterested in the comfortable life he could offer?

The time is 11:30. Cece's come to dread weekends when she's not working, when her idle mind can wander and double in on itself. These are the slivers of time when she misses her old job, the murmurs of a thousand commuters in Grand Central Station, the jockeying, shoulder to shoulder in a crowded subway, the sense of importance, no matter how manufactured.

Outside, the splash of water. Bernard's ears perk up. Lorraine's skimming the pool. An aggressively friendly *ping* from her phone. An email—her latest credit card statement. The urge to simply flip her phone over and go about her day is strong, overpowering almost. Cece has a vague sense that she's spent more than she has. Usually responsible and manically frugal about her finances, she's let herself go recently, spending here and there, nothing ostentatious or excessive: takeout a few nights a week, drinks at the Whaler, and a few items (a bathing suit, sandals, and a sundress she found flattering) from the outlets in Clinton. True, the clothes weren't exactly a necessity, but everything had been on sale! And what good was trying to start over without any new clothes? It occurs to Cece that it's not a matter of whether her checking account will be in the negative after paying this credit card bill, but by how much. "Eat your vegetables," her father always used to say. "They aren't pleasant, but they are necessary." He was a stickler, especially when Cece started swimming competitively, about her nutrition. "There are things in life you just need to do, no matter how unpleasant. Drinking broccoli water is one of them," he'd say with a grin. And what could she say? He would always drink it with her, a playful scowl on his face.

Eat your vegetables, Cece thinks, eyeing the damage on the credit card statement and then logging on to her bank's website. If she pays the bill today, she'll be in the red, not by a lot, but that isn't really the point. Cece Downing doesn't exist in the red; Cece Downing's entire existence has been about avoiding this exact situation. She hasn't been in the negative since she invested fifteen dollars in a lemonade stand with her sister in sixth grade that went belly up. This isn't supposed to happen to people like her, Cece thinks while she moves money over from her dwindling savings account so she can pay the bill.

It's not very much fun, worrying about money. There is a fatiguing quality to it, a dull, benign but bothersome headache, ever present but somehow hidden. Cece regrets splurging on the pastries for Davi and Santiago. They hadn't achieved what she'd hoped, and worse, they'd been purchased on credit. Maybe it's about time Cece tried some of Lorraine's home brew after all.

Three hard kombuchas later, sprawled on a lounge chair, bathing suit straps dangling around her shoulders in an effort to combat her egregious farmer's tan, Cece gazes through smudged sunglasses at the placid pool water. A yellow Walkman Velcroed to her wrist, straw hat darkening her face, Lorraine rests on a bright pink inflatable donut. Whether she is awake under the wide brim remains unclear. The world feels softer here, rough edges buffed, colors dulled to a pleasant hue. Cece sprays some SPF 35, just enough to discourage potential skin cancer while still getting a tan (hopefully), and skims her other emails. SAVE DEMOCRACY, DONATE NOW; 30% OFF J.CREW SUMMER SWIMWEAR; $0 INTRO BALANCE TRANSFER FEE OFFER INSIDE—Cece is particularly thankful for Lorraine's fermentation skills as she confronts the deluge of junk mail and solicitations. There is a sense of satisfaction and accomplishment from deleting them with a flick of a fingertip. It feels good to declutter, even if it's only digital junk.

There are other emails, unread, automatically siphoned to a different folder so Cece won't have to confront them head-on. Given the current financial circumstances, Cece finds herself more amenable to her mother's help, maybe even a better-paying job. She has no right, but she's still angry at Santiago for not being nicer to her. Kim's emails are plentiful; it's her preferred mode of communication. "I like being able to organize my thoughts," she always says.

Cece plods from one email to the next without any clear sense of direction. She doesn't know what she's looking for. How does her mother know so many people? For the briefest of moments, Cece finds herself in awe of Kim . . . the sheer number of people in her network. How many professional connections does Cece currently have? And why stop there—how about personal connections? Cece doesn't dwell too long on that last question, lest it torpedo the remaining day. Drinking and feeling sorry for yourself—never a good combination. Of the many jobs—retirement readiness, claims analytics, and embedded value—nothing piques Cece's interest, at least not enough to pull her from her midday torpor. Then she sees it: catastrophe and disaster modeling. Sure, it's still just reinsurance (insurance for insurers), but Cece likes the idea of using data (historical and scientific) to predict the likelihood of future occurrences. She knows it's the three hard kombuchas talking, but she lets herself imagine, daydream. This company would be different—humane and professional. They would value her.

While Lorraine drifts into the far end of the pool, Cece rings up her mother, who's ecstatic to hear from her. "Let me give Tina a call," she says, the sound of a scribbling pen and tearing paper filling the background. "She's not in that division, but she's a big deal at the firm."

"It's a Saturday," Cece says, doing her best to enunciate her words.

"It's no big deal. Tina and I go way back. I did some pro bono work for her a few years ago. She owes me big-time! I'll get back to you ASAP."

The line is dead before Cece can say goodbye. Lorraine does a lazy lap around the pool, using her right hand as an oar, humming a familiar show tune. Cece leans back in her chair and tries to recover the boozy equilibrium she'd discovered earlier in the day. Was going back into actuary work so soon a mistake? Wasn't the whole point of doing all this—working at Rayburn, moving to New London—to get some perspective? Money—or lack thereof—has a way of changing one's perspective, and even if Cece's still coming to terms with it, Morgan's dishonesty, or maybe that's too strong a word . . . his opacity, then, makes Cece feel like she's flailing. She's tired—more tired than someone her age ought to be, and if this is life's way of throwing her a line, she had better grab it, before she drowns.

The kombucha tingles on her tongue. It might be nice, she thinks, to get back on track, to not have these kinds of worries, the ones that make her feel dingy and small. She lets herself look at Jonathan's message again: Just checking in. I know you said we shouldn't talk, but I'm worried about you. Is this really what you want?

A pang warms Cece's chest. Guilt? Regret? She's forgotten how kind and thoughtful he can be. When had she known they were in it for the long run? When had she known they had a chance? Jonathan had been forthright about his feelings for Cece; although if she's honest, his unbridled assuredness in their budding relationship caused her to feel uneasy and skittish, like a dog scrabbling across hardwood floors. They'd been dating for five months, and Jonathan invited Cece to spend Christmas with him and his parents. They'd rented a not-so-rustic cabin in Stowe for the season. Jonathan and his parents were big skiers, and Cece quickly gathered that this wasn't just any old vacation. The Von Trapp Family Lodge with all its pomp and holiday cheer, daily après-ski, and daunting slopes drenched in downy white—was a deeply held tradition. There was only one problem; she'd never skied. This unfortunate fact was treated like a genetic defect by Jonathan's mother, who physically recoiled when Cece mentioned it was her first time at a ski lodge.

The next morning, Jonathan stayed with Cece on the bunny hill for the entire day, and when her hamstrings ached and her ankles grew stiff, he whisked her back to the lodge where they sat in front of the roaring fire and sipped hot chocolate. Cece couldn't help but apologize. She was a drag on the family vacation. While his parents were hitting the slopes, Jonathan was stuck babysitting her.

"I'll gladly spend the entire weekend with you on the bunny hill," he said.

"What if I'm no good? What if I don't like it? Your mother nearly fainted when I told her I didn't know how to ski."

"She has very strong feelings about skiing. She thinks it's a life skill. Like swimming," Jonathan said with a chuckle.

"That's what I'm worried about," Cece said, before she realized what she'd revealed. She cared. Cared about what his parents thought of her. Cared whether they could imagine her in their son's future.

If Jonathan noticed her slipup, he didn't harp on it. Instead, he stood up and tossed another log on the fire where it crackled and popped, sparks pinging against the chain screen. He eased down next to Cece and pulled her close, his wool sweater itchy and rough against her cheek. "Don't mind my mother. I like you, Cece, which means my parents like you. It's simple. They've got no say in the matter."

Cece had her reservations, but at the time, it seemed cynical and foolish to doubt Jonathan, especially while they enjoyed the warmth of the crackling fire, amidst the merrymaking of skiers still in their gear, elbowed up to the bar, their faces red and chapped.

Bone-chilling cold, fingertips numb, nose ruby red . . . the crisp Vermont air seems an impossibility now in this summer heat. How far away that memory feels . . . She stares at Jonathan's text message. A response would be easy enough. Prolonged radio silence feels rude, immature even. But what to say? How to play it? Honest, guarded, deceitful to prove a point, alluring to get her way? I'm okay, she types. You don't need to worry about me. I hope you're managing.

She leaves the last question of his message unanswered. At the moment, she doesn't know what she wants, although the kombucha is providing a clarity of sorts, a distinct desire. Such assurance in anything, let alone her feelings, seems ludicrous. Does she want to see Jonathan? Yes. Maybe. But she doesn't want to type it out, to be faced with the visual evidence whenever her mood inevitably changes. *Is this really want you want?* She's already moved on, moved out, slept with another man (once, twice). But of course, she hasn't really gotten over him, them—not really, it seems. This particular revelation should elicit discomfort, even panic in Cece, but she finds herself unbothered, her body featherlight, her mind deliciously sluggish, infused with the singular pleasure of day drinking.

"What a load of shit," Lorraine bellows, yanking her retro headphones down around her neck. She paddles toward the steps, a magenta sarong wrapped around her waist, her tanned and wrinkled bosom straining against her one-piece. "NPR must be running out of content."

"That so?"

"For someone who doesn't like hard kombucha, you sure drink a lot of it," Lorraine says, elbow deep in the cooler. "You drank me out."

"Sorry."

"What do you say we take this show on the road? You got plans today?"

"You're looking at them," Cece says, happy to be on better terms with her landlord. She prefers this Lorraine to the one lecturing her on archaic zoning laws or the inadequacy of the EPA.

"I've got some friends who run a rum distillery over in Stonington. We could check it out. They always show me a good time."

Cece agrees heartily. Nothing sounds better than continuing the party. If she doesn't stop, if she can keep moving forward, she won't have to think. "What were you listening to?"

"I'll tell you in the car," Lorraine says, shaking the keys in her fist. "But I'll give you a hint: It involves your stupid generation. Millennials!"

8

Windows down, Lorraine guns it, the station wagon lurching forward as they merge onto I-95. Once they've found a comfortable cruising speed, Lorraine reaches into the back seat, one hand on the steering wheel, the other flailing wildly among opened boxes and loose manila folders. The tires hug the breakdown lane, a resounding *dududududududuudu* vibrating up through Cece's seat.

"Take a look at these," Lorraine says, retrieving a handful of pamphlets and dropping them in Cece's lap. "Just got them back from the printer."

They are surprisingly good quality, the paper thick between her fingers. The front page depicts an idyllic wetlands. Below, in bloodred letters:

STOP THE DESTRUCTION OF MAMACOKE COVE!

RAYBURN EXPANSION MEANS MORE:

MORE TRAFFIC!

MORE POLLUTION!

MORE ENVIRONMENTAL DESTRUCTION!

On the inside pages:

If you want to make your voice heard, sign below to let your town legislators know that you oppose the overdevelopment of Mamacoke Cove and the destruction of historic New London. We can't let big-money interests make decisions about our town. Just like you, we want to create new jobs for New Londoners, but not at the cost of what makes our city special. If Rayburn Oyster Company is allowed to expand, there's no telling how many other companies will follow and overdevelop the area we call home. By signing this document and providing your email address, you agree to be put on our mailing list to receive weekly updates. We will be organizing protests, lobbying efforts, and a show of force at the next zoning commission hearing. Make your voice heard!

The pamphlet is tantamount to NIMBY propaganda, the worst kind of fearmongering. Rayburn Oyster isn't some kind of giant corporation, but that doesn't serve the narrative, so the truth's been warped, or done away with altogether, it seems. When Cece had initially heard about the opposition to the company's expansion, she found herself sympathetic to the nature lovers, who argued the cove's natural beauty would be ruined by more oyster racks and boat traffic, but now she's hardened against Lorraine's cause.

"What do you think?" Lorraine says, snapping her eyes from the road to gauge Cece's excitement.

"They're something."

"Aren't they? We'll paper the town with these things. Rayburn doesn't stand a chance. You'll have to tag along next time we go out to get signatures."

"Absolutely," Cece says. She won't, of course, but she can't tell Lorraine that. She needs to stay in her good graces for as long as possible. Then again, maybe she should help the cause . . . Why is she so intent on defending a company who'll most likely fire her within the week? No matter, Cece thinks. Today isn't the day for ruminating.

Crammed between her already sweating thighs, her phone vibrates: It's good to hear from you, Cece. I know you don't need me worrying about you, and I know you said you need your space. I just hate the way we left things.

Space. She'd asked for space. What is this space that Cece has been so preoccupied with? Why did she think space—physical, emotional—was the panacea for her ills? What had it accomplished? Looking back on the last month, Cece surmises that she's filled it with floundering loneliness and poor decisions.

"I just don't understand what this FIRE movement is about. I mean, what compels people to do such things?" Lorraine shouts into the wind.

Cece starts typing and then stops. "What is it?"

"FIRE: financial independence, retire early. The whole NPR interview was about these people, people your age who are dead set on retiring in their forties. Have you ever heard of such a thing?"

The term sounds vaguely familiar. Cece catches her face in the side mirror, freckled from the sun, wrinkles setting in around the corners of her mouth. Screen swiped open, she fires off a response, an invitation. Me too. What's the worst that can happen? "Desperate times call for desperate measures."

"What's that supposed to mean?"

Cece doesn't expect Lorraine to understand. It's not her fault she's a boomer. She can't be blamed for her home's skyrocketed value or her tenure-track gig at a small liberal arts college. "People are trying to figure out the best way to live."

"That's not living. Socking away seventy percent of your income, living like some monk, waiting for retirement. What's the point of making money if you don't spend any of it? Young people should be traveling, having fun . . . Fun, Goddammit!" Lorraine says, slapping the steering wheel.

Three dots—Jonathan's responding. "You're offended by this thing . . . the FIRE movement."

"No . . . not offended, just miffed. What would drive someone to spend their twenties and thirties—the best damn time of your life—penny-pinching and budgeting? It makes me sad. *Sad* is the word I was looking for."

I want to see you, Cece. I'm at my parents' place.
House-sitting.

Cece wants to say something to Lorraine about wage stagnation, housing scarcity, and student debt, but she suddenly finds the conversation uninteresting and tedious. Jonathan's parents' place is only twenty minutes from Stonington. Cece pulls up the distillery's website and sends him the link.

I'm on my way to a distillery in Stonington with
a friend. It would be good to see you.

After weeks of silence and denial—yes, denial—it feels good to write something so direct, to send it out into the universe, come what may. Cece loosens her seat belt. She should have peed before they left. Her mind drifts. She still remembers the first time she'd seen the house in Weekapaug, driving up the white-pebble driveway framed by English lavender and drooping peonies, the grand New England shingle-style home emerging, framed by the ocean. Something in Cece softens, has been softening for quite some time, perhaps. What had she thought? Hadn't she hoped they might vacation there during that summer and every summer after that? Hadn't she allowed herself to wonder whether they might inherit the property one day?

Lorraine leans forward and spits on the side mirror, working her thumb counterclockwise while she says something about needing to get the car washed. Was *friend* the right term? Certainly not. Cece doesn't know what constitutes a friend these days, but right now, she's grateful to her landlord, if only because she hasn't seemed to take Cece's flightiness personally. Sure, Lorraine's a little out there, and she'll undoubtedly evict Cece from the pool house if she discovers who she's working for, or has slept with, for that matter, but right now, scalp tingling, the world hazy and soft, these are merely details, inconsequential details.

THE DISTILLERY IS housed in an old velvet mill. Sun pours down through the skylights onto the buffed concrete floor. The space is spartan: high-top tables are sprinkled around the cavernous room;

on the back wall, a makeshift gift shop offers up T-shirts and baseball caps. The operation—a massive copper boiler outfitted with a serpentine array of curving steel tubes—sits behind a glass partition. The whole thing reminds Cece of those old diving suits, the ones with the bulbous metal helmets and circular glass windows.

Willa and Thomas, Lorraine's friends, are her near carbon copies, jumbled gray hair, Birkenstocked feet, the scent of patchouli oil pungent. They bring a flight of rums to the table, and Cece acts like she can tell the difference between the light and dark. Mostly, it all tastes like sugar and caramel. Thomas fetches a bag of freshly made popcorn from an old-timey machine in the corner. Everything's on the house, and Cece is happy—stomach warm, fingertips buttered and salty. Willa and Thomas require no encouragement to tell their story: met in DC at an anti–Vietnam War protest in 1971, fell in love, moved to New York City, made their nut in the real estate market, and eventually retired up here, where they decided the best way to spend their golden years was making small-batch rum inspired by their many trips to Martinique.

"And how did you all meet?" Cece asks, her finger feeling sluggish and delayed while she points between the group.

"Ages ago," Lorraine says with a smile, "I had a research fellowship based out of Caracas, and I did a lot of bopping around to all those little islands. St. Lucia, Barbados, and Martinique, which is where I met these two. They might not look like it now, but they could dominate a karaoke machine."

There is more talk of the old days, when everything seemed easier, when life wasn't dragged down by the heaviness of things.

Would Cece ever look back on this precise moment and think the same? She finds herself envious of Lorraine's life—the places she's lived, things she's seen and done. Would such a life have brought Cece happiness? Probably not—they are not the same, cut from entirely different cloths; and yet she wonders, waving off another flight, opting for water instead in the hopes of appearing mildly sober if Jonathan decides to show. There's talk of a grand tour, but Cece declines. To her relief, no one seems to care, too absorbed in talking about the glory days: the time Lorraine slept with a French aristocrat and got everyone invited on his yacht; the night they snuck into an all-inclusive resort and charged everything to a stranger's room.

Cece doesn't know how long the group's been gone when she looks up from her phone to see Jonathan standing before her, brown hair tousled, a white linen shirt half-tucked into his khaki shorts. Face tanned, the whisper of a beard on his cheeks, he has an easy look about him that fills Cece with a strange sense of belonging, like she's come home after a long trip away. "May I sit?" he says.

Throat tightening, Cece resists the urge to cry. Inexplicably, tears well. The rum, she thinks. The rum. Get a hold of yourself. "Of course."

"Where's your friend?"

"My friend."

"You said you were here with someone."

"Right. Yeah. Lorraine . . . She's my landlord, but she's cool . . . It's a long story. She's around here somewhere. Rum?"

Jonathan demurs. "It's a little early for hard liquor. Don't you think?"

Cece flips her phone over. When had they started drinking? "I guess so."

"What the hell," Jonathan says, elbows on the table. "Don't think I've had straight rum since that terrible New Year's party we went to last year."

"That was an exceptionally terrible party," Cece says. They touch glasses; everything is warm and tingly at once. "Why did we go to it again?"

Jonathan scrunches up his face. "That one was my fault. Had to impress one of the higher-ups at work."

Cece remembers. Dripping ice sculptures, buttoned-up finance bros with their idle chatter, steam peeping through manhole covers on their way home, Jonathan's arm around her.

"You were always game for those work functions. I don't think I appreciated it enough at the time."

"They weren't so bad."

"Oh, but they were. They were awful! You'd always get relegated to the significant-other table, talking about God knows what. I don't know how you did it."

A chuckle sneaks up on Cece, and she finds herself smiling. "There was a lot of interior decorating talk . . . wallpaper, sconces."

"You're a saint."

"It was nothing."

"Work was crazy back then . . . postponed dates, reheated meals, eighty-hour workweeks. You were my rock."

"We had a plan. Failure wasn't an option."

"Maybe that was the problem," Jonathan says, blue eyes flashing, "I mean . . . that's a lot of pressure, to make things work."

Cece is trying to listen, but she's having trouble, vision narrowing, the room spinning out. She focuses on the soft indentation where Jonathan's chest meets his neck at the base of his throat. "I'm sorry about the way we left things. I guess I . . ." The rum threatens a return, sloshing in her stomach, saccharine and perfumed. "I freaked out."

Jonathan moves instinctually to take her hand but pulls it back, realizing what he's doing at the last moment. Pure muscle memory. "That's on me."

"Your family must hate me, especially your mother."

Jonathan pushes a hand through his hair and cracks a smile. "Quite the opposite. It raised your estimation in their eyes. My mother was relieved. It seems like you weren't the only one who thought we were rushing."

"You mean she thought I was only marrying you for the money," Cece says, surprised by how easily the truth comes with a little alcohol. It's satisfying to say aloud what she's always suspected. After all this time, honesty seems like the best chance at recovering something between them.

Jonathan scratches his stubbled chin. It's strange to see him with any facial hair. He was meticulous about shaving every morning before work. "Maybe," he says, eyes cast down in disappointment. "I've been thinking a lot about what you said before, about us moving and starting a family . . . I haven't been very understanding . . . about our differences."

"Our differences?"

"Where we're from. How we grew up. I didn't consider how hard you've worked to get where you are, and how you might feel giving it all up."

Jonathan's contrition catches Cece by surprise. "Pretty sure I should be the one apologizing here. Aren't you angry? Upset with me?"

"I was. You didn't exactly let me down easy, Cece. You just sort of picked up and left. But mostly, I was worried about you. I mean, did you just make the decision then and there? Or were we in trouble before then and you just never said?"

There are so many moments Cece can recall, not glaring warning signs or fluttering red flags but the subtlest of intuitions, so small and insignificant that even now, she doubts them, cannot give them credence; and yet, at the time, they'd added up to something, something big, something she felt she couldn't ignore. Jonathan's preference for taking a taxi instead of the subway, his habit of discarding hotel towels to the bathroom floor after one use, the reverence with which he spoke to her father, even after she'd told him how difficult he'd made her life after she quit swimming. Alone, none of it was terribly bad, but it balled up into a collective feeling—a want—to get out, to escape. The proposal and his response to her firing were the last things to tip her over. But now, with Jonathan seated before her, cheeks cherry red from the rum, eyes searching, she feels foolish, like a child who's fallen for a cheap magic trick. Is she really giving him a hard time about being nice to her father? Would any other woman in the universe judge a man for flagging down a cab instead of riding the subway? Yes, they'd been in trouble long before she'd returned the engagement ring, but none of that seemed like Jonathan's fault, at least not now.

The desire to propel them forward, to rescue them from rehashing the past, swells in Cece's throat. Looking back, digging up petty injustices—nothing good can come of it. "I'm sorry," she manages. "I panicked."

Something like relief works its way into Jonathan's shoulders, his body slouching forward. He gives her a tired smile and is about to say something, but then Lorraine is at their table, asking about this good-looking boy Cece is flirting with, and why she hasn't been properly introduced.

Thankfully, Jonathan says they're old friends, which will save Cece some explaining on the drive home. The revelation that Cece's been living in Lorraine's pool house for the last month elicits an eyebrow raise from Jonathan. Cece assures him it's not as terrible as it sounds. She doesn't say anything about the oyster farm or the impending job interview when he asks what she's doing for work, offering up vagaries instead.

"Enough about Cece," Lorraine says, who smells like she's had a few more drinks on the tour. "What do you do, Jonathan? Actually, no, no—let me guess."

Jonathan gives Cece a look, as if to say, *Where did you find this kook?* Lorraine's first two guesses aren't far off—accountant and lawyer—and Cece isn't sure how she feels about it. Jonathan grins. He's clearly enjoying this.

"It's got to be finance, then—private equity, something like that," Lorraine says, seemingly pleased with herself.

Jonathan is genuinely enthused, like someone's just read his palm. "How did you know?!"

"I have a knack for this sort of thing. Plus, I saw a fancy car out there. I'm guessing it's yours. And I don't think Cece here would be friends with a trust-fund kid. I knew you had a job!"

Jonathan takes it all in stride. "I'm impressed."

Lorraine settles onto her stool. "So private equity, yes? But what kind of private equity? Specifically, how are you screwing the American people? Buying up single-family homes and flipping them? Taking over nursing homes and maximizing profits?"

"Well . . . I can't say we . . . I'm not really involved directly in those sorts of things. It's a big firm, you see . . ."

"Oh, that's fine, just fine, I was only joshing you. Forgive me, rum always makes me say silly things, and what do I know, I'm just a geriatric botany professor!"

Cece mouths an *I'm sorry* to Jonathan from across the table.

Willa and Thomas stop by and whisk Lorraine away—something about a food truck outside and the best tacos al pastor she's ever had in her life, which seems impossible in a place like Stonington, Connecticut.

"She can be a lot sometimes."

"A character for sure," Jonathan says.

There's a commotion as a group of elderly tourists make their way into the tasting room—a sea of sun hats and white knee-high socks.

"Thanks for coming."

"Thanks for texting back."

"Why don't we try that food truck?"

"I have to get back, actually," he says. "I may or may not have left a few friends hanging to meet you."

"Sorry about that."

"Let's make a plan. How about next week? Maybe you can give me a tour of your pool house."

Cece can't think of a worse idea. The last thing she wants is Jonathan walking around the rubble of her crack-up. "Or we could meet somewhere in the middle again."

They make their way out into the parking lot, passing picnic tables and hulking cloth umbrellas. Cece suddenly understands what Lorraine had meant back inside as Jonathan stops next to a shiny, electric-blue sports car. He clicks a button on the key fob, and the roof starts retracting, shrinking in on itself. Cece knows nothing about cars, but even she can tell this one is expensive.

"Too flashy?" Jonathan asks, sun behind him.

"No . . . not at all. I like the color."

"I had to do something nice for myself after you threw me over. Cliché—I know. Dumped guy buys Porsche."

Cece winces. It's difficult—hearing it in such plain terms. "Why'd you text me anyway? I mean, I'd understand if you never wanted to speak to me again. I didn't exactly handle the situation with grace."

Hands in his pockets, Jonathan lets out a long breath, his cheeks deflating like a balloon. "We were good together, and I'm not one to give up easily, and while I hate to admit it—I think you were right to call things off. We weren't ready, but that doesn't mean we should throw it all away."

Cece is trying to remember why it seemed so entirely necessary to throw it all away, but she can't seem to. "I'm still figuring stuff out," she says, as much of a warning to Jonathan as to herself. She almost tells him about her potential job interview in the city but stops herself. Exercise some self-control, she thinks. It wouldn't kill you. The rum still on her lips, the sun warming her face—she is doing her very best not to do something incredibly stupid.

Jonathan is close, the powdery smell of laundry detergent and sunblock, his chin perfectly dimpled. "We've got time."

From somewhere, Lorraine's laugh on the wind. Cece can't help herself, leaning in for a quick kiss, the sun splotchy on her eyelids. His lips are soft and forgiving. The rum's telling her to keep going, to get in his car and drive to Rhode Island without a second thought, but she pulls back. "Hope that was okay."

Jonathan chuckles. "Do you remember our first kiss?"

"On that trail in Central Park."

"Yeah, and that runner screamed at us for blocking the path."

"That's New York for you. Then again, I'm pretty sure we were standing right in the middle."

Jonathan squeezes her hand and slides into his car. "Let's get back there."

Cece watches him leave. There, Cece thinks. How do I get back there? How do we get back there?

July

9

Cece arrives at the docks early, the sun chasing away the gray dawn sky. What transpired over the weekend has lent her fresh perspective on her situation, and while she's prepared to give the job her best (her father didn't raise no quitter), she's also prepared to be let go.

On the dock, it's only Santiago. Davi, it turns out, has been recalled by his mother due to a poor showing on the PSAT. No more helping his father until his grades improve.

"He must be disappointed," Cece says, thinking back to those terrible years of test preparation: handwritten index cards with archaic vocabulary words, algebraic equations, and mazelike word problems.

Santiago gives a shrug. "She doesn't want him to end up doing this for the rest of his life. Can't say I blame her."

"Does Richie know?"

Santiago nods and pulls a cigarette from the pack in his shirt pocket. "You're with me today."

"Out on the water?"

"Where else?"

Cece digs her tongue into the back of her teeth to hide her excitement. Act like you were expecting it! Like you deserve it. "When do we start?"

"Right now," Santiago says, returning the unlit cigarette to the pack.

"What did Richie say when you talked to him?"

"He asked me whether I thought you were up to the job. I told him I didn't think so, but we're down a man, so here we are."

Had Santiago been overruled? Cece wondered.

"Richie wants you learning everything about the operation today, so pay close attention. You'll still have to wash the bags, too, when we're finished."

Finally! Cece thinks. It doesn't matter that she wasn't able to convince Santiago or Richie of her capabilities. She's getting her shot—thank you, Davi—that's all that matters. Now she just needs to make it count. "Sounds good," Cece says and takes a step toward the boat.

Hand out, like a crossing guard, Santiago stops her. "A single fuckup today—a knot tied wrong, a buoy missed, an oyster damaged—you're gone. Understand?"

Cece squints into the rising sun and gives him her best smile. "Loud and clear."

"Good."

He doesn't waste any time running through his departure checklist. He speaks quickly while they move around the deck of the skiff, showing Cece where to top up the oil, how to check the fuel lines, filter, and battery terminal for corrosion. He flips switches on and off, illuminating the dashboard in an array of yellow and green. "This is your radio," he says. "First aid and life jackets are under there." He taps his stubbled chin and looks over the boat, like he's misplaced something. "You also want to check your other fluid levels: steering, hydraulic, and coolant. All of that is right here. Questions?"

"No."

"Remember, the biggest mistake amateur boaters make is not respecting the ocean. They think just because they aren't going out far or for very long they don't need to take the necessary precautions, but that's wrongheaded. Whether you're on a cruise ship or a pontoon boat, it's your responsibility to be prepared if anything should happen."

Cece does her best to remember every detail, down to the knots tied around the deck cleats. Once Santiago has gone through his checklist, they push off and set out into the cove, the tide low, waves merely a suggestion. He puts Cece at the helm and points her where to steer—a mass on the horizon, cages floating on the placid surface. He lets her get a feel for the boat, throttling up and down. Compared to the swift machine she'd ridden earlier with Morgan, this boat feels more like a utilitarian barge, pulling against the waves like an oar through seaweed.

The rest of the morning is spent rotating racks, which ensures each oyster receives the same amount of nutrients to maximize growth rates. Santiago demonstrates how to pull alongside a row of floating bags and flip them using a long pole with a hook at the end. Once flipped, Santiago gives each bag a strong shake to clear any excess sediment. Since these oysters are in their most mature stage, they only need to be flipped every four to six weeks, he explains. After demonstrating a few more times, Santiago hands the job off to Cece while he pilots the skiff, correcting her with a blunt directive whenever she skips a step or messes up. The oysters rattle in their cages, their shells the color of moss-covered stones. Waves slap a rhythmic beat against the fiberglass body of the boat, and Cece's forearms burn—one hundred fire ants biting in unison. Only briefly does she dare to look up to see how many racks are left. Rows upon rows, effortlessly bobbing in the blue-green water, mocking and malevolent.

"Only flipping this batch today," Santiago says, like he's reading her mind. "Those ones over there," he says, "those won't be moved until next week."

Cece pretends not to hear him and keeps rotating the cages, afraid that if she stops, she won't be able to keep going. The sun is high and warm on Cece's cheeks. The boat moves under her feet, undulating to the infinite push and pull, and for a moment, Cece wishes she could stay here, in this strange equilibrium of perpetual movement. There is no stillness, no stagnation, only the tides. The ocean—briny and sweet—fills her nostrils, and she inhales sharply, flipping her last one in the row. The floating bags don't look like much, but Cece is overcome with a strange sense of pride. She feels foolish—but then again, why not feel pride? There's a concreteness to the job she likes, Cece realizes, while they uncouple bags and haul them aboard, the oysters shining a dull white green in the sun.

Before their lunch break, Santiago and Cece transport the harvested oysters back onto shore where he starts up the grader and shows her how the merchandise is cleaned, measured, and sorted into specific buckets. He'll drive these over to Mystic, where they'll be shipped to local restaurants tonight.

"So, these are ready to eat?" Cece yells over the roaring grader, shells clattering, water spray shifting sun into rainbows.

Santiago only nods. When they've finished grading, he packs the oysters away in ice-filled bins and stacks them in his pickup. If he's even mildly impressed by Cece's capabilities, he doesn't let on. He hasn't cracked a smile all day.

"What should I do while you're gone?"

"You can hose down the grader. Just don't touch the settings. And those could use some freshening up. Paint's in the warehouse," he says, pointing to a pile of sun-faded buoys before hopping into his truck.

Cleaning the grader is quick, and Cece takes a break to eat the ham sandwich she brought from home for lunch. She unhooks her waders and shucks off the heavy rubber boots before walking along the dock, the wood rough and warm. Shielding her eyes, she looks out into the cove, out where the oyster bags are floating, like rows of seals sunning themselves, and even though she is tired and spent, her mind still spinning from Santiago's breakneck orientation, she is filled with a deep sense of satisfaction, not just from a job done well, but from proving herself. She knows the work is easier now while the summer breeze is refreshing and the days are long, but even when she imagines the wintertime, the freezing white chop, the howling wind that cuts down under your layers, she can't find any objections. At least she'll feel alive; at least she'll be outdoors, making her way in the world, the real world, not a cubicle or a conference room, no laptop screens or client calls, just her and Mother Nature.

The euphoric sense of self-actualization is short-lived; the paint is ancient, and it takes an excruciating thirty minutes just to pry the tops off the rusted cans. It's obvious at this point—Santiago wants her to quit, which at the moment, only makes her more determined to stick it out. If he hadn't antagonized her, Cece might have quit within the week, seeing the job at Rayburn Oyster for what it was, a desperate and ill-fated attempt to run away from her problems. But now. Now she wants to stay, to thrive, just to spite him.

Cece's painted six buoys when Santiago returns. She keeps working while he saunters over to the grader and reaches into the hopper, his upper torso disappearing momentarily. There's a commotion when he starts it up, grating gears and clattering metal. Cece's heart is in her throat while Santiago curses and hits the emergency shutoff. The metal rollers from the conveyor belt lie in the gravel, glinting in the sun.

"What did you do?" he shouts, stomping toward her. "I told you not to touch anything."

Bewildered, Cece rises, paintbrush in hand, legs shaky. "I washed it. Like you told me to."

"Then how do you explain the rollers being loose? You must have hit the chain and jacked up the gears."

"That's impossible. All I did was spray it with water," Cece says, surprised by how incredulous she sounds.

"How would you even know if you messed something up? I told Richie you'd screw up again."

Something bubbles up in Cece, an indiscriminate rage pushing through her very pores. She's been set up. Sabotaged. She knows it. "What were you doing by the grader anyway? You were messing with it right before you turned it on. How convenient."

"Don't blame me for your incompetence. Who's Richie gonna believe? The guy who's worked with him for the last eight years or some girl? Do me a favor: Go home before you break anything else."

There's no argument there. He has her beat, Cece realizes. Even if she can prove to Richie that Santiago set her up, what would he say? What could he do? Santiago is infinitely more valuable to the company than she is . . . "What's your problem with me anyway?"

"No problem at all," Santiago says, a toothy grin breaking his face. "You just have no business being anywhere near an oyster boat. You haven't done a damn thing to earn the job, and Richie'll see that now."

"I see," Cece manages to say. The fight's gone out of her. She'll sound like a crazy person if she goes to Richie accusing Santiago of sabotaging her. She watches him walk down to the water, his head buoyant, shoulders thrown back. Balled into fists, her hands shake, nails digging into her fleshy palms. *The world's not fair, Cece,* she remembers her father saying. *If you want to win, if you want to dominate, you've gotta go out there and take it. No one is gonna hand it to you. Winners win. Winners beat losers.* The sentiment had seemed easy enough to follow in the swimming pool, but in life, without lanes and judges, stopwatches and rules, Cece is drowning in the deep end.

The tears don't threaten until she's halfway across the bridge. Cece fights them back, breathing through a runny nose, her vision blurring. Even in private, she can't give Santiago the satisfaction. The piercing trill of Cece's phone fills the car. It's her mother. Cece has the sudden urge to pick up and confess the truth: She hasn't the faintest idea of what she's doing. But she knows this won't produce the result she's hoping for. While Kim might offer a few banal words of encouragement, she'll eventually circle around to something like *I told you so*, and so Cece takes the call but swallows her tears and makes her voice blithe and airy.

Kim has good news. The interview at Global Risk Management is all set for Monday. "Go buy some new clothes if you need to," Kim says, her voice bouncy and festive. "Use my card. You need to look sharp."

"A week from today?"

"No time like the present?"

An hour ago, she would have said not a chance, but now, it seems incredibly imprudent not to take Kim up on the offer. What choice does she have? "Monday works."

Her mother is pleased; Cece can tell by how energized she sounds, a frenetic optimism. "Thanks, Mom," she says, concealing the welling sense of dejection in her stomach.

"Tina says it's a great company. She talked you up plenty."

"Does Tina even know my qualifications?"

"I told her all about your experience, and at this stage, everyone's qualified. It's about who you know."

Cece thanks her mom again and promises she'll pick up some new clothes. She's grateful for the offer; most of her work outfits are still boxed up in the self-storage unit. Taking the interview isn't committing her to anything, Cece tells herself, but she needs to pivot. If things at Rayburn are truly finished, she needs a contingency plan. Who knows? Maybe she'll love being back in the city; maybe the interview will crystalize things for her . . . What she wouldn't do for some crystallization, Cece thinks as she turns onto her street. When she spots Lorraine out in the yard, she finds herself unable to take her foot off the gas. The last thing she wants to do is stop. She can't face anyone, especially Lorraine, just yet. A block later, Cece pulls over behind a minivan and cuts the engine. She just needs a second—that's all—to collect herself.

The car clicks and clacks, heat rippling off its paint-faded hood. Big, ugly tears come easily then while Cece gasps for air. Forehead on the steering wheel, arms hanging loose at her sides, she lets herself go. Cracking up over such a silly and pathetic thing like losing a summer job only makes Cece cry more. Of all the things that have transpired since she left Jonathan—fleeing to New London, moving into Lorraine's pool house, messing around with Morgan—the job at Rayburn Oyster Company was the one thing that gave her a sense of purpose, no matter how trivial. Flipping baskets, sorting oysters, scrubbing the boat—she was contributing to something . . . giving something tangible to people. Cece had felt a kinship—not with Santiago or Davi, but with the ocean and the sun, and the surrounding community that consumed the Rayburn product. Passing crowded outdoor tables at happy hours in New London, fine-dining restaurants in Mystic, seaside shacks serving up fried seafood baskets—Cece had felt a profound sense of pride. But now that's all gone, thanks to Santiago's jealousy and malice. The tears, Cece understands, are for the fleeting glimpse of a different life she might have lived. They are for a return to the known path, the predictable and the trustworthy. They are for Cece's brief and paltry attempt to alter a future that had seemed designed for her . . . by whom? Her mother, her father, herself? It's who she's always been—cautious, rational, and pragmatic. Who is she kidding? She should take the actuary job in the city if she can get it; she'll be better off. There's no denying that. Cece puts her face in her hands and squeezes her eyes shut until she sees stars. Who can she call? Breaking up with Jonathan has revealed just how alone she really is. Kim is out of the question. Her father's advice has always been more inspirational than substantive: *You miss 100 percent of the shots you don't take; if you fail to prepare, you're prepared to fail; you're never a loser until you quit trying.* These trite slogans might have worked when she was swimming, but today they seem to perfectly incapsulate all of Cece's worse qualities—a quitter ruled by fear. Wynonna is her last resort, but what would her baby sister have to offer in the way of comfort and advice? Shouldn't it be the other way around? Shouldn't Wynonna be the one calling her, panicked about a date, stuck in a joyless job, filled with existential dread? But, of course, she isn't. Far from it, in fact. Happily married, mother to two ludicrously rambunctious boys, a dedicated stay-at-home mom—she has made a life, while Cece has made a mess.

A gentle knock on the window freezes Cece. She is distinctly aware that she's openly sobbing in a parked car a block away from where she lives. "I'm fine," she says through spread fingers. She dares not look. "Please just leave me alone."

"It's me," the voice, soft but forceful, says.

Morgan. Of course. As if her day couldn't get worse. She can only imagine how she looks: hysterical and puffy faced. In a moment of paralysis, she wonders what would be more unattractive: letting the snot run from her nose or rubbing it away with the back of her hand.

Cece groans and puts the window down. "Hi."

"I'm on my lunch break. Everything okay?" he says, rocking back on his heels, hands fiddling with the buttons on his paint-speckled plaid shirt.

Cece laughs at the absurdity of it all. "Yes," she says with a genuine smile, not because she's happy, but because it's all she can do . . . laugh at this disaster she calls her life. She pushes her hair out of her face. "Just a bad day at work."

"Sorry to hear," Morgan says, hands in his beard. "Anyone you need me to thump?"

"You joke," Cece says and falls into a fantasy involving Morgan tossing Santiago off the dock into the water, where he flails and splutters.

"What can I do to help?"

"It's okay."

"I'm here, Cece," Morgan says and spreads out his arms. "Just tell—"

"I don't need you to solve my problems." It comes out harsher than she wants, but she's worn thin, too tired for niceties and decorum. Even if she were to accept his help, Cece knows Morgan isn't the solution. The sooner she realizes that, the better. Would she like to be consoled, to be held and told none of this is her fault? Yes, unequivocally yes, especially by Morgan . . . Mr. Shipyard, but where would that get her? It would be comforting, God knows it would feel good, but wanting to feel good has only gotten Cece into trouble of late.

Like she's got a gun pointed at him, Morgan raises his hands. "I hear you. Loud and clear."

Cece puts up her window, reclines her chair all the way back, and closes her eyes. She listens to Morgan's boots crunch on the sidewalk. The prospect of facing Lorraine is simply too much. She'll wait until dark before she heads back. Bernard will just have to make do.

ON THE RADIO, there's news. An unprecedented heat wave is sweeping the globe: 104 in London, 105 in Belgium, in Paris, a godless 114 degrees. And in New Haven, Connecticut, a sizzling 102 and climbing. Unprecedented. What does that word even mean anymore? Cece wonders while she looks for a space in the cool darkness of the parking garage on York Street. Every summer it seems there's some new threshold passed, a new study published outlining the absolute and unalterable demise of humanity. Earth is ringing its fire alarm, but no one seems to be listening, but is Cece any better? Here she is, driving instead of taking the train, readying herself for her date with Jonathan in an air-conditioned museum—preoccupied with the concerns of her miniscule human life, not even a speck in the grand scheme of things. And yet, it feels important! Necessary!

All it takes is a brief walk from the parking garage to the Yale University Art Gallery for the heat to take its toll on Cece's wardrobe—blouse clinging to her lower back, shorts darkening at the first sign of sweat between her thighs. She's already regretting the decision to keep her hair down, bleached by the sun, a hot compress on the back of her neck.

Jonathan is predictably punctual, waiting in the lobby, pamphlet-sized map in hand. Even in this weather, he's wearing faded khakis and sneakers. Heat didn't bother him, Cece remembers. He never broke a sweat, not when they biked through the Tuscan countryside that one summer, not when they took a weekend trip to DC to see the sights, humid air thick like stew. No—Jonathan always ran cool, dry to the bone. Cece, on the other hand, is like a cold bottle of beer in summer, dappled and soggy. Today seems no different, her upper lip salty, underside of her bra damp. Nevertheless, she endeavors, light on her feet, the edge of a smile on her lips.

They hug, which seems right, although it's odd to be this formal after everything they've been through. Then again, maybe this is what they need. To start over, to go back to the beginning. Jonathan has promised to go as slow as Cece wants, and she intends to hold him to it, if only because she can't imagine going any other speed. She isn't quite sure what she's hoping for—a moment of clarity, a sign—but there's comfort in the familiarity of things.

"Where should we start?" Jonathan asks. "The ancient civilization stuff looks interesting."

Six months ago, Cece might have deferred to Jonathan's preference, but she has no real interest in looking at rusted knives and spearheads. She still remembers the hours they'd spent staring at the medieval suits of armor at the Met during one of their earlier dates. Back then, it didn't matter that she was terribly bored by the endless versions of silly-looking chain mail and flamboyant jousting paraphernalia, but now, she feels no desire to please.

"They're supposed to have some incredible modern and contemporary art. Let's start there."

"Sure," Jonathan says, unbothered by not getting his way.

A museum was a strategic choice by Cece—a space that required minimal conversation, hushed tones, and lots of walking. Cece commends herself on the decision as they move slowly from exhibit to exhibit, the parquet floor creaking beneath their feet. Patrons dot the rooms, standing statue-like before gold-framed paintings entranced by the audio guide, headphones squeezed against their inquisitive ears. There's another reason they are here instead of Jonathan's parents' sumptuous beach house or a rooftop bar in the city, places where Cece finds it difficult to focus and see things for what they are. Here, there are no distractions, no window dressings, no chance for luxury and comfort to camouflage reality; she can see her relationship with Jonathan for what it is, what it might be. Among the studious drawing students huddled at their easels and perpetually perturbed security guards in their dour blazers, Cece can observe Jonathan on an even plane, objectively.

They chat idly, pointing to pieces they vaguely recognize. Jonathan seems content to follow Cece's lead while she lingers in front of specific paintings, puzzling over the artistic choices. She'd always wanted to take an art history class in college but hadn't been able to justify it. An impressive orange and lavender Rothko arrests her attention. There's an immersive quality to it, and Cece catches herself holding her breath while she scans the subtle shifts in color within the rectangular shapes. Jonathan stands beside her, arms crossed, wristwatch glinting in the dim light. "I like this one," is all she can say.

"I never totally got abstract art, but this is intense. That's a serious orange."

"Is this where you tell me anyone could have made this?"

"No way! I mean, you've gotta know something about color theory to pull this off."

Cece catches a security guard watching them from the corner of the room, the white baseboards scuffed black from his restless heels. She wonders what he sees. Does he think they're a couple? Is he calculating how long they've been together, whether they've got a shot? Or does he just think they're those kinds of friends who are super close—the ones with the pact that they'll marry if they're both still single at forty? And what might Cece think if she saw her with Jonathan, just as they are now? Would she think they make a good couple? Or would she wonder why a guy like him would ever date a girl like her? Or would it be the other way around? Cece wants to ask Jonathan why he's persisted, why he's willing to give them another chance, but there's nothing less appealing than insecurity, and so she remains silent.

They peruse the other rooms, sometimes together, other times apart, letting the artwork pull them in whatever direction it might. They find a rhythm of sorts, a silent dance where they take turns pointing out details and flourishes that strike them. To no one's surprise, Jonathan is drawn to Roy Lichtenstein's depiction of an exploding military jet with a comic-book-like

BLAM written above. His excitement and wonder remind Cece of how much she enjoys his boyish enthusiasm and near complete and utter lack of self-consciousness.

As they make their way to the American wing of the museum, Jonathan catches Cece's hand and squeezes it, a grin on his face, and then lets it fall. "This is fun," he says. "We should do it more often."

"I think you'd get bored," Cece says. "I might get bored."

They stifle their laughter, but not before eliciting a few icy glares from other patrons. A nervous electrical current bounces in her chest. They were always good at this, going on dates, being out in the world, anonymous but together. Cece remembers this feeling well: when they walked down crowded city sidewalks, when they stood side by side at monotonous social events, pinching each other's elbows whenever their tone swerved into snarky, when she'd doze off on road trips and wake to find Jonathan at the wheel, alert and poised, checking his mirrors, passing people with ease. She remembers it so clearly now—safe, protected within the walls of an impregnable castle perched on a mountaintop, immune to the buffeting winds of fate.

Only halfway through the American collection and Cece is exhausted. This happens to her in museums. One moment she's brimming with energy and insight, the next she feels as if she could sleep for days, spent from the endless act of perceiving, studying, and analyzing. Jonathan's energy also seems to be flagging, and they agree to cut the rest of the visit short in favor of an early lunch somewhere nearby.

They snake their way through the collection of American

paintings, giving a cursory glance before moving swiftly on, compelled by the promise of lunch. And even though her head is light, and her stomach is grumbling—she's only had coffee this morning and a zero-fat yogurt—Cece finds herself drawn to a painting on a far wall closest to the exit. In the foreground, men at work, their faces are bland and featureless, only brushstrokes, except for one, the man in front with a thick rope looped around his shoulder. He is bigger than the others, sporting a distinct beard, a streak of red under his eye. A bruise? A cut? Behind the laborers, an enormous wooden boat under construction, the frame bowed, like the ribs of a giant. Cece is drawn, as if by invisible threads, to the big man's hands wrapped around the rope, clasped as if in prayer. Morgan—the last person Cece wants to be thinking about, but now that he's entered her mind, she can't help but fixate: What's he doing at this precise moment? Is he wondering what she was crying about the other day? Does he ever think of her?

For lunch, Cece recommends Louis', an unpretentious sandwich-and-burger spot on Crown. She's on a strict budget, especially with her job at Rayburn up in the air. She'd planned on going to talk to Richie the day after her fallout with Santiago, but she hadn't been able to muster the energy.

"I was thinking tapas," Jonathan says. "This new place just opened up. The chef has a great restaurant in the city, too, really good."

Mediterranean certainly sounds more appealing than sandwiches, and with no illusions about who'll be footing the bill, Cece is more than willing to yield to Jonathan's preferences.

The restaurant, with its sleek surfaces and cream-colored tablecloths, reminds Cece of all those fine-dining establishments native to Midtown, the ones catering to patrons with little food sense but plenty of money. Accompanying the tapas are a lot of frills: edible flowers, foam, a hovering trio of waitstaff. There's a stiffness to the ambiance that grates on Cece, but any qualms she has quickly evaporate upon sampling the food: croquettes with downy potato centers, luxurious ham sliced paper-thin that melts in her mouth, fried squid that is at once both crunchy and featherlight. The wine, the wine! From somewhere she can't pronounce, chill and crisp on her tongue, the taste of wet stones lingering on her lips. She'd forgotten how nice it was to eat and drink well; she'd forgotten how easy it was to let Jonathan take control. What sequence dishes ought to be served, what wine paired best with their meal, what dessert would leave them satisfied but not stuffed—he decided it all. Cece quickly found herself relaxing, sinking into the plush velvet cushion of her seat.

"Anything promising on the job front?" Jonathan asks, dabbing at the corners of his mouth with a thick napkin.

That's right, Cece thinks. She never told him about the oyster farm job, the job she doesn't really have anymore. Still, she wants to see how he'll react. The timing had been bad at the distillery, although if she's being honest, timing didn't have much to do with it. She doesn't know how Jonathan will react to hearing about her work at Rayburn. Then again, why should it matter? Isn't this new version of Cece supposed to be different? How can she expect things to go differently for them if she makes the same mistakes?

She takes the plunge. "I've been working at an oyster farm for the last month, but it's just temporary. I actually have an actuary job interview on Monday in the city."

"An oyster farm . . . like a place where they grow oysters . . . in the ocean."

"That's pretty much it," Cece says, watching Jonathan for any signs of disapproval. "I've been really enjoying the work. It's completely different from what I'm used to doing . . . Lots of manual labor."

"Sounds like you really like it."

"I guess I do . . . I don't know. With your job, don't you ever wonder whether you'd be happier doing something else for a living? Or whether you're missing out on some other career because you've been on the same path for so long?"

Jonathan scans the silk-draped ceiling. "I guess I've never thought about it. There's always something to do, but that's just the nature of the financial market. It never sleeps. You can always be doing *something*. And what makes me happy isn't necessarily the work, but the things I get to do with the money I earn, like that trip we took to Italy together, having this lunch with you, or driving my new coupe with the top down. Those things bring me happiness."

"When you say it like that, it doesn't seem like such a difficult decision."

"You're having second thoughts about your oyster career?"

"What would you say if I told you I wanted to keep working on this oyster farm?"

"I'd say go for it."

"Be serious."

"I am."

"A month and a half ago, we were engaged, now you're okay with me going into aquaculture, a field I know barely anything about."

"Married, a house and kids. Do I want those things? Absolutely, but it doesn't mean we have to have them now. And if you're really into this oyster thing, you should explore it, but you should have a plan. How much time are you willing to dedicate? When will you call it quits if you don't meet certain benchmarks? Is it something you want to make a career out of? Do you want to scale up the business? Or do you want to start your own farm? I'll support it. Heck, I could even give you seed money to get it off the ground. Just show me a road map, Cece. I need to understand where you're going, but if you shut me out and panic, then I'm in the dark. I'll admit, I got out a little over my skis. All my friends are getting married, and my parents haven't exactly been subtle about how much they want to be grandparents. I'm not immune to that kind of pressure. But after I told my parents about us breaking up, I think they understood."

"But what if I never know for sure about any of those things?"

"Is this the same Cece Downing who passed her actuary exams faster than anyone else at her company? The same Cece Downing who finished first in the two-hundred-meter backstroke with a partially torn labrum? You don't give yourself enough credit."

"I'm just saying—what if we reach an impasse?"

"Then we reach an impasse, but at least we'll know we reached it instead of bailing out before. Plus, Cece, we were good together, and we can be again."

Cheeks warm from the wine, the arches of her feet aching

from their walk around the museum, Cece finds Jonathan's logic unassailable. He's right; they were good together. Cece feels the tension drain from her temple—the concerns of stability and money easily healed with a quick glance into her imagined future. This is steady ground, rock solid. And yet, like a shout in a storm, the whisper of a question teases at the corner of her mind. "Why are you giving us another shot? I mean, I've screwed things up spectacularly. Why aren't you out there painting the town red?"

Jonathan laughs, a lighthearted laugh. "We spent four years together, Cece. That's the longest I've ever been with anyone. Same for you, too, I think . . . It's a known quantity, what we have together. There aren't any surprises, in the best possible way. It's bedrock between us, and I want to see what we can build together. I'm old enough to recognize something good. When I was younger, I always judged a relationship by things like passion and desire, and you need those things, too, but a relationship can't survive on just those emotions. As for painting the town red—you know that isn't really my style."

Later, many years later, Cece will recall this lunch in detail. She will remember the honey-colored curtains framing the front window of the restaurant; she will remember the sound of the wine bottle sinking in its bucket with each melting ice cube; she will remember the hint of vanilla on her lips from the *torrija* they ordered for dessert. She will remember Jonathan handing his credit card to the waiter without looking at the bill. But now, here, Jonathan seated across from her, Cece is only aware of her gratitude for this man who is willing to forgive her colossal blunder. And while she won't say it aloud for fear of ruining the moment, she's thankful to him for seeing past her foibles and her shortcomings, her anxieties and her indecisions.

Jonathan insists on walking Cece back to her car in the parking garage. Without Yale students in session or the weekday commuters, downtown is oddly quiet, the streets vacant and hushed.

"Thanks for the today," Cece says after opening her car door. "I didn't realize how much I needed it."

"Anytime," Jonathan says. He looks like he wants to say more but doesn't.

"I'd prefer if we left things undefined . . . if that's all right with you."

"Sure," Jonathan says with his trademark confidence. "It's not like we're involved with other people or anything."

Cece thinks of Morgan, his beard against her neck, hands on her lower back, chapped lips that tasted like woodsmoke and molasses. It had only happened once—no—twice, but that didn't mean anything. It was foolishness and lust—there was no depending on such whims. This, Cece thinks, Jonathan in the flesh, is real. This is something she can depend on.

10

Just calling to wish you good luck, not that you need it!"

Cece instinctively lowers the volume on her phone, paranoid that her mother's voice might somehow blare throughout the train car. Boxed in, knee to knee, commuters are buried in their screens—a few old-timers peruse newspapers. Before she can respond, there's a click on the other end. Inconceivably, her parents still have a landline.

"Barry, is that you?"

"Who else would it be?" From the sound of his voice, Cece surmises her father is in the kitchen, most likely at the island having his trademark breakfast of black coffee and an English muffin.

"I'm talking to Cece." Kim's annoyance mingles with the birdsong in the backyard.

Cece can see her parents very clearly, living in the same house but occupying two completely different spaces.

"What's this job I hear you're going for?"

"Risk management firm. Mom had a connection."

"Sure you want to jump back in so soon? You've been grinding for a while."

It's strange to hear her father advocate for rest and reflection; after all, this is the man who, when Cece was in high school, rose at daybreak to ferry her to and from morning swim practice. This is the man who walked the length of the pool, while she swam, with a bullhorn shouting instructions in a crackling voice. Is he getting soft in his old age? Is Kim right? Has Barry Downing grown complacent?

"Let me talk to Cece, Barry."

Coffee is slurped. "All right. Don't lose your head. Say, Cece, when are we getting Bernard back? It's getting lonely here without him."

"She's bringing him down next weekend. We discussed this. Now, will you get off the line, Barry? Aren't you supposed to be at the hardware store?"

"Your mother is keeping me busy, Cece. Idle hands are the devil's workshop and all that. Remember, Cece, just focus on you. Don't worry about what anyone else is doing in their lane. You'll get the job if you want it."

The line clicks off and Kim lets out a long, exasperated sigh. The birds have gone quiet. "See what I'm contending with?"

The carriage door clangs open to reveal a burly conductor in a blue MTA uniform, ticket scanner swinging from his belt, a hole punch in his right hand. "Tickets! Tickets! Last stop before Grand Central Station is Stamford. Stamford!"

"What do you expect, Mom? He's practically retired. How many clients does he have left? Two, three?"

"I should have seen this earlier. I did, of course. I just never did anything about it," Kim says, more to herself than Cece. "This isn't some new thing, you know. Other than with the swimming. His swimming, your swimming. He's never been a very serious person. Sure, when business was good, when the money came easy, he was happy to dash off to the office, but he got complacent. I told him! The internet was coming. But he wouldn't listen. He stuck his head in the sand, and now look where we are."

The refrain is a familiar one. Wynonna and Cece could practically recite her mother's complaints when it came to Barry's Luddite tendencies, but this feels different. Kim's voice is strained, her words steeped in anger and resentment. "These were supposed to be our golden years. Instead, I'm working for two."

Cece doesn't think this is the best time to point out that Kim is only still working because her definition of retirement includes two homes and at least one international trip a year. If Kim wanted, she could retire today, but that would require cutting back on certain luxuries and imagined futures. "Maybe he'll get more clients," Cece offers, even though she knows it's an impossibility.

"Maybe," Kim says distractedly. "Don't tell your sister about any of this."

"About what?"

"This conversation."

"What *are* we talking about?"

"I have to run, Cece; otherwise, I'll be late for my spin class. You're a shoo-in for this job. A shoo-in!"

The line goes dead. A man dressed in an ill-fitting suit sitting across the aisle glares at Cece, seemingly for talking on her phone.

She ignores him and looks out the window at the backs of row homes and apartment buildings, backyards cluttered with discarded playsets and rusted bicycles.

Vividly, down to every detail, Cece can still recall the day Barry announced they'd landed the Condé Nast account; or more accurately, she remembers what that deal brought the family: a monthslong vacation in Montauk. They rented a stately home overlooking Fort Pond. Wynonna and Cece spent their days biking into town, sailing Sunfishes, and marveling at the tanned lifeguards at the ocean beach. It was a summer like no other, a summer when Barry never said no—mini golf, dinner at Gosman's, even surfing lessons—to anything the girls wanted to do.

"Wouldn't it be nice to do this every summer?" Kim was saying. It was their last night in the house. Barry had picked up lobsters for dinner. The sun clinging to the horizon outside, an orange orb purpling the sky, dunes wavering in the dusky air.

Barry stuck his head out from the kitchen. "Certainly would."

"What's stopping us from getting a place like this for ourselves?"

"I can think of a few hundred thousand reasons."

"Other families manage it. Why shouldn't we?"

"Dinner's served!" Barry shouted. "Grab your lobsters. Corn and bread rolls are on the table."

Much later, after the plates had been cleared and the girls had left and returned with Carvel ice cream, Barry and Kim sat on the porch, summer cocktails in hand, looking out at the darkness, the wind salty and wet. Wynonna had already gone to bed, exhausted from the sea and sun. Wanting to make the most of her final hours, Cece had settled on the couch to watch *The Andy Griffith Show* on the only TV channel that worked. The screen door rattled in its frame. Stubborn sand clung to Cece's ankles, and she rubbed them together absentmindedly while the black-and-white screen flickered in the darkening room.

"You shouldn't say things like that in front of the girls," Barry was saying, his voice nearly one with the wind. "You'll just get their hopes up."

"What's wrong with dreaming big?"

"There's big and then there's delusional, Kim. You know we can't afford a second place, especially out here."

"The business will keep growing. The Condé Nast deal is huge. You've finally got some momentum. Now you can build on it."

Eyes heavy like lead, blanket pulled up to her neck, Cece was half listening, sleep beckoning like a lighthouse. She was mildly aware of her father's growing silence. Her mother's advice . . . or was it hope, strung out, left to dangle.

"I don't want us to get overextended," Barry said, his voice soft and easy like freshly laundered sheets. "We've got to pace ourselves."

"Not everything is like swimming, Barry . . . What happened to all our big plans?"

Cece can never remember her father's reply. Maybe she'd finally dozed off; maybe he'd reassured Kim with a promise and a kiss on the forehead; maybe he'd only nodded and hadn't said a word, looking out to where he knew the ocean churned.

THE LOWER LEVEL of Grand Central Station is abuzz. Commuters disembark from train cars, a gyre of backpacks, creased newspapers, and noise-canceling headphones. The solid mass trudges across the platform. A few intrepid youngsters break off and duck around steel columns, looking to gain a few precious seconds. Even in these dingy catacombs, the air thick with grime and axle grease, there's an infectious energy. Cece remembers it well, the collective sense of purpose gaining strength with each step. And then the churning river splits into a hundred tributaries, each winding their own separate way: the M42 across town, the 4 local heading uptown, the 7 to Queens.

Cece takes the shuttle to Times Square and hops on the 2 downtown. She hasn't been to the financial district in a year, maybe more. The only time she ever ventured to this side of the city was when Jonathan had to work late, and she wanted to surprise him with an impromptu dinner date. When the weather was nice and the days were long, she'd sit in Zuccotti Park with a good paperback and wait. Things seemed simpler back then, when her biggest concern was trying to decide between Italian or Indian for dinner.

The offices for Global Risk Management occupy a mammoth skyscraper Cece doesn't recall. Half of the city is unrecognizable, the skyline a patchwork of freshly erected glass and steel. She takes a seat in a chair that looks more comfortable than it is after she checks in. While she waits, Cece tries to remember some of the literature on the company's website about catastrophe and disaster modeling. It's always important to show you've done your research. Now that she's here, questions assail Cece's relative sense of calm. Is she really so confident in her mother's connections? Are her qualifications that impressive? Or is this surrender? Cece wonders. Is this what it feels like to have nothing to lose? Her argument with Santiago and impending dismissal from Rayburn Oyster should be making her nervous, desperate even, but Cece is surprised to find the opposite seems to have happened. She's already been fired from one job, soon to be two, what's another failed interview? Hire me, don't hire me, Cece thinks, rising to meet a woman her age wearing a neatly cut gray suit and shaking her hand. I'll be just fine.

The first woman she speaks with is unnervingly kind, and Cece gets the distinct sense that someone's greased the skids before her arrival. She can hear her mother extolling the virtues of connections and networking. For once, she agrees. There are questions about her previous work experience at Ernst and Young and why she thinks she's a good fit for the company. Shuttled from room to room, shaking hands, firm but not too firm, confident but not cocky, Cece does her best to take it all in: gray-walled cubicles, clacking keyboards, and glowing monitors. More than once, she's shown tables and charts of data and asked how she'd interpret them. What problems does she anticipate? How would she solve or minimize them? There are a few women throughout the day, but most of the people she meets are men in their late thirties with soft hands and clean haircuts. They are the types of men who cycle maniacally long distances on the weekend, Cece imagines, to places like Nyack and Beacon. They are the types of men who enjoy the morning jockeying for a seat on the commuter trains. Her second-to-last meeting is with Maddox Hickock, the head of the climate disaster department, the man who would be her supervisor if she gets the job. Maddox occupies a corner office, and Cece's reminded of just how high up they are. He beckons for Cece to sit and offers her kiwi-infused water from a pitcher. She declines, wondering if this is something he always has in his office, or if it's merely for special occasions like this—interviewing semi disgruntled actuaries who've fallen on hard times.

"This is mostly ceremonial. Your credentials are impeccable. Plus, Tina and I go way back," Maddox says, moving out from behind his standing desk. He's wearing a pair of white laceless sneakers. "She was singing your praises."

Cece resists the urge to confess that she's never met Tina and that whatever Maddox has heard is merely secondhand flattery from the most unreliable of sources, her mother, but she holds it together, forcing a laugh down into her chest where flattens. There's an absurdity to the whole process she's trying to ignore. What's with the sabotage? Cece thinks to herself. You need this job, remember?!

In the leather lounge chair, Cece crosses her legs and tries to readjust her pants without making a scene. She's not used to wearing suit pants, and everything feels tight and restrictive. The backs of her heels are rubbed raw from the pumps she picked out. How quickly those callouses have softened.

"References." Maddox pulls back an immaculately white shirtsleeve and checks his watch. "Will they have anything bad to say?"

"I don't think so."

"They never do."

A sharp pain pinches under Cece's right breast—a rogue bra wire. She's grown accustomed to wearing only sports bras while working at Rayburn.

Maddox continues. "I think we're doing some really interesting work in the field. Cutting-edge stuff. Risk mitigation in the climate disaster arena is a priority for the company."

"Because we're living through a climate catastrophe?" The question comes out harsher than Cece intended, and she punishes herself by pushing her tender toes into the front of her shoes. Shut up, she thinks. The door's been opened, you've got the keys, all you have to do is walk through. This isn't the time to get on your moral high horse.

Maddox's waxy face hardens. "Catastrophe sounds a bit bleak. Our firm doesn't just react. We help companies and communities build more resiliency in an unpredictable world. You'd be helping us with that process. Looking at where we could improve and what we need to safeguard against."

While he talks, Cece's eyes wander beyond the uncannily smudge-free glass, where she catches a glimpse of the Hudson, a shimmering streak of blue. On the sun-dappled water, gliding triangles of white tack into the wind. Cece wonders what it's like out there today . . . if the waves are more green than blue, if the boom groans when they come about, sails slack only for a moment and then, in an instant, billowing and full against the sky.

Maddox extends his hand. The interview is over. "Just one last question. A formality, really. Could you shed some light on your departure from EY? You were with them for quite a while."

There's no use lying. If Cece is under serious consideration, which she is, Maddox is going to call her former boss. She weighs her options, even though they aren't really options at all. "I was let go," she says. "There was a big merger. They said my position was redundant."

"Do you actually believe that?"

Cece understands this is where she is supposed to lie, where she's supposed to side with the company in the name of efficiency and cost cutting. This is where she lauds her own firing, a company gal through and through. A little lie, the whitest of lies—that's all it takes. She thinks back to the day not so long ago, sitting across from those men, those boys, knowing smirks brushed across their smarmy faces. A fib, only a fib, then it's yours. She can practically hear the final-lap bell, ringing brightly, lungs on fire, the end in sight. "No," she says, "not really."

"Why then?" Maddox says, like he's sharing a secret.

Cece's gaze drifts to the window again. What exactly is she doing here? Why is she sucking in her stomach and smiling until her cheeks hurt? "Probably because I'm too qualified, and I'm a woman."

Maddox produces a pained smile and drops his gaze, like he's embarrassed for Cece. He traces the inoffensive pattern on the carpet with the toe of his shoe. Cece can feel him wanting to reply, a rebuttal, or maybe just a dismissive laugh, but he only shows his white teeth and says, "Well, that's certainly an explanation." Then he ushers Cece out of the office like a nurse who's just discovered their patient has a highly infectious disease, congenial but speedily and firm. "If you have any other questions," he says, handing her a card, "don't hesitate to reach out. Patricia in HR is your next stop."

Patricia is a woman with voluptuous hair and thick glasses

who runs through the company's benefits packages, and even though Cece has effectively ruined her chance of an official offer and is starving—Joe's Pizza is only a few blocks away—she forces herself to pay attention. In addition to a substantial pay raise, roughly five times what she might earn at Rayburn, there are countless other benefits she won't be receiving, thanks to her momentary lapse: There's a 401(k) with more-than-generous employer matching, top-of-the-line healthcare benefits, life insurance, funds for adoption or surrogacy programs, and a seemingly endless list of other perks (discounted SoulCycle memberships, free Citi Bike access, and an open invitation to a multitude of social events hosted by the company).

"Impressive," Cece says, sliding the bulky folder into her Longchamp bag. She's already regretting the act of sabotage—shortsighted and impulsive.

"I think you'll find that we're more than competitive when you stack us up against our peers."

"How about oyster farms?"

"Come again?"

"A bad joke," Cece says before thanking the woman for her time.

A few hours later, while Cece waits to board the train home, she can't help but notice the dinginess of her subterranean surroundings. Fluorescent light bangs off the gum-stained concrete, grim-faced commuters prepare for the long trip home to the far-flung suburbs of Fairfield, Wilton, and Milford. Cece feels foolish—the optimism and promise of the morning evaporated, ground to fine dust. Was it hubris? Naivety? She'd left all this—the office job, the city, with its perpetual motion—for a reason.

What had made her think she could return? Desperation, she supposes. Money, certainly. But there must be another way, she thinks, a better way.

FROM THE OVERGROWN azalea bush next to the shed—profanities. It's dusk, and Cece's carrying her heels, suit jacket folded under an arm, finger lifting the fence latch. For a moment, she thinks she's mistaken, and she waits, ears trained. In the direction of the pool house, Bernard's impatient yap. Bathed in purple twilight, the bush shakes, as if someone's trying to uproot it.

"Lorraine?"

"Cece? Goddammit . . . Is that you? I'm stuck."

Upon closer examination, Cece spots one of Lorraine's Crocs sticking out from the underbrush; farther afield, a ladder lies in the tall grass. Moving quickly, Cece works to part the branches, revealing a sideways Lorraine smooshed between the shed wall and the bush.

Cece reaches for what she thinks is a hand. "Are you hurt?"

"Fine, fine. Just got my leg caught under me."

A canvas drop cloth is twisted around Lorraine, and Cece works hard to pull it free. After a final tug, Lorraine stands before her, paint chips in her hair, a pair of safety goggles dangling from around her neck. "What happened?"

"I've been meaning to repaint that shed for three summers. I finally had some time today, but that damn ladder gave out on me," Lorraine says. She touches her ankle gingerly and winces. It already appears double its normal size.

"How long have you been stuck there?"

"Oh," Lorraine says, cocking her head to one side and shaking out her hair. "A few hours or so."

"Jesus, you could have died. You can't be doing stuff like that. You should just hire someone. What if I hadn't come home?"

Lorraine waves away Cece's concern. "But you did. What's with the getup?"

Cece sees that her reprimands won't have the desired effect, so she decides to let it go. If Lorraine wants to die because she needs to scrape some paint off her decrepit shed, so be it. Cece can barely take care of herself; she's not about to start looking after others, too. "Job interview in the city."

"You don't seem pleased."

Somewhere on the street, a screen door slaps, and a car starts, the engine turning over once, then twice before catching. "It didn't go well," Cece says. "Mostly because I didn't want it to."

Lorraine picks something off the tip of her tongue and flicks it into the night. "Ooooo! Sabotage. So, you didn't want the job?"

"No," Cece says. "I guess not."

"Do I need to start worrying about your rent check being late?"

"It's not like that. I've got something going on now, but this was a better opportunity. A no-brainer."

"How so?"

"It's a real job. Generous benefits. Well paying. Good company, too. Kind of like my old gig."

Lorraine shrugs. "I never met a real job I didn't just hate to death."

Bernard's barks crescendo. "I don't know . . . I just think there's something wrong with me."

"Could be something wrong with you if you take it, too," Lorraine says, before patting Cece's shoulder with a filthy hand and hobbling off to the house.

Reminder to self, Cece thinks. Don't end up like that—alone, at risk of perishing at the hands of a ladder.

AFTER A LONG shower, Cece takes Bernard out for a walk around the neighborhood. Twilight deepens to night, and Cece wonders if the answers to her questions are out there somewhere. What will she say to her mother? How will she explain her reasoning when she can't even explain it to herself? Kim will surely call her every name in the book: entitled, spoiled, and delusional. She won't fight it. She's deserving of her mother's wrath. And what will Jonathan say? Will he understand Cece's predicament? Will he see the choice she sees?

A creature of habit, Bernard quickly veers in the direction of Morgan's house, but Cece isn't in the mood to remember her mistakes. It was fun, a whim—now it's time to forget it. She has bigger concerns at the moment. If only he didn't live so close!

Bernard quickly embraces their detour, snout to the broken sidewalk, vigorously inspecting the new sights and smells: crabgrass sprouting through cracked pavement, newly bloomed irises, purple and majestic, a forgotten recycling bin still on the curb. With flip-flops on, the breeze feels good against her oxygen-starved feet as she walks down to the water, seeking respite from the lingering heat. Tree branches hang low, and Cece ducks underneath, shrouded momentarily in cooler shadows. From open windows, the murmur of televisions and calls for dinner.

Bernard strains the leash and tugs them forward. Cece, not ready to leave her reverie, holds firm, until she looks up and sees the reason for his excitement. In the distance, two figures—one big, one smaller—walking toward her. Cece doesn't have to see his face. She knows that gait and bulky frame, baseball cap pushed back on his forehead—Morgan. She looks back, hoping she might be able to retreat into the darkness, but it's too late; Bernard is barking, Morgan raises his hand in a tentative wave. Is this the other woman? The girlfriend? The wife? Cece wonders, preparing herself for the worst. Men are dogs! Why had she ever let herself forget it? Maybe he's the one who should be dashing down a side street! But the figure is too adolescent, awkward, and rangy. A girl. Twelve or thirteen if Cece has to guess. "Is he friendly?" she asks as they move closer.

"Absolutely," Cece says, looking at Morgan for some kind of explanation.

Bernard licks the girl's open palm inquisitively and promptly rolls over, groveling for belly rubs. She obliges him, running her cherry-red fingernails through his fur.

"This is Lacy, my daughter," Morgan says. "Lacy, this is my neighbor Cece."

"Nice to meet you," the girl says without looking up. "Your dog's really cool. What's his name?"

"Bernard. He's actually my parents' but I'm watching him for a while."

Morgan mouths a silent *I'm sorry*. Cece is too bewildered to respond. Morgan is a father.

"We were just going for our postdinner walk," Morgan says. "Lacy's visiting from Providence." His eyes are wide, and it seems like he's trying to communicate some unsayable thing to Cece from across the space between them.

"How nice," she says, peering down at Lacy's fingernails. Do they match the nail polish she found in Morgan's medicine cabinet? Had all those things—the makeup, the tampons—belonged to her? Cece is paralyzed by her suspicions and potential folly.

"Everything going all right?" Morgan says tentatively, like he's wading in rocky waters.

Remembering her hot tears, the stifling car, Cece blushes. The world seems intent on her humiliation. "Much better," she manages.

"That's good," Morgan says, a broad smile peeking through his beard to assure Cece there are no hard feelings. "Haven't seen you around much, that's all. I was getting worried."

"Yeah. Uh . . ." Cece says, looking down to gauge the girl's interest in the adult conversation happening above. "Work's been a little crazy."

"I thought you might have had a change of heart, or maybe there was something else."

Cece's forgotten this feeling—like someone's whipping egg whites in her stomach—and does her best to breathe.

Morgan continues before she can say anything and make a bigger fool of herself. "I was gonna text you, but then I realized we never exchanged numbers, and I can't exactly go knocking on your door. Lorraine'll have my head."

Bernard sneezes and Lacy is up and standing between them, wiping a hand on the back of her shorts. Cece apologizes for the dog, but the girl just shrugs. "Do you really live next door? I've never seen you around."

"Not exactly. I live a few houses over but on the same street."

The clarification doesn't seem to sway the girl. "Can I have the key, Dad?" she says, hand outstretched to Morgan. "Me and Zoe are supposed to watch our show."

"Don't be rude, Lacy. Your show can wait."

"It's bad enough that I have to come down here—now you're cutting into my *O.C.* time with Zoe."

Cece enjoys seeing this different side of Morgan, defeated and exasperated, caught between deciding whether to admonish his daughter or apologize to Cece. "Zoe is her friend back in Providence," he explains. "I better go."

"I was obsessed with that show in high school."

"It's the best," Lacy proclaims as she walks away, her figure colt-like, all legs and knobby knees.

Morgan hangs back, stalling. "You sure everything's okay over at Rayburn? The offer still stands. I can clock someone if you need me to."

"I was in the city today, actually. Interviewing for an actuary position at a risk management firm."

Cece thinks she can spot Morgan's brow furrow. "I thought you were trying to get out of that line of work."

"I'm just keeping my options open. You never know."

"Right," Morgan says and buries his hands in his pockets.

Cece isn't sure why, but she's feeling defensive, like she's done something, betrayed a promise. "You seem disappointed."

"Me?" Morgan flashes a thin smile. "No, not at all . . . So what's going on at Rayburn?"

In the dark, Cece can't read his face, whether he's actually hung up on her actuary work, or if she's just being paranoid. She lets it go, too tired to analyze and ruminate. "I haven't exactly endeared myself to the other workers . . . They hate me."

"I find that difficult to believe."

"Fine. They don't respect me."

"They're giving you the greenhorn treatment."

"Something like that."

"The trick is . . . with men like that. Hard men. You've got to insist on yourself. Listen. Be respectful. Do the job. But keep going, keep putting one foot in front of the other—even when they tell you to stop."

Job advice isn't exactly what Cece wants from Morgan, even if it seems sound. She has other needs presently. "Give me your phone."

Morgan obliges.

"There. Now you've got my number."

"Great," Morgan says. "I thought maybe you'd had a change of heart and thrown me over."

"To be honest, I did, but maybe that was a mistake. I seem to be making a ton of those lately. Does that matter?"

"Not really."

Lacy turns back. "Dad! *O.C.* Zoe!"

"I want to see you, but just as friends. Until I figure some stuff out."

"Whatever you need," Morgan says, and then he's gone, feet

pounding the pavement, his keys jangling a merry tune from his belt loop. Ahead, in the patchy darkness, Lacy laughs, easy and ephemeral. Cece stays in the street until they turn to shadow, and then she continues toward the river, thinking about how absurd and farcical life can be in spite of itself.

11

When Santiago pulls into the gravel lot for work on Tuesday morning at Rayburn Oyster Company, Cece is there, seated on the rear bumper of her car, rubber waders on, hair tucked under a baseball cap. Before he can turn off his truck, she's standing, gloved hands on her hips, eyes shaded by sunglasses. Santiago pretends to look for something in his console—probably toying with the loose coins and candy bar wrappers. Cece watches him intently. He grumbles under his breath, wipes his nose with the back of his hand, and steps out.

Cece puts herself in front of him. She doesn't want to walk and talk. This is too important. Insist on yourself!

"I figured you'd quit when you didn't show up yesterday," he says.

"I had some business to take care of, but I'm here now."

Santiago leans and spits. "I don't think that's how this whole employment thing works, but you can explain yourself to Richie. He's stopping by later this afternoon to check out the grader. The one you broke, remember?"

Cece turns on her heels and strides to the warehouse without another word. She waits until Santiago heads out on the boat before enacting her plan. If successful, maybe she can garner a modicum of respect from Santiago and keep her job. And if she fails? She fails. It's not like she can fall any further.

Gathering what she thinks are the necessary tools, Cece approaches the broken oyster grader with baseless optimism. Santiago's wrapped it in caution tape, just in case there was any doubt about its functionality. After some searching, she locates a sticker, faded and peeling, with a customer service number. It takes a few guesses before she gets someone. On the other end, a youthful-sounding representative from Sorting Solutions Inc. named Brian. The morning heat is already palpable, and sweat pops and runs as Cece explains her situation. And while Brian sounds sympathetic, he reminds Cece that his job is only to order replacement parts and schedule maintenance.

"But you must know how these things work, right?" Cece says, undeterred. "I don't have time to wait for a technician to come out and fix this thing. Surely you can walk me through some troubleshooting steps."

"I have a general understanding of the products we sell, but I really don't think I should be helping you. I'm not a certified tech. I'm just the guy who answers the phone."

Cece yanks off the fluttering tape and stuffs it in her pocket. "The thing is, Brian, I need to fix this grader before my boss gets here, and if I don't, I'll be out of a job."

There's silence on the other end of the line, but Brian hasn't hung up. She can hear him thinking, mulling over her plight.

"Just give me fifteen minutes of your time," she continues.

"And if I can't fix it, you'll never hear from me again. If I break it, that's on me. I won't mention I called you guys."

More silence and hesitation, the distant drone of an office air conditioner. Cece holds her breath.

"Is the grader disconnected from the power source?"

Cece wants to shout with glee and profess her immeasurable gratitude to Brian, but she controls herself. "Yes."

"Okay," Brian says cautiously, like he's worried someone might be listening. "I can walk you through a few things."

Cece explains what had happened when the grader broke. The grinding noise, the rollers coming loose.

"Sounds like a drive chain issue."

"Okay, so what am I looking for?"

Without being able to show Brian what she's seeing, the going is slow, and Cece knows she's way out of her depth, but she's already gone too far, caught in the current. There's no going back. She successfully identifies the drive and elevator chains, and conveyor belts. They work backward. Process of elimination. Cece's hands are slick with grease, but she doesn't care, checking for bent or corroded teeth, debris, too much slack, too much tension. "It's just like a bike chain," Brian says over speakerphone. "Look for anything that would stop it from moving smoothly."

At the sound of a boat motor, Cece's eyes dart out to the water, but it isn't Santiago. She's still got time. "If it's the gearbox," Brian is saying, "you're out of luck. I'm not messing with anything electrical."

After double-checking all the sprockets and chains and finding nothing, Cece begins to lose hope. If the problem was an easy fix, Santiago would have done it himself, unless, of course, he wanted to highlight her incompetence in front of Richie. That's probably his big plan. He's invited Richie here today to make a big show it. Breaking another piece of machinery, plus skipping work on Monday—she's as good as gone. Sweat burns her eyes. A horde of gulls yap and circle an incoming fishing boat. "Maybe we just call it, Brian. I appreciate your help."

"But won't you be fired?"

"Wouldn't be the worst thing," Cece says. "I don't even know what I'm looking at anymore."

"You said the rollers fell off first, right?"

"Sure, at least I think so."

"Maybe the chains and sprockets aren't the problem."

"I'm all ears."

Following Brian's instructions, Cece hefts all the rollers back into place, cuts a long piece of string and lays it flat across the them. She's looking for a gap or sag, something that might indicate where the frame could be warped or bent. Then, toward the front of the grader, she spots it, a small area where the roller track bends inward, like something crashed into it. It doesn't matter how it happened, although Cece suspects Santiago (he was the only one who loaded the oyster crates onto the grader). What matters is how she can fix it. A hammer is the first thing that comes to mind, which seems exceedingly stupid.

Brian seems dubious. She could cause more damage. Cece acknowledges his concern, but she's short on time. Out in the bay, she can see Santiago flipping bags. It's slow going with just one person, but he's making good progress, and he'll be back on dry land soon. She thanks Brian profusely before hanging up and fetching the smallest hammer she can find. After much agonizing and lining up, Cece gives the steel frame a confident whack. The earsplitting clang draws the ire of a few crows who have taken up residence atop the warehouse roof. She runs the string across the rollers again. Almost, she thinks, and strikes the same spot. This time the string looks straight and flat, the rollers run on the track smoothly. It doesn't look pretty—the frame dented and stippled—but Cece isn't worried about appearances right now. As long as the grader is up and running, no one will go looking for a problem.

It takes another hour to put everything back in place: chains tightened and greased; bearings double-, then triple-checked; bushings scrubbed; guard covers reattached. Cece is meticulous but quick in her work. Richie will be stopping by at any moment. The grader needs a test run, but when Cece finally looks up, tools scattered around her in the hot gravel, she spots Santiago heading into port. There's no time. After hastily cleaning up the area, Cece gives everything a final once-over and heads back to the warehouse.

Cece doesn't move when Richie's truck pulls in. Eyes closed, she's seeing stars, so she waits, seated on the cool concrete floor, back against a tool chest. Not until she hears Santiago's nasally voice does she will herself up, with a confident smile across her face, and step back out into the sun. The men are gathered around the grader, hands on their hips, expectant, like it's a tamed circus animal, ready to perform a trick.

"What seems to be the problem?" Richie says. "You're saying someone broke it?"

Santiago grins at Cece as she approaches. "Let me show you."

Cece can barely look while Santiago plugs in the grader and walks over to the start button. His finger lingers over the switch; he's enjoying this, no doubt. Determined to face the moment, Cece forces herself to watch. The machinery comes to life with a rattling chuff. Water sprays, gears churn, belts whirr, rollers roll, smooth like butter. Triumph wells in Cece's chest. If only she could call Brian and tell him they'd done it!

Bewilderment paints Santiago's tanned face. Richie scratches his stubble. "What am I supposed to be looking at?"

"Wait. You'll see."

"She's running fine, Santi. This is a waste of my time."

"Someone must have fixed it. But I'm telling you, she broke it the other day," Santiago says and points at Cece.

Now it's Cece's turn to relish the moment and watch Santiago flail. "I don't know what he's talking about."

Flustered, Richie looks back and forth between them, the grader whirring and thunderous. "Will someone shut that thing off? I can't hear myself think."

Santiago hits the kill switch and stands bashfully while water dribbles and drips.

"Now, I understand you two have had your differences, but you can't be blaming each other and causing problems. I won't have it—"

"But she broke—"

"Cut it out," Richie says and holds up a hand. "It ain't broke. So either you're trying to make Cece look bad, or she fixed it. Either way, you're wasting my time."

Cece compels every muscle in her face to repress the smile that's threatening to break. This feels good.

"Now, what's this I hear about you skipping out on work yesterday?" Richie says and glowers at her.

"I . . . uh . . ." Cece splutters.

"She was here," Santiago says. "That was my mistake."

"I'll give you the day off, Santi," Richie says, "if you wanna go get your eyes checked. Maybe you need glasses."

"Maybe," Santiago mutters.

Richie's already halfway to his truck, sandaled feet ghostly white in the sun. "Get along, you two. We're a team, Goddammit."

Sun blazing overhead, a stiff breeze off the water, Cece relishes her victory. Santiago inspects the grader carefully, like he's expecting it to fall to pieces at any moment. "You fixed it," he says.

"Sure did."

"What was the problem?"

"Dented frame. The rollers weren't tracking properly."

Santiago chews a thumbnail mercilessly. "Okay," he says. "We're good."

They walk toward the boat where full racks wait to be offloaded. "About missing yesterday. It won't happen again. Thanks for covering for me."

Ahead, the boat floats effortlessly. Dock lines creak. "Let's go to work," he says.

IT'S LATE, CLOSE to ten, by the time Cece pulls into her parents' driveway. The Friday traffic had been interminable on I-95 and then the Merritt, stop-and-go all the way from New Haven to the bridge. Oddly enough, Cece had been more than happy to languish, bumper-to-bumper, the only worry being Bernard's bladder. Sitting in her car only meant more time to revel in her breakthrough at work, more time to replay her days out on the boat, working in tandem with Santiago, as a team. Piloting them out of the harbor, flipping cages, measuring and recording oyster size, pulling mature oysters and hoisting them onto the boat where the cages shed seawater and glistened in the sun. On land, they'd worked the grader seamlessly. Santiago showed her how to adjust the belt speed and the water pressure for the nozzles. Finally, she'd earned his trust. He showed her how to pack the bins with ice and prepare the oysters for shipment. For their labors, they had twenty bins filled with fresh, ready-to-eat oysters. With the help of a hand truck, they stacked them in the back of the pickup. Santiago cursed Richie (that cheap bastard!) for not buying a forklift. Maybe when they expanded, he said. Then the operation would be too big not to buy more equipment.

They'd clocked out together at five. A breeze swept in off the water, cooling the sweat on Cece's brow. Santiago grabbed two bottles of water from the storage shed fridge and tossed one to Cece. They drank thirstily, nothing but the sound of gulls in their ears.

"See you Monday," Santiago said. "Good work today."

Santiago's muted praise had sustained her all the way from New London to Tappan.

There are only a few lights on in the Tudor's slender windows. Bernard whimpers from his crate, familiar with his surroundings. Before Cece can get the cage half-open, he's out, bounding up the stairs to where Kim stands on the brick landing under the porch light, circular and golden.

The summer vacation seems to have done her mother good, or maybe it's her new blond highlights and youthful athleisure wear. Over the past few months, Cece's noticed a subtle shift in her mother's wardrobe, coinciding with a budding obsession with personal fitness. When Cece and Wynonna were kids, Kim would deride New Jersey for all its shortcomings, only crossing its borders for cheap gas and lack of sales tax on clothing, but lately, she's been venturing deep into the Garden State, to Ridgewood, Paramus, and Woodcliff Lake for classes at the likes of SoulCycle, Pure Barre, and Orangetheory. And while Cece doesn't necessarily approve of Kim's newfound love for Lululemon crop tops and skintight yoga pants, she must admit there's a new vivacity in her face and certain tightness to her figure.

"Thanks for watching him all this time," Kim says, stooping to give the dog a brief pat before opening the door. Bernard shoots through the gap in search of Cece's father. He's always been Barry's dog.

Cece gives her mother a hug. "You look amazing, Mom."

"I don't know why I didn't take these classes before. It's a real community. And the endorphin rush. I'm addicted. I've got a hot yoga class tomorrow. You should come . . . I swear, I feel better than I did when I was your age."

Cece can't imagine anything worse than group exercise with feisty middle-aged women. "Where's Dad?"

"In the kitchen making grilled cheese sandwiches. He was worried you'd be hungry."

"He's cooking?"

"If that's what you want to call it."

Barry isn't known for his prowess in the kitchen. Whenever Kim worked late when Cece and Wynnona were younger, dinner had been served at a variety of hours: Wise potato chips and tuna fish sandwiches at 5, or grilled cheeses at 7:45, or more than not, something canned with boiled hot dogs at 10 p.m. "Don't tell your mother," he'd say to the girls, making them feel as if they were part of a grand conspiracy. "She'll have my head if she knew we were eating this junk." Kim knew, of course, but she never reproached Barry in front of them, at least when they were younger. Back then, Kim was still an adherent to the values evangelized by popular parenting books at the time, the ones that encouraged parents to present a "united front," saving all disagreements for the privacy of their bedroom. And even if Kim hadn't read all those books, she was too tired from working long hours at the law firm to supplement Barry's paltry income —when his advertising business was still in its infancy—to start a fight.

The house is just as Cece remembers. The formal dining room table, unused since Thanksgiving, is cluttered with framed photographs. Most of them are old, pictures of Wynonna and Cece when they were young: high school graduation, family vacations at the beach, Cece standing on a podium draped in gold metals. There are a few new additions, all of Wynonna and Devin, staged photos with their kids, like they're auditioning for J.Crew's next fall catalogue. From the den, the murmur of a sports announcer. Cece already knows its swimming. A shiver slinks up her back, shoulders tense, forearms goose bumped. Even after all these years, the early-morning wakeups, the sting of chlorine . . . her body remembers.

From the kitchen, the sound of sizzling cheese and a hundred "good boys." Barry is kneeling on the terra-cotta tiles rubbing Bernard's belly. While Kim seems downright effervescent, the same can't be said for Cece's father, who's returned from their summer excursion stouter and plumper than she remembers. His gray widow's peak more pronounced than ever, the war has almost been won by his receding hairline. Seeing her father like this—dressed in a BUCKNELL SWIMMING T-shirt and stained sweatpants, a week's worth of stubble papering his face—softens something in Cece, if only for a moment. This man—diminished and disheveled—is not the man she's been holding grudges against in her imagined memory. Cece remembers the anger in his voice, the sheer disappointment in his eyes when she refused a third shoulder surgery, told him she was done swimming. For Cece, swimming was hell; or rather, everything surrounding swimming: the practices, the workouts, the dieting, every second of her life structured, measured, and weighed. The actual swimming, putting one arm in front of the other, was pure bliss, but her father had ruined that for her, taken it too far. Yet Cece can't be so sure now, seeing him, happy to see her, showing off his shirt with a smile on his face, talking to her about the latest results from the World Aquatics Championship. Barry doesn't remember the tears, the tantrums, and later, the grievances and flat-out refusals to continue doing something that only served his ego. She'd told him as much, screamed the truth in a small booth at a pizzeria in Lewisburg, where families had turned and gawked—this father and daughter at loose ends. He'd listened then, sat there and taken it. Still, here he is, hugging Cece, talking to her about a new display case he made for all her medals, like none of it was ever awful, like it was the happiest time of her life.

Bernard keeps his whining to a minimum while Cece polishes off two grilled cheese sandwiches with a tall glass of iced tea. She notices Kim eyeing her, but she doesn't care. Ever since she started working at Rayburn in earnest, Cece's appetite has only grown. Bernard, pleased to be home, sits patiently, nails clicking on the tile, in anticipation of a scrap. If this is the extent of his begging, Cece will take it. Her parents would run her out of the house if they knew what Bernard ate while under her care. Cece likes to believe they have a pact, one signed in leftovers.

Cece wipes her mouth with a paper napkin. "How's work, Dad?"

"Solid as ever. I mean it's not like the '90s, but there's still the Newark office. And sure, we might have fewer clients than we had twenty years ago, but the ones we've got are loyal."

Cece watches her mother while Barry talks. If she's bothered or stressed by the seemingly dire straits of the business, she doesn't show it, tapping away on her phone with freshly manicured nails, an amused smile on her face.

"You're not worried at all?" Cece says, searching her dad's face for a bluff.

"Me? Not a chance. We've always found a way. Just in a slump. But we'll run into something soon. We're doing a big physical installation for Beefeater at the duty-free shop at JFK. I'll show you the prototypes. You'll love them. We got a huge cardboard cutout of Big Ben."

Barry has never been one for doom and gloom. Forever the

optimist, he never met a challenge he didn't think he could overcome. He could always swim faster, flip turn tighter, dive deeper. Failure was never an option. It's in his DNA. What does Cece expect? He's an athlete at heart. It's not over until it's over—like he always used to say. He won't admit the business is doomed until he files for bankruptcy, and even then, he'll have all sorts of harebrained ideas about how everything will be okay. Another saying he always used to say: Everything will be okay in the end, and if it's not okay, it's not the end. He especially liked that one when Cece was running wind sprints. When Cece was younger, she was awed by his tenacity, his refusal to say quit. Now . . . now it feels closer to delusion, but all she can do is smile and kiss him good night before he shuffles upstairs.

"Aren't you worried about Dad? The business?" she asks her mother when she can hear creaking floorboards overhead.

Kim finishes typing something and locks her phone. "Huh?"

"Dad. The business is in trouble, and he doesn't seem good."

"The business has been in trouble for almost two decades," Kim says, eyeing a dish her father didn't put in the dishwasher. "He was the one who said the internet was a stupid idea. Look who's stupid now. Every year, his client list gets smaller and smaller."

"Is everything okay? I mean in terms of money."

"Shouldn't you be worried about your own situation? Any updates on the new job? I need to call Tina and see if she's heard anything."

Cece desperately hopes she's gone, with at least New York between them, before Kim finds out about the sabotaged interview. "You know what I mean."

"Sure," Kim says, standing up and pushing in her stool, "I know what you mean. I know we'd be royally screwed if I weren't bringing in money, working like I'm some entry-level associate."

Cece is about to apologize—for what, she doesn't know—but her mother is already giving her a hug and a kiss on the head and saying something about needing to catch her nighttime wind-down yoga class on the Peloton. There are fresh sheets on her bed, and if Cece wants to go for a run in the morning, she'll be up at six.

IT'S A STRANGE sensation, Cece thinks, lying in one's childhood bedroom. As the eldest, she'd had first choice. Naturally, she'd picked the one on the third floor, farthest away from Wynonna and prying parental eyes. Other than a few minimal changes—a new comforter and rug—the room is the same from Cece's high school days. The corkboard adorned with friendship bracelets and faded photos remains propped on the dresser. Miraculously, the Backstreet Boys poster taped to the wall above the headboard hasn't fallen. The desk, where she'd spent countless hours typing up lab reports, memorizing flash cards, and solving parabolic equations with her graphing calculator, sits in the far corner of the room, her old computer hulking and obsolete. At the time, high school, with its grueling social landscape and endless assembly line of work, had seemed like the closest thing to torture. And yet, looking about her, Cece finds herself missing the rudimentary sense of purpose she possessed back then—be respectful, study hard, go to a good college. When had things gotten complicated? Or was she simply refusing to grow up?

From the second floor, shuffling feet, the rattle and gurgle of the hallway toilet. Cece swipes open her phone and texts Wynonna. She remembers her sister's call, Kim's complaints about Barry, and wants to fill her in on what she's seeing now: her dad's slippage into malaise, her mother's indifference and newfound youthfulness. Cece can smell the stench of defeat in everything, from the paper plates at dinner to the fine coating of dust on the mantel.

The text to her sister goes unanswered. Other than that one time, has Wynonna noticed anything off about their parents? Then again, can Cece even trust what she's seeing? She's the older sister who leaves, then comes back on a whim, flitting in and out of family life. Her observations are suspect, not to be trusted, painted through with distance and absenteeism.

Jonathan's a terrible texter, but Cece still considers messaging him until she realizes it's nearly eleven. He sticks to a strict sleep schedule: in bed by nine, awake by five. When they'd first met, she'd found the habit endearing, illustrative of his determination and strong work ethic. Then, when things had gone south, she'd found it boring. Now, lying in her childhood bed, wondering what's up with Barry and Kim, she doesn't know what to think. The sad truth is, Jonathan probably understands Cece's parents better than she does.

Still no response from Wynonna. Usually, Cece can rely on the kids causing chaos with her sleep schedule. The morning—out on the water with Santiago—feels like years ago. She can hardly remember that feeling, standing on the deck of the boat, the world in perpetual motion beneath her feet.

The whole situation feels ridiculous, basking in the memories of high school, worrying about her parents like they aren't grown adults, like she can actually fix their problems. Cece can only laugh at the absurdity, opening up the camera on her phone and snapping a photo of the Backstreet Boys poster and sending it to Morgan. NYSNC or Backstreet Boys? You know where I stand. If there is intention behind her message, Cece is only vaguely aware of it, like the dull ache that permeates her surgically repaired shoulder whenever it's about to rain.

Can I say neither?

Blasphemy.

I was more of a Foo Fighters, Smashing Pumpkins fan.

That tracks.

I'm choosing to take that as a compliment. Does Lorraine know you're redecorating?

Cece wonders where Morgan is: sitting at the kitchen island with a glass of whiskey, or in bed, head propped up against the headboard, one of his many books splayed on his chest? Don't get carried away, Cece thinks to herself. Just imagine him on the toilet. That's where most men are when they're texting anyone.

At my parents'. My old bedroom to be more specific. Had to drop Bernard off.

He'll be missed. Lacy took a real liking to him.

It was nice meeting her.

Three dots. Then nothing. Should she explain why she got spooked and put distance between them? *Sorry, Morgan, I was snooping through your medicine cabinet and mistook your daughter's makeup for another woman's, and even though I'm a perfectly well-adjusted and mature adult, I decided to cut you loose instead of having a conversation about it. And yes, I realize that we weren't even serious and I had no right to be angry, but I was, which was confusing, and now it's even more confusing because I've started seeing my ex-fiancé, but I'd still very much like to be friends, just not friends who act on the obvious sexual tension between them because . . . because, well, I don't think I've been acting like a serious person lately, and Jonathan is a serious person. And just look at my mother. She didn't marry a serious person, and look where that's gotten her . . .* No, of course she can't say any of that. What can she say? What can she even admit to herself?

Morgan replies: I should have told you about her. I was gonna, but I wasn't sure how, and then you sort of disappeared on me.

Cece doesn't know how to do this. How do you end something that never had a beginning? What did her swimming coach used to say in high school? Honesty was the best policy. Then again, that coach was a total bitch. Then again, maybe partial honesty can count for something. You don't owe me an explanation. And it wasn't anything you said or did. Ever since I got fired, I've just been sort of confused, and us sleeping together, while absolutely wonderful, wasn't exactly helping.

There's no response. Not even three dots. Cece locks her phone screen and presses it against her chest. How fitting that she'd be having this conversation in here, surrounded by the now cringeworthy evidence of her impressionable teenage years. At least she was making up for lost time. There'd been no room for romantic flirtations in high school. While most of the girls her age reveled in the world of crushes, innuendo and subterfuge, Cece had only wanted clarity, something factual and true.

A cheerful ding. Morgan. An anticipatory swell fills Cece. Are you "it's me, not you-ing" me? That's my move. Nobody steals my move!

Cece's never been more thankful for Morgan's levity and seemingly endless ability to not take anything too seriously.

There's more: But seriously. It's no big deal. It's not like I've got my shit together . . . can't really expect the same from other people.

Cece starts typing and then deletes the message, bottom lip chewed raw between her teeth. What is she so afraid of? Things are already in motion; she's made her decision. Telling Morgan about Jonathan won't change anything. Except that it might. It most certainly will—of course it will! And Cece isn't quite ready to let go of whatever is between her and Morgan. Whatever potential friendship they might be able to cultivate will evaporate with news of her reconciliation with Jonathan. Cece wants to keep Morgan in her life—even if it's selfish, even if it means withholding this bit of information. It isn't really lying; she's not leading him on. It's not as if they're planning a future together. That's an impossibility, even without Jonathan in the picture. From where she stands, Morgan's life seems nerve-wracking, filled with potential concerns of money and stability, the means to build a future, and that was *before* she met Lacy. And even if she wants it, Cece can't afford unpredictability and risk. She has enough of that in her own life at the moment.

Still, Cece finds herself imagining. Imagining what Morgan might do if she were to tell him about Jonathan: reads the message and tosses the phone across the room in anger, laughs uproariously at the craziest woman he's ever slept with, scoffs with disdain, or the worst of all, turns off the lights and sleeps a dreamless sleep, content to be rid of a clingy woman he'd barely known.

Cece thinks about admitting to snooping through his medicine cabinet but stops herself. Thanks for being so understanding, she types, a twinge of guilt needling her. How long is Lacy staying with you?

Kind of up in the air. My ex and I are still working on a more regular visitation schedule. She isn't exactly making things easy.

Maybe we can get together after she leaves.

I think she'd probably prefer another person to hang out with. All her friends are up in Providence. I took off a few days so we could get some time together, but I'm worried we've already run out of things to do. Her phone seems infinitely more interesting than her old man.

You are very old. I don't think she really liked me.

That's just the way she is. All teenagers, really.

We'll figure out something to do then.

Have you talked any sense into your landlord about the oyster farm? Last I heard she was knocking on doors collecting signatures for some kind of petition. I don't think everyone in the neighborhood is taking kindly to it.

I'm afraid not. Lorraine is her own woman.

Oh well. It was worth a shot. Better get some shut eye. Text me when you're back in town. I'll tell Lacy to expect you.

THE HOUSE IS eerily quiet when Cece comes downstairs the next morning, a crick in her neck from the overly soft pillows. Like she needed more evidence she's getting old. A few crumbs on the kitchen island serve as the only evidence of someone eating breakfast. From the window over the sink—no sign of Kim, her car gone from the shrub-lined driveway. Cece shouts her father's name, then the dog's, but there's no answer, not so much as a bark. She moves from one room to another, a silly panic setting in, feeling like a kid who's lost their parent in the grocery store. She's about to go outside to do a loop when a thud sounds from the basement.

Stairs creak beneath her feet, fluorescent lights hum overhead, the smell of mildew and sawdust mingling into a strange brew. Barry is bent over in concentration at his workbench, a flat pencil behind his ear.

"You're awake," he says, spinning around on his stool.

"Where's Mom?"

Barry stands, his head nearly touching the exposed beams. "She lit out of here pretty early after her run. She was in a bad mood . . . something about you blowing off an interview."

"Shit."

"You two had some sort of agreement?"

"She set up a job for me, but I blew the interview, partly on purpose . . . mostly on purpose, I guess."

Cece's expecting Barry to be upset with her or at least reprimand her for wasting her mother's time and energy, but he seems preoccupied.

"Aren't you angry?"

Barry rubs his stubbled chin. Crumbs dot his flannel shirt, and Cece wonders if he's the culprit for the mess upstairs. "I just want you to be happy. Your mother does, too, of course. She just goes about showing it differently."

Cece has never heard her father speak critically of her mother. Even when they'd fought terribly, he'd always presented a united front. "What's going on with you two?"

"We've just hit a rough patch—that's all."

"What about the business? Things sound worse than usual."

"Business could always be better, but it'll turn around. I have faith."

"Mom doesn't operate on faith, Dad. You know that."

"Let me show you something," Barry says.

Cece follows him to the far corner of the basement, under the air ducts and past the boiler and boxes filled with Christmas ornaments, where she's confronted by an enormous wooden armoire with glass doors. Inside, shelves lined with all her high school swimming trophies. On the top shelves, her Patriot League plaques from her time at Bucknell. Below, her high school awards in the shape of New York state, and toward the bottom, where the shelves grow crowded and cluttered, countless ribbons, crystal cups, and engraved plates from her youngest years of competition. He's even saved the cheesy participation trophies from when she first started competing, the ones with little gold men on top, crouched, ready to dive. They hadn't had any with women figurines, but Barry hadn't cared. And there, in a simple black frame, her certificate from the YMCA for completing her first swim class. Cece remembers—hands gripping the foam board, legs kicking up froth, Barry at her side, up to his stomach, wet hair painted against his chest, hands at her sides. Looking back, she doesn't know where her father ended and she began. It had always been swimming. There'd been no conversation about enjoyment or fulfillment, but had she needed one? Was the passion innate or cultivated? She'd never know. And wasn't that Barry's fault? He was the adult, the parent. The anger comes quickly, like a flash flood, and Cece's about to remind her father of all the pain and suffering she's endured because of swimming, because of him, but then she sees his face, full of admiration and gratitude, and she understands that this is perhaps all her father has—a case full of his daughter's trophies in his basement—and she can only bring herself to hug him and tell him it looks great. If he wants to run sandpaper over those memories until they are smooth, so be it. What will Cece gain from setting him straight, pointing out every misremembered moment? Only fleeting satisfaction, she suspects.

"I'm proud of you, Claire," Barry says, adjusting a few crooked trophies. "I know we had our differences about the surgery, but you were always a fighter. You can do anything you put your mind to."

"Why are you telling me this?"

"I need you to watch Bernard for a little longer, if that's all right. Your mother was supposed to be here . . ."

Cece feels a familiar twinge—anticipation—crouched on the starting block, bathing suit cutting into her hips, waiting for the gun, waiting to dive and sink or swim. "Are you guys getting a divorce?"

Barry shakes his head in a defeated kind of way. "No . . . God, no . . . nothing like that. Your mom just wants some space," he says, tugging at the cuffs of his shirt. "She's getting her own place for a bit, and I can't watch Bernard on my own, with work and all."

Even though Cece's suspected something was wrong, she can't believe what she's hearing. Her parents, on the verge of divorce. Hadn't they made it through the hard part? Careers, kids, paying for college—now is when they're supposed to spend more time together, enjoy each other's company. Maybe that's the problem. Cece wonders if her father actually believes what he's saying, or if he's trying to soften the blow. Surely, he must have seen the signs. "Did Mom tell you why she's unhappy?"

"This isn't on you, Claire. We'll figure it out. We've had troubles before, and we've always come out through it."

"How are you gonna take care of yourself, Dad? Mom does everything around here."

Barry reaches for Cece, his long arms wrapping her in a tight embrace. "This isn't your problem to fix."

"Does Wynonna know?"

He lets her go. "No. Absolutely not. She can't hear about this. She's not like you."

"Like how?"

"You've got strength, kid. You always have. I don't know what's going on with you right now with work and the extracurriculars, but I know you'll figure it out. You've always had a strong sense of purpose."

"What if that's the problem? What if what I want doesn't make sense? What if my purpose isn't my purpose at all, but some stupid experiment?"

"Remember what I used to tell you before each swim?"

Cece rolls her eyes. "You're gonna have to be more specific. You were a walking cliché back then, Dad."

Barry chuckles. "What did I say right before your second shoulder surgery, when you told me you were scared?"

The raw antiseptic smell of the operation room, the pinging monitors . . . she remembers. "If you aren't scared, you're not trying."

"Exactly. And what happened? You came back stronger, better than ever."

"When was the last time you were scared with Mom?"

Barry makes his way up the basement stairs, varicose veins popping in his right calf, hand gripping the banister all the way up. In the kitchen, he calls Bernard's name and shakes a bag of treats. Upstairs, nails scrabble on hardwood. "Like I said, fixing your parents' problems isn't your job." He rests a hand on her shoulder and gives it a squeeze, his eyes watery and big. "But point taken."

12

The email comes through while Cece's picking up Bernard's unsettlingly warm poop at a rest stop on I-95. She can't begrudge him too much; she'd forgotten to take him for a walk before they'd left—her father in the rearview mirror, wearing the same clothes as yesterday, waving goodbye, a look of bemused worry on his wrinkled face.

Dear Cece,

I've lived long enough to learn when to take time to cool off before getting into some heated, pointless argument. This morning was one of those moments. Imagine my disappointment and embarrassment when I called Tina to hear about how my accomplished, brilliant daughter knocked her interview out of the park, only to hear that she'd done quite the opposite. Blaming your previous company for letting you go? Challenging your potential supervisor on the mission of the company? You could have simply said you didn't want the job. At least then I wouldn't have wasted my time.

I can't pretend to know what's gotten into you, Cece, but if you're dead set on self-destructing, I'd appreciate it if you kept me out of your blast range. Not all of us want to go down like the *Titanic*. Is this really what you've decided to do with the privilege and opportunity afforded to you? I cannot understand this change, Cece. Everyone loses their job at one point or another, everyone has relationship trouble, but you don't blow it all up. I can only hope that you've reconciled with Jonathan. He is a good man, Cece. He is dependable and yes, he is rich, and that matters. There, I've said it. Sure, money doesn't buy happiness, but it buys so much else: space, time, safety, and consistency. You might not think much of these things; you're still young. But trust me. There is nothing worse, nothing dingier, than getting old and worrying about money. I don't know why I've never said it so plainly to you before, perhaps because it sounds crude, but it only sounds crude to those who are unwilling to admit its truth.

I'm sorry I wasn't there this morning when your father told you. I imagine it came as quite a shock, or maybe not. You've always been more perceptive than Wynonna. The truth is, Cece, your father and I have been drifting apart for quite some time. Marriage is a funny thing. Sometimes I think it was easier when you girls were young, and we were busier than bees. Sure, we fought more. God, the screaming matches we would have, but in the end, cooler heads would always prevail because we had you two, and we knew there were necessary sacrifices that had to be made. And I'm glad I made those sacrifices, but now that you and your sister are out of the house, there's less to distract us from ourselves. The vacation was a last-ditch effort to try and save things, but it feels to me like this has run its course, and I refuse to be still and atrophy just because that's what good wives are supposed to do. Your father and I spend very little time together as is. I've never been busier at work, perhaps by choice, and he's grown only more like himself. He's a creature of habit. Just getting him out of the house feels like a feat. People don't change as they get older; they just get more like themselves—at least that's what my mother used to say. None of this takes into account the matter of your father's business, which moves closer and closer to insolvency with each passing day. I can safely say that the company hasn't turned a profit in three years. We're only above water because I've redoubled my efforts and have found my own steady stream of income. But I am tired. Tired of his delusions, tired of pulling more than my weight. I don't want to grow older and more resentful than I already am, which is why I need to leave. Staying will only harm the both of us. I've found a good community of women in my exercise classes. I'm telling you, I feel like I'm forty again. I wake up energized and hungry. You can understand, Cece, can't you? I'm not asking for your forgiveness; I'm just asking you to understand. I imagine this is a lot for you to process. Call me if you want. I haven't told Wynonna yet, please don't say anything, I want to tell her myself. In fact, I'll give her a call now. The last thing I want is your father breaking the news to her. And just in case you're wondering, I'm still mad at you about blowing off that interview.

I love you, Cece. So does your father. I hope you'll eventually understand why I'm doing this.

Love, Mom

Cece finishes the email and slides her phone into her pocket and stands up from her seat at the picnic table. Semitrucks rumble by, kicking up dust and grime. From the welcome center, a steady stream of weary travelers sated by McDonald's and Starbucks. Only Bernard's impatient yaps bring her back to the moment. In so many ways, her mother is right, which only makes Cece angrier, mostly with herself. Of course, she should have rebuffed Kim's connections and help, but that would have required honesty and forthrightness, two qualities Cece is woefully in short supply of.

The tears come fast and hard before Cece can stop them. How absurd and juvenile, she thinks, running the back of her hand under her nose. Crying! Why is she so upset? Hadn't she suspected something was going on? Even so, Cece finds herself overcome with the keen sense that something is ending, not a perfect union, but a union, nonetheless. Her parents' marriage had lasted nearly four decades—a not-so-insignificant amount of time. Cece wonders how long her parents might have lasted if not for her and Wynonna. She wonders what makes a strong marriage, a good marriage, one capable of weathering not just the small tragedies of life, but the inexhaustible whims of the human heart for change and reinvention. Except there was no changing with Barry—he'd very much preferred to stay the same—and now her parents were on the brink.

Cece doesn't know how to hedge against such risks. Two months ago, safely ensconced in her job and relationship with Jonathan, right before the proposal, she'd have turned to the numbers, to probable outcomes. The best indicator of the future was the past, and the only way to guarantee success, in anything, was to analyze the risks and uncertainties and act quickly and decisively to account for them. But even then, Cece understands, cajoling the dog back into his crate, there are no guarantees.

BERNARD SNIFFS AROUND the unfamiliar apartment. It feels strange to be back in the very place Cece absconded from, filled with conviction and malice. Had she failed? Run back to the friendly confines of her relationship with Jonathan, tail between her legs? It doesn't feel like she's given up, but somehow, she suspects she's faltered somewhere.

Jonathan had sounded anxious on the phone when she'd asked if she could stop by, but now that she's here, in the apartment, her old apartment, there's no doubt he's happy to see her. Bernard lends the place an air of domesticity, and Cece finds herself slipping into a reverie of their future together, a future filled with family gatherings and warm chandelier light, cooing infants, and the sumptuous ease of a full and busy life.

There's time to kill. Even though it's Saturday, Jonathan has work calls and meetings. The three massive computer monitors in his office tell a story in a foreign language, with greens and reds, jagged lines and blinking decimal points. After being cooped up in the car, Cece decides to take Bernard for a long walk to stretch his legs. Jonathan promises to text her once he finishes up, his voice already distant, his mind drifting from the present to his spreadsheets and inbox, tickers on repeat—an infinite loop of inscrutable data.

The South End is bustling with young professionals, techy-looking men in stretchy pants and half zips, skinny women in pastel-colored running shoes and tight ponytails. Bernard pauses outside a crowded brewery patio, and Cece is amazed by the number of families seated at the beer-hall-style benches and standing around cornhole boards. Fathers cradle swaddled infants to their chests, hoppy beer painting their upper lips. Mothers push luxury-looking strollers back and forth with idle feet. This portrait of parenthood feels less daunting to Cece, nearly attainable.

After Bernard's tired himself out, Cece finds a bench in the shade along the water and checks her phone. Nothing from Morgan, and why would there be? Instead, an ominous-sounding text from Wynonna: Check your email. So, Kim had told her.

Cece,

Did you know about this? Mom just called me to say she's leaving Dad. This doesn't make sense. They've been together for almost forty years, are things really so bad? What did I miss? This can't be the solution, Cece. Sure, they bicker, but what married couple doesn't? A little tension is normal, don't you think? What the hell is Mom thinking? She can't just drop Dad and start a whole new life. She's sixty-two! What does she actually think is out there?

I imagine you're handling this much better than I am, but aren't you angry with Mom? I hung up on her when she told me the news. Sure, she's sacrificed a lot for Dad's business, but that was her choice. No one forced her to do anything. I just don't see how she can do this to him. I know he's far from perfect, and yes, he's probably the most stubborn person I've ever known, but he doesn't deserve this. What about the vows they took? When I told Mom I was marrying Devin, she couldn't shut up about how a good and stable marriage was the best way for a woman to secure her future. And now look at what she's done. I just keep thinking about Dad trying to make himself dinner every night. Maybe that was part of the problem, but it's not his fault. Men of his generation just never learned how to do that sort of thing. Now what's he going to do? Subsist on grilled cheese sandwiches? What are we going to do, Cece? Sooner or later, he's going to need help. And no offense, but you're still figuring things out, and Devin and I have our hands full. The boys just finished up summer camp, and it's pure madness here. I can't stand the idea of him being alone in that big house. He isn't the perfect father, but whose father is? Whatever his shortcomings, they don't justify Mom's behavior.

I hope you're taking all of this okay. I'll call when I've calmed down. Maybe I shouldn't be this angry, but I can't help it. I feel like she's been lying to us the entire time. I'm sure you have a much more enlightened perspective, but for now, I'm just angry.

Love, Wynonna

Cece wouldn't call her reaction more enlightened. *Realistic* is probably the better word for how she sees the world lately. She understands how Wynonna feels. Kim had always heralded the virtues of marriage, the importance of finding a good match and worthy partner to propel you through life, someone who would stand by you when waters grew rough, and they always grew rough, she used to say. Maybe Wynonna feels the impending separation of their parents more acutely because she's the only one of them who's taken the plunge, followed through on their mother's advice. For Wynonna, Kim's departure is an admission that she was wrong—and what might this truth reveal about Wynonna, or the entire enterprise of marriage?

Betrayed . . . it's not how Cece feels, exactly. And even while she worries about her father, she can't help but be impressed by her mother's fortitude and unrelenting optimism . . . or maybe it's something closer to cold pragmatism. After all, isn't she following the same advice she used to drill into her daughters all those years ago? Kim seems determined to deny her fate, stuck in a stale marriage with a man who has little interest in evolving or maintaining, even improving, their current financial state. It is a terrible thing, Cece thinks, growing to the age when you can see your parents for what they are: frail, imperfect creatures who once spoke with confidence and authority because that is what their children required.

ON THE TELEVISION, Diane Lane is standing on a dock staring out to sea and looking exceptional in a worn flannel shirt. Cece finds her beauty distracting. She's a fisherman's wife, after all!

"You're cool with this?" Jonathan asks from the kitchen.

The microwave whines, the pop of kernels fragrant and urgent. "With what?"

He emerges from behind the half wall, a questioning smirk on his face. "Staying the night. I told you. I'm fine with easing back in. Taking our time."

"Totally," Cece says, louder than she means. "It's not a big deal."

"Great," Jonathan says, over the beeping.

Jonathan had wanted to eat out, but Cece had convinced him to order in from their favorite Thai place. She'd made sure to eat light in anticipation of something happening. If she'd had any doubts about whether she was doing the right thing by trying to make this work with Jonathan, the implosion of her parents' marriage has only reinforced her reasons for coming back. There's always going to be risk, of course, but with Jonathan, the percentages are just better. Plus, Jonathan is a good man, a kind man. A man who forgave her, even if Cece never did come clean about everything. A small, unimportant detail, she thinks, while they settle into the couch. By the front door, Bernard eyes them with suspicion, and she wonders what he thinks about all this.

Cece doesn't dare mention anything about her parents' marital problems. Nothing ruins the mood like divorce and family dysfunction. Cece has plans. She resists shoveling popcorn in her mouth and drinking too much wine while the movie drags on, pondering the best way to initiate things. It's odd—strategizing like this, like Jonathan's a stranger, like they don't know the rhythms of their bodies. The AC kicks on and Cece pulls a blanket over them. In the dark room, the television flickers: Bearded men in orange rubber waders. Green ocean spray. The boat's heaving prow. Of all things, must they watch this? All she can think about is the grumble of Morgan's pickup truck, his baseball cap pushed back on his pale forehead. It's nothing, Cece thinks to herself. It's a silly thing. It doesn't matter. Soon they'll retire to the bedroom, where Jonathan's bed is the perfect height for him to stand and pull her to the edge, hands grasping her hips. She hopes the months apart have made him hungry and a little bit mad. She needs him to lose himself with her; otherwise, what's the point?

Cece turns to kiss Jonathan only to find him asleep, snoring lightly. Disappointment and relief flood her chest, and she laughs silently to herself at the absurdity of it all before resting her head on his shoulder and closing her eyes, the movie playing out on mute. When they wake in the early hours of morning, they look at each other bashfully and pick stray popcorn from the folds of the blanket while an infomercial flashes electric blues across the walls. They shuffle to bed. Even with the lights off, Cece knows her way around the bathroom, the hand towel in its usual place, the toilet handle requiring an extended depression in order to flush fully.

Jonathan is half-awake when she comes to bed and slides in next to him, the smell of freshly laundered sheets nostalgic and familiar.

"I fell asleep," he says to the room.

"You were tired."

"Work's been killer."

Cece hears Bernard out in the kitchen, his anxious whine and slow walk to his foreign water bowl where he drinks noisily. Oh, to be an animal! A thoughtless beast! A sweat breaks out on her neck, lungs full, heart working hard, blood in her belly, blood in her toes. She can't will herself to move, but she would, she will, if only he touches her first. That will do the trick! Jonathan rolls onto his back and rearranges the sheets. He clasps her hand in his. "It's good to have you back."

Cece finds herself sinking, gloriously, into the mattress. She's forgotten how nice it is to sleep on a Tempur-Pedic bed . . . and on these six-hundred-thread-count Egyptian-cotton sheets. "It's nice to be back."

"I've been thinking about attending my high school reunion," Jonathan says, "in August. Any chance you'd join?"

Cece is somewhere else, the memory foam pillow cradling her heavy head, the central air-conditioning washing over her body in waves of snowflaked cool. Outside, the dim hum of streetlights and the occasional faraway siren. Hips loosen, and the knots in her shoulders melt. She will sleep well tonight. "Sure," she hears herself say, "I'd love to."

Jonathan only squeezes her hand softly, his breath going quiet and deep. In the apartment, only the drone of energy-efficient appliances. Even Bernard has settled in for the night.

In the morning, Jonathan's possessed with the idea of visiting Rayburn Oyster Company. "I've never seen an oyster farm," he says over toasted whole wheat bread and orange juice. "At least show me where you guys are planning to expand. I wanna see the site."

Cece can't tell if his interest is earnest or manufactured, but she realizes it doesn't matter. He's trying—that's what matters. "When would you like to go?"

"How about this morning? I've got nothing. We can take your car up and I'll catch the train back."

The idea makes so much sense Cece has trouble finding an answer other than yes. It's Sunday, so Santiago and Davi won't be in Noank, which is perfect. It's not that she's embarrassed for them to meet Jonathan; she just wouldn't know how to introduce him. Ex-fiancé now friend / potential fiancé again? Either way, they would give her shit.

IT'S MIDDAY WHEN they get to the docks in Noank. The Sunday crowd is already out on the water, leaving dozens of empty slips, squares of placid water reflecting the clouds above. Before taking Jonathan down to the water, Cece shows him the warehouse where all their equipment is stored. She can't help brimming with pride as she points to the towering stacks of oyster cages she's cleaned, the meticulously organized buoys, and the enormous floor-to-ceiling pegboard wall she reorganized to hold all their shop tools. A musty aroma—dried seawater and motor oil—lingers in the stale air.

"You had to have seen the place before to appreciate the neatness," Cece says after she sees the bewildered expression on Jonathan's face. Of course, what she might see as a well-organized symbol of all she's accomplished this summer, Jonathan might just see a dank room filled with things.

Not to be deterred, Cece shows him the oyster-sorting equipment next and explains how the process works. Jonathan lets out a low whistle and runs his hand along the grader. Cece explains how they move the bags from the boat to here, where they go through the process of tumbling, sorting, and washing. Encouraged by his enthusiasm, she points out what makes this unit special: the adjustable spray bar, the self-aligning conveyor belt, and the sliding chute doors. Cece almost starts regaling Jonathan with the story of her heroic repair job but stops herself, worried he'll find it boring.

"Looks like a serious operation," he says. "I wonder what the overhead costs are on this whole setup."

They make their way down to the water, and while they don't have time to go out on the boat, Cece hands Jonathan a set of binoculars and points to a spot in the near distance where oyster bags float like thousands of mermaid purses on the calm blue-green water. She tells him how the oysters are first spawned and fertilized at their hatchery, then moved to one of their outdoor nurseries in the surrounding bays and coves. Once they've matured, that's when they bring them out to open water for their final growth phase where she and Santiago clear seaweed off the bags and flip them when necessary.

"This is even more involved than I was imagining, Cece," Jonathan says, binoculars still pressed to his eye sockets.

"Let me guess," Cece says, something close to satisfaction swelling in her throat. "You thought it was some little rinky-dink outfit."

Visibly flustered, Jonathan protests. "I didn't have anything to go on. I mean, you didn't tell me it was so big. You . . ."

"Relax. I'm just giving you a hard time. Wanna see the cove where Richie wants to expand?"

"I'd love that," Jonathan says.

THEY DRIVE BACK to the pool house and down toward the water, past the boatyard, to a dead end where a worn trail leads through rebellious forsythia bushes. Cece is aware of taking a specific route so as to avoid Morgan's house—a fact she only half recognizes as they drive. If Lorraine hadn't shown Cece how to access the cove on foot, she might never have known about this path—a favorite of local nature enthusiasts and hikers.

Through the trees, glimpses of cedar-shake waterfront homes and still water. The trail is meticulously maintained, the underbrush conveniently cut back to combat the ticks. Darkness gathers, and then they're free of the tree line, low marshland ahead, and then the cove, a lush blue-gray paint spill, surrounded by low-lying grasses, towering oaks, and the occasional home, placed a polite distance from its neighbor. Cece can see Lorraine's point; she understands how Richie's oyster bags might disturb the natural beauty of this place, but soon enough they'll feel like they've always been here, like these sun-faded homes. And in truth, Cece wonders just how many times a year the residents of these houses look out and admire the pristine beauty before them.

To Cece's surprise, Jonathan has all sorts of questions about the intended expansion. They walk to the water's edge, or at least to where the grass turns to marsh, the ground wet and squishy. Jonathan wants to know where the bags will be situated and how many. He wants to know how the oysters will be transferred once they get large enough. Questions about output, logistics, margins, and profits flow from him like he's a seed investor of a promising startup. While Cece does her best to answer all his questions, he slips an arm around her waist as they look out over the water. There's an unencumbered giddiness to him, and Cece finds herself letting go and easing against the crook of his arm, while she details Richie's vision for the company and its expansion.

Jonathan turns to look at Cece and puts his hands on her shoulders. "I want to invest."

Cece can only laugh. The words don't make sense. "This isn't the stock market, Jonathan."

"It's investing all the same, and if Rayburn is expanding, you'll need an infusion of capital. There are all sorts of costs to consider: permitting, more equipment, more boats, more employees."

The idea is so ridiculously audacious Cece is dumbstruck. It seems silly, paranoid even, in hindsight, to have thought Jonathan would have reservations about her new job. Sure, working on an oyster farm is a stark change from her old actuary job, but she should never have doubted his support. Isn't this what Cece's been waiting for? His encouragement and devotion? And if it is, Cece thinks, then why does something nag at her, like a run in her stocking, threatening to split wide open? Why is she resisting? What is she afraid of?

"I don't even know if the farm is profitable," Cece says, unsure of what she's trying to protect.

"Then we'll make it profitable," Jonathan says excitedly. "I see how happy you are here, Cece, and if you're this passionate about the business, then I want to be a part of it. And once the project gets approved, you and Richie will need all the help you can get. Who knows—maybe we buy Richie out eventually and run it ourselves? You could take care of the aquaculture stuff, and I'll handle the money side. Maybe we settle down around here. There's no reason I can't work from home, and it's closer to my parents."

Is it Jonathan's spontaneity or his obsession with turning Rayburn into another asset Cece finds disconcerting? "You'd really do all that?"

"Is this the thing you were born to do? Is this the thing that makes you feel most alive?"

Cece looks out at the serene water, Jonathan's body warm against her. "It's the closest."

"Then let's make it happen. I'm good with money, Cece. Let me do the one thing I'm good at. Let me invest in Rayburn and help you build something."

Jonathan's gesture—his absolute support, his unrepentant enthusiasm, his belief—is proof alone of his unconditional love. Is it not?

CECE RECOGNIZES THE familiar sound, the feeling in her gut, before it registers who's driving by when she and Jonathan emerge from the thicket into the cul-de-sac. Morgan does a circle around the cul-de-sac before slowing down, and Cece finds herself infinitely thankful they left Jonathan's sports car in Stamford. And even though she hasn't done anything wrong, or at least anything terribly wrong—a few small lies here and there—Cece is filled with palpable anxiety, ears hot, fingertips swelling, the air suddenly thick. With Jonathan behind her, Cece waves at Morgan—a wave, she hopes, that indicates there's no need to stop or have idle chitchat, but of course he does, a broad smile on his face. Quiet follows after Morgan's cut the engine, putting an end to the possibility that Cece can escape this unpleasant predicament.

"Coming from the cove?" he says, his hand tan and paint-flecked against the turquoise truck door.

Cece is aware of Jonathan's nearness. A shadow of recognition flickers over Morgan's face, darkening his features, brows bent, jaw set in a hard line. Jonathan says nothing, waiting for an introduction, it seems, the way Bernard waits by his food bowl before dinner.

"This is Morgan," Cece says, toes cramping in her sandals. "He's my neighbor."

"Jonathan. Pleasure to meet you. I'm . . ." Jonathan steals a glance at Cece and chuckles. They have yet to discuss the formal title of their current situation, a point of ambiguity Cece had embraced until now. "We're still figuring that out, but let's go with friend."

Cece tries to suppress what must look like relief flooding her face, that is until Jonathan puts an arm around her and pulls her close.

Morgan peers questioningly at Cece, his unruly eyebrows raised in what? Alarm? Jealousy? Pity? Then the look is gone, wiped from his face, like it was never there at all. "Not really neighbors. I live a few houses down."

"Some truck," Jonathan says, oblivious to Cece's nervous canter from one leg to the other.

"It's a truck," Morgan says.

Cece doesn't think Morgan's going to put her on the spot—he's not malicious—but she's not taking any chances, imploring him with a subtle look: *Please don't say anything; please don't ruin this for me.*

Morgan puts a hand through his beard, his gaze probing Jonathan's countenance for something. "I better get going. I'll leave you two to it."

Before Cece and Jonathan can reply, the truck growls to life, and then its out of sight, only a low rumble and heady hint of exhaust lingering in the air remain.

"Weird guy," Jonathan says.

Now it's Cece's turn to look for something—what, exactly, she has no idea. But Jonathan's already forgotten the moment, walking to her car.

The street is suddenly quiet, save for the chatter of songbirds, and Cece is filled with gratitude for her luck and Jonathan's blissful easiness with which he moves about the world.

13

Business is booming. At the docks and on the boat, Cece moves with the kind of quiet confidence that only comes from repetition. A single task—dropping a cage, priming the motors, and sorting oysters—done so many times it's become an extension of her. There is no thinking, no second-guessing; there's only the invisible checklist in her head that needs to get done before the sun slips to other side of the world, where other fishermen, just like her and Santiago, are rising before daylight breaks to push their boats from the shallows and cast their nets.

Some days, Santiago lets Cece take the boat out by herself while he stays on dry land to help Davi with his SAT vocabulary words. The prep classes aren't working the miracles they'd expected, and Santiago has promised his wife they'd use whatever free time they could to cram, a condition for Davi joining them again. Cece is more than happy to work alone, thrilled by this newfound responsibility. It's a strange feeling to be trusted by Richie and Santiago to get the job done, and she doubles her efforts, working as fast as she can without cutting corners. Pretty soon, she's finding enough time in the day to harvest the day's catch, sort the oysters, and maintain the equipment on the docks. "Take it easy," Santiago says from the shade of the maintenance shed, a stack of oil-stained index cards in front of him. "You'll put me out of a job."

Cece runs a forearm across her mouth. "I'm seasonal. Remember?"

"Richie's gonna need all the help he can get with the expansion over in Mamacoke."

"I thought that was all tied up in—"

"Bureaucracy," Davi says with a big smile. "One of my words."

"Exactly," Cece says.

"Nah," Santiago says, and spits onto the hot gravel, "can't stop progress. It'll happen. Richie's got a plan."

Cece just smiles and heads back to the docks, where she washes down the boat with fresh water and sets up the cages for tomorrow. There's a distinct pride she's beginning to take with the work: the appearance of the boat, the timeliness of their deliveries to the distribution center, and the quality of their oysters.

A few weeks later, Richie calls Cece down to the office. Her efforts haven't gone unnoticed. Product is being delivered faster than ever without any complaints about quality. To boot, Santiago's put in a good word for her. Even though Richie is delivering welcomed news from behind his slovenly desk, his dour tone and ragged nails tell a different story. His face, already wrinkled and worn, is cavernous today, cheeks hollow, dark circles under his bloodshot eyes. He wants to know if Cece's willing to see the other side of the business. "The money and the bullshit," he says with a weary smile.

Cece looks around at the swollen filing cabinets and stacks of manila folders overflowing, she imagines, with long-forgotten invoices, bank statements, and tax documents. "You mean like secretarial work?"

"Not necessarily. You'd be learning about how the business really functions. The numbers and such."

"I prefer to be out on the water."

"I figured," Richie says, sounding roundly defeated. "It's a funny thing. My son was the opposite. Didn't want anything to do with the boat or the oysters themselves. You know . . . get his hands dirty. Was only willing to putter around the office. Imagine that. Something like six generations of Rayburns working on the water's gonna end with me. It wasn't always oysters, you know . . . It was whaling back then, when New London was something to behold. Those were boom times, but they didn't last. We hunted sperm whales to near extinction, then kerosene came along. Those were lean years, or so I've heard. Between then and now, there were other ventures, boatbuilding, some commercial fishing. My great-grandfather was the one who got us into our current line of business. You've gotta remember, that was when we still had wild oyster beds . . . I've seen old photographs. Just about the most beautiful thing you could see. They've all mostly disappeared, of course, gone the way of the sperm whale . . . but we're keeping on. That's why we've got to secure this Mamacoke expansion and grow the industry sustainably."

"Where's your son now?"

"Brooklyn. He works for a company down there. Renting out virtual spaces or something. I don't quite understand it. What even is a virtual space? Doesn't make sense."

She wonders if this is how Kim feels about Cece's current employment ventures, bewildered and flabbergasted at her daughter's unwillingness to follow the plan, the path she'd laid before her. Before she can offer Richie comfort, he's on to the next thing, trying, in vain, to organize reams of opened mail on his desk. There's something sad and pathetic about witnessing his attempt to bring order to the chaos of the office, but Cece resists the urge to help. She can't be relegated to paper pusher. She won't allow it.

Something clatters to the floor, envelopes and documents flutter and slide. Richie curses his clumsiness and gets on all fours. Cece helps clean up and spots an official-looking letter.

July 19, 2018
Richard Rayburn
P.O. Box 348
Mystic, CT 06355

Dear Mr. Rayburn,

Pursuant to the bylaws of New London County, the Zoning Commission hereby notifies you of a Town Hall meeting scheduled for noon at City Hall on 8/22/2018, at which the matter of building permit #956718 will be discussed. This meeting has been convened in response to the collection of at least two hundred signatures (the threshold for convening a public hearing) of residents who oppose the proposed project.

As stipulated by the County's regulations, residents who have expressed opposition to the issuance of this permit are entitled to a public forum to voice their concerns. While the majority sentiment expressed by the public may be considered in the Commission's deliberations, please be advised that the Zoning Commission retains sole and final authority over the approval or denial of the building permit.

We respectfully request your presence at the Town Hall meeting to present any pertinent information or responses to the concerns raised by the public, as this may inform the Commission's review process.

Sincerely,

Hollis P. Angstrom

Chairperson, Zoning Commission

New London County

"When did this arrive?" Cece says.

"What?"

"This notice about the town hall."

"Last week, I think," Richie says through labored breath. "Pain in the ass, really."

All summer Lorraine had been hard at work building a grassroots opposition. Now they were running like a well-oiled machine, blanketing neighborhoods with their fearmongering pamphlets and hosting summer barbecue socials with like-minded NIMBY folk. There were even rumors of a protest at the Rayburn farm in Noank. There'd be no compromising with Lorraine. Cece knew she wouldn't rest until having it out in a public forum.

"What will you do?" Cece says, trying to smother the panic in her voice.

"I'm still working on that. I mean, I knew we'd have to jump through some hoops in terms of permitting. But I wasn't really anticipating any serious pushback," Richie says while he stands and stretches his long legs in their faded blue jeans. "The build permit was supposed to be granted already, but with all this damn public outcry, the board delayed it and scheduled this town hall instead . . . The thing is I thought it was a done deal, so I went ahead and secured financing for the project and purchased the necessary equipment . . . brand-new tumbler, new racks. I even put a down payment on a second boat. If this thing gets pushed back, Cece . . . maybe I can hold out a few months, but I stand to lose everything."

So, this isn't just the Mamacoke expansion, Cece realizes. The whole business might go under. How could Richie have been so foolish? Why hadn't he waited to get final approval before sinking money into the project? Cece knows that isn't how it works. He hadn't done anything wrong—she's just angry, furious even, at the prospect of losing Rayburn completely, the only job that's ever truly sustained her. Just when she's found her footing, Lorraine and her zealots are going to wipe it all away. They don't care about the environment or the historical preservation of the city; the only thing they're interested in preserving is their property values. Even though she's aware of it happening, even though she can identify it, Cece starts to spiral. Worst-case scenarios loom like rogue waves on the horizon. Without the oyster farm, without Santiago and Davi, Cece will be forced to take another actuary job, commute to the city, wear pantsuits, eat obscenely priced salads at her desk. Admit her mother was right . . . Without this, there'd be nothing tying her to this place. If Rayburn closes, she'll be forced to contend with her desire to remain in New London for reasons beyond the job—an act of self-reflection she fears deeply.

"When's the first payment due on the loan?" Cece asks, the vaguest outline of an idea forming in her head.

"Thirty days, but it's not the first installment I'm worried about, it's the second, third, and fourth. These activists could tie this project up for decades. I've seen it happen."

"Why didn't you mention any of this? Does Santiago know?"

"I thought you said you didn't want to deal with the money and the bullshit. This is most definitely the bullshit."

"Maybe I've changed my mind. Ballpark. How many payments can you make?"

"Four. Five at the most."

"Then we have time."

"For what?"

"To sway public opinion." Cece can see Richie isn't following her. He is a man who has had no use for politics, local or national, until this moment. "We can get out there and knock on doors. Collect our own signatures. I bet there's a ton of support in the community for more jobs."

Richie works his hands together like he's holding an imaginary bar of soap.

"Look, right here," Cece says. She points to a line in the letter. "While the majority sentiment expressed by the public may be considered in the Commission's deliberations, please be advised that the Zoning Commission retains sole and final authority over the approval or denial of the building permit."

"We still have a chance, you mean."

"Correct," Cece says, "and if we can bring our own list of signatures and make our case, there's a good chance it'll be approved."

"It's worth a shot, I suppose," Richie says dubiously. "Where do we begin?"

For once in a very long time, Cece knows exactly what she needs to do. "Leave that to me."

CECE KNOCKS ON Morgan's front door and then retreats to the top step of the stairs. She has no real right to ask anything of him, especially after running into him with Jonathan, but she's desperate. Pride be damned—she needs his help to save Rayburn. From the backyard, the whine of a saw. Cece picks her way around the side of the house where she finds Morgan standing in a cloud of sawdust, bright orange earplugs crammed into his ears, extension cords crisscrossing the lawn. Cece gives him a big wave, but he remains bent to the task, lips pursed, guiding wood slats with both hands, the saw spitting out scraps like spent sunflower seeds.

A few more cuts, the saw powered down, Morgan stands before her brushing sawdust from his beard and pant legs. Two red indentations grace the sides of his nose from the now-removed safety goggles.

"Remember when you asked me if there was anyone I wanted you to thump?" Cece says.

Morgan slides his backward hat around to face forward. "Sounds like something stupid I would say."

"It was appreciated at the time," Cece reassures him. She'd expected him to laugh or at least crack a smile. "I can come back. If you're busy . . . I mean, I know you're busy. I can see you're working . . ."

"Just trying to finish up a few projects I've been neglecting."

"Totally. I get it," Cece says, flustered at her own presumption of Morgan's availability. "I'll stop by another time."

She turns and goes back the way she came, stepping gingerly on moss-covered bricks.

"What's the problem?" Morgan says before she's out of earshot. "Guys from work still giving you a hard time?"

After Cece hurriedly explains the situation—the impending town hall, Richie's financial gamble, their immediate need for signatures—Morgan says he knows where they should start.

"You'll help me, then?"

Morgan tugs a rumpled plaid shirt on over his threadbare V-neck. "Sure thing."

"We can do it another day, if you're busy, that is."

"Sounds time sensitive."

Cece can't deny this fact. "What about Lacy?"

"She's up at her mom's place. Coming back down tomorrow."

"Too bad. She could have joined. We need all the help we can get. Should we take my car?"

"Know where we're going?"

"Not necessarily."

"Might make more sense for me to drive, then."

After retrieving the pens and clipboards from her trunk, Cece jumps into Morgan's pickup truck and they head downtown. How many times has Cece heard this truck from a distance and turned to watch, anxious and expectant? Now she's inside, the cab just as she imagined, a leather bench seat, worn and grooved, the back seat a tangle of power tools, paint cans, and extension cords. Don't be weird, Cece thinks to herself, and redirects her attention out the window. The silence grows between them. She wants to ask him why he was acting strange the last time she saw him. But speaking Jonathan's name aloud will ruin everything; it will force them to have some kind of definitive conversation that ends with them not spending the day together. Her job—Richie—requires her not to bring it up, Cece thinks to herself. It's the right thing to do. Still, she's antsy, the silence working on her like some kind of medieval torture, compelling her to reveal . . . what? Anything. Everything.

"My parents are getting a divorce," she blurts out. It feels more real now that she's said it aloud. Morgan's the first person she's told. "Or at least I think so. My mom is moving out."

"Sorry to hear," he says. "How are you taking it?"

Cece scolds herself. What did she expect him to say? *Thanks for this incredibly revealing and depressing information, Cece. I'm so glad you've told me this.* Then again, maybe this is good, maybe this plants them firmly in the friend zone, sharing their messy lives, unconcerned with appearances.

How is she taking it? Well? Fine? All in stride? "I guess I don't really know. My sister is upset. They've been together for almost forty years."

Morgan lets out a low whistle. "Siobhan, Lacy's mom—we didn't make it six years. I've come around to the opinion that a good, decent marriage is about the toughest thing a person can try to do. And even when you find it, you've got to work to keep it good. There's no slacking off, or at least that's what it seems like. I wouldn't know."

"Why did you guys break up? You and Siobhan?"

Morgan seems to be weighing how much he wants to tell Cece. "We weren't good for each other . . . Maybe that's unfair to her . . . I wasn't ready to be a father."

"But you are now."

"I'm trying."

"My parents were good for a while, I think. But people change. Or they don't change at all. Both can bring problems. It just seems like one big crapshoot. No one knows if they'll love or even tolerate each other in five, ten, twenty years, but they do their best to assess the risk and take the leap."

"I don't know how much assessing goes into it. People are spontaneous and pretty reckless in my experience."

Cece picks at the frayed leather seat under her thigh. "Maybe that's my problem. Too much assessing."

"Is that why you called things off with Jonathan? Too much risk?"

A pang of guilt needles between Cece's ribs. How much truth does this particular moment require? How much truth will absolve her? And what does she owe Morgan? Since when did friendship make things more complicated? Truth, in all its variations, seems like the best policy; after all, Cece could use a friend right about now, even if it comes at a cost. She forms the words in her head and recites them back to herself before she says them aloud. "Kind of the opposite. You probably already guessed, but we're trying to make things work again."

From the side, Cece studies Morgan's face. She doesn't know what she's looking for. Relief? Disappointment? What does she want him to do with this information? His demeanor betrays nothing, no inner turmoil, no gloom—a perfect statue radiating stoicism. "Seems like a nice guy."

Cece fights the desire to defend Jonathan's personality against any potential perceived assholery—he isn't one of those mindless finance bros; he wasn't in a frat; he's offered to invest in Rayburn Oyster—but she chews her cheek instead, sensing that Morgan would prefer to drive in silence.

There's something else that stops Cece from breaking the soundless morass that settles between them like river mud. Morgan's demeanor, his tight grip on the steering wheel, his eyes narrowed and straight ahead, like he's determined not to look at her.

Whether the palpable tension can be attributed to their not-so-forgettable sex a month ago or Cece's proclamation that she's back together with Jonathan remains unknown. Is Morgan angry with her, disappointed? Disappointed would be much worse. Or maybe she's just being paranoid. He has a lot going on. Maybe this newfound taciturnity can be easily attributed to the ex or something else entirely. He's helping her, after all. Take the win, Cece thinks. Windows down, the wind gusts deafeningly, eliminating any need for conversation. Cece is infinitely thankful when they hit nearly every green light on their way across town.

Morgan insists they start on Perry Street and work their way north. Cece is less familiar with this part of the city and is happy to follow his lead. The roads grow more rutted, the homes cramped together and divided into multifamily apartments. Low-slung power lines hang across streets like loose stitches in the sky. Gray satellite dishes teeter on sun-faded shingles. Air conditioners lean precipitously out of windows. From a chain-link-fenced yard, a dog yaps.

"Just a little different than Mystic," Morgan says with a chuckle.

Cece wonders if this is some sort of test, if Morgan's seeing how far she'll go outside her comfort zone. If it is, she's determined to pass. She may have given up on being an actuary; she may have embraced risk and taken her leap of faith (or foolishness), but Cece has never met a test she hasn't wanted to ace.

They decide to split up to cover more ground. "How about a bet?" Cece shouts while she crosses the street. "Person with the lower number of signatures has to buy the other a drink at the Whaler tonight!"

"Let's focus on getting actual signatures first."

"Spoken like someone who's afraid to lose!"

Cece recites her script to herself while she climbs the rickety steps of the first home. She pulls back the screen door and gives three confident raps. Somewhere, a car alarm blares. From inside, rustling, like someone is moving boxes out of their way. A sliver of light. A woman in a nightgown peers at Cece through enormous glasses.

Smile, Cece thinks. Smile! "Hi, my name is Cece Downing.

Do you have a moment to chat about an important matter in our city?"

The woman regards her with vague suspicion. "I already have cable."

Cece presses on. "I'm collecting signatures to support the expansion of an oyster farm right here in New London County. If approved, our project would generate both seasonal and permanent jobs for our local economy."

"Who'd you say you were with?"

"I'm collecting signatures on behalf of Rayburn Oyster Company. We're trying to expand our business into New London."

From across the street, Cece hears Morgan's hearty laugh. From the sounds of it, he's already ahead of her by one.

"I don't want to put my name down on any kind of list," the old woman says. Before Cece can reply, the door crunches closed.

Undaunted, Cece heads to the next home where a young mother in a velour jumpsuit answers the door angrily. "I was just putting my kids down for a nap." She points to a laminated sign below the mailbox. INFANTS MAY BE NAPPING. DON'T RING DOORBELL! "Can't you read?"

Cece apologizes profusely through the din of wailing infants and hurries off. After stopping at every home and apartment on the block, Cece is dismayed to find she's only managed to collect a single signature from a teenager who was supposed to be in summer school and signed his name only after Cece promised not to tell his mother. Back on the sunbaked sidewalk, sweat dappling her upper lip, Cece can't help but be impressed by Lorraine's determination. The woman had gotten something like two hundred signatures—a feat and testament to her maniacal zeal. Not helping matters is the fact that Morgan appears infinitely more adept at this than her, holding up a hand and shouting, "Five already!"

The next line of homes over proves more fertile ground, and Cece gets three signatures in a row. At the mention of new jobs, people nod and sign their names. "I remember when a man could make a decent living for his family around here," says an elderly man seated on his porch. "I used to build subs down at General Dynamics. Nowadays, folks are working two, three jobs to make ends meet. Driving for Uber and all that nonsense."

"We're hoping our project will create more jobs."

"Where'd you say you're putting this farm?"

"Mamacoke Cove."

"Mamacoke?" The man removes his Red Sox hat and scratches his head. "You've got about as much luck building a riverboat casino as you do putting anything up in Mamacoke. White folk up there won't abide it."

"That's why we're collecting signatures to present to the zoning commission."

The man chuckles. "They do love their kayaking."

Cece thanks the man and encourages him to attend the town hall. With each signature, her steps grow lighter. There is something invigorating about being out in the community and speaking to people, even those who don't want to sign their name. Then there are those who don't answer the door at all, those who would prefer to look through a peephole or stare down at Cece through a gauzy curtain. But no matter! There are always more she can rally to the cause! Her script tightens. Her delivery sharpens. She highlights the benefits Rayburn will bring to New

London while laying out the opposition, those who are weaponizing well-intentioned zoning laws, historical preservation, and environmental policies to stop the city from growing. It's hard going, and after her fifth block, Cece's losing her voice and her cheeks ache from smiling. For all her efforts, she's only collected twenty-five signatures. How would they ever get a high enough number to rival Lorraine's efforts?

Dejected, she makes her way back to Morgan's truck. Losing their bet is the least of her worries. Inexplicably, Morgan's doubled her number.

"What did you tell them?"

He starts the truck. "The truth."

"And what's that?"

"I told them we need more here. More jobs, more opportunity, more everything, and people who oppose this project, people like Lorraine, those college old heads—they're standing in our way. They're all about free love and reminding you where they were when MLK and Kennedy were assassinated, but when it comes to growing this city and creating jobs, half-decent jobs for hardworking folks, a lot of Black folks, mind you—well. They'd rather not. Not in their backyard at least. Civil rights are well and good, as long as they don't fuck up your property value."

Cece is taken aback by this flash of anger. She remembers what Lorraine told her about the incident at his house back in January, when the cops were called. As quickly as it enters her mind, she pushes it down. "Did something happen?"

Morgan shakes his head. "Work's been slow. A few guys got laid off."

"Did I meet them?"

"Mickey and Wesley? No idea."

"Wasn't Mickey the guy who fixed the engine for me?"

"Sure," Morgan says, already battening down the hatches, his eyes still and unblinking. "We've known it was coming for a while. Building boats, fixing boats. It's not exactly a booming business. It's just . . . this place, this city, they used to build things here, things they could be proud of. And now, not so much."

"If we get enough signatures, we can do something about it. The zoning commission will have no choice but to listen to us. I'm knocking on doors from now until the meeting. And I'll get Davi and Santiago to help. Two hundred names is doable."

In the cab, Morgan lunges for his pack of cigarettes on the dashboard, then seems to think better of it. "Why do you care so much?"

"What do you mean?"

"You're going back to your old life, applying for that actuary job in the city. What's it to you if Rayburn can't expand or the boatyard goes belly-up?"

Cece chooses to ignore the opaque reference to Jonathan. If it's just plain old jealousy, she can handle it, but what she isn't prepared for are Morgan's opinions on her career. The actuary position is long gone, not hers even if she wanted it (which she doesn't)—Cece's self-sabotage had seen to that. She hadn't said anything to Morgan about it, her change of heart and commitment to Rayburn, she realizes.

"I can't figure you out," Morgan says before she can say anything. "Why go back to a job that clearly doesn't make you happy?"

The choice between her old career in the city and Rayburn

Oyster has been settled for quite some time in Cece's mind, but she bristles at Morgan's exasperation. Even if she has no intention of returning to Manhattan's grind and tumult, even if she's done with risk models and painting by the numbers, that's her call . . . What makes Morgan think he knows what brings her happiness? And why does he feel like he can voice his displeasure with so much knowing? The sensible thing to do, the mature thing to do, Cece thinks, Cece knows, would be to tell him the truth: She's out of the actuary game for good, committed to Richie's business ventures, big and small. This, however, would require wisdom and dispassion, two things Cece is short on at the moment.

"Some parts of it made me happy," Cece quips. "The money was good."

Morgan seems intent not to press the subject, eyes on the road and his mirrors, on anything but Cece. "The money," he says. "Can't argue with that."

They pass the Whaler. Drinks are off, apparently, which feels petty and small. Cece can feel it building, the urge to win the argument, to prove she's right, even if she's not entirely certain what it is she's after. But then Morgan's slowing down, and Cece realizes they're already back at his house. She considers coming clean about the actuary job, but he's already out of the truck, the door shutting with a resounding *clang*.

She hurries after him. "Thanks again."

"No problem," he says and hurries toward the house. "Happy to help."

"Hey," Cece says. "Are we okay?"

Morgan stops and turns. "All good," he says. "I just thought you cared about this place, about Richie's business. I thought all of this was more than just a distraction, but I was wrong, and that's okay."

Before Cece can respond, Morgan is giving her a firm wave—neither unfriendly nor friendly—and bounding up his front stairs. She stands outside, arms crossed, the clipboards digging into her stomach. She looks at the puny number of names she's managed to collect and compares them to Morgan's prodigious list. How had the day gone south so quickly? Why hadn't she just told him she wasn't considering the actuary position any longer?

Better get moving, she thinks. The last thing she needs is Lorraine spotting her in enemy territory. She's tempted to march back to the house and declare her pro-Rayburn activities, but the truth is, she still needs a place to live, at least for now.

August

14

Cece awakes to the sound of rain drumming on the roof of the pool house. Even with the air conditioner on, the room feels subtropical, the air wet and sticky. The downpour intensifies outside, except it isn't just rain, Cece realizes. Someone's knocking on her door. Bernard is fast asleep, further proving his uselessness to potential home intruders. She reaches for her phone, but it's dead, nothing but a black screen.

"Who is it?" she croaks.

"Morgan and Lacy."

Only after Cece mumbles something about needing a minute and stumbles to the bathroom does Bernard rise from his slumber. Cece quickly gives up on looking presentable and gargles some mouthwash before opening the door.

"Hey," Morgan says, holding a black umbrella aloft, mostly over Lacy. His navy-blue T-shirt is soaked through to the skin. Lacy crosses one foot in front of the other, her painted toenails cheerful and pink in their flip-flops. Behind them, power lines quiver and the rain bends sideways. Cece would invite them in if she had the room, if the place were a place at all, but all she can do is pull the door snugly behind her and say something about Bernard trying to escape.

The kitchen light is on in Lorraine's house, and Cece thinks she sees the curtains move in front of the big sliding door, but she can't be certain. This won't end well.

"Sorry about this. I tried calling but it kept going straight to voicemail. I . . ." Morgan trails off and kneads his temple. He looks tired, eyes bloodshot, his beard more unkempt than usual. "Something's come up. I know this is last-minute, but could you watch Lacy? Just for today. My lawyer called, and I need to drive up to Providence."

"Sure," Cece says, surprised at how quickly the words come. "Give me fifteen minutes, and I'll come by the house."

"Thanks," Morgan says, his voice strained. "Really, you're saving me here. I would have asked someone else, but—"

"Really, it's no problem. I'd love to hang out with Lacy. We can do fun girl stuff, isn't that right?"

Lacy moves slightly behind Morgan. She has no interest in partaking in Cece's mock enthusiasm.

"I owe you," he says, and hustles Lacy back down the path and out the gate.

Cece waits outside her door, rain spattering her cheeks, and watches them disappear down the street. There's no movement from inside Lorraine's house, and Cece hopes she's avoided certain eviction.

"WHAT'RE YOU LISTENING to?" Cece ventures. Her morning coffee hasn't kicked in, and she's groggy, sitting cross-legged on Morgan's living room floor, the sun freshly risen, the early dawn rainstorm forgotten like a dream. The house feels different in the morning, cozier.

Ensconced in the sofa, Lacy yanks her headphones down around her neck. "You wouldn't know them."

Cece doesn't press her luck. She's more than a little out of touch with the trends of the youth. If this conversation is going to go anywhere, it needs to be played on her turf. "Any updates from Newport Beach? What's going on with Seth and Summer?"

"Ugh," Lacy says, interest flickering across her face. "They're dating other people."

"Season two."

If Lacy is impressed by Cece's recall, she hides it well. "I mean, I know they're gonna get back together. I've seen the show, like, fifty times, but it's still upsetting. They're meant for each other."

Cece smiles, remembering when she used to believe in things like soulmates.

"What was it like," Lacy asks, "when the show first came out?"

Buoyed by the girl's interest, Cece tells her how it was a massive hit, how her friends used to argue at their lockers and in their homerooms about who was hotter, Ryan or Seth, about how Marissa's death went viral before going viral was a thing.

"Did people really freak out?"

"It was all anyone could talk about."

"Zoe and I watch all the episodes together. It's like our thing. But we've had to do it over the phone this summer, since I started coming down here," Lacy says, her voice slipping from exuberant to distant.

Cece says nothing, does nothing, for fear of making a misstep and setting the girl off.

"My parents are fighting again," Lacy says.

Cece tries to arrange her face. "Adults have disagreements all the time. It's completely normal."

"Did your parents fight when you were a kid?"

"Like, have big arguments?"

"You know," Lacy says, toying with her headphones, "lots of yelling. Plates and glasses always getting broken."

Cece should say yes, yes her parents fought all the time, so as not to scare the girl, but then again, shouldn't Lacy know this sort of thing isn't normal? She remembers what Lorraine told her about the police outside Morgan's home that one winter evening. Did he pose a threat to Lacy? Is his wife trying to get full custody? Because she fears for her daughter's safety? "Lacy," Cece says, her voice raspy and low, "how bad is your father's temper? Is he violent?"

Lacy stares at Cece, dumbfounded. Then she doubles over and laughs. "That's a good one," she says between gasps for breath. "My dad doesn't even let me kill the ants that come into our kitchen. He makes me take them outside. No . . . it was always my mom back then. Dad would do some tiny thing or another, and next thing I knew, they'd be yelling. Sure, he yelled, but she was always the one who started breaking things and threatening to call the cops. Then, last winter, when she was dropping me off, they got into it again. Bad. Just like old times, and she threatened to call the cops, and then she actually did it. I thought she was bluffing, but they showed up, lights flashing, hands on their belts, like they expected my dad to put up a fight or something. Eventually they ended up leaving because my dad hadn't really done anything."

"But you like staying with your mom."

Lacy gives her signature shrug. "I like being near my friends. And besides that one big blowup, my parents really don't fight anymore. Now they just sort of stare at each other."

Cece feels foolish. She'd believed the neighborhood gossip about Morgan from Lorraine. And why? Because he drove a rusty pickup truck and worked down at the boatyard? Because a man his size surely enjoyed throwing his weight around? If Cece's being honest, wasn't the idea of Morgan having a brush with the law part of his initial appeal? The risk, the mystery—she'd wanted it. And now? Now she's been embarrassed by a thirteen-year-old girl. A girl who seems to have a far better understanding of the world than her. If Cece's instincts and perceptions are this flawed, what else is she getting wrong?

"Let's go somewhere," Cece says, desperate to change the subject for her own sake.

"It's, like, seven in morning."

"How about the supermarket?"

"Seriously?"

"Come on. It'll be nice to get out of the house."

Lacy rolls her eyes but doesn't protest, which Cece takes as a win.

PERUSING THE AISLES of ShopRite, Cece does her best to act as if nothing is amiss, as if Morgan didn't just rush off to Rhode Island and leave Lacy in her care. Sure, the girl's been warming up to her, but Cece feels wholly incapable of looking after a teenager. Or is it adolescent? She doesn't now the correct terminology, and even though Wynonna's kids have years to go before reaching the girl's age, Cece has half a mind to call her for advice. How does one entertain a thirteen-year-old? Cece thinks back to her own childhood even while recognizing the unhelpfulness of the exercise. Being the bookish and goal-oriented girl she was, Cece's summer before high school had been filled with sleep-away camp (a necessary social adventure), reading all the required books for her history and English courses ahead of time, and attending a young scholars program for promising STEM students at Princeton (her idea, not her parents'). No—nothing from her youth would be helpful in relating to Lacy. Even still, Cece hopes there might be something she can do for the girl: distraction or comradery. Witnessing her own parents argue and fight, their marriage fracturing around her, has been disquieting and uncanny at Cece's age. She struggles to fathom how gutted and empty she'd feel if she knew her parents' marriage was beyond repair at the fragile age of thirteen.

Life—Cece finds herself begrudgingly admitting—is messy, full of contradiction and risk, but children are an entirely different proposition. She's avoided the conversation completely since getting back together with Jonathan. The prospect of marriage and a house in the suburbs is something she's come around to—

she wants those things; she wants stability and permanency. As for the bringing of life into this world—Cece thinks she ought to figure out her own life first.

With Lacy silent and sullen, whatever inroads Cece had made earlier seem to have washed out. They're in the bakery section, and Cece's doing her best not to keep checking on Lacy, who's hanging back a few feet, like she'd rather be left behind than risk association.

"Donut?" Cece says, opening up the flimsy plastic pastry case. Maybe she can bribe the girl with sweets. It's not the worst idea she's had. "We can eat them while we shop."

Lacy observes Cece like she's a statue in a museum. "Before we pay for them?"

"It's not a big deal."

Lacy buries her hands in her jean shorts pockets. "Isn't that illegal or something?"

"All right, then. Negative on the donut."

They walk on in silence, a wonky front wheel pulling the shopping cart to the right. Does Morgan expect her to cook Lacy dinner? Cece realizes he didn't say exactly how long he was going to be. No matter—she's helping out a friend in need.

"You're not a vegetarian or anything, are you? Or have any food allergies?"

Lacy gives her head a shake, deep into her phone, freshly painted nails flitting across the screen like water striders on a placid pond. She's gone nonverbal now. Not great. For the first time, Cece feels like the curtain's been lifted, ever so slightly, on Morgan's life, beyond his eclectic book collection and expert home-cooked meals, beyond his paint-spattered forearms and quiet eyes—to reveal what, exactly? Cece should feel some sense of satisfaction, or perhaps contentment, but she's surprised to find herself disappointed, even saddened by the state of his life. An unstable job, ongoing custody battle, and a kid . . . these are not the outcomes of a life well planned.

"Have you ever had nachos for dinner?" Cece asks, hoping to break through to the girl.

"No way. Dad wouldn't allow it. Does that even constitute a meal?"

Finally. She speaks! "You clearly haven't had Barry's famous nachos."

"Who's Barry?"

"My dad. And trust me. They're amazing," Cece says, detecting something close to a smile on Lacy's pale lips. They do the rest of their shopping with purpose, Cece ticking off the essentials—ground pork and beef, taco seasoning, Colby Jack, tomato paste, and jalapeños. Her father's recipe always called for black olives, but Cece remembers how she and Wynonna would always pick them out, and she assumes Lacy'll do the same.

At the checkout, a teenage boy with neck pimples wearily scans their items, and Cece does her best to ignore the total on the receipt. It's been a while since she's gone grocery shopping for two. On their drive home, Cece finds herself apologizing for the state of the car. Lacy shifts in her seat, discarded to-go bags and empty water bottles crinkling beneath her feet. She cranes her neck and surveys Cece's back seat. "What's all that?"

Cece had almost forgotten about the heaps of clothes: rubber waders, nylon shorts, long-sleeved shirts, and a sun hat. "Work stuff."

Lacy looks at her quizzically. "You work at a shipyard, too?"

"Me? No. I don't know the first thing about fixing boats. That's my oyster-farming gear."

"I didn't know you could farm oysters."

"To be honest," Cece says, shifting gears and taking the hill, "I didn't know much about the business either before I started, but it's pretty cool. I'll show you sometime if you'd like."

"I hope not," Lacy says. "No offense, but I don't plan on spending a lot of time down here. This whole shared-living thing is just temporary until my parents sign the new custody agreement."

They come to a stop at an interminably long red light. Without a steady breeze this morning, the air is heavy and thick. An old Cadillac rolls through the intersection, base thumping. Cece fiddles with the air-conditioning in vain. "Is that what this morning was about?"

Lacy looks like she might give Cece the silent treatment or make a snide comment, but she doesn't. Instead, the girl turns her attention back to her phone and says, "My mom thinks I should stay with her full time."

A voice inside Cece's head is telling her to stop, leave it alone, but something—her curiosity about Morgan, her growing attachment to Lacy—won't let her. "What about you? Don't you like spending time with your dad?"

"Sure," Lacy says, her voice indifferent and distracted, "but all my friends are in Providence. Plus, he's the one that decided to move away. It wasn't so bad splitting time between them when he lived nearby."

Even if she wants to tell Lacy there are all sorts of reasons why people break up, or parents decide to separate and move away,

Cece can't argue with her logic. She should know—thinking about her mother, desperate for a third act in life, or her, abandoning Jonathan at the thought of wedding bells, then returning . . . for good.

The light flicks green, and Cece coaxes the car into first. Lacy lets out an audible sigh and slips her phone under her thigh.

Proceed with caution, Cece thinks to herself. The girl's just started opening up to her. "Everything okay?"

"Just my friend Brittany. She's all into this boy from Bishop, and I keep telling her to be careful."

"Bishop . . ."

"It's a fancy private school. I don't even know where she met him, but he's been texting her nonstop, trying to convince her to come to some party . . . Brittany doesn't wanna go without me."

"How would you even . . ." Cece trails off. This isn't her territory. "You're not interested in going?"

"A party? Thrown by Bishop boys? Plus, I'm convinced it's some kind of *She's All That* situation. Why else would he invite some random public school girl?"

"How do you know about that movie?"

"*She's All That* is like the original *O.C.* Brittany and I are obsessed with it, which makes this whole thing even more annoying. She should know better!"

"Well, it sounds like you're a good friend. Brittany's lucky."

"You don't have to say stuff like that," Lacy says.

"What do you mean?"

"Like you're my parent."

Cece is flustered but determined not to let on. The day isn't even half-finished, and the last thing she needs is for the girl to see just how ill-equipped she is to be trusted with any kind of supervision. She needs to maintain the veil of adulthood as long as possible.

Lacy nudges some garbage on the floor with her foot. "Are you my dad's girlfriend or something?"

Cece can only keep her eyes on the road, mindful not to slam the brakes and send them careening onto the sidewalk. She hears herself say something that doesn't sound half-bad, confident but not dismissive. "I sure hope not. I already have a boyfriend."

This piece of irrefutable evidence doesn't seem to sway Lacy, who seems fixated on the mundane view of underpasses and gas stations outside the car window. "My bad. Forget I said anything."

Drop it, Cece thinks, take the win, but she can't help herself. She wants to know. She needs to know. "What made you think I was his girlfriend?"

Lacy's already back on her phone again. "Just the way he looks at you, I guess."

Cece is suddenly hyperaware of how she might appear. Hand white-knuckling the gearshift, shoulders hunched forward, strands of hair in the corner of her mouth. Get a hold of yourself, Cece Downing!

THE NACHOS ARE a hit, and to Cece's relief, they seem to have bought her some cachet with Lacy, which takes the edge off the news that Morgan's running late. From his intermittent text messages, Cece discerns that all is not going well, and even while her anxiety crescendos at the idea of having to entertain Lacy for a few more hours, she's determined not to let on about it.

Luckily, Bernard is providing endless amusement. The dog is grateful for the unrelenting attention from Lacy as he spreads himself out on the living room floor, whimpering for more belly rubs. Cece peruses the on-demand movie options. Lacy had suggested they have an *O.C.* marathon, but Cece thinks the girl can expand her horizons a bit.

After Lacy nixes *Notting Hill* (too British) and *Roman Holiday* (too old), they land on *You've Got Mail* (Tom Hanks, the volleyball guy?). Lacy's intrigued by the idea of a world when the internet was strange and new. The three of them—Lacy, Bernard, and Cece—settle into the couch. The movie feels older than it should: no cell phones in sight, the Upper West Side void of chain stores, the city itself seemingly exclusively populated by White people. Even so, Lacy seems interested, the times between glances at her phone getting longer and longer. The movie isn't anything groundbreaking, but Cece welcomes the innocuous distraction from her current life. She doesn't want to watch something that makes her think too hard. And despite the film's predictability, Cece finds herself full of loathing for Tom Hanks (even if he's gallant and dashing) and cursing Greg Kinnear's ostentatious character. Lacy agrees wholeheartedly. Meg deserves better! They shout in unison at the television screen. It's been ages since Cece's seen the movie, and the end catches her off guard, the way it tugs at her heart. She has to turn away and dab at the corners of her eyes with her shirtsleeve to hide her tears. It's embarrassing. She never used to cry about anything—movies, books, life—but now it seems like anything will send her over the edge.

Lacy doesn't need encouragement to share her opinions. She has lots of questions about why everyone thought Tom Hanks was attractive back in the nineties. And while she mostly enjoyed the movie, she didn't like how Tom Hanks's character hangs out with Meg Ryan's character multiple times even after he discovers she's the woman he's been talking to online. "Think about it," Lacy says, folding her legs underneath her on the couch. "He basically tricks her into falling in love with him."

Cece doesn't see the big problem and chalks it up to a generational divide. Through the living room shades, the sun is setting, and Cece feels lethargy take hold of her. Perhaps nachos as a main course wasn't the best choice. She goes to the bathroom to freshen up, where she runs the tap and splashes water on her face. In the mirror, Cece looks different, hair lighter from the sun, nose brown. The woman looking back at her—makeup-less and weathered—is foreign to her, and Cece wonders whether Jonathan has noticed this change in her features; she wonders if he's expecting the old Cece (smart business suits and tidied hair) to appear when they move back in together.

Being in this bathroom again . . . the medicine cabinet slightly ajar, the bristles of Morgan's toothbrush stubby and frayed. How different Cece's circumstances are now. If only she hadn't snooped around . . . The doorbell chiming stops Cece from going any further down that road. She dries her hands and turns off the light.

From the front door a muffled conversation. By the time Cece recognizes the voice, she's halfway into the living room and it's too late. Lorraine stands in the doorway, hair pulled up in a chaotic bun, pen on a string swinging from her clipboard.

"This lady wants me to sign her petition even though I told her I don't live here," Lacy says.

Lorraine scowls at Cece. "Can't say I'm surprised to see you here."

Lacy looks between them. "You two know each other?"

"No one here wants to sign your petition," Cece says, stepping between Lacy and the doorway. She suddenly feels protective of the girl. "And you're just snooping is all. You know Morgan would never sign anything for your cause."

"I thought he might have changed his mind. Even a broken clock is right twice a day."

"Now I know who you are," Lacy says, her voice eerily cheerful and buoyant. "You're that old, cranky lady who lives down the block."

Lorraine ignores the girl. "I knew you were desperate, Cece," she says and peers inside the house, "but this is a cry for help. I can only assume you've taken his view on things about Rayburn's expansion."

"You've got it backward. I recruited him. As an employee of the Rayburn Oyster Company, I was able to make a pretty compelling case."

Lorraine's beady brown eyes go wide. "You're a spy! Richie sent you to live with me."

"Don't flatter yourself," Cece says, relishing the words. "It was a complete coincidence, but once I heard you talking bad about him, I kept my mouth shut."

"And now what? You've been plotting? Reporting my plans back to him? You *have* been spying on me!"

Cece had never really conceived of it as spying, but seeing Lorraine writhe in anger and humiliation is mildly entertaining; after all, this is the woman trying to put her out of a job. "Let's just say you haven't been the only one collecting signatures. What? Did you think we wouldn't be prepared for the town hall?"

"And to think I let you drink my good wine."

"Just admit it—this has never been about the cove. You just don't want more people coming around."

"This is about protecting our natural resources and maintaining the authenticity of our neighborhood."

"You think a few rows of oyster bags are gonna destroy an ecosystem? Do you even know what oysters do? They clean the water!"

Lorraine seems to have gotten over the shock of Cece's betrayal. She pushes the pen through the clipboard. "I'll expect you off my property by the end of the week."

"Suits me," Cece says, her cheeks hot, fingernails itchy.

"Well, I best be going," Lorraine says and spins in her Birkenstocks. "You two behave, now. We can't have the cops getting called every time there's a row in this house."

"What's a row?" Lacy asks after Cece's slammed the front door closed.

"It's nothing," Cece says, clutching her hands to make them stop shaking. What's just happened? *Suits me*—what had she been thinking?! Now she'll have to find a new place to live. Lorraine! Cece hates herself for once thinking so fondly of her, for looking up to her!

"Was she talking about when the police came? When my parents were fighting?" Lacy says.

Cece is too drained to lie. "Yes."

The girl goes quiet, a different quiet from her usual sassy silence. She moves to the couch, Bernard sniffing at her heels, and plops down into the cushions. Cece wants to comfort the girl but doesn't know what to say or do. There's so much she doesn't know about the situation, and even if she did, she's no mature adult, dispenser of wisdom.

After a while, Lacy speaks, her voice agitated and uneven. "My dad isn't a bad guy."

"I don't think he is."

"But people in this neighborhood do. People like that woman."

"People don't always know what's really going on. They just pass judgment," Cece says, the guilt welling in her chest.

Lacy chews her bottom lip. "What I said before. About my dad leaving. That isn't entirely true. I mean, he did leave, but that's only because my mom asked him to . . . or at least I think that's what happened. I don't know all the details, but I know it wasn't all his idea. I mean, it's not like he abandoned me."

"No one thinks that."

"I just get angry, you know? I wish he didn't live so far away."

Cece wants to sit next to Lacy and embrace her, hold her close, but she doesn't know how the girl will react and is wary of crossing boundaries. Lacy already suspects she's her father's girlfriend. Cece can't risk confusing her more. "You can be as angry as you want," she says. "That's your right."

By now the house is dark, and Cece turns on some lights. She lingers in the kitchen to give Lacy space. She drinks a tall glass of tap water, then another. Cece feels closer to Morgan than she ever has, like she's glimpsed the *real* Morgan, like he's finally let her in. Except that he hasn't. Whatever she's learned or understands about him is because of Lacy. And what she knows now—

Siobhan's temper, his money problems, his daughter—only makes everything seem more convoluted. And even if it were possible . . . even if they tried . . . could such a man, a good and decent man, make Cece happy, with all his material limitations?

The faucet leaks, a steady and ominous *plunk*. Why had she gone to the door? She should have just stayed in the bathroom and let Lacy handle it. Where will she move? Jonathan's place, of course—he'll be more than happy to take her back. It's the simplest solution. It makes sense. She can commute from Stamford up to Noank. The drive will be hell, but she doesn't see any other option.

It's around nine thirty when Morgan pulls into the driveway. Cece's sitting on the porch stairs and finishing her third glass of wine (she deserves it after today), citronella candles burning at her feet.

He takes his baseball cap off and runs thick fingers through his matted hair. He looks worn-out, puffy bags under his eyes. She offers him a seat next to her, which he accepts after lumbering up the stairs, stepping gingerly, as if he might wake his daughter inside.

"Sorry. I had no idea that was gonna take so long. Siobhan's lawyer is a nightmare."

"That must mean they're good."

"Yeah. That's what I'm worried about."

"She's trying for full custody?"

Morgan glances at her in the candlelight. "Lacy told you that?"

"She mentioned something about it."

"She say anything else?"

Cece doesn't have the heart to tell him the truth. "She misses her friends."

Morgan studies his hands. "Sounds about right."

"We had a good time today," Cece says, trying to lighten the mood. "We made nachos, watched a movie."

"Thank you again. I hope it didn't put you out."

"I had a great time with her. She's fantastic," Cece says, surprised to find that she means it.

Morgan reaches out to take Cece's empty wineglass. "I can take that for you, unless you'd like to come in for a nightcap."

"I better not. I have a double shift on the boat tomorrow."

They stand up, a polite awkwardness simmering between them. Cece's head is heavy. The last forty-eight hours have left her thoughts jumbled and hazy, like she's looking through smudged binoculars. Just yesterday, she was ready to declare Morgan just like all other men, jealous and arrogant. It was easier then, to dismiss his petulance as frivolous and egotistical, but after spending the day with Lacy, Cece's having trouble letting go.

"Can I ask you something?"

"Anything."

"Yesterday, when we were collecting signatures, were you annoyed with me? About considering the actuary job?"

"I've been meaning to apologize. I was out of line. What you do for a living isn't my business."

"You sure it's about that and not something else?"

"Like what?"

Why can't she accept his apology and move on? What does she want to hear? "You only started acting strange after you met Jonathan, and I told you we were giving it another try."

Morgan bristles at the question, that familiar exasperation creeping across face. "Look, Cece. You saved me today. I don't know what I would have done if you couldn't have watched Lacy, and I'm thankful for it. Let's just leave it there."

"I wasn't ever considering the actuary position in New York."

"Why didn't you just say that?"

"Because I didn't need some guy telling me what jobs will or won't make me happy. Besides, it's not like that's what was bothering you."

"Meaning?"

"Meaning you only started acting distant and annoyed since you met Jonathan."

There's a part of Cece that knows what she's doing, poking and prodding, hoping for an argument, a moment where Morgan loses control and says what she suspects but he refuses to admit or say aloud: He's jealous of Jonathan. He wants Cece to himself; just being friends won't cut it.

"I don't think he's right for you," Morgan says and puts his palms out, like he's admitting defeat.

"What's that supposed to mean?" Cece says, acutely aware that her plan is already backfiring. *She's* the one who's flailing, whose cheeks are flushed, heart hammering in her ears.

Eyes still, Morgan regards her like a wild animal caught in a trap. "This is stupid, Cece."

"No. Now that you've said it, I want to know. I deserve to know why someone who's barely known me for two months is an expert on my type."

"I don't picture you with someone like that . . . his whole look. I mean, give me a break. There's no way he doesn't absolutely bore you to death."

"So it's his money. Someone with money can't interest me?"

"In my experience, folks with that kind of money aren't always good people."

"It's a moral objection, then," Cece says, aware that her voice, unfortunately, sounds shrill and deranged. So much for keeping her cool. She's the one being goaded, it seems; and yet, she can't stop herself. She wants to break this wide open.

"I'm not objecting to anything. I'm just surprised."

"Well, maybe you don't know me as well as you think."

"Clearly."

"And you're wrong about Jonathan. He's a good guy."

"Okay."

"Stop agreeing with me."

"What are we even talking about, Cece?"

"We're talking about friendship. And friends don't sabotage each other when something good finally comes along."

"We've got different definitions of friendship."

"Then maybe we ought to see less of each other."

Morgan yanks his baseball cap on and moves to his front door. "I couldn't agree more."

"Great!" Cece says, trying to hide her surprise. What had she been expecting?

15

Jonathan's outrage is sexy. Over the phone, he's threatening all manner of lawsuits against Lorraine. How dare she violate Cece's rental agreement for her political beliefs! It's discrimination; it won't stand! Cece's forgotten this part of him, the part that's like a dog with a bone when it comes to a personal injustice, real or imagined. There was the time he got them moved up to first class on a flight when her chair's recliner was broken, the time he extracted a formal apology from a theatergoer after he bumped into her at the coat-check line, or the time he shouted down her first landlord in Manhattan when she threatened to withhold Cece's security deposit over a dirty stove. Jonathan's always been there for Cece when she needs him, and this time is no different. Except that Cece isn't interested in exacting her pound of flesh from Lorraine. The town hall in three weeks will do that for her. Right now, she needs to start packing. Only after she reassures Jonathan that this is what she wants does he drop the issue.

At first, Cece had resisted the idea of moving back in with Jonathan. It wasn't just about her responsibilities at Rayburn; she was worried her need for a place to stay was clouding her judgment. Even if she knew she and Jonathan would eventually live together again, she hadn't realized it would be so soon. The power dynamics at play in their relationship when they first broke up were clear, nearly equal. Sure, Jonathan made more money than her, but her actuary job had allowed her to split their expenses, except for their more extravagant international trips. Her new situation—soon-to-be homeless, earning a pittance on an oyster farm—has the potential to swing the pendulum of power entirely to Jonathan's side. It isn't something Cece's pleased about, but then again, she doesn't feel like she has much choice. Not that Jonathan would ever leverage his newfound position. He'd been nothing but generous to Cece since they'd decided to get back together. It's all for the better, Cece thinks, while she tapes the cardboard boxes together that she got for free from the liquor store.

Cece had messaged Morgan asking about Lacy earlier that morning. They hadn't left things on the best of terms last night, but Cece's grown fond of the girl and is worried about how she's holding up. Hours later, Cece trying to will herself asleep, he still hasn't responded, and she can't help herself but fire off another communiqué—a dumb observation about the absurdity of buying new cardboard boxes for moving when that's all anyone uses to put out their recycling. Would you think less of me if you saw me dragging boxes out of your trash?

Monday morning, and still no response from Morgan. They've officially entered silent-treatment territory. It seems he's taking her proclamation about them seeing less of each other seriously.

She was a fool to think they could be friends anyway, especially after sleeping together, and Cece begrudgingly acknowledges that Wynonna was right: men and women simply can't be platonic. Still, Cece had held out hope, delusionally, it seems. Jealousy was not a trait she had expected from Morgan, and yet, it is undeniable. Everything had gone sideways after the two men had met and she'd been forced to break the news of her reconciliation with Jonathan. It all felt so juvenile and small. Couldn't Morgan understand her position? Couldn't he just be happy for her?

Cece is saddened by the idea of leaving without saying goodbye to Morgan and Lacy. After work, the packing goes faster than Cece anticipated, which only serves to highlight how little of a life she's built here in New London. Roving dust bunnies clotted with Bernard's hair wander the pool house floor. A lemony, fresh scent wafts in from the bathroom where Cece's scrubbed the floor and shower with Pine-Sol, determined to leave her summer residence better than she found it. From his perch on the bed, Bernard eyes Cece warily while she moves around the empty space, wiping down baseboards, double-checking the condiment tray in the fridge, scraping the grime from the crack where the sink meets the linoleum countertop. The security deposit is not an insignificant amount, and Cece refuses to give Lorraine any excuse to withhold it. There's something else, too. Guilt. Lorraine's the one acting like an irrational zealot, but it still doesn't change how Cece feels, like a traitor and a coward. They haven't crossed paths since last week, and there's been no movement from the main house—curtains drawn, not so much as a whisper.

Bernard's ears perk up at the purr of an engine outside. It must be Cece's mother. She's picking up the dog before Cece drives down to Stamford. By the curb, Kim emerges from a silver BMW, eyebrows freshly plucked, heavy rouge reddening her cheeks, a tight-fitting halter top straining against her bosom. If this weren't her mother, Cece might find the scene comical, but Kim is very much her mother, so instead, Cece is closer to deeply concerned or potentially embarrassed.

"It's a rental," Kim says, sitting in the dining nook, "the closest I'm gonna get to driving a luxury car. You should see your face."

Cece considers clarifying that her look of shock is only partially related to the car but decides against it. She's waiting for the avalanche of disapproving glances and comments about the cramped quarters and low ceilings, but Kim seems uninterested in picking a fight. Cece's decision to get back together with Jonathan has its benefits, after all.

"By the way," Kim continues while she takes out her phone, "I can't take Bernard just yet. I need you to watch him for a few more days."

"Isn't that why you're here? To bring him home?"

"I'm on my way up to Boston. I'll get him on my way back."

"What about Dad?"

"He'll be fine. He's not infirm, you know."

"I think you're overestimating his ability to function without you."

"He's quite capable," Kim insists.

"I don't know if Jonathan's apartment allows pets long term."

Cece waits for a response while she fills two Solo cups with water from the tap. Her mom says nothing, typing furiously on her phone, sandaled foot bouncing anxiously. Cece recalls all the moments her parents cajoled her and Wynonna to get off their phones and talk to them like human beings.

In a huff, Kim fires off whatever message she's been typing and puts her phone down. "What were you saying?"

"What's in Boston?"

Kim flips her phone over and checks it before turning her attention back to Cece. "I'm meeting an old acquaintance. We were friends when I was at Fordham. You don't have to look at me like that. What are you, the morality police now? Nothing ever happened between us, but there was always something there—tension. Anyway, we reconnected on Facebook. It turns out he's a widower. We got to chatting, and he's invited me up to his place in Brookline."

Cece drains her water and studies the ceiling. Too fast—everything is happening, dissolving too fast. She finds herself amazed at the speed at which a family can fracture and fall away. "Don't you think you're kind of rushing things?"

Kim regards her with a patronizing look. "There's no such thing as rushing at my age. I've got ten, maybe fifteen good years left, and I intend on enjoying them."

"What about Dad?"

"What about him?"

"Are you actually getting divorced?"

"We're taking a break. That's about as official as he can get. You know your father."

"And Wynonna?"

"Not speaking to me at the moment. Now, before I go, I need

you to look at some photographs for me. I require your millennial expertise."

"What kind of photos?"

"For my profile. I'm on SilverSingles and eharmony," Kim says, and shows Cece her phone, swiping through a dizzying array of photos: oddly angled selfies, hastily cropped photos, evidence of Barry in the form of a shirtsleeve, a hand, a shadow.

Cece recoils. "Mom, this is nuts. I'm not doing this with you."

Kim shrugs. "Suit yourself. God knows I can't talk to Wynonna about any of this. I thought you'd be able to handle the situation with a little more maturity."

"You can't just expect everyone to fall in line. I mean, I support your decision to be happy, Mom, but don't you think it's kind of disrespectful to Dad? Moving on like this? So quickly?"

"And what would the requisite period of mourning look like to you and your sister? What's a satisfactory length of time for me to be depressed and downtrodden? Perhaps you and Wynonna would prefer I just become an old spinster and live alone for the rest of my life. Then you'd never have to imagine your mother actually enjoying her life."

"Don't be ridiculous."

"Time is all we've got, Cece. Can't you see that?"

Cece can only nod.

"I need to get on the road. I really hate driving at night," Kim says, tossing her phone in her Saint Laurent tote and standing. "Send Jonathan my love. I'm thrilled you two are giving it another shot. Nothing in life is a guarantee; every relationship, every marriage is a crapshoot, so you've gotta look at the constants and bet on those, but I don't have to tell you that. You're the risk analysis expert."

Walking with her mother out to the curb, Cece waits for the inevitable criticisms of her continued work at Rayburn and now-infamous job interview in the city. Sure, Kim's happy about her decision to reconcile with Jonathan, but there's no way she'll let Cece give up on a stable and profitable career without a word. She'd pushed Cece too hard, spent countless hours helping her with summer enrichment program applications and supplemental college essays, turned a blind eye to Barry's maniacal swimming practice regimens in the name of character building. But the moment passes without incident, and it occurs to Cece that for once, her mother is more preoccupied with her own life than her daughters'.

"WHAT DO YOU mean he sounded weird?" Cece says. She's fifteen minutes away from her parents' house, navigating the familiar back roads in the dark, eyes squinted, nostalgia around every corner.

"He just seemed out of it," Wynonna says. "I cannot believe Mom just left him alone. You said she was only supposed to stay in Boston for a few nights."

"I guess she extended her stay."

"It's selfish, Cece. She's acting like a spoiled teenager." There's muffled commotion on the other end of the line. Cece only picks up bits and pieces. "You put them down, Devin. I'm talking to my sister . . . She's going there now to check on him . . . I know it's not ideal!" More shuffling. A sliding glass door. "Sorry. I'm back."

"I'll update you when I get there."

"Thanks for checking up on him. I told Devin earlier this is untenable. He can't be left alone."

"He's not infirm."

"Is that what Mom said? It sounds like something she'd say. You don't understand, Cece. People dad's age, they can go into a steep decline without anyone to socialize with. It's not a matter of supervising him, but he needs people around to keep him active, physically and mentally."

Cece does her best to calm Wynonna down and assures her she'll report back when she sees their father. The lights are on when she pulls into the driveway. Ringing the doorbell, she arches her aching back and bends down to touch her toes, sending lightning through her hips. After listening to Wynonna's panicked voicemail, she'd rushed home to let the dog out before getting on the road. Barry wasn't returning her calls, and Wynonna had quickly shifted into worst-case scenarios. Nothing from inside the house. Worry grips Cece. Maybe her sister is right.

After trying the doorbell again, Cece picks her way around the side of the house, the usually pristine landscaping looking shabbier than usual, hedges jutting into the pathway, grass tall and unruly between the bluestone pavers. From the backyard, an alien orange glow against the night sky. Cece nearly trips over herself as she runs under the rose-covered arbor to find her father standing, hands buried in sweatpants pockets, gazing into the blazing firepit.

"Cece? That you?"

"What are you doing, Dad?"

"Summer bonfire," he says, like it's the most commonsense thing in the world. "Remember how much you and Wynonna used to love these?"

"You haven't been picking up your phone."

He holds up his phone, light dancing off the screen. "No juice."

"Wynonna was worried. I came down to check on you."

"Tell your sister to stop worrying. I'm not geriatric just yet. Let's go inside. You must be starving. Let me just put this fire out."

Cece examines her father while they head indoors. He looks grungier than usual, hair unkempt, stains of all color and size on his pants. Does he have a musk? An odor? She wonders when he's showered last. The kitchen appears to be relatively clean, a few dishes in the sink, crumbs on the island. Wynonna will be happy to know their father is doing just fine.

He opens the fridge and peers inside. "What do you wanna eat?"

Cece perches atop a stool. "Did you already eat dinner?"

"Hard to say," Barry says, head buried in the fridge, his voice cavernous. "Can't remember. We don't have much. There's yogurt if you want that."

"When was the last time you went grocery shopping?"

Barry doesn't say anything, distracted by the undecipherable date on a packet of cold cuts.

"Dad?"

"Yeah?"

"When did you go to the supermarket last?"

Barry seems to weigh the risk versus reward and then puts the deli meat back and closes the fridge. "Your mom got some stuff before she left . . . I just remembered there are some frozen meals in the basement freezer."

"What have you been eating for the last few days?"

"Your mother made a few things before she left, and those frozen meals have been getting me through. I ordered pizza last night. Had it delivered. Forty dollars for a whole pizza. Highway robbery."

Cece's alarm starts to grow. Perhaps Wynonna is right. Barry can't be left to his own devices. "I'm not hungry, Dad. Don't worry about it."

"Let me just go down to the basement and see what's in the freezer."

While Barry plods down the rickety wooden stairs, Cece does some snooping in the refrigerator. Pizza isn't the only thing Barry seems to have ordered. Chinese take-out boxes line the shelves. There's a carton of expired milk and a few suspect-looking jars of olives. Cece calls her sister.

"It's not terrible, but it's not great either," she says.

With Wynonna's urging, Cece digs through the recycling bin in the pantry and uncovers a treasure trove of empty Campbell's soup and deviled ham cans emitting a sweet metallic smell.

"It's like a 1950s time capsule," Cece whispers.

"But how does he seem to you?"

"I don't know, Wynonna. A little schlubby? Like a man who's letting himself go a bit while his wife's out of town?"

"You mean he isn't showering. He stinks."

Cece is reluctant to disclose this piece of information but does, nonetheless. "There is a definite stink."

"And you still think he can take care of himself when Mom decides to abandon him for good?"

Abandon feels like a strong word, but Cece must admit her sister has a point. "What do we do? I can't take him, Wynonna. I'm supposed to be moving back in Jonathan."

"What? When did this happen?"

"It's a long story."

"Okay . . . This really isn't ideal."

"I know."

"I need some time, but I'll figure it out. And please, give Dad a multivitamin or something. He's gonna get scurvy."

"Right."

"Cece."

"Yeah?"

"I'm glad you're back with Jonathan. You deserve to be happy."

Cece hangs up and shuts the pantry door just as her father emerges from the basement, grinning from ear to ear, his arms overflowing with Hungry-Man frozen dinners. Not ideal, she thinks. Unequivocally, not ideal.

EVEN BEFORE THE docks in Noank come into view, Cece can hear them—the protestors. The group is small but loud—twenty or so people with handmade signs lining the entryway of the gravel parking lot: PEOPLE OVER PROFITS; SAVE MAMACOKE COVE; HANDS OFF MOTHER NATURE. A young man with stringy long hair wearing an olive-green T-shirt directs chants through a bullhorn. No sign of Lorraine. Nothing good will come from this, Cece thinks. It's only a matter of time before the local news shows up. She's got to hand it to Lorraine. It's no easy task mobilizing people like this. As she pulls through the main gate, a loud *crack* sounds, and Cece flinches and ducks for cover. In the rearview mirror, Cece watches yellow yolk run down the back window. There's no time to be livid, though, as she catches sight of Santiago emerging from the warehouse wielding an enormous pipe. His eyes are white and wild. Davi hangs back, a look of helpless terror holding him prisoner.

Cece guns the car and then slams on the brakes, putting herself in between the protestors and Santiago. The engine still running, she jumps out of the car and lunges in front of Santiago.

"I'm gonna bust them good, Cece. They're trying to shut us down."

Two hands pressed against his chest, Cece pleads. "Richie wouldn't want this."

"Richie ain't here. Our jobs, Cece. They're coming after our jobs." He brushes her aside easily and keeps marching, swinging the pipe menacingly. If he gets to the protestors, he will hurt them—Cece has no doubt.

"They want you to hit them. Don't you see? They're trying to provoke you!" Cece shouts. "They're doing this because they're desperate. You assault any of them, and we're done. You might as well close Rayburn yourself."

The fire leaves Santiago as quickly as it came. His arms go limp. The pipe clangs to the ground. Santiago turns to leave, but not before spitting a wad of thick phlegm in the direction of the protestors. "Never worked a day in their lives," he growls as he passes Cece on his way back to the boat. She calls Richie to tell him what's happening, only to find out there's a demonstration at the office in Mystic, too.

"They've been going strong for about an hour," he says. "Making a real scene."

On the other end, Cece can hear the steady chant of protest. "Is there a woman there? In her sixties, curly hair, probably wearing sandals."

"Sandals doesn't really narrow it down," Richie says. "But yeah, there's someone who fits that description. She's on the bullhorn."

So this *is* all Lorraine's doing. Had she always planned to protest the Rayburn locations, or is this revenge for Cece's betrayal? Her alliance with Morgan?

"An acquaintance of yours?"

"Regrettably, yes."

"Small town," Richie says, sounding resigned to whatever situation he's looking at through his office window. "How's Santiago? Give the protestors a piece of his mind?"

"There was a pipe involved, but I talked him down."

Richie chuckles. "He runs hot."

The background noise goes hushed, like a hand over a speaker. "A spokesperson from the zoning commission reached out about the town hall. She said I should have some prepared remarks and be ready for any questions the members might have."

A horn pierces through the tumult. Cece watches as protestors circle, signs held aloft, faces locked in grim resolution. A stubby middle finger appears from the driver's side window of a dump truck as it rumbles by.

"What do you need from me?"

"Just make sure Santiago doesn't crack any skulls," Richie says.

The din on the other end of the line grows louder, more persistent. Cece thinks she can make out the crackling feedback from an amplifier. "Aren't you worried about them?"

"Not really. I called in a few favors."

Cece doesn't know what he's talking about until two trailers carrying enormous motorboats show up outside the gate and park directly in front of the protestors so no one can see them from the road. Cece heads to the warehouse where she runs an inventory of their supplies, the steady chant of the protestors keeping her company.

DAYLIGHT IS FADING. Cece's taken off from work an hour early to move the last of the boxes to her alarmingly small trunk. Cece's ears are still ringing from the protestors' chants. They were kind of catchy, she must admit.

It feels strange, leaving under such hostile circumstances. All week, the curtains in Lorraine's house have been drawn. She's watching; Cece just doesn't know from where. On her way back to the pool house, she stops to survey the view of the tranquil garden and pool, the scent of freshly cut grass thick on the air.

She'll miss this—the peace and quiet, the illusion of escape. She'll still be in the area for work, but she knows it won't be the same. Living on Lorraine's property, in this quaint and tree-lined neighborhood, the echoing screeches and whoops of children playing in the night—there is something here . . . ineffable and fleeting. A mosquito buzzes by Cece's forehead, and she swipes at it. Nostalgia's a dangerous thing.

Bernard paces the empty rooms of the pool house and sniffs every freshly exposed area. After doing a final sweep, Cece puts the keys in an envelope and licks it closed, the glue bitter and astringent.

"About time we went, don't you think?" she says to Bernard, who is sitting on his haunches, his eyes moving warily to his crate.

Cece takes out her phone and checks her messages for what feels like the millionth time this week. Her last text to Morgan remains unanswered, taunting her. She'd gone so far as to call the phone company to make sure she'd paid this month's bill. It isn't like him to ignore her texts; then again, maybe it is. What does she know? Cece has driven by his house more than she'd care to admit in recent days, each time left more despondent at the sight of lights on inside.

It occurs to Cece that she is not as good of a person as she thinks she is. She thumbs out a message, then deletes it. What is she apologizing for? Leading him on? Trying to maintain a friendship on the most tenuous of terms? Living her life? Occam's razor says jealousy—the reason for his radio silence. So typical of a man, to tell you they can be friends with you only to hold it against you in the end. Cece is caught off guard by her anger, or maybe it's simply hurt.

Even though he doesn't look like he needs it, she decides to take Bernard for one more walk around the neighborhood. The last thing she wants is to pull over somewhere on I-95 for some canine emergency, at least that's the rationale she's going with. After heading down to the river, following their familiar path along broken sidewalks and overgrown hedges, Cece hangs a left and turns around in the now-infamous cul-de-sac. The night air grows inky and soft. Cece presses on, doubling back from where she came, working up the courage . . . After more circuitous routes, she finds herself, bug bitten and sweaty, in front of Morgan's home. His truck—the truck that started it all—sits parked on the street. Cece's pulse quickens, her heart in her throat. Nails scrabble on the pavement. The dog pushes forward, straining against his collar, eager for the familiar. The living room lights aren't on—no glowing TV or yellow reading lamp. Towards the back, a golden square of light washing over the side yard—Morgan's bedroom, if she's remembered the layout of the house correctly. *Time is all we've got.*

Up the stairs, Bernard at her heels, restless and expectant, Cece's knocking on the door before knowing what she will say or how she will explain her intrusion. In not-so-uncertain terms Morgan has told her this is the end. He'd accepted her declaration. *Then maybe we ought to see less of each other.* And yet, like a petulant child, she is here—knocking on his front door. She waits, the solid oak door absorbing the sound, swallowing it whole. Nothing. Cece knocks again, this time with the fleshy side of her hand. She wonders what might happen if he opens the door. She lets her mind drift to those first days of summer, wine on her lips, Bernard yapping, Mr. Shipyard, Morgan.

The dog whines and paces back and forth. She's about to knock a third time, but she stops herself. Enough, Cece thinks. Enough. She makes her way down the porch, steps grumbling, and heads back. The side yard lies in darkness, the lamplight snuffed out, the grass a cold blue in the moonlight.

16

"Jon Boy, is that you?!" a voice booms across the quad.

Jonathan turns, Cece on his arm, to locate the voice. A redheaded man squeezed into a blue blazer at least one size too small bounds toward them, his fiery locks bountiful and flowing.

"Logan?" Jonathan shouts and leaves Cece to greet the Viking.

"Fifteen years, and you still walk like a stiff. Recognized you from a mile away."

A scuffle breaks out, and Cece isn't sure whether to laugh or come to Jonathan's aid. Then the two men are laughing and fixing each other's collars. "This is my girlfriend, Cece," Jonathan says. They'd agreed beforehand that *girlfriend* made the most sense. None of the people at his high school reunion knew about the unsuccessful engagement, and he seemed more than happy to go back in time, to a place before he ever proposed.

Cece shakes the Viking's hand.

"Logan. We were floormates."

"Logan played on the lacrosse team."

"Jon was more of the chess-club type," Logan says, giving Jonathan a nudge.

"You told me you played in high school," Cece says, eager to catch Jonathan in a lie, to find out some mysterious secret or imperfection about him.

"Logan's just being an ass. I was on the team . . . mostly rode the bench for four years."

It's pleasing to see Jonathan on his heels. It had never occurred to Cece that he'd gone through his own stages of social awkwardness, that he hadn't always been this poised, all-knowing man.

"Shit. It's been years, Jon Boy. What are you up to? No. Let me guess. Making gobs of money."

"That's putting it a bit indelicately. But yeah. I'm in finance."

"Indelicately—listen to you, man. Big words! What about you, Cece?"

It's the question everyone either dreads or looks forward to at any high school reunion: What do you do? Cece considered lying. Jonathan would understand, and perhaps even appreciate it.

Working in risk management as an actuary is a respectable job, a real job, one that makes real money. None of Jonathan's classmates would find the job terribly interesting, but they wouldn't find it weird, either. It wouldn't cause raised eyebrows and demand follow-up questions like telling people you work on an oyster farm. And while Jonathan hasn't said anything, she gets the distinct feeling that he cares a great deal about what these people think of him. But if things are going to work between them this time around, Cece needs to start being authentic to herself, and Jonathan will just have to deal.

"I work on an oyster farm."

"No shit. I've never had an oyster. They freak me out."

"It's a great opportunity," Jonathan says. "We're looking to grow the business."

While the three of them walk to the palatial white tent on the green, Logan tells Cece and Jonathan about his medical sports equipment business based out of Jupiter, Florida. It sounds a bit like a pyramid scheme to Cece, but she doesn't say anything. She's too busy taking everything in, from the brick, ivy-covered buildings to the impressive athletic complex. Cece knew Jonathan's alma mater was storied and grand, but she hadn't comprehended that it would put her college to shame. It makes sense now—his confidence and self-assurance. Cece would like to think that she might have come to possess these qualities earlier in life had she attended a school like this, but she has her doubts. In the distance, the recently renovated library (by the looks of it) sparkles in the summer sun. Old oaks cast shadowy respite on the pedestrian paths, and Cece can see it now: students in ties and skirts hustling from the dining hall, teachers in tweed blazers and worn leather satchels lost in thought. Even without the bustle, it feels magical, and Cece finds herself thrilled by the school, with its history and tradition, its gold-framed oil portraits, and engraved trophies. If her mother could see Deerfield Academy for herself, what might she think? Would she be elated? Her eldest daughter walking among the privileged and moneyed like she belongs?

Steam rises in thick white plumes around the tent, the aroma of boiled corn and lobster on the wind. This must be the famous lobster bake, Cece thinks to herself. She hadn't needed to be sold on attending the event with Jonathan, but that didn't stop him from assuring her that the school pulled out all the stops for reunions: catered meals with open bars, concerts by the a cappella group and jazz band, an alumni soccer game, and a massive dance under the big tent. He'd even signed them up to sleep in his old dorm room so that Cece could get the full experience, and while the thought of sharing an extra-long twin bed made her back hurt, Cece was excited by the prospect of getting to know the version of Jonathan that had existed before they'd met.

Picnic tables twenty deep squat in rows under the soaring tent. Red-and-white gingham tablecloths flap in the wind, secured by enormous steel buckets. "Lobster bake, baby!" Logan shouts and runs ahead to a table where a few other couples are already seated: a predictable collage of khaki shorts and floral dresses.

"Thanks for coming," Jonathan whispers in Cece's ear as they pick their way through the crowd. "I'm glad you're here."

"Me too," Cece says, pleased with herself for buying a yellow-and-white-checkered Ophelia dress from Tuckernuck and a pair of baby-blue Jack Rogers sandals for the event. The purchase had been excessive, foolish perhaps, but it had felt good to buy something for herself. Her feet accustomed to her rubber waders, the grass is foreign and strange against her toes. She'd decided to stick with the sandals at the last minute despite her egregiously pale feet.

There are introductions all around once they get seated at their table. A few names sound familiar to Cece, people Jonathan has stayed in touch with since graduating, names she's heard mentioned in passing. There's talk of marriage and children, divorce and home buying, the various ills of getting older. Cece notices that Jonathan and Logan are the only men at their table who have yet to marry. If this detail bothers Jonathan, he doesn't show it. They'd gotten back together with the express understanding that Cece could take as much time as she needed. The last thing he wanted to do was rush her. And yet, surrounded by his old classmates, his lacrosse buddies, dormmates, and something called the Dr. Wales Latin V survival group, Cece is surprised to find herself ready, even eager, to be rushed. Grown-ups—that's who these people are, she thinks. Adults. Isn't it about time she grew up? Isn't it about time she admitted what she wants?

The lobster is succulent, the drawn butter warm, the red potatoes steamed just right (not too mushy), the summer corn perfectly sweet. The boys, or maybe just Logan, are drinking beers at an impressive rate, and Cece volunteers to grab the next round from the bar. She stands in line behind a group of women reminiscing about the best places to hook up on campus. "Remember when Mr. Thornburg would catch you during rounds?" one girl says. "Don't remind me. Pervert alert!" The group devolves into laughter. Cece wants to think she could have thrived in a place like this, but something tells her she would've drowned. She might have been able to cut it academically, but socially . . . this place, these people? She wouldn't have stood a chance, but now she's with Jonathan. She's older and wiser, and while she might feel a little out of place, she's stopped caring whether she belongs.

The bartender is a young kid with a mop of black hair and the hint of a mustache. The group in front of Cece puts in an order for five Aperol spritzes. He looks at them, befuddled, his black standard-issue polo already showing sweat stains. "Like a wine spritzer?"

"Aperol. It's a bitter," a woman says.

"An aperitif," another one says.

"You think he knows what an aperitif is?" another voice cackles.

The woman who originally ordered sighs. "Just make it five white wines."

Cece shrinks into herself while she watches the kid hurriedly retrieve a bottle from the cooler, fingers pink from the ice water, and fill the wineglasses. The women swoop in and snag their drinks, and then they are gone as quickly as they'd come, laughter trailing behind them.

Cece approaches, trying to imbue her face with some kind of silent understanding between her and the kid. She's not like those women. She knows how it feels to be a financial-aid kid and work an on-campus job. She knows what it means to earn a buck, to work with your hands, to sweat in the summer sun for anything but a proper tan! Is he a local kid, Cece wonders, or is he a current student? It doesn't matter, but she's determined to make up for his previous customers.

"Just five beers," she says.

"What kind? We have a bunch."

Cece feels around in her bag for her wallet. The tip jar is woefully empty. "Whatever's easiest."

"It's easiest if you tell me."

"Right," Cece says, her fingers identifying what she hopes is a five-dollar bill. "How about five Heinekens?"

The kid disappears under the table and emerges with five green bottles. He wraps each one in a thick paper napkin.

Cece drops the money in the tip jar and wrangles the beers by the neck. "Thank you," she says, but the kid is already walking away to help another customer.

THROUGH THE OPEN window, the sound of boisterous laughter and inebriated mumbles. Cece tosses and turns in the impossibly narrow bed, mattress springs seeking out the tender areas of her back. The small oscillating fan provided by the school labors under its colossal duty, pushing hot air around a room not meant to be inhabited beyond the first week of June.

Jonathan is still out, drinking and carousing with forgotten friends, maybe even old flames. Cece had thought she might grow jealous or petty upon meeting one of Jonathan's high school dalliances, and even though there've been jokes among his friends, gentle ribbing, and raised-eyebrow innuendo, she is surprised to find that she doesn't care. After all, she's the one he's with; she's the one he's brought to his fifteen-year reunion—not these other women.

Outside, the revelers have gone quiet, and Cece moves to the window in the hopes of a cool breeze. In the distance, under a shadowed tree, a circle of people stand swaying silently. Cece waits for her vision to adjust to the darkness. Something—a bottle, a glass—catches the moonlight while it's passed from hand to hand. Ears straining, elbows digging into the windowsill, Cece looks on. At first, it's barely discernable, a low hum in the night, like a forgotten lullaby. Then the chorus grows, a melody shakes forth from the swaying circle, men shouldered up against one another, leaning forward, fingers snapping to some familiar beat. This must be Deerfield's famous all-male a cappella group, reunited once again under the near-full moon. Cece has never cared much for song, and if pressed, she might say that a cappella is just fine, but she never understood why it was elevated to such venerable status, especially in high school and college. At Bucknell, the all-male group had quite the following, and Cece remembers thinking it comical that a group of singing boys might attract as much attention as a soccer game. And yet, for all her past pessimism, Cece finds herself enjoying the sweet serenade echoing in the summer night.

Eventually, the crowd breaks up and the men stagger off in groups of three and four. Giving up on sleep for the foreseeable future, Cece throws on some clothes and heads downstairs, but not before making sure to keep the door unlocked, just in case Jonathan comes back while she's gone. It's strange, making her way through a building made for kids. The hallway seems narrow, the wood floors creaking beneath her feet, the low ceilings pressing down from above. She wonders what the space must be like when school is in session: doors open, boys mingling in the hallway, jockeying for position in front of sinks in the bathroom, violating each other's personal space in the way most young men do. Then it's lights out, and the faculty dorm parent, perhaps a man with white wispy hair, is bellowing up and down the halls, threatening detention and worse. And then it is quiet, save for the dripping faucets and clanging pipes. A hush falls over the campus—boys and girls in their respective dorms, faculty grading papers by lamplight, bemoaning the familiar mistakes, the cooks and janitors soaking their cracked and knotted hands.

The night air is cool, a welcome respite from the furnace that is the dorm room, and Cece takes off walking, imagining herself a wide-eyed scholar on this learned campus. On the quad there are voices—men drunk—shouting about one thing or another.

Cece sticks to the path, her presence obscured by the old oaks overhead. At first, she isn't certain, but then she recognizes Jonathan's voice. She wants to join him but thinks better of it. It's his high school reunion. Let him have his fun. She's about to keep on walking, determined to do a full loop around campus and walk herself to exhaustion, when she hears the admission of a secret, the hint of a misdeed, and she finds herself slowing down and creeping closer and crouching—she's ashamed to admit—behind an enormous boxwood bush.

Logan strikes an imposing figure on the field. Cece recognizes a few other moonlit faces from the people she's met throughout the day. Jonathan stretches his arms over his head. Beer cans pop and fizz. A toast to something.

"I can't believe we didn't get nabbed," Logan says.

"Logan might as well have been running his own pharmacy," someone shouts.

"I was just providing a service, my friends. Not my fault if the school had a rampant pill problem!"

"But you *did* get caught," Jonathan says, his words soupy. "That old fucker. Mr. Erdinger caught you with that huge bag of pills in your book bag."

"Wasn't there a rumor that he was a Nazi?"

"He sure graded like it."

Clouds shifting, the near-full moon spills across the quad, the men swaying to some invisible tide. "Innocent until proven guilty!" Logan shouts, bowing before them. "If you'll recall, the backpack was mine, but the drugs were not. And after all, how could they be? A legacy, captain of the lacrosse team? No, gentlemen. I'm an upstanding citizen. A Deerfield man! Those drugs belonged to an interloper, an imposter!"

"Fuck. I forgot about that. Did we really pin it on that kid?" a voice in the darkness asks.

"Sure did," Logan says, "but he had it coming. Fucker was trouble from the minute he stepped on campus."

Jonathan drains his beer and tosses it onto the quad where it tinkles softly in the grass. "How the hell did you convince Mr. Hech the drugs weren't yours?"

"Oh, you mean our fearless headmaster? That quivering little weenie. You don't remember, Jon Boy? How many beers have you had anyway? Methinks you've gone lightweight on us. You all vouched for me—said you saw him put the drugs in my backpack. He was jealous and trying to frame me."

"Fuck."

"Fuck is right."

"What happened to him?" Jonathan says.

"Expelled," Logan says, "if memory serves. Perhaps we ought to pour one out."

By the time Cece stands up, her leg has fallen asleep, and she limps gingerly back to the path. After a disagreement over their tennis acumen, the men have meandered off toward the lower courts in search of rackets and balls. There is talk of a one-thousand-dollar wager. From the other end of campus, the steady thump of base. Some, it seems, are not keeping their powder dry for the dance tomorrow night under the big tent. Jonathan has promised it will be glorious, and a tad debauched.

The walk feels displeasing to Cece now, and so she heads back to the dorm that once seemed regal and storied but now looks run-down and grimy. The hallway walls are a sickly yellow under the fluorescent lights, and Cece dreads returning to Jonathan's old dorm room with its tight quarters and miniature window. Why does she care about some injustice from years ago? Of course, Logan is a terrible person, but she had already deduced that fact within five minutes of conversing with him. And it's not like he and Jonathan are still friends. Cece is comforted by the fact that Jonathan doesn't seem to have remained close to any of his Deerfield compatriots. He's jettisoned them, become his own person with his own values, values Cece quite enjoys. Sure, he did something stupid for a friend; he lied. What kid hasn't lied? And who is she to judge? She wasn't exactly truthful with him about the goings-on this summer.

Cece puts the fan on high and rolls into bed, the rubbery mattress squeaking. And even as she affirms Jonathan's goodness to herself, she can't help but let her mind drift to whoever this boy was—the victim of Logan's cruelty. She wonders how he came to be at Deerfield; she wonders if he ever got a second chance. She wonders, eyes fluttering, breath heavy, sleep coming to her at last, what any of this—life and its oddities—means at all.

THE HANKERING FOR a proper cup of coffee and the desire to escape her cramped confines drive Cece from bed. The campus is still asleep, bathed in early-morning mist. The air is cold and crisp—a quality of New England summers Cece's come to appreciate. It will burn off quickly, and Cece will be left marveling at how she could have ever doubted the midday heat.

Coffee in hand, a brisk walk to clear her head, Cece returns to find Jonathan still in bed, the room air stale and pungent, last night's beer, and maybe some liquor, pushing through his pores. A pitiful groan rises from the huddled mass, arms bent over his eyes. He croaks for help, and Cece administers Advil from her toiletry bag with bottled water from the vending machine downstairs.

"You're a lifesaver," Jonathan mumbles before he clutches the pillow under his chin and dozes off, legs hanging off the end of the bed.

Cece sits at the tiny desk in the opposite corner of the room and watches him sleep. She can't remember the last time he was hungover. He'd never been a big drinker—something Cece had appreciated about him. Everything in moderation, he always liked to say. Maturity and sense—these had always been Jonathan's calling cards, and Cece is happy to have come back, to have embraced the good between them. Perhaps if she were a more reckless woman, a stronger woman, she might have thrown caution to the wind, run off with Morgan and dedicated herself to oyster farming without a safety net, but this is not her; she understands this about herself, and unlike in the past, when she's grown disappointed in her shortcomings, Cece is perfectly happy where she is.

Despite reeking of alcohol, Jonathan has an angelic quality about him, a certain innocence painted on his slumbering face. It's difficult imagining him playing any role in getting someone wrongfully expelled from school. Cece's already determined not to bring it up. It isn't her place. After all, she was the one eavesdropping. And what would come of it? She knows Jonathan is a good person. He's never given her a reason to think otherwise. In truth, he's the one who should be questioning Cece's morals, except he hasn't. He's been here this whole time, waiting for her to finally make up her mind about what kind of life she wants, and she has. She has!

Jonathan emerges, pushing himself up on one arm, hair mussed, eyes bloodshot. "I'm sorry. I'll be useless to you this morning."

"It's your reunion. I'd be worried if you weren't hungover. Best rally for tonight!"

Jonathan groans and folds the pillow over his face.

"You need sleep."

More whimpers. "I should be good in a few hours. What're you gonna do?"

"Check out the library. Dig through the archives."

"I believe it took us until 1976 to racially integrate. Not our finest moment."

Cece waves him off and gathers her things to leave, but not before pulling the blinds down and patting Jonathan's clammy forehead. He's fallen asleep again before she gently closes the door.

THE LIBRARY IS not the monastic, sunless building Cece had expected. The red brick with its Colonial Revival columns exudes a quiet sense of assurance. The space must have been renovated at one point, and Cece finds herself in awe of the perfect blending of old and new: enormous windows filtering natural light, wood-paneled walls adorned with oil paintings of old, dusty White men, a circular staircase that reminds Cece of something out of a science fiction movie.

The school archives are stowed on the lower level, where the air grows musty and damp. The aroma brings Cece a strange sense of comfort. She's missed the smell of old books, of cracking glue and ageing paper. In college, she practically lived in the library, hording the small study rooms, roaming the stacks of the quiet study floor to stretch her legs. Things were simpler then, when she used to think a 4.0 GPA would ensure a life without trouble, when she was convinced one's future might be charted out on graph paper.

It takes some searching, but eventually Cece finds the year book section—a seemingly endless row of green-and-black-bound books. She traces the golden lettering with a finger until she arrives on 1999, when Jonathan would have been a freshman. Senior-year Jonathan can wait; Cece's more interested in seeing a gangly, awkward version of him—if such a thing exists. The first book disappoints, and all Cece finds is a stock-looking photo of a young Jonathan in a blue blazer, green tie, and khakis, standing in the back row with his classmates. All the boys stand in the back rows, their faces youthful and optimistic. In front, the girls in white dresses, their hair blond as wheat in the summer sun. If Cece was hoping for something to give Jonathan grief about—an ill-fitting suit jacket, an adorable cowlick—she's sorely disappointed. There's an uncanny maturity and professionalism to the class picture, as if the participants were aware it might be dug up by nosey investigative journalists when they invariably run for US Senate.

Cece decides to speed up the process and skips a year. She holds out hope for a photo of interest and pulls Jonathan's junior-year yearbook off the shelf. Thumbing through the thick pages, she's pleased to find a photo of young Jonathan playing chess. Now *this* is the kind of detail she's been looking for—something she can tease him about. She takes out her phone and snaps a picture for later use. There's more gold in the subsequent pages: Jonathan standing on the sidelines of a lacrosse game, mop of hair covering his face, shoulder pads comically large on his skinny frame; Jonathan acting in a play, a newsboy cap on his head. The full class photo arrives in the middle, and Cece presses the pages down on either side of the spine. In the back row, it's easy to make out Logan with his shock of red hair. There are a few other familiar faces from the lobster bake. At the far end of the top row, she spots Jonathan—taller and more filled out. She's surprised at what two years does—how quickly he seems to have gone from boy to man. Her eyes drift to the girls in front, bosoms fuller, legs longer. They are not yet women, and yet they very much are.

Cece is about to close the book—her curiosity sated—when something catches her eye. A boy, two rows down from the top, his blazer dull and shabby, his face somber and unsmiling. It can't be. It's impossible. Cece hunches over the pages to get a closer look, back aching, heart hammering. The broad shoulders, the square jawline—it's unmistakable.

It can't be, and yet it is. A young Morgan, lost among the

swirling crowd of green ties and white dresses, looks at the camera, at Cece, his eyes narrow, almost angry, and even though he's surrounded by his classmates, there's a loneliness about him, as if everyone is leaning just a few inches away from his invisible ignominious sphere. Cece snaps the book closed. Don't be ridiculous. It's only someone who looks like what Cece imagines a young Morgan would look like. A doppelgänger, a bizzarro version of him, a scholarship kid, evidenced by his worn jacket and unruly hair. Cece looks at the photo once more and confirms her mistake. For whatever reason, she'd wanted it to be Morgan, but now she sees—the face is all wrong, the shoulders too hulking. To put her suspicions and paranoia at ease, Cece flips to the back of the book to read through the class names. She runs down the list with a thumbnail, hair in her eyes, nerves tittering. She suspects that if anyone comes across her in this moment, they will think her mad. She stops. Her thumbnail is white and ghostly. *Morgan Wells.*

Cece reaches for the following year. A terrible lump lodges itself in her throat. Only after opening the book and riffling through the pages does she notice the blood trickling from a paper cut on her fingertip. She finds the class photo and sits down. She spreads the book out on the floor while sucking on her finger to stem the bleeding. Everyone is where they should be. Logan with his red hair, Jonathan on the far end, his remaining youthful features now given way to a professional exterior, the girls in front in their white spring dresses. No Morgan. Cece searches the faces again. Nothing. She feels like she's out at sea, the waves rolling, the deck pitching back and forth, her stomach sloshing, threatening to come up. The boy Logan and Jonathan were talking about last night, the boy they got expelled. It was Morgan.

She understands now. The look on Morgan's face upon seeing Jonathan at the cul-de-sac, one of recognition and contempt. Worse—Morgan had recognized Jonathan almost instantaneously while Jonathan had barely registered him.

It wasn't jealousy, then—the reason for Morgan's silence. It was something else entirely. It was hatred for the man and profound disappointment in Cece for choosing him and abandoning whatever it was, however tenuous and ephemeral, between them.

Cece deserts the yearbooks—pages smeared with blood—scattered on the floor. She feels filthy and ashamed, an accomplice in some terrible wrong she doesn't fully understand. She makes her way upstairs and staggers out of the library and into the bright, unforgiving sun and wretches, hands to her knees, into a freshly mulched bed of roses.

"Looks like someone had too much fun last night," a stranger says as they walk by.

Eyes burning, mouth sour, Cece ignores them. Her mind drifts, nothing to nothing, an ocean of blank space. Legs numb, heart thrumming, she zigs and zags back to the dorm with some vague idea of what she thinks she should do, what she wants to do.

All the around her, the campus has sprung alive. Organizers stand under nylon tents holding campus maps and canvas swag bags. Overachievers are out for their morning runs, clad in neon and leggings. Couples, high school sweethearts, Cece suspects, walk hand in hand, bathing in one another's contented smiles. On the verdant quad, industrious robins dig for worms, and somewhere overhead in the trees, mourning doves coo. All of this—the storied institution, the well-bred men and women, the happy, perfectly matched couples, the world an oyster of endless opportunity and prosperity—she'd wanted it. And doesn't she still? Isn't this why she's here? Isn't this why she's come back to Jonathan? Because he's always been the only one who can provide what Cece needs? Security, stability, predictability.

The dorm staircase reeks of beer and piss. Cece holds her breath and tries to gather her thoughts. She needs a plan, a course of action, but all she can think about is Morgan. How different his life might have turned out . . . Cece feels complicit in it all. Just last night, she'd slept well, a dreamless sleep, unbothered by the story. Before she'd known the kid was Morgan, she'd been more than willing to rationalize Jonathan's behavior, to forgive him for some boyish antics. It was ages ago! Who didn't do things they regretted? And now? Cece doesn't know, her solitary footsteps ringing in the empty hall. She should write it all down before she confronts Jonathan, but there's no time. Cece wants answers . . . answers to what, exactly? She isn't quite sure, but she needs to know Jonathan is remorseful; she needs to know he regrets what he did. And what then?

To her surprise, Jonathan is awake. Two Advil and a Pedialyte from Logan have done wonders. He's showered and clean-shaven, a towel wrapped around his waist.

"Is everything okay?" he says, pulling out the desk chair and offering it to Cece. "I'm supposed to be the hungover one, remember?"

"I'm fine."

"Is that blood? Jesus, what happened?"

"It's nothing. A papercut. I wanted to talk to you about something."

Jonathan still looks alarmed by the dried blood on Cece's hand. She doesn't know where to start . . . how to broach the subject. Jonathan offers her bottled water, which she drinks as slowly as possible. Always have a plan, her father used to say when she was swimming. Every stroke, every kick should be in service of a goal, a mission. Anything else is a waste, or worse, a mistake. But this isn't swimming, and since she was fired, since the job at Rayburn, since Morgan, Cece hasn't been one for plans and premeditation.

"I overheard you guys talking last night," she blurts out.

"Oh," Jonathan says, seemingly miffed. "You're gonna have to be more specific. There were a lot of guys around last night, and I wasn't exactly of sound mind."

"Logan," Cece stammers. "I overheard you and Logan talking about that kid you got expelled."

Jonathan tugs a shirt over his head and pulls on boxer shorts under his towel. He's never been one for nudity in front of Cece, which has always struck her as deeply funny, but she'd never said anything, even when he insisted they always turn off the lights before sex. "What were you doing out?"

"I couldn't sleep, so I went for a walk. You guys weren't exactly quiet."

"No. I can't imagine we were," Jonathan says, tidying his hair in the mirror.

"Well?"

"Well, what?"

"Is it true? What Logan said? About that kid getting kicked out for drugs that weren't his?"

"Logan's an idiot. Half the things he says are lies and the other half are exaggerations."

"It didn't sound like a lie."

"What do you want me to say?"

"Is it true?"

Jonathan grabs his Shinola watch and squints while he struggles with the glossy leather band. "It's not one of my prouder moments."

"You just let it happen?"

"It was a long time ago."

"You could have said something. You could have stopped it."

"The kid was a bad egg, Cece . . . I'm not saying he deserved it, but it was only a matter of time before he got expelled for something. He didn't belong at Deerfield."

"How do you know that?" Cece says, her voice rising, piercing and shrill. "How can you be so certain?" It catches her off guard, her anger and fury, like it's always been inside her, like it never left since their first breakup.

Predictably, Jonathan remains calm, regarding her emotional outburst with a scientific curiosity, like she's a new species he's discovering for the first time. "What's gotten into you, Cece? One minute you're doting on me, the next you're on some righteous crusade against me and my friends. What's this really about?"

"It's about the truth!"

"I don't think so. I think you're having second thoughts,

again," Jonathan says and chuckles to himself. "I must be the dumbest person alive to give this a second go. Everyone told me—my friends, my family—not to take you back. But I didn't want to quit. I'm not a quitter, Cece. But I have eyes, Cece. Last night, I was watching you judging this place . . . my high school buddies. You want it all so badly. Why else would you be with me? Why else would you have come back? But you won't let yourself enjoy it. You've got to poke it and prod it, pick it over until you find something you don't like about it, and then you do what you're doing right now."

Jonathan's friends . . . his family . . . It stings to know she is a topic of discussion, a blight on his otherwise wonderful life. "So then why did we get back together? If everyone keeps telling you how terrible I am."

"Because I know the real Cece," Jonathan says and takes her in his arms. "Remember her? The one who finished her CAS exams faster than anyone else at her company, the one who always knew what she wanted. The one who was never afraid of the future, because she'd already considered every possible outcome."

It's easy for Cece to be seduced by this version of herself; it's a version she's cultivated over the years to ensure she never had to confront what she finds herself face-to-face with now: a future she no longer recognizes, a person she does not like. She closes her eyes, grinds her molars. "A kid's life was ruined because of you and your friends."

"I'm sure he turned out fine!" Jonathan says, exasperation seeping into his voice.

"But he didn't!"

"What are you talking about?"

"Morgan. You met him the day you came to New London. When I showed you the cove. You saw him and you didn't even recognize him. I didn't understand why he was staring at you, but now I do. He's in the class photograph in the yearbook for your junior year, but then he's gone in twelfth grade."

"That's ridiculous. Do you hear yourself? You sound like a crazy person. A crazy person, Cece."

"He knew you, Jonathan. He knew exactly who you were."

"So you know the guy. I mean, it's a hell of a coincidence, but I guess that's what you get for slumming it in New London this summer. It was years ago, Cece. It's not like I can go back and undo what Logan did. Why do you care so much? What does any of this have to do with us?"

"He's my friend!"

Jonathan retreats to the bed and sits down. His eyes are calm, his voice contemplative. "I get it now. You like this guy. You don't actually care about whether I'm a good person, or whether Logan ruined his life—you just want an out. You've met someone else, and instead of being up front about it, instead of being honest with yourself, you're starting a fight in the hopes that I'll end things for us."

The veracity of Jonathan's observation—an observational truth that was not evident to Cece herself until this very moment—leaves her speechless, her mouth agape, words caught somewhere in her throat. Jonathan regards her with a kind of sagacious displeasure, like a college professor listening to an undergraduate pleading for an extension on their midterm paper. He shakes his head and fishes his loafers out from under the bed. "It's my reunion weekend. All my friends are here. I'd prefer if we didn't have a big blowup . . . I'm all tapped out. We're just different, Cece. There's no shame in admitting it. I know that now."

Jonathan's maturity is enraging, but Cece knows he's right. The fire's gone out of her. Logan, Jonathan, the rest of his friends—they are of this place. And why should she hold it against them? It's like faulting a fish for swimming, a wave for rolling. Her pocket vibrates but she ignores it. He is right. Of course, he is always right. Even now, she can't vilify him—make it easier to leave, less risky. She goes to her suitcase and zips it closed. "I'll just get going."

"You don't have a ride."

"I'll figure it out."

Jonathan throws up his hands as if to extricate himself from the situation entirely. "Do whatever you want."

Cece pulls out her phone. It's Richie. "I'm sorry about the way this all ended."

"I'm not," Jonathan says. "It's brought me clarity, and now I don't have to waste any more of my time."

Cece feels the heat rise in her chest, the need to defend, to attack Jonathan for being *so* Jonathan in all things, but then it dies. She lets him have the last word (a sign of maturity, she hopes) and slips out into the hall, suitcase rolling behind her, and picks up the call.

"We've got a problem," Richie says. It sounds like he's calling from a high school cafeteria, voices echoing in the background.

According to Richie, he's done nothing wrong. It was all just a big misunderstanding, but that isn't how the police saw it, which is why he's calling from the county jail.

"Assault?! What were you thinking?"

"All I did was yank a banner out of the guy's hand. I was just going about my business. He was the one being aggressive."

"They're holding you just for that?"

"He might have taken a spill."

Cece's mind whirls. "What can I do?"

In an oddly steady voice, Richie tells her he needs two things. The first is that he's using up his one call on her, so she'll need to contact his lawyer. The second is that she'll need to head back to New London as soon as possible.

"Why?"

"The town hall is tomorrow, remember? There's no guarantee I make bail by then. You need to be prepared to give a statement, serve as a representative for the company."

"What about Santiago?"

"Don't kid yourself. He's too rough around the edges. My time is up here. You're the only one who can do it."

Images flood her mind: Cece fumbling for words at the microphone, palms slick, tongue turgid, onlookers chuckling to one another at her frazzled gibberish. "I'm terrible at public speaking."

"And you think I'm any good?"

"But I don't know anything about the company. What am I supposed to say? This isn't the plan."

"You'll figure something out," Richie says.

"There's got to be another—"

The line goes dead, and all Cece can do is stare at her trembling hands.

17

The tall ships have yet to sail into harbor for the maritime festival, leaving New London's skyline empty and bare. The old church steeple stands alone, slender and gray. The rising sun bounds off the placid waters and glows on the redbrick train station, stout and proud. Row houses cramp the streets, side by side, ready to face the day. Fall beckons.

The planning and zoning commission meeting at city hall isn't until noon, but there's already a crowd forming—a rarity for downtown—of local news vans and overzealous reporters in heavy makeup and neutral-toned suits. Word of the protests and Richie's arrest has sparked interest, and there's nothing the media would like more than B-roll of civil unrest between protestors on the granite steps. People are picking sides, apparently, environmentalists and NIMBYs pitted against tradesmen and fishermen of all stripes. From the images on the grainy motel television, it's clear to Cece that very few people understand the issue and instead have latched on to their chosen cause to align with their personal politics. Richie was nice enough to put Cece up at a local motel since staying at Lorraine's is no longer an option. His lawyer seems confident he'll make bail in time for the meeting, but Cece isn't taking any chances. Index cards with scribbled notes litter the carpeted floor like confetti. Still no word from Morgan. Cece doesn't know what she's expecting. At least they'd reached the two-hundred-signature threshold in support of Rayburn's expansion. That had to count for something, right, all those names? She'd had no problem recruiting Santiago and Davi to collect signatures, especially once the protests had started.

Bernard lounges on the unmade bed, no doubt overjoyed at the lack of rules. Cece looks over what she has for an opening statement on Rayburn's behalf. Her more composed thoughts are barely enough to fill two flash cards. On the muted television, a man in oil-slicked overalls is being interviewed. He keeps pointing to the horizon. The camera zooms in on his wiry mustache. Cece recognizes the next interviewee, the long-haired guy with the bullhorn from the protest in Noank. He's holding up a sign: KEEP MAMACOKE COVE CLEAN! Cece turns the TV off and sits in the musty room, the synthetic comforter rough on her palms. The instant coffee she'd brewed an hour ago is already burning a hole in her stomach. She knows she should eat something else, but the idea of taking her chances with the continental breakfast in the lobby is enough to make her queasy. Sunlight pries through the yellowed track blinds. Phone unplugged from the frayed charger, Cece decides to text Morgan (what dignity does she have left to maintain?) before she heads out.

Hope to see you at the town hall. Could really use some of that trademark nonchalance. I'm terrified of public speaking!

CECE CAN HEAR the tumult behind the heavy oak doors before she enters, a maelstrom of concerned citizens: NPR-loving neighborhood advocates, representatives from the Teamsters Local 493, nature enthusiasts, and ornery dockworkers. She's arrived exactly five minutes late to avoid any awkward conversations, but mostly just Lorraine. The Beaux Arts–styled room, with its grand coffered ceiling inlaid with gold leaf motifs and imposing columns, teems with a nervous energy. News cameras line the back wall, lenses trained on the dais; three empty chairs sit behind an impressive oak table where three microphones are neatly arranged. For the masses, a sad-looking microphone stands resolutely near the front of the room, ready to absorb the plentiful threats, pleas, and protestations of the crowd. Someone's used red tape to make a giant X on the floor, indicating where the good citizens of New London should stand if they want to be heard.

Cece looks frantically for Richie with some mad hope that he'll arrive just in time to save her from complete humiliation, but no such luck. Reluctantly, she snakes her way through the jumbled mass, a haze of axle grease and patchouli oil. Murmurs ripple through the crowd, necks crane, and heads turn as members of the commission enter from a side door and take their seats at the front of the room. Cece is sandwiched between a burly man with steel-toed boots and a gray-haired woman in a forest-green tank top. Her breath comes quick, her throat burns. She looks up and focuses on the ceiling, with all its ostentatious detail to quell the panic attack. An elbow, a shove, and she's moving, pushing through the mass, quaking with anticipation.

Cece scans the room surreptitiously. Lorraine is standing in the crowd, arms crossed over her enormous bosom, a red bandana struggling to contain her curls. She's not so much looking at Cece as burning a hole through her chest.

If the panel is taken aback by the turnout, they don't show it, pulling eyeglasses from the insides of their jackets and handbag, opening spiraled notebooks, and clearing their phlegmy throats. The spokesperson, a tall, wiry man with a mop of white hair, leans close to his microphone and calls the meeting to order. The crowd settles into a resentful silence.

"The town hall concerning Rayburn Oyster Company's proposal to expand their business operation into Mamacoke Cove is now in session," the man says in a plodding tone. "Now, it seems we have a few more attendees than usual, so it behooves this body to remind everyone in attendance the purpose of this town hall."

"You're bought and paid for!" a man shouts from somewhere, his voice sonorous and venomous.

An uproar swells through the crowd. Clenched fists menace. Veins bulge. Lorraine, in the middle of it all, seems to be relishing the civil disobedience. Unphased, the wiry man taps the microphone with a slender finger, sending pops through the speakers. "May I remind you . . . May I remind you that this commission has voluntarily opened our doors to the public. If you cannot be civil, we will simply conduct our business behind closed doors."

As he speaks, two state troopers in neatly pressed gray uniforms filter in from a side door and position themselves not so inconspicuously in view of everyone, their gray campaign hats comically large. Cece works hard to suppress a nervous giggle. The rest of the room—taking them more seriously—settles down and grumbles among themselves.

"The purpose of this town hall is to allow residents to express their opinions regarding the current project before this commission. And while the public does not possess the power to approve or deny the project, the commission is charged with carrying out the will of New Londoners in good faith. In addition, the opposition to the project has obtained more than two hundred authentic signatures; as a result, their spokesperson will be allowed extended time to speak."

A woman in her seventies wearing a canary yellow cardigan much too heavy for summer leans over and whispers something in the chairman's ear, who raises a prickly eyebrow and nods solemnly. "Having received more than two hundred authentic signatures in support of their expansion, we will also be hearing from a Rayburn representative."

A chorus of whoops rises into the steamy air. Something like guilt wells in Cece's chest. She hadn't done much. Most of the credit belongs to Santiago, Davi, and Morgan—especially Morgan. Where would she be without him? Cece wonders. Nowhere good, it seems. Cece wishes he were here to witness their success, even if he just glowered at her. An appearance would at least mean he still cares. The big doors crack open, and Cece's heart bounces into her throat; she cranes her neck, expectant and hopeful, but it's only another cameraman.

"We'll first hear from"—the chairman checks a piece of paper that has just been slid to him—"Lorraine Fields and those who oppose the Rayburn expansion. Richard Rayburn and those *for* the project will follow. Please keep your comments to three minutes long. Everyone who wants to speak should have picked up a number when they entered. If you don't have a number, please do not get up to speak. Going forward, I expect this to be a civil dialogue. If at any time this commission feels that the conversation is counterproductive, we reserve the right to close the meeting to the public. As usual, our scribe, Ms. Williams, will take meeting notes, which will be posted within seventy-two hours. Are there any questions before we proceed?"

A voice booms from somewhere in the far corner of the crowd: "Where can a man find a decent job around here?!"

Hands on their duty belts, the state troopers peer into the crowd, their beady eyes glinting beneath their wide-brimmed hats.

"The commission calls Lorraine Fields."

The crowd parts for Lorraine as she makes her way to the microphone, Crocs squeaking with each step. A collective hush shrouds the room. Lorraine defiantly holds aloft a yellow legal pad. "In my hand are the voices of more than two hundred residents of New London who do not wish to see the last remaining vestiges of our county's natural beauty destroyed by industry and corporate greed. In my hand are the names of people in our community who care about the air we breathe and the water we drink. In my hand are the names of people who are rightly concerned about increased traffic on their roads and waterways."

"You'd think we were building a nuclear power plant," a man says in Cece's ear. It's Santiago. He must have just arrived.

"Any news on Richie?" Cece whispers.

Santiago shakes his head but gives her a thumbs-up, like he's always been her biggest champion.

"As a collective," Lorraine continues, "we are prepared to present this commission with numerous data points and findings regarding the following: environmental concerns in accordance with the Clean Air Act, Clean Water Act, and Migratory Bird Treaty Act, as well as concerns about traffic patterns and home values."

"The commission asks that you save all presentations of data for another date, Ms. Fields," the chairman says, his voice tinged with annoyance.

"Should this commission fail to stop Rayburn's expansion, we are prepared to file a lawsuit to halt any construction."

A tumult rises from the audience: chairs scraping, hands clapping, muttered swears and threats.

"This kind of escalation is unnecessary, Ms. Fields. The commission has yet to render a decision."

"Nevertheless, we are prepared to protect what is ours. We will not sit by idly while a panel of bureaucrats decide the fate of our town. We will fight and we will win!" Lorraine shouts, before sitting down to a mingled roar of boos and cheers.

A flurry of residents follow, none as vociferous as Lorraine but all equally aligned in their mission to stop Rayburn's expansion. There's the avid birder who claims that oyster boats will scare away the native wildlife; the kayaker who maintains that oyster baskets pose a danger to the waterways; the retired pharmaceutical executive who believes the entire operation will be an eyesore, a blight on the cove. There are others, less articulate residents who are just happy to have an audience for the public airing of their grievances. The elderly man who wants to bring back coin-operated parking meters; the grumpy sanitation worker who reprimands everyone for throwing trash in the town's new recycling bins; the opinionated barista who takes the opportunity to shame everyone for their poor tipping habits. The chairman does his best to move them along. Cece reviews the notes she's jotted down for her speech. Her handwriting suddenly seems unintelligible, and she decides to ditch them. If she's going to lose to Lorraine, she might as well go down speaking from the heart.

Cece hears the chairman call Richie's name. The microphone suddenly seems very far as Cece makes her way to the front of the room. The audience eyes her with suspicion and optimism, a hundred hopes and recriminations The panel regards her with confusion over their reading glasses. This is some kind of mistake, Cece thinks. Has it really come down to her? Surely there must be someone more qualified. She looks to Santiago in one final plea, but all he does is give her an enthusiastic fist pump, his plaid shirt and greasy hair in stark contrast to the grandeur of the room. Cece imagines she's crouched on the platform, swim cap squeezing her skull, goggles snug around her eyes, the water, glossy and inviting. Before the gun, she does like her father tells her and visualizes her start, slowly uncorking her body like a spring; her body bending like an arrow loosed from a bow and piercing the surface, arms out, fingers pressed together—the tip of the spear, fearless and unforgiving, leading her to victory.

The microphone pops, and Cece begins, her voice foreign and

new. "Thank you, Mr. Chairman. Mr. Rayburn apologizes for his absence this morning. He's attending to another matter."

A collective snicker rolls through the room.

"For the record, my name is Cece Downing. I'm an employee at Rayburn Oyster Company. As noted, we too have collected more than two hundred authentic signatures. These signatures represent the will of a significant number of New Londoners who recognize the jobs and opportunities a Rayburn expansion will bring to the area. The truth is, the latest GDP numbers for the county show a significant downturn, something locals are feeling acutely. I've been going door to door and speaking to residents, and there is a deep sense of unease and resignation about the city's chances for an economic rebound."

Cece can't see the crowd behind her, but she's aware that the energy is flagging. When Lorraine had spoken, there'd been muttered agreements and the silent pumping of fists. But now, as she leans on her old skills as an actuary, citing statistics and numbers, evidence and fact, she feels the wind die, her sails fall slack. Even the chairman seems disinterested, doodling on the printed agenda and glancing at his wristwatch. Things are slipping away. She pauses, her tongue pressed against her teeth. The audience waits. What would her father say? If you're behind, if your stroke is off, if you're getting your ass kicked, beat them at the turn—get it back! Underwater, the wall approaches, Cece flips, curls her body inward; she anticipates the wall perfectly, feet against tile, and then she's uncorking, pushing off, lengthening her back, powering up to the surface.

Cece leans closer to the microphone, mouth dry, lips chapped. She remembers what Richie told her, about his family, about how he came to be here, in this place. She remembers the conversations she's had going door to door; she remembers the way the men talked at Morgan's shipyard; she remembers everything she's learned about this place she's called home for the last three months, a place she wants to call home for a long time to come.

"While I am sympathetic to those who share Ms. Fields's perspective, I cannot say I find her arguments to be in good faith or in the best interests of this community. I would ask this commission, this collection of residents who claim to care about this town and its people, when was the last time you heard about jobs getting created around here? When was the last time you heard of a company adding jobs instead of sending them overseas? When was the last time we were proud to call ourselves New Londoners? And I'm not talking about those liberals up at the college or those self-righteous cadets at the Coast Guard Academy! I'm sure as hell not talking about the white-collar bastards at Pfizer and the politicians in Hartford who stole land right out from under your feet—land belonging to a number of folks in this room, I'm willing to bet—in the name of economic development! I'm talking about residents I met while gathering signatures. Good people. Hardworking people. People like Richie Rayburn. His family goes back six generations in New London. Back to when the whaling industry built this town. His great-great-great-grandfather earned his way as a lamp keeper on the Niantic, and his wife worked as a seamstress and volunteered at the Seamen's Friend Society. For nearly two hundred years, the Rayburns have worked as fishermen, boatbuilders, and eventually oystermen. That's their legacy. Riche's trying to build something. Now, I'm not a CEO or a politician. And we're not promising revitalization miracles or magical economic growth, but we promise you this: We will make sure Rayburn creates jobs, good jobs, decent jobs, and we'll do it sustainably. You've heard a lot about all the negatives of the business, but none of these folks want to talk about the benefits. We're going to grow this company, and when we get this approved, Rayburn plans on hiring as many New Londoners as possible!"

Cece is breathless, blood thudding in her ears.

The room erupts with deafening cheers and whoops. Boos are sprinkled throughout, but they're quickly drowned out by applause. The floor quakes under thunderous boot stomps, and Cece can only smile. The chairman taps his microphone and calls for order but to no avail. Among the sea of chaos, Cece catches sight of Lorraine standing stunned, clipboard clutched to her chest, bodies jostling around her. On the left side of the room, Cece recognizes a few guys from the shipyard standing on a bench high-fiving one another. She wonders if Morgan made it after all.

When the chairman finally regains order, he informs the crowd that they will deliver a decision tomorrow by 4 p.m. "The commission would like to reiterate that our decision, while informed by these hearings, is not decided by public opinion."

"If you don't stop it, we will!" Lorraine shouts. "We'll sue!"

People are already shuffling out the door. They came for a show and are leaving satisfied.

"That is your right, Ms. Fields," the chairman says, "although I would note that suing to stop a project that has significant public support would certainly hurt your standing in the community."

With a disgusted wave and something that looks like a middle finger, Lorraine is gone.

WALKING DOWN THE front steps, the midday air surprisingly cool for August, Cece feels as if she's accomplished something, which is foolish, she knows—all she did was listen to the community and to Richie. Still, it's like she's a part of something now, something that's bigger than her.

Taking the marble stairs two at a time, she spots Morgan, she's certain, a few steps ahead. She bounds forward, shouting his name. She wants to revel with him in their most certain victory. But when Morgan turns around, his face is darkened in a grim frown. He hears Cece. He sees Cece, of that she is most certain, but instead of waiting for her to catch up, or breaking into one of those smiles, the ones where his teeth glint through his thick beard, he simply turns and keeps on walking. There is a moment when Cece almost calls out again. Perhaps there's been some error. He thinks she's someone else, he misheard her, but she quickly understands this is no mistake.

By the time she catches up to him in the parking lot, he's halfway in his truck.

"What's with the silent treatment?"

Morgan doesn't move, one foot on the hot pavement, the other in the cab. He drums out a rhythm on the top of the rusting cab. His shoulders heave, and then both feet on the ground and he's facing her. He's gotten more color since the last time Cece's seen him.

"We agreed to see less of each other."

"By less you mean not at all."

"There just didn't seem much use in carrying on like we were."

"What do you mean?"

"Don't do that . . . play dumb. You're smarter than that."

Cece can feel her face reddening, shame spreading like wildfire. "So why did you come?"

Morgan tugs a purple handkerchief from his pocket and cleans imaginary grime from his big hands. "Guys from the shipyard asked me to tag along. Moral support."

"I see," Cece says, trying to quell the anger she has no right feeling.

"I gotta get back," Morgan says. "I'm on my lunch break."

"Let's grab a sandwich, then. I know a killer place. Richie showed it to me."

"I'm good, Cece," he says and gets into his truck.

"I know what happened," she says, because it's the only thing she can think that will keep him here, if only for a few more seconds. "I know what happened at Deerfield. I know Jonathan was a part of it."

Morgan's face is stony and tight. "He told you?"

"Not exactly, but I found out."

"I bet he doesn't even remember me."

Cece doesn't have to say anything. She can't lie.

Morgan laughs a bitter laugh and picks at the steering wheel with a jagged thumbnail. "That tracks."

"I didn't know," Cece says. "I had no idea he . . . If I had . . ."

"What? Dumped him on moral grounds? Don't make me laugh."

"Okay. I deserved that."

Morgan shakes his head and readjusts his baseball cap. "I get it; I was just your summer fling, your hall pass before you went back to Jonathan and your comfortable life. I thought I could do it, okay? I knew those were the terms, and I had no right, but I started wanting something more, something real."

"But it was more, it is more."

"Who are you kidding, Cece? Your little speech up there about the community? About being a New Londoner? How long have you lived here? Three months? Not even. You're no local. This is just your working-class cosplay phase, and I played a part, and sure, I was happy to; I'm not saying I'm blameless. But you took it further than you needed to. It could have just been that one night, but you wanted more, but then you didn't . . . You chipped away at me."

The truck starts with a sputtering grumble, the air thick with exhaust.

"I left him," Cece shouts over the noise. "We broke up."

Morgan shifts the truck into reverse and checks the rearview mirror and says, "What do you want, a medal?" And then he's gone, the roaring engine sending waves through Cece, like she's a buoy at sea, rising and falling to the whim of the waves.

18

Forty-eight hours later, Richie and Cece are dining at an upscale spot called the Oyster Club in Mystic's historic district. There is cause for celebration. The expansion has been approved by the zoning commission, and even the threat of legal action from Lorraine isn't enough to dampen Richie's spirits. He's still riding high after the assault charges were dropped. He's convinced she won't follow through with it, so for now, they drink to victory.

Late-summer tourists mingle around their two-top, jostling for a position at the bar and sliding into booths, voices booming upward to the white coffered ceiling. With his Teva sandals and black jean shorts, Richie cuts a striking figure against the sea of khaki, linen button-downs, and pastel dresses.

"This really wasn't necessary," Cece shouts over the din.

"Are you kidding? You sold them, Cece. It was all you," Richie says. "Plus, we're this restaurant's oyster supplier. Everything's comped tonight. And the owner also owes me big-time. He crashed into my truck last summer after too many martinis. I didn't call the cops."

Magically, a bottle of white, along with bread and warm butter, appears, but Richie insists they touch none of it. Not until the oysters have arrived, which they promptly do, a dozen gleaming bivalves on a bed of ice and seaweed. The waiter expertly navigates the already-frosting tray onto a metal stand. It reminds Cece of pizza places she'd go to as a kid, where the whole family would split a pie, elevated above paper plates and red plastic cups of soda. Embarrassingly, Cece knows nothing about eating oysters, a fact Richie is intent on remedying.

"First," Richie says, his finger lingering over an oyster, "we're smelling. They should smell like an ocean breeze. Second, we're checking for plumpness or meatiness. Third, we're looking for them to have a glossiness to them, a sheen, like they're swimming in a liquor of sorts. Check all those boxes, you've got a good one. You can tell these are ours because of the green shell, see?"

Cece studies the half shells, glistening under the lights. She thinks about the whine of the winch and the rush of water through the cage. She thinks about Santiago, eyes inscrutable behind his sunglasses, a cigarette dangling on his smiling lips. Pride wells up in her chest, and she hopes Richie can't tell how hard she's trying not to cry. Everything's making Cece cry these days, even the good stuff. She'd spent the night in the same motel watching bad television and raiding the vending machine. Luckily, the minibar had never been refilled, so there was no risk of drunkenly texting Morgan and making a fool of herself. He'd been clear as day. He didn't want anything to do with her anymore. Cece doesn't blame him. She'd foisted friendship on him, knowing, deep down, there was something more there. She'd used him to make sense of her own screwed-up relationship with Jonathan. She'd betrayed his kindness and his patience, and for that she is truly sorry.

"Finally," Richie says, his eyes glinting in the candlelight, "the last thing we're looking for has less to do with our oyster and more about the guy or gal shuckin' them. See, you want to keep the oyster intact, and you want to keep as much of its juices in the shell. The last thing someone wants to eat is a cut-up oyster. This one's perfect; it looks like someone just opened it with a key. And of course, a good shucker never breaks off parts of the outer edge. There's nothing worse than picking bits of shell out of your mouth while you're trying to enjoy a taste of the ocean!"

"When do we eat them?"

Richie gives his nod of approval. Wine is poured. The first few oysters are eaten without any fixings: mignonette, cocktail sauce, horseradish, or even lemon. To Cece's surprise, she finds herself tasting all the things he'd told her to pay attention to. They're refreshing and clean, a metallic tang lingering on her tongue. Once they've eaten a few without accoutrements, Richie relaxes his rules. The owner, a tall, handsome guy with black hair, comes by the table and introduces himself, but the name is lost in the chatter of the dinner rush. He thanks Richie for his impeccable product and melts into the muted light of the foyer, no doubt embarrassed about the aforementioned martini-induced car accident.

They order another dozen oysters, some local sourdough, mussels, and corn bread. Richie checks the wine, pulling it from the chilling bucket, but doesn't order more, which Cece finds slightly disappointing. She was hoping for a license to get a little more than tipsy this evening. "I've been doing some thinking," Richie says, fingering his oyster-shell necklace. "I'd like you to do more around here. Give you more responsibilities."

"I'd make a terrible secretary," Cece says. "I promise you."

"I'm talking about making you the supervisor for Mamacoke."

All Cece can do is laugh. "What are you saying?"

"I'll need another set of eyes on that operation."

"What about Santiago?"

"He can't be in two places at once."

"But I don't know anything about the business. Not really."

"I could teach you. Unless there's something else you'd rather be doing."

No, Cece thinks, there's nothing, nothing in the world she'd rather do. The prospect of partnering with Richie and helping grow Rayburn Oyster fills Cece with a nervous, vibrating energy. It wouldn't just be a job; it would be a life, something that required tending and attention. "It would be an honor," she says, the words catching in her throat.

"Those are good tears, right?" Richie says.

Regaining her composer, Cece dabs her eyes with the heavy cloth napkin. "Absolutely."

"That's just grand. Just grand."

"Does this mean I get a say in who we hire?"

"Sure does," Richie says. "Have anyone in mind?"

"I'd like to hire from the shipyard near where I was staying this summer. A few guys got laid off there, and I know they'd appreciate the work."

"Let's bring them in for an interview this week."

"Just like that?"

"Just like that. We've gotta get things moving now that the expansion's been approved," Richie says. "Stay as long as you'd like at the motel until you find a decent place to live. I catered the manager's second wedding on the cheap, so he owes me a favor."

"I'll start looking for a new place first thing tomorrow."

"I still can't believe you were living on that lady's property this whole time . . . What did you say her name was?"

"Lorraine."

"And you're saying she organized the whole protest?"

"Pretty much."

"Well, I appreciate you sticking it out with us, even after she kicked you to the curb."

Cece thinks about the cozy pool house with its low-slung ceiling and miniature windows. She thinks back to the beginning of summer, when she used to sit on the front porch with Bernard and wait to hear Morgan's truck rumbling up the hill, Mr. Shipyard. "It was time to move out anyway," she says.

OUTSIDE THE HANGAR, the shipyard is desolate. Under the baking sun, pickup trucks tinkle, heat rippling off their hoods. Morgan's truck is parked in the shade under the only tree at the far end of the lot, which means he got there first. Cece's only has thirty minutes before she needs to head back to Santiago in Noank, so she parks and hustles across the gravel lot, dust coating her rubber boots. Morgan will be in the trailer, but that's not where Cece is going. She's looking for information on the men who were fired.

The hangar is cool and subterranean. Cece half expects stalactites to be hanging from the towering ceiling. At the far end, welders are at work, sparks dancing in the dark. A few men are congregated around a piece of plywood on sawhorses, pencils in their hands, eyes trained on a blueprint. They pay Cece no mind. If anyone recognizes her, they don't say anything. Cece decides to try her luck with a pockmarked kid eating an egg salad sandwich. He's sitting on a cooler with an energy drink between his boots.

"Any idea where I can find Mickey and Wesley?" Cece says.

"Black Wesley or White Wesley?" the kid says.

"Not sure. All I know is he repaired my engine. They repaired a boat engine for me."

The kid takes a bite of his sandwich and chews it methodically. "That's Black Wesley, but I'm pretty sure those two got laid off a few weeks back. You'd have to go talk to the supervisor." He jerks his head toward the trailer.

"That's not really an option."

The kid shrugs. "Try Bob. He's Mickey's uncle or somethin'. He should be somewhere out in the yard painting boats."

Cece thanks the kid and leaves him to his sandwich. It doesn't take her long to spot Bob. An enormous human with a beer gut the size of a Sub-Zero fridge, he greets Cece with an enthusiastic handshake that leaves paint between her fingers. He pushes his

Oakley sunglasses up on his sunburned forehead and asks what he can do for her.

"Hell of a thing for you to do," Bob says after Cece explains why she's looking for Mickey and Wesley. "Hell of a thing. Those boys would sure be appreciative of a steady gig."

With Mickey and Wesley's contact information in hand, Cece thanks him and takes her leave as quicky as possible. She has the distinct feeling that if she'd stayed for a moment longer, Bob would have offered her a beer from his secret cooler he has hidden somewhere.

On her way back to her car, Cece instinctively glances toward the trailer. The blinds are drawn, but there's movement, she thinks. Wishful thinking, Cece reprimands herself. Focus on the job, she thinks. Keep your shit together before you start thinking about anything else. That's what had gotten her in trouble the first time around. She'd do things different this time around. She'd do them right.

So lost in thought is Cece that it takes her a moment to recognize Lacy standing before her. Cece looks around wildly, trying to identify the illusionist who's playing tricks on her.

"I saw you from the trailer," Lacy says, as if to allay Cece's fears of the supernatural.

"Oh" is all Cece can manage. She wonders how much if anything Morgan has told his daughter, his daughter who is back, which means he hasn't lost the custody battle just yet.

"What're you doing here?"

"Two guys were fired a few weeks ago. I'm going to offer them jobs at Rayburn—now that we're expanding."

"That's nice of you."

Cece can't tell if Lacy's being facetious. The girl had undoubtedly noticed her absence the last few weeks, but had Morgan given a reason? "They're good workers. They deserve jobs."

"My dad is always saying work makes the man."

Cece can't resist. "How is your dad?"

Lacy ponders the question, crossing and uncrossing her pale, gangly legs. Cece is happy that at least she's been wearing sunblock at the beach. "About the same as the last time you saw him."

Cece doesn't know what she wants from the conversation, so she scrunches up her nose and looks into the sun.

"Is it because of my mom and dad?" Lacy says finally. "Is that why you don't come around anymore? Is it because of that lady who knocked on our door and told you about the cops getting called?"

"What? No," Cece says, and she squats down so she's eye to eye with Lacy. "That's not it at all."

"Then why are you acting weird all of a sudden?"

Cece searches the ground for answers. She wonders if Morgan is watching them from inside the trailer. From somewhere deep within the hangar, a hammer clangs. "I made a mistake," Cece says, meeting Lacy's gaze. It is a strange and unnerving sensation to admit your faults and shortcomings to a thirteen-year-old. "I took your father for granted. I wasn't a good friend."

"I fight with my friends all the time, especially when they borrow my favorite outfits without asking, but we always make up."

"What's your secret?" Cece asks.

"That's easy," Lacy says, like it's the most obvious thing in the world. "You just have to admit you were wrong. And eat some humble pie, at least that's what my dad always says."

"That simple, huh?"

"That simple," Lacy says cheerily and skips back to the trailer.

To put off spending the evening cooped up in the drab motel room (she still hasn't found a decent apartment), Cece picks up Bernard, who is none too pleased about his cramped confines, and drives directly to the Whaler after work, where she's become a folk hero of sorts. Or at least, someone who doesn't have to buy her own drinks for a while. Word got out quickly about what she'd said at the town hall, and now everyone at the bar, including the bartender, won't let her spend a penny. She's also personally classified Bernard as Cece's service animal, which means he can preside over the Whaler's modest craft beer selection for as long as he pleases. Cece feels a modicum of satisfaction at her acceptance by the local clientele. For once, she's a part of something; she's welcome—shortcomings and all.

The work crowd hasn't quite arrived yet, and Cece elbows up to the near-empty bar and orders a beer, something cheap and easy to drink. On the television, the Yankees are in the playoff hunt. The game hasn't started yet, but the pregame show is on, the talking heads rattling on about what storylines to follow. Two plumbers sit at the far end of the bar complaining about the price of gas. At a high-top table, an old-timer sits hunched over her whiskey straight. Strange, Cece thinks, how fast things happen, how they can come together in an instant, a moment of pure random chance, and then fall apart just as quickly, like they meant nothing at all. The bartender puts a bowl of mixed nuts in front of her. Craving something stronger, Cece orders a seven and seven and fires off a message to Richie, telling him she set up interviews for Mickey and Wesley. They seemed thrilled by the prospect of a steady gig.

There's a voicemail from Wynonna, no doubt concerning their father. Cece should listen to it right away, but instead, she stuffs the phone deep into her jeans pocket and takes a long drink, sucking the sugary goodness through her teeth. It numbs her forehead, and she holds the cool glass against her cheek, ice sloshing. It can wait five minutes.

There are pressing matters (Where will she live? Is Richie's faith in her unfounded? Who'll take care of Barry when Kim inevitably leaves for good? What'll her family say when they find out Cece's left Jonathan for the second time?), but for now, all she can manage is the decision to sit in this local bar and feed Bernard cashews from her outstretched palm. For all her successes this summer, all her victories, big and small, Cece can't ignore the nagging emptiness that irritates her like a single grain of sand in a bathing suit—a constant reminder of where she's been, where she'll never go again. Soon, it will be autumn, and Cece doesn't know how to make sense of it all—time passing, the seasons changing with relentless predictability. She has the distinct and terrifying sense that she's lost or losing something.

"Everything all right here?" a familiar voice says.

Cece closes her eyes and dares not open them, lest it be a

dream, a hallucination. She doesn't believe it until the bartender says Morgan's name. She feels him sit down on the stool next to her. Bernard whines, struggling against his leash.

"Funny seeing you here."

The serendipity is all too much for Cece. "How did you know . . ."

Morgan points to the bartender, who's dumping ice into the sink. "Wish I could say it was fate, but I asked her to give me a call if you came around."

"Why?"

"I heard what you did for Wesley and Mickey," Morgan says, his eyes quiet, shoulders tight.

"It was the least I could do. Richie's the one who signed off on it. I just suggested it."

"After the town hall. I was a little harsh."

"No. Not at all. I needed to hear it. You were right, about everything," Cece says. It feels good to surrender, to admit what she's wanted this whole time.

Morgan rests his hands on Cece's knees, assured and steady. "Lacy told me what you said."

It is good to be touched. Cece feels like a boat in a storm, tossed this way and that. Her throat aches. It is so much easier this way, to sail with the wind, to roll with the waves. What's the use in fighting Mother Nature? "I'm ready to eat humble pie."

Morgan smiles a reassuring smile. "That won't be necessary, but we can't stay here," he says. "You know my rule about getting more than one drink at a bar so close to home."

"It is a very good rule."

"Let's go back to my place."

"I'd like that very much," Cece says, "and so would Bernard."

"Good. I have a lot to tell you."

MORGAN TELLS CECE then—seated on his couch, his hands in his lap, Lacy in her room listening to music with the door closed, Bernard curled up on the rug—about how he came to Deerfield in the first place, and how he left, or was forced to leave, and the terrible ways in which his betrayal at the hands of a few cruel boys shaped his life into the thing it is today.

By any standard, let alone those of his family, Morgan was a bright boy. Where his half brothers struggled in school, often spending more time in detention and summer school than class, Morgan excelled. He was a mystery to his father and stepmother, nose buried in a novel or history textbook whenever he wasn't helping out at the family boatyard. Where Morgan was from, perfect grades didn't get you into places like Deerfield; mostly they got you nothing, except for maybe the admiration of your teachers. A few made comments about how he could look forward to a full ride to UMass when he graduated from high school.

Mostly, Morgan's academic aptitude was treated with a combination of curiosity and distrust, and his siblings often enjoyed placing random boat blueprints in front of him and watching him calculate the volume of a hull or the angle of a sail in his head. Morgan never enjoyed this activity; it made him feel like a circus animal, but he partook nonetheless, as it seemed to entertain his siblings.

It was during one of these moments of mathematical wizardry

when one of their father's clients was walking through the boat yard and noticed him. Morgan remembers the man vividly, dressed in a white linen suit, wavy white hair peeking out from under the brim of his fedora—he seemed to Morgan like a character in a novel. The man was intrigued by Morgan's demonstration and gave him a few more problems to solve, which he did with ease.

"That's my boat over there," the man said, pointing to a sloop Morgan's father had been working on for the last nine months. "Hoping to get her in the water this summer."

Morgan paid the man no mind, now uncomfortable from the attention.

"Name's Cody. Doug Cody. What's your name?"

"Morgan."

"Nice to meet you, Morgan," the man said, and then he was gone as quickly as he'd come, his leather shoes tapping on the concrete, his suit the color of vanilla-bean ice cream.

It wasn't until the next week when Morgan's parents sat him down on their springless couch and explained that Doug Cody wanted them to send him somewhere called Deerfield Academy, and he was willing to cover all the expenses. He was an alumnus and board member of the school, and he explained how they had scholarships for kids like Morgan. Kids who were bright but didn't possess the necessary resources to attend a fine institution like Deerfield.

"It's like a school for the gifted or something," his father said.

And so it happened that Morgan stepped foot onto Deerfield's campus in the summer of 1999 for orientation. He never saw Doug Cody again.

From the outset, it was clear to Morgan, and everyone around him, that he didn't belong. From his coarse Outer Cape accent to his single blazer, there was little doubt he was a scholarship kid. The students were generally nice about it, but Morgan could sense a quiet distancing, especially in his dorm, as if his very presence meant others couldn't be themselves. They had to curtail their talk of skiing in the Alps or summering in the Hamptons around him. They had to lend context to every conversation when he didn't recognize a neighborhood in Manhattan or a Caribbean island. In short, they pitied him—but not enough to be his friend. None of this bothered Morgan particularly, or at least he never let on about it. Only one time, during the ninth grade class photo, did he falter, slipping away from the other students, embarrassed by the haircut his stepmother had given him at home over break.

He knew it was a gift, him being here—a thousand-, no, a million-in-one chance—and he intended on making the best of it. And while Doug Cody had thought Morgan was bright, Morgan had his doubts after the first semester. His classes were demanding, his teachers rigid and unforgiving. They doled out reading at an endless pace, tearing his essays apart as if they were paid in spilled red ink. Still, Morgan kept on—determined to prove himself worthy of the scholarship. And so it happened that he lived in the library and fell in with the international kids, who, while rich, didn't seem as intent on keeping him on the outside.

When the year ended and the summer came, when everyone else was heading off to internships and far-flung European countries, Morgan decided to stick around and take a job at the summer camp. It paid good money, and it would give him time to prepare for next year, which was somehow supposed to be harder than freshman year, but really, he couldn't bear to go home. He was afraid of how much he'd changed and what his parents might think of him, but mostly, he was worried they'd set him back somehow. Slowly but surely, he'd started to make his way in this new world, and he didn't want them limiting him, as terrible as that sounded. He stayed on campus all summer with nothing but a box fan to keep cool.

By the time the fall semester of his second year ended, Morgan was pulling straight A's and catching jealous glances from classmates when teachers commended his contributions in the classroom. His comments were insightful and perceptive in Harkness discussions in English; his scores set the high mark in math and science; his oration skills were nuanced and powerful in speech class. He tried out for the rowing team and didn't make it, but at least he tried. Girls started paying attention to him, and for the first time in his life, Morgan understood what confidence was.

As junior year approached, Morgan doubled his efforts, shunning all distractions real and imagined. By now, he'd come to experience some manner of popularity, and while he'd once been ignored, he now found himself the object of attention, not just of girls, but of boys, too. In particular, a group from the boys' lacrosse team who lived on his floor in the dormitory took a liking to him and invited him to various social gatherings, but he politely declined. Princeton and Harvard were now chief among his priorities, and having tasted academic success, the singular joy of learning deeply and fully, he saw no goal more worthy than the pursuit of knowledge. Not even 9/11 or the subsequent war in Iraq could distract him. By the end of his junior year, with stellar

SAT and ACT scores in his back pocket, Morgan allowed himself to dream of what college life might look like.

So, it was to his immense surprise and distress when the headmaster called him into his office and informed him that he was being dismissed from Deerfield Academy for drug possession and violating the school's honor code. Morgan had only spoken to Mr. Hech once before, when he'd needed to draw on his financial-aid funds early for an additional textbook. He was a severe-looking man with a thin mustache. He wore a black vest and carried a pewter pocket watch. Upon delivering the news, he peered at Morgan through his black-rimmed glasses like an owl watching its prey.

Morgan maintained his innocence, but Mr. Hech said he'd already made up his mind. The evidence was overwhelming. Eyewitness testimony from two other boys saw him slip the drugs into Logan Baxter's bag prior to his being apprehended. And there were others willing to go on the record about Morgan's scheme to frame Logan.

"You're lucky we aren't involving the police in this matter. Deerfield has been more than generous in the matter of your finances. It is deeply disappointing that you would feel the need to take even more from a school that's already given you so much."

Years later, Morgan would berate his younger self for sitting in silence, for not protesting more, for not demanding an appeal, some sort of hearing, but in that moment, it seemed the entire institution was against him, and what did he know about institutions and power?

Panic and confusion gripped Morgan. He saw no possible recourse. It was their word against his, and who was he? "But what will I do? I can't go home."

"You most certainly will. As for what you will do—well, you should have considered that before you decided to partake in this little plot of yours. Now, will your parents be picking you up, or do we need to arrange your transportation home?"

Morgan was given twenty-four hours. He moved about the room mechanically while he packed his single duffel bag. Paralyzed by deciding which books to bring home, he left them all on his bookshelf. What use did he have for them now? In a stupor, he shuffled down the hall of his dorm. A taxi idled outside. When he emerged with his luggage, the cabbie popped the trunk and gave him a head nod. From the back seat, Morgan looked out at the campus. He didn't know whether to commit the image to memory or look away and make it easier to forget the place entirely in the years to come. The lacrosse team was practicing on the main field when Morgan drove by. The team stopped and watched him go; Logan took off his helmet and waved goodbye, his toothy grin terrible and careless. Morgan spotted Jonathan on the sidelines, his face ghostly white, his lips thin and quivering.

What followed was a time when Morgan cared not what happened to him, so great was his despair. With a formal dismissal from Deerfield Academy, he stood little chance of gaining admittance to another school of its caliber, and even if he could have, who would pay for it? He often thought about contacting Doug Cody and pleading his case, but whenever he sat down to explain himself, he was overwhelmed with shame and anger. In some small way, he blamed himself . . . for what, exactly, he didn't know.

Morgan eventually gathered himself enough to finish out his senior year at the local public high school. His parents never got the full explanation of why he never returned to Deerfield to finish his education. He told them the scholarship had run out of money, and they took this as the truth because things like scholarships and boarding schools were impenetrable black boxes to people like them.

When the National Guard set up a table in the entryway of Morgan's high school, he found himself stopping and talking with the spokeswoman. She wore green fatigues and spoke enthusiastically about the benefits of serving one's country. Morgan didn't care much about serving his country, but he couldn't stand the idea of sticking around home, working for the family business. He took a pamphlet and gave the woman his phone number.

Six months later, he was stationed with an artillery battalion in Iraq fighting for freedom, working hard to forget about the last four years of his life. After being discharged, he met Siobhan, and Lacy was born soon after.

"I hadn't thought about Deerfield in a long time," Morgan says, leaning back on the sofa. "But I can't forget their faces, even if I wanted to."

Cece wants to reach out and hold him, but what right does she have? It all makes sense now. The books, the mysterious and captivating ways in which he never seemed to add up. Even though she's played no part in the demise of his dreams, she can't help but feel responsible somehow.

"Why didn't you tell me?"

"It's not really the kind of thing that comes up in conversation."

"I guess not," Cece says, her voice low and tremulous. "I'm sorry for what they did. It's unforgivable."

"I made my peace with it," Morgan says, "at least until I saw you with him."

"I think I'm beginning to understand what a terrible judge of character I am."

Morgan smiles bitterly. "We all have our prejudices. God knows I've got mine."

Cece feels complicit, guilty by association. The betrayal is too great. How could they ever come back from this? How could Morgan look at her and not see Jonathan's face through the taxicab window? She'd thought there was hope—a chance at reconciliation—but that all seems impossible now.

She's taken up enough of his time, not just now, but this entire summer. What has she brought him other than uncertainty and the pain of old wounds reopened?

"I should go," she says and stands abruptly.

Morgan looks up at her from his seat on the couch.

Bernard only follows Cece with his eyes, hesitant to leave the comfort of the rug. Cece tugs on his collar, but he is unmoved.

Morgan is standing now, hands on his hips. "Why'd you leave him?"

Cece wishes she could say it was because she can't be with someone who did what Jonathan did; she wishes she could claim moral outrage. But deep down, somewhere mysterious and frightening, Cece knows the incident at Deerfield, and perhaps her entire weekend there, crystalized what she'd known all along and had been unwilling to admit. She would have led a privileged, comfortable existence with Jonathan, but a dull one—filled with all the trappings of living but none of its truth. It was the kind of life Cece desperately wishes she could convince herself not just to want, but to inhabit, wholly and happily. But if the summer has proven anything, it is that she's as stubborn as she is foolish.

She attaches Bernard's leash. "I couldn't imagine a future together."

Morgan nods and looks at the floor, as if the wood grains might reveal some deep and unknown truth between them. "Where'll you stay tonight?"

A cool breeze sweeps in through the open windows. Outside, cicadas *thick*, their calls furtive and longing. "Richie put me up at a motel until I find a place of my own."

How did it get so late? Where did the time go?

Cece reminds herself to breathe, ears buzzing, throat tight. "I know it's too late, but I'm sorry," she says. "I was afraid . . . of how you made me feel. It was selfish, hoping I could just keep you in my life as a friend even when I knew, deep down, what you wanted . . . what I wanted . . . I just wanted—"

"Why not stay here?" Morgan says, as if it's the simplest thing in the world, as if they've just met for the first time at the Whaler, when Springsteen had played on the jukebox, when they'd walked around the neighborhood, cocktails in hand, Bernard tugging on his leash, Morgan beside her, forever patient, forever there.

At first Cece says nothing because she's misheard him. Magical thinking, fantastical optimism. After all this—he wants nothing to do with her. *She* wants nothing to do with her! And then he's close, arms around her.

"I didn't think that was an option."

"You're thinking again," Morgan says, his beard teasing and prickly against her cheeks. "That's the problem."

19

In his baggy sweatpants and faded UNIVERSITY OF TENNESSEE SWIMMING T-shirt, Barry more resembles The Dude than the once-proud athlete Cece recalls so vividly from her adolescence. He stalks the perimeter of the detached garage in Wynonna's backyard like an animal wary of a trap. In a bind, Devin had called in a favor of his friend who was a local contractor, and he'd started converting the garage into a proper guesthouse. Devin had even lent a hand to speed things along, cutting out windows and putting up drywall. If he's bitter about having to park his shiny truck on the street, he's hiding it well. The place still needs plumbing and electric, but it looks better than anything Cece could have expected. She is thankful for Wynonna.

The air in Charlotte is sticky like molasses. The sisters, side by side, watch their father. From inside the house, the sound of children roughhousing. Devin is grilling steaks for dinner on the deck that overlooks the subdivision, where Cece imagines he can see fifty houses identical to this one. Maybe she's been too hard on her sister, too judgmental. Wynonna seems happy; her family is big and loud and must fill up her life in ways Cece could never imagine.

"Go inside, Dad. Check it out," Wynonna says. "Just don't touch anything. We're still waiting on city inspectors."

Cece's back barks from the merciless U-Haul seats. She's made the drive from New York with her father in two days, only stopping once at a profoundly disappointing Best Western for a night of fitful sleep. Barry had wanted to make the drive in a single shot, but his bladder had quickly put an end to those aspirations.

Wynonna runs a hand under her nose and sniffles. Cece pulls her close, and then her little sister is trembling, her voice woolly and low. "I'll never forgive Mom."

Cece doesn't say anything for a long time. Barry moves from room to room in the garage, his figure determined and plodding. "I know you're angry," she finally says.

"And you're not? You don't just give up. That's not how marriage works."

"I'm more resigned than anything."

"I just can't fathom it, Cece. Mom. At her age? Starting over. It's laughable."

"She did try, Wynonna. Maybe we wish she would have tried for longer, but she couldn't. And now she's trying to make up for lost time . . . I can't blame her for that. I know the feeling."

Wynonna stiffens, shoulders tight, back rigid. "I can't forgive her, Cece. I just won't."

"No one's asking you to, Wynonna. Certainly not me."

One of the boys bursts through a sliding door, and Wynonna quickly wipes her tears and conjures a smile before he asks for the precise location of a toy. Wynonna scrunches her eyes, thinks for a moment before she says it's in the den under the coffee table. The boy scampers off, confident in his mother's superpower. She is no longer her little sister, Cece realizes, not really. This life, this family—this is her creation, her monument to humanity. A triumphant yelp from an open window—the toy has been found, just where Mom said it would be.

"Thanks for taking Dad," Cece says. "Really, I don't know what I would have done." And it's true. When Kim had informed everyone of her intentions to move out, Cece is ashamed to admit her first concern was not for Barry's well-being, but for his living situation. Who would look after him? Who would take him in when they eventually sold the house? It couldn't be her; she didn't even have a place of her own, not really, and the thought of caring for her father just when Rayburn Oyster was expanding seemed like a cruel twist of fate.

"It's nothing," Wynonna says like she really means it. "We have the room, and the kids will love having him around. Once we get some furniture in there, it will feel like a real home."

"You've built a good life down here, Wynonna. Have I ever told you that?"

"You should visit more."

"I will. I don't know why I haven't."

Wynonna puts an arm around Cece as if to absolve her of any guilt. "You've been a little busy."

"Understatement of the summer."

"And now?"

"Less complicated. I met someone."

"What's his name?"

"Morgan."

"What do you like about him?"

Cece rests her head on Wynonna. She's always been taller than her sister; she got their father's genes—taller than most, back broad, legs long. Nestled in the crook of Wynonna's shoulder, Cece looks at the twilight world sideways. Bats squeak overhead, their bodies seamless and fragile against the indigo sky. "He makes me feel like I'm living life, not just passing through it," she says.

Barry emerges from the garage, his silhouette more upright and buoyant than before. He makes his way toward his daughters in the dying light, sandaled feet padding the grass, his steps lighter. Devin calls out to tell everyone dinner is served. Kids rumble through the house. Somewhere, a neighbor's dog yaps. Barry embraces his daughters, pulls them close and holds them tight. "I count myself lucky," he whispers. "Who's got it better than me?"

Cece wants to say something, protest her father's optimism in the face of most certain tribulation, but it is easier to stay like this—together—and let be what will be.

THE LATE-SUMMER CROWDS have descended on Mystic. Up the coast, I-95 brims with cars, swollen like a flooded river as families make their yearly pilgrimages to Newport and the Cape. The more ambitious, those who seek natural and pristine beaches void of human interference, venture farther north, to Harpswell and Brooklin. They pass by these once-great centers of American industry brimming with New World promise with names like New Bedford, and Providence, Salem, and New London, impatient and hurried.

American flags line Bank Street, and Cece is thankful for those who don't stop in this fair city. Without any traffic, it takes her fifteen minutes to get from Mamacoke Cove to the beach. On account of the holiday, Richie had called it at noon after they'd finished surveying the spot where they're intending on installing the first thirty oyster spat bags. Even though the business is still being picketed by Lorraine and a few remaining NIMBY zealots, they decided it was best to proceed while the weather was good. She is still threatening to sue, but Cece and Richie have come to the conclusion she's more bark than bite.

After paying the twenty-five-dollar parking fee, Cece digs her bathing suit out of the back seat and changes in the car, driver seat reclined, a thick orange beach towel wrapped around her midsection. There is nothing that reminds her more of summer than this—hot fabric against your thighs, the floormat rough and pebbled under your bare feet.

Flips-flops on, beach bag full of all the necessities—outrageously protective sunblock, a dog-eared book, and a floppy hat—she makes her way down the path toward the beach. From the food truck, the sizzle of hot dogs. Kids shout and clamor in front of an Italian-ice cart, their bodies toasted by the sun. The air cools as Cece nears the beach, the path grows narrow, the dunes rising steeply. There is a moment where she can smell the ocean before she sees it, and Cece slows, her heels sinking in the sand, and she breathes in deeply—the brine and baked sand—and she is paralyzed with happiness. As she crests the hill, only a teary-eyed boy with a boogie board breaks her reverie. He wails—something about his older brother not sharing. She surveys the beach, the Sound curling up its sandy leg one wave at a time. Mothers wade in the shallows with diapered toddlers. A few regulars in swimming caps do laps beyond the buoys, their strokes steady and even. Cece's heart beats double time. She's about to check her phone when she sees them, hugging the string of boulders at the far end of the beach. Morgan, his dark blue linen shirt billowing in the wind, stands and waves. Cece holds her hand over her chest and presses down on her collarbone, just to make sure she isn't dreaming. Lacy, a tangle of limbs, rises up from the sand onto her elbows and beckons Cece enthusiastically.

"Richie's working you to the bone," Morgan says after Cece puts her things under the umbrella. Lacy's lying facedown, the sea drying on her back, headphones on.

"I'm doing it to myself. We're trying to get all the bags installed before winter," Cece says. Now that Cece's a supervisor, she feels even more responsibility for the project's success, and she's overseeing everything during the expansion process, from the hiring to the deliverables.

"Well, look at you," Morgan says. He glances at Lacy, whose face is turned away, and steals a kiss.

It's a foreign sensation, being this way out in public. Cece still hasn't gotten used to this new reality, waking up in his bed—now their bed, she supposes—and sitting together on the front porch sipping coffee before work. They are together, irrefutably. An item, one might say. And how strange it is! They've fallen into the patterns of daily existence that make Cece feel like they've done this already in some previous life. Cece keeps waiting to be struck with a sense of panic or fear that they've moved too quickly, that they've misjudged each other terribly, but no such feeling arrives.

"Gross, I heard that," Lacy says and blows a raspberry into her elbow.

"Be nice," Morgan says, his voice more embarrassed than stern.

"It's okay," Cece says, eager to work her way back into the girl's good graces. Ever since she moved in, it's been touch and go. Some days Lacy is cheerful and warm, willing to talk about her friends and the coming school year, others she is cold and standoffish. Morgan apologizes on her behalf, but Cece explains this is simply life with a teenager. Lacy's mother ended up losing her effort to gain full custody, so Lacy's spending the three-day weekend with them before she heads back for school. Morgan and Siobhan agreed on a visitation plan that works for everyone. Lacy will spend one weekend a month in New London with her father. It's not what Morgan wants, but it's only a compromise if no one's happy, at least that's what his lawyer said.

Cece playfully jabs Lacy's arms. "How about those swimming lessons?"

"I just got comfortable."

"You didn't strike me as a quitter," Cece says, whipping the towel at Lacy's toes and jogging into the water.

"Hey!" Lacy shouts and shoots up and bounds after her.

Perhaps hoping to raise Cece's estimation in his daughter's eyes, Morgan had talked up Cece's swimming prowess and collegiate accolades, and while Lacy didn't seem particularly interested in Cece's athletic career, she did ask if Cece could teach her. Obviously, she could already swim, but she wanted to learn the proper technique. She'd watched the summer Olympics two years ago and grew infatuated with the American team, especially Katie Ledecky, who seemed unstoppable. Lacy wanted to know how to do that—how to move with power and grace, how to breathe and shape your body, how to cut through the water like it was the most natural thing in the world.

Cece waits for Lacy, water up to her waist, feet on rippled sand, right before the drop, where the depths are chilled and dark. This is only their second lesson, but Lacy already knows the drill. She levels out in front of Cece, who puts a hand under her midsection. They review the basics: streamlined body position (head down, neck neutral, legs and hips even); elbows high on the stroke.

The girl is weightless in her hands.

"When I let go, you go. Give me fifteen good strokes."

Lacy gives a confident nod, but Cece can see she's already running through the checklist in her head. "Give it a try," Cece says. "Just like the other day."

Lacy puts her head down, brown hair fanning out like a seashell. Cece slips her hand away, and the girl goes, arms rising and falling, legs kicking up white foam. Cece remembers when she did the same thing with her father. She remembers how awkward and uncoordinated her body felt when she tried to remember every little rule, how her legs and arms felt disconnected from her torso and shoulders, like she was a marionette without her strings. While a bit choppy and halting, Lacy's form isn't half-bad, but the coordination just isn't there. Cece gives a thumbs-up. Perhaps she's approaching this the wrong way.

They move closer to shore. Cece can feel Morgan watching them intently from the shade of the umbrella. Once Lacy can stand, Cece reviews the basics again and then tells Lacy to watch her and pay special attention to how level her body stays with the surface of the water. Lacy appears dubious but willing.

Cece eyes an orange buoy twenty-five yards away. A good target as any, she thinks. She wets her face and hair, and then she's taking her first stroke and then her second, head down, body straight but not rigid, her arms rising and falling, fingers squeezed tight. Legs pump. The first breath comes, a shock of sunlight against her closed eyelids. Everything moves in unison, and quick enough, she isn't swimming at all—just moving. She pushes herself, lungs burning like they used to, back stretching like it used to, the water no longer an obstacle but a path. Her chest opens, the air comes, salty and sweet. Cece doesn't need to peek. Straight and true, she knows she'll hit her mark, as long as she keeps swimming.

SOON ENOUGH, THE summer will end just as it began, quickly and without warning. Lacy will return to school, where she'll boast of her newfound swimming talent and continue watching *O.C.* reruns religiously. Lorraine will eventually give up protesting Rayburn Oyster, but she still won't acknowledge Cece or Morgan, which is mighty awkward, considering they're basically neighbors. A few seasons down the road, Morgan will offer to cut her hedges, and she won't say no, which he'll interpret as the door remaining open to some sort of reconciliation. Cece will call him crazy, but deep down, she'll hope he's right. Speaking of things that might seem crazy but are, in fact, not at all, Cece's mother will find her second chance at love, thanks to the internet. "Who knew there were so many men out there!" she'll say to Cece over the phone.

Wynonna won't ever fully get over her parents' divorce, especially with Kim moving on so quickly, but like most things, time will do its work, and Cece will eventually feel her sister softening. After an initial period of transition, one marked by hard conversations and reality checks, Barry will be perfectly happy living in Wynonna's guesthouse. Surrounded by grandkids and without a spare moment to think, there won't be a day that he beats himself up about selling his print advertising business at a loss. The only thing he'll grumble about is having to give up Bernard, since Wynonna's kids are allergic.

After recovering from being jilted a second time, Jonathan will begrudgingly take his mother's advice and start dating more "suitable" women, "good girls" who'll understand him. And it won't be long before he's married with a big house full of children. Only sometimes, when he sees oysters on the menu at a restaurant or drives by the exit for New London, will he think of Cece. It will be a fleeting thought, and he'll be thankful to have escaped a period of his life that no longer makes sense to him.

As for Cece, she'll see Rayburn's expansion through to the end, and when Richie gets too old for the job, his back crooked and his eyes bad, he'll put Cece in charge full-time. Morgan and Cece will talk about moving from New London to Mystic to be closer to the office, but they like it here. After all those years, Morgan will nearly be finished renovating the house, and it will be summer soon. Morgan will plant his colossal vegetable garden and cook dinner on the grill while Bernard lounges on the back patio, eager for a treat. Cece will get off work early because she's good at paperwork, and they'll eat summer fluke and drink white wine while the citronella candles flicker; and later, before they've grown too heavy with lethargy, they'll mix their usual nightcap and take Bernard for a walk around the neighborhood. They'll lean into one another and chuckle and point to the spot where they first kissed. Not as rambunctious and overzealous as he once was, the dog will tire and slow his gait. He'll whine and sit down in the middle of the street. Morgan will chastise him for his laziness but will oblige him. Later, they'll head back, neighborhood homes casting curtained light onto yards and sidewalks. The heat from the summer sun will rise from the ground and mingle with the wind coming off the water. Cece will loop her arm in Morgan's; she'll feel his quiet presence. Close to home, Bernard will break into a trot, and Cece will feel her own pace quicken, and she'll smile to herself in the darkness at all the good things to come, whatever they may be.

ACKNOWLEDGMENTS

A book is never a solitary endeavor, and I am grateful to a number of people for their help throughout the process.

To my brilliant and clear-eyed agent, Catherine Cho. Thank you for your expertise, infinite wisdom, and most of all, belief in my writing

To the insightful Melissa Pimentel. Thank you for your notes on an early draft of this book.

To my superstar editor, Lindsey Rose. I cannot thank you enough for your patience, generosity, and keen editorial eye. This book would not exist without your advocacy, and I count myself blessed to have you as my editor.

To Emily Canders, Isabel DaSilva, and the whole team at Dutton. Thank you for everything you do, seen and unseen, to support my books.

To my beautiful wife, Jennifer. Thank you for always making room in our busy lives for my writing, even if it means listening to my alarm go off at 4:30 in the morning.

And to my daughter, Emma. Thank you for giving me a glimpse of what the future might hold and what I ought to be writing toward each and every day.

ABOUT THE AUTHOR

A native of Nyack, New York, **Soon Wiley** is the author of the novel *When We Fell Apart*. He currently teaches English in the Upper School at Greenwich Country Day School, where he also serves as chair of the English department. He resides with his family in Connecticut.